P9-DMA-134

★ OPERATOR DOWN ★

Also by Brad Taylor

One Rough Man
All Necessary Force
Enemy of Mine
The Widow's Strike
The Polaris Protocol
Days of Rage
No Fortunate Son
The Insider Threat
The Forgotten Soldier
Ghosts of War
Ring of Fire

Short Works

The Callsign
Gut Instinct
Black Flag
The Dig
The Recruit
The Target
The Infiltrator

OPERATOR DOWN

★★★★★★★★★★★★★★

BRAD TAYLOR

A Pike Logan Thriller

DUTTON

DUTTON
An imprint of Penguin Random House LLC
375 Hudson Street
New York, New York 10014

LIBRARY OF CONGRESS CATALOGING-IN-PUBLICATION DATA
Names: Taylor, Brad, 1965– author.
Title: Operator down : a Pike Logan thriller / Brad Taylor.
Description: New York : Dutton, [2018] | Series: A pike logan thriller ; 12
Identifiers: LCCN 2017035102 | ISBN 9781101984819 (hardback) | ISBN 9781101984826 (ebook)
Subjects: LCSH: Logan, Pike—Fiction. | Special forces (Military science)—United States—Fiction. | Special operations (Military science)—Fiction. | Terrorism—Prevention—Fiction. | BISAC: FICTION / Suspense. | FICTION / Action & Adventure. | GSAFD: Suspense fiction. | Adventure fiction.
Classification: LCC PS3620.A9353 O64 2018 | DDC 813/.6—dc23
LC record available at https://lccn.loc.gov/2017035102

Printed in the United States of America
1 3 5 7 9 10 8 6 4 2

BOOK DESIGN BY CASSANDRA GARRUZZO

To Ben Sevier,
for seeing the potential in an unknown

To put on the garment of legitimacy is the first aim of every coup.

Barbara Tuchman

1

★ ★ ★

Being a spy is a lot like being a bank robber. In espionage—as in crime—it's always the little things that get you. You can plan for an entire operation, allowing for one contingency after another, foreseeing when and where things might go wrong, but you inevitably miss the little things. A drop of sweat on a doorknob, drywall shavings left behind after the installation of a bug, a nick from a tension wrench in the brass plate of a lock. Small things with huge impacts.

In this case, the little thing happened before Aaron Bergmann had even left Israel, when a travel voucher routed through Mossad headquarters included a man who had been specifically excluded from the mission read-on. For a specific reason. And that little thing would prove devastating for Aaron and his neophyte apprentice.

Casually tapping the tablet in front of him, Aaron said, "Alex, turn just a tad bit to the right. I'm missing the man on the left."

Across the table from him Alexandra Levy shifted slightly, her face aglow. She said, "This is so exciting! Straight out of a James Bond movie."

He chuckled, then said, "Right there. Good." He hit record on the tablet.

Alex stiffened a little bit, as if she were posing for a photographer, holding her angle. She whispered, "That thing will really read their lips? Tell us what they're saying?"

Aaron said, "Yep. If you can keep the camera on them, but don't look so rigid. Relax a little. I'll tell you if it shifts off."

Aaron continued manipulating a piece of software in his tablet, something that was highly classified and usually reserved for active Mossad agents. A simple button camera in Alexandra's blouse was tied by Bluetooth to his tablet and seemed to be out of a 007 movie, but in truth, both were commercially available to anyone who wanted them. The secret was the software churning through what the camera sent it.

Artificial intelligence for facial recognition had grown by leaps and bounds in recent years, and the Mossad had taken that in a different direction, focusing on the spoken word. They'd replicated the human act of lipreading in the cyberworld, designing a software suite that could decipher what was being said without hearing sound.

Alex relaxed her body a bit, contrition floating across her face. "Sorry. This isn't my expertise. You should be doing the camera work."

He laid the tablet on the table and took a sip of beer, saying, "You're doing fine. This beats working in the diamond exchange, right? Keep up the talent and I might recruit you for my firm."

She grinned and said, "No, no, this is enough excitement. I enjoy being able to help—I've never even been to Africa—but I'll stick with my boring job."

There was no fear in the statement. No realization of the risk. It was like she thought they were executing a high school senior prank. She had no idea of the threat level.

That would come later.

She glanced over the balcony toward their target and said, "Besides, I don't think your partner would agree to that. I think she hates me."

Three people sat at the table they were filming, two white and one black. Their target was a man of about thirty-five, and unlike the rest of the patrons in the restaurant, he was dressed in a suit as if he were still working in his office in Israel. The other white man looked like he was about to head out on a safari, wearing cargo pants and a shirt that had more pockets than a photographer's vest. He had shaggy blond hair, ice-blue eyes, and a feral quality. Aaron had seen his type plenty of times before, but only in war zones. It intrigued him.

The final man was tall, with a thin mustache and coal-black skin. He was dressed like a local but didn't act like one. Ramrod straight, he showed not a whit of humor. Had they held the meeting at a café in downtown Johannesburg—where the target was staying—they would have attracted attention by their very disparate appearances, but they didn't here. Which explained why Aaron's target had chosen this restaurant. The one thing remaining was to find out why the meeting was occurring.

The only man Aaron recognized was the one the Mossad had asked him to track—an employee of a diamond broker in Tel Aviv. The other two were a mystery, but he'd know about them soon enough, when they reviewed the footage later.

The primary problem with the lipreading software was choosing a language—try to lip-read German when the target was speaking Chinese and you'd get gibberish. Here, in the township of Soweto, just outside the city center of Johannesburg, South Africa, he was sure they were speaking English. There was no way the black man spoke Hebrew, and he would be astounded if his target from Israel spoke something like Swahili or Afrikaans. No, they'd be speaking English, and the fact that his method of recording the conversation came through in visual rather than auditory form was a plus in the current environment.

The outdoor balcony they were on belonged to a restaurant called Sakhumzi, as did the patio holding the target's table. Just a stone's throw from the historical houses of Nelson Mandela and Bishop Tutu, in the section of Soweto known as Orlando West, the restaurant hosted a smorgasbord of local food and native performers and was a permanent stop for tour groups large and small traveling to see the ghetto made famous in the uprising against apartheid. Because of it, there was a constant drumbeat of laughter and clapping—something that had no effect on the lipreading software. As long as Aaron could keep a line of sight with whoever was talking.

Aaron focused on the computer, tapping icons and ensuring three computer-generated squares remained over the men's mouths. He said, "Position is good. Keep that." When he hadn't responded to

Alex's statement, she repeated, "Your partner doesn't care for me at all. I thought she was going to throw me out of your house."

Aaron looked up from the tablet and said, "Shoshana? She doesn't hate you. She's just mad because I brought you instead of her. She was aggravated at me for the decision. It's nothing personal."

Making sure not to disrupt the camera angle, she said, "I don't think so. When you left the room, she was . . . a little scary."

Aaron laughed and returned to the tablet, offhandedly saying, "You need to get to know her. She's not all knives and death threats. She just acts that way. She understands that she didn't have the knowledge base for this mission. When we fly back, I'll take you to dinner. The three of us."

Alex smiled and said, "I'd like that. I think she thought . . ."

Aaron looked up from the tablet and said, "Thought what?"

"That we . . . I mean, you and me . . . might . . ."

Aaron scoffed and said, "You're twenty years younger than me."

She said, "Yeah, but it was the Mossad that asked me . . . *you* asked me . . . I mean, they wouldn't do that unless it was for a reason."

Aaron realized she thought she really *was* in a movie. And that she was hitting on him. A twentysomething *sabra* who worked inside the Israeli diamond exchange, she was no doubt attractive, with brown hair, brown eyes, liquid skin, and a quiet intelligence surrounded by an innocence he no longer possessed. He would have hunted her like a wolf a decade ago, but no longer. She deserved to live in her innocence. His entire existence was ensuring people like her could do so. He decided to put an end to the fantasy.

"Alex, I picked you because you understand the diamond market. Yes, you're attractive, which meant I could use you to blend in, but I need your knowledge. Period. You watch the tape, you tell me what they're talking about within the diamond world, and I write an assessment. That's it. This isn't a complex thing. We're not here to save Israel from Blofeld. We're here to save Israel from embarrassment. That's all. It's a simple mission."

Turning red, she tilted forward and whispered, "What does that mean? I wasn't suggesting anything."

He said, "You're screwing with the camera angle. Lean back."

The target at the table answered a cell phone.

Aaron said, "Shit. Lean back—now."

Alex did so abruptly, causing the camera to sway wildly. Aaron said, "Stay still."

The man turned away from them, still on the phone.

Aaron said, "We need to move. *You* need to move. Stand up and go to the bathroom. Walk by the table and get me a shot of his face as long as you can. Stop and ask the table for directions, but not to him. Let him keep talking on the phone."

Hesitantly, Alex stood. More forcefully than he wanted to, Aaron said, "Go."

She did, sidling between the throngs of tour bus patrons and locals, threading between the tables and down the stairs, the picture on Aaron's tablet jumping left and right. She reached the patio and it stabilized. She walked toward the restrooms, then stopped at the table, asking directions. He recorded about a fifteen-second snippet of the phone conversation, unsure if the software would be able to utilize the footage because the target's face was partially obscured by his smartphone.

He glanced over the balcony to see the interaction, and she broke contact, doing a passable job of being a tourist. He saw no outward interest in the interruption.

Aaron ignored the rest of the feed, wondering if Alex would be smart enough to cut it off if she really chose to use the bathroom. She did. Or maybe the Bluetooth simply lost contact because of distance. He grinned and took a sip of his beer, surreptitiously giving the target table a side-eye.

The Israeli was asking a waitress for the check. Aaron immediately picked up his phone and called Alex, telling her to return.

The men tossed some rand on the table, preparing to leave, and he saw her coming across the patio. She mounted the stairs to the balcony and he stood, saying, "Hopefully they take the same car. If they split up, we'll stick to the target."

Hidden by the balcony railing, they let the group exit the restaurant, then followed, getting to the parking lot just as they were loading a single car. A part of him spiked at the action, since they'd arrived in two separate cars.

He should have listened to his sixth sense. Lulled by the minimal threat of his mission, he thought he had his bases covered, but he had forgotten a hard truth he'd learned in the past: In warfare, the enemy gets a vote.

2

★ ★ ★

As we crossed the lobby to the Las Vegas Venetian casino, another gaggle of bearded men went by, all wearing cargo pants and baseball caps with Velcro patches. Half of them toted some form of corduroy nylon backpack, which also sported a variety of gun-porn patches, depicting things like *ISIS Hunter* or a Punisher skull.

I said, "I have never seen this many supercommando 'operators' in one place in my life."

Knuckles laughed and said, "Yeah, this event brings 'em out of the woodwork, no doubt. But make no mistake, the real deal's running around in here as well. In fact, keep your eyes peeled. The odds of us running into someone we know are pretty high, so be prepared to throw out the cover story."

Working in cover was the worst when you did it in an area where the locals potentially knew you. Whenever that happened, the nastiest thing that could occur—besides getting your fingernails pulled out by the enemy—was running into someone who knew who you were in real life. It was the surest way to blow the hell out of what you were pretending. An FBI agent infiltrating an outlaw motorcycle gang would be in dire straits if he bumped into a friend from law school.

In this case, Knuckles was still active-duty Navy and I was retired Army. In the world of the Taskforce, when we were out in the badlands earning our ISIS Hunter patches for real, he was a civilian employee of my company, but if another SEAL from his past saw him here, they'd know that was bullshit, so we'd created a story that was plausible should that happen to either of us.

It was my first trip to the fabled SHOT Show in Las Vegas, the largest gun show on earth, and the interior of the Sands Convention

Center was literally stuffed with booth after booth selling various weapons, accessories, and outdoor gear. It was Mecca to people like me, and the Taskforce sent a contingent every year to prowl the halls looking for anything new that we could incorporate into our mission set. Back when I was on active duty, as the team leader, I'd always let a junior member of the team make the trip, and Knuckles, my 2IC, had been a few times before.

Given how he was dressed, I was surprised they let him in.

In contrast to the bearded ones, he looked like he had come to protest the convention, with his long hippie hair, Che Guevara T-shirt, and lack of any tacti-cool paraphernalia. He was even wearing a leather necklace with a bronze peace sign the size of a fifty-cent piece—either as irony or as a challenge. With him it was hard to tell, but if someone took it as a challenge, they'd be sorely wishing they hadn't. Unlike a lot of the posers at the convention, he was most definitely an Operator.

While the trip *was* a little bit of a boondoggle, we did have a specific mission. We'd just come from a booth manned by a company called ZEV Technologies—a maker of high-end aftermarket components and custom frame/slide work for Glock pistols—and had sealed a deal to test some pistols for our specific applications.

Although we already had our own armorer support that we used to hone our combat weapons, Kurt Hale—the commander of the Taskforce—was wondering if we weren't just reinventing the wheel and wanted to see if it would be better to simply farm out the work. After talking to ZEV, I was beginning to believe he was right, only our wheels were something from a Conestoga wagon while ZEV was racing around on run-flats.

We pushed through the crowd and entered the cavernous Venetian casino, working our way to Las Vegas Boulevard. We exited into the sunshine, leaving the commandos and gamblers, only to be hit by Guatemalan refugees trying to hand me cards with hookers offering their services. One of the strangest things about Vegas.

Knuckles said, "What did you think?"

"Seriously? I think we should have flown here with the entire team's Glocks. No question they can do better than our internal armorers. Nothing against them, but did you work the one they had on display? Better trigger than ours by far."

Knuckles took a left toward Caesars Palace, passing the gigantic Venetian hotel, saying, "So forget about any other vendors?"

He had a point. While we didn't fall under any official DoD rules about contracts, it would be stupid to latch on to the first one we found. We had a list of potential companies that could meet our goals, and it wouldn't be right not to at least check them out. But I was pretty sure where I would end up on my recommendation to Kurt.

I said, "Naw, we should hit 'em up as well, but we only get two days out here, and I want some Vegas time. I'll send Retro and Jennifer to go hunt them down."

"Retro isn't going to like that, and Jennifer's not exactly an expert."

Retro had been a teammate of mine since Jesus was wearing diapers, but all things come to a close sooner or later. He was set to retire from the military at the end of the month and had truly come out here for vacation. Kurt knew he wasn't needed but had let him come along as a little retirement gift. Unbeknownst to me, in all our time together, he absolutely loved playing craps, and his wife frowned on gambling. I learned he had planned on spending his entire time in the casinos betting away his per diem like a drunken sailor.

As we were planning to leave for the trip, he'd begged to come along, getting a seat through Kurt, then had turned around and told his wife he was desperately needed for national security, which she bought. As they say, "What happens in Vegas . . ."

I said, "It's not going to kill him to take a break for a few hours, and as far as Jennifer goes, she could learn something."

Jennifer was my partner in Grolier Recovery Services—our company—and, outside of some serious weapons training I'd given her, had no military experience. She wasn't qualified to judge whether a vendor was worthy and wasn't needed on this trip either, but I'd paid for her to come along out of my own pocket because, well, she was a partner in more ways than one. She'd planned on spending her time at the pool—or, if the weather was too cold, in the spa.

I felt my phone vibrate and saw it was her. I said, "Speak of the devil."

I answered, "Hey, we're on Vegas Boulevard headed home. What's up?"

"Kurt wants to talk on the VPN. Secure."

"About what?"

"Apparently, about a mission. In Vegas."

3

★ ★ ★

Aaron Bergmann left the parking lot of the Sakhumzi restaurant, keeping a few cars between him and his target, blending in with the traffic on Vilakazi Street. In short order, they had left what was sarcastically called by the locals the Beverly Hills of Soweto, crossing out of the Orlando West neighborhood and into Orlando East.

Making sure he was still screened from the car in front of him, he turned to Alex and said, "What's the video telling us?"

Alex, in the passenger seat, said, "It's got nothing about diamonds or the diamond exchange. They're talking about weapons. The black man is being called a general, and he's asking the blond guy how many soldiers he has. Our target's only contribution is saying that money is no object."

She looked at him and said, "What's going on? This isn't about blood diamonds. It's not about embarrassment to Israel or the diamond exchange."

They entered a single-track road leading to two giant power-plant towers looking like they belonged in a nuclear facility, only they were now painted with multicolored graffiti and artwork. *Why would they be coming here?*

He said, "Get off the video. Google this place. What's here?"

She did, just as they passed a sign describing the towers as a fun park, with bungee jumping, paintball, and other adventure sports. Aaron let the target car roll past the parking lot, seeing it continue on to a cluster of abandoned buildings. He pulled over to the side of the road, caught by a stream of patrons exiting the park, the sun beginning to set.

He said, "Give me something. What is this place? I'm about to lose the target."

Looking up from her tablet, Alex said, "It's an old coal-fired power plant. It closed in 1998. In 2008, it reopened as a bungee-jumping place called Orlando Towers. Since then, it's expanded into a bunch of different adventure events. Something called 'SCAD Freefall' and other things."

"That's no fucking help. Who owns it? Why are they here?"

Alex snapped back at his tone, looked fearful, realizing she was failing in her duties. She said, "I have no idea. I don't know how to ascertain that."

Aaron glanced forward and saw the car drawing away at a slow pace, passing through the remains of the power station. It pulled into an alley between two brick buildings that looked like a setting from a *Saw* movie, the doors hanging askew and the windows broken. He had to make a decision.

He said, "Switch seats with me. Give me the tablet."

They did so without opening any doors, playing a game of Twister, arms and legs flapping back and forth in an awkward dance, him keeping an eye on the car to their front. It began to disappear through the crumbling buildings, and he made a choice that would prove fateful.

"Keep going. Slowly. Keep the car in sight, but don't turn down that alley. Stop before they can see us in the rearview mirror."

She did so, turning on the headlights to counteract the dying sun. He immediately snapped, "Off, off, turn them off."

She reflexively twisted the stalk hard enough to break the plastic, shutting out the lights. She looked at him in a panic, and he patted her hand, saying, "Take a breath. We're okay."

She exhaled and then inched forward, past the tourist park and into the abandoned buildings. She leaned toward the windshield in the gathering gloom and said, "I see the car in the alley. It's pulled over next to a trash pile."

He said, "Park it here, in the shadow of the buildings. Whatever they're doing, we're not going to see. We've gone far enough." He pulled out a night vision monocular and handed it to her, saying, "Keep an eye on the car. I'm going to cycle the video."

He powered up the recording from the restaurant, the conversation between the men spit out at the bottom of the screen by the software package, looking like closed captioning at a sports bar. He saw that Alex was correct. The men were discussing weapons, strategy, and money. The deputy prime minister of Lesotho, Makalo Lenatha, was mentioned, then the black man spoke, and Aaron finally had a name: Lieutenant General Jonathan Mosebo, head of the Lesotho Defence Force.

The readout continued, and he learned that the general was being unceremoniously fired by the prime minister and was none too pleased about it. The other Caucasian, a man called Johan, calmed him down, and the talk continued along nebulous lines about force structures and loyalties.

Nothing to do with diamonds. *What the hell?*

The phone call came, the target answering, and he fast-forwarded through Alex's short walk down the stairs. When she appeared by the target's table, he slowed the video down again, and the scrolling sentences at the bottom turned into gibberish. Confused, he punched a couple of icons on the software package, then realized what the problem was: The man wasn't speaking English.

He's speaking Hebrew.

Aaron glanced up from the tablet and saw that a single streetlight had come on, providing enough feeble illumination to potentially compromise them. He began manipulating the software package, saying, "How're we looking?"

Alex said, "Good. I haven't seen any movement from them at all."

Which should have been an indicator.

He loaded the Hebrew suite into the software program, saying, "Get the car turned around and out of the ring of that streetlight. We'll stay for a couple of more minutes, but this isn't worth burning ourselves.

There's more going on here than just blood diamonds. I need to assess and report back for guidance."

She started the vehicle, and he rewound the video feed, getting to the start of the phone conversation. She did a U-turn, parking the car on the opposite side of the street, now facing toward the exit of the dilapidated power station.

He hit play, and the screen cleared. The software suite could only lip-read the target's end of the conversation, making the readout a little confusing, but eventually, one sentence stitched the others together, clearing the state of play like fog hit with the morning sun.

I have a tail? From Mossad?

The text across the bottom of the screen hung still as the man on the other end of the line talked. Aaron saw the words on the tablet, not wanting to believe them.

His voice grating low, he said, "Get out of here. Now."

Alex said, "What?"

The man on the other end of the phone quit talking, and the screen spit out the target's response. *You want me to take him out? Are you sure?*

In that millisecond, Aaron realized that he was no longer the hunter. He was the hunted. They had been led here for a reason.

He bolted upright and saw men appearing like wraiths from the dilapidated buildings, an anthill kicked over, running toward the car.

He shouted, "Get the fuck out of here!"

The driver's-side window was smashed. He saw Alex's head yanked out of it, a man trying to pull her from the car by her hair. He exploded forward, grabbing the man's wrist and slamming it backward, into the shards of glass that remained in the window. The man screamed, releasing Alex's head. Aaron leaned over and jammed his foot on the accelerator, causing the car to burst forward. The men dove out of the way, with one flipping onto the hood. Alex shouted, and the car skipped into the curb, bounced back, and headed straight into the wall of a building.

Aaron grabbed the wheel, but not soon enough. They slammed into the brick, the vehicle stopping in a grinding of metal. His door was ripped open, hands jerking all over his body, spilling him out. He hit the ground hard, felt a fist hammer his temple, and heard Alex scream again.

A visceral fear flooded him, the adrenaline coursing through him in a spastic jolt. Like a father defending his family against overwhelming odds, knowing he would lose, he began doing what he knew best.

He turned to fight.

4

★ ★ ★

Knuckles took a sip of his club soda and said, "This is bullshit. I should not be burning myself for this mission. We should be using Jennifer. It's easier, and you know it."

I kept my eye on Retro at the craps table and said, "If GRS is to remain in play for the follow-on mission, I only have two guys here who I can burn. You and Retro."

"You don't have to burn me. I can do the follow-on mission. Retro's the one retiring."

I took a sip of my own club soda and gave him the side-eye. I said, "You're slated to train Carly. You want to ditch that for a simple Alpha follow-on mission?"

Carly was a Taskforce CIA case officer who had been granted the honor of attempting to achieve Operator status in the Taskforce. Only the second female to be allowed to try, after Jennifer. It was an open secret that she was dating Knuckles, and he'd fought like hell to get her a shot, with Kurt agreeing only after I'd given my concurrence. She needed some serious training to even begin to think about succeeding, and Knuckles had been detailed to conduct it. His willingness to ditch that for a simple surveillance mission with no chance of high adventure was a little strange, to say the least. Especially after how hard he'd fought to give her the chance.

He toyed with his napkin, then said, "Real-world missions take precedence. That's all."

"So I should burn Jennifer so you can go on a *potential* trip, when she has no commitments and you do? What would Carly say about that?"

He remained quiet, and I knew something was different. We were so close, I could read a tick of his eyebrow and learn volumes. But I wasn't sure I wanted to push.

He balled up his napkin and said, "You heard Kurt. This has a whole lot more behind it than a simple Alpha mission."

Earlier, after leaving the convention center, we'd returned to our hotel room at Caesars Palace to hear what Kurt was thinking. Waiting on the elevator to arrive, Knuckles had broached a topic that was also on my mind: "What the hell do you think this is about? We can't operate on US soil."

The Taskforce was an extrajudicial force—which was a Washington, DC, way of saying it was illegal—but it still had some rules. One of those was that we only operated overseas, hunting bad guys in bad-guy lands. Home soil was the purview of the FBI and others.

I said, "No idea. But it does make me wonder why Kurt was fine with me coming out here with a full team when two guys would do."

The bell dinged, and Knuckles said, "Well, this could be fun, but I'm smelling a shit sandwich. Like always."

I chuckled and said, "So working with me is always eating shit?"

We hit the fourth floor, and he said, "Pretty much."

We'd entered my room to find Jennifer and Retro expectantly waiting, the laptop on the desk connected to the Taskforce through an unbreakable VPN. Jennifer's eyes were alight, relishing a mission beyond sitting by the pool. Retro looked like he wanted to kick me.

I shut the door and said, "Okay, before I get on, what's the deal?"

Retro said, "The *deal* is Kurt wants to do some sort of surveillance mission here in Vegas. Against our charter, I might add."

I looked at Jennifer, and she said, "Apparently, there's an arms dealer he wants us to track. Some guy who's got a booth here at SHOT." She glanced at Retro and raised an eyebrow, saying, "I think it sounds fun. Retro's a little angry."

He said, "I'm *not* angry. I just think it's a little sleazy cutting this trip short for a mission that we're not even allowed to do."

Which meant he was pissed. His answer brought a grin to both

Knuckles and me because in the twenty-two years that he'd been running missions, he'd never cared about the rules.

I held up a hand and said, "Okay, okay. Don't worry about your craps weekend just yet. Dial Kurt up. Let's see what this is about."

We connected, waited a bit, and then Kurt Hale settled in front of the camera. He turned around to look behind him and said, "Close the door, George."

When he returned to the screen, I saw his lips curl into a ghost of a smile. "How's Vegas?"

I said, "A little boring, to tell you the truth. I understand you want to spice things up."

He laughed and said, "You find a vendor for the work on our pistols?"

"Yeah, I got the one that I think we're going to end up with, but we haven't checked out the others yet."

"Good. Don't worry about the others. Just send the information you have."

"What's up, sir?"

The camera feed disappeared, and in its place a target card appeared. A single PowerPoint slide that had the specifics on someone we were hunting.

Name: Tyler Malloy

Citizenship: United States of America

Professed Occupation: Arms dealer

Activity: Intercepts indicate possible facilitation of weapons transfers to groups designated as Foreign Terrorist Organizations by the Department of State. Currently attempting to gain trigger components suitable for nuclear weapons. Currently licensed in good standing with Department of State ITAR protocols.

Threat: Low

Authority: Alpha only, secondary protocol

Next to the information on the slide was a picture of a thick-necked guy of about twenty-eight, with the ubiquitous "operator" beard and a pronounced Jay Leno–looking jaw. He was giving his best *I'm a badass* scowl.

I said, "What's this guy's story?"

The slide vanished, and Kurt reappeared on-screen. "He was an enlisted Marine for four years, one tour in Helmand. After that, he became an independent contractor for a company called Blue Spoon. He ended up in Bulgaria training a bunch of Syrian 'moderate' rebels under the failed CIA program. While he was there, he seemed to figure out where the money was really made, which was supplying the arms for the fight instead of getting paid by the hour to train up a bunch of farmers. Blue Spoon was buying a ton of AKs and other old Soviet arms from Belarus and Bulgaria, and he spent his time there learning the trade and building personal contacts. Eventually, he went out on his own, using those contacts and undercutting Blue Spoon pricing until his little company became the sole supplier. That was three years ago. Now he's a real player, selling everything from tanks to missile launchers. He's moved far beyond the small train-and-equip program for Syria."

I said, "And we're tracking him because why, exactly? The card says he's a nobody, low threat and secondary protocol. Hell, according to the Oversight Council, he's not even worth a primary mission. He's a standby target in the *if we have the time* category. He'll probably get arrested by the FBI for breaking ITAR if we let him run it out."

"Except he's apparently got some ideas about purchasing nuclear components, and we don't know why. The guy is amoral with respect to buyers, and while we don't really give a shit if he sells some AKs to someone who passes them to Hezbollah, nuclear components are something else entirely."

I brought up the elephant in the room. "Sir, he's an American. We're on American soil. We can't operate here. I get President Hannister loves us, but surely he didn't authorize this."

Kurt vanished from the screen and a new picture appeared. An older man in a foreign military uniform, with a receding hairline and tiny piglike eyes. He looked like a caricature of some old Soviet propaganda poster. Kurt said, "This is Stanko Petrov—Tyler's unofficial right-hand man. Formerly a colonel in the Bulgarian Army from the Warsaw Pact days, he scraped by after the fall of the wall until he met Tyler. He's the man who got Tyler his start in the arms trade. He now acts as a sort of combination personal security slash personal assistant to Tyler. Everything that Tyler's planning to do goes through him. And he's Bulgarian."

I smiled and said, "Ahhh . . . Sooo. Approval because we aren't officially tracking an American. We're tracking a Bulgarian. Nice. Where's his target card? What's the Council's level of operational approval for him?"

Kurt reappeared and said, "He doesn't have a card. Look, Pike, this guy has an iPad mini that's glued to him like a third hand. Everything Tyler does is executed through Stanko, and that iPad will have it all."

I glanced back at my crew, now on unfamiliar ground. Usually it was I who was begging to break the rules. Now my commander was ordering me to do so. I wasn't sure how I felt about that. It was easy to rage against the machine when the machine kept you in check. It was something else when the machine itself began to go off the rails.

I said, "Sir, you sure about this? Did you talk to the Oversight Council?"

He exhaled and said, "No. They don't care about Tyler, and truthfully, neither should we, but I've got a feeling about him. He's not a good guy. He can pull his small-time shit and stay off the radar, but he's up to something, and that something is potentially big. I don't want to *react* to a threat. I want to *prevent* it from occurring."

I paused, not responding. He said, "Pike, all I want you to do is attempt to access the iPad. If you can't, you can't. Just get me details on where and when his next overseas trip is, so I can begin executing Alpha authority against him. Let me deal with any fallout. I'm not asking you to thump him on the head. When I learned he was at the SHOT show, it was the perfect coincidence."

I considered his words. In truth, it sounded easy enough, and, honestly, I could use some high adventure. If Kurt thought it good enough, then I wouldn't question, although I'd keep the overstep in mind. Because I'd personally saved the president's life on a previous mission, we now had his ear, which meant we'd get to do whatever we wanted with our intelligence, but cutting out the Oversight Council might not be the best thing for the nation, because it would be up to the Operator on the ground to determine what was right in the future. And I was that Operator.

Not liking the role reversal, I relented, with a caveat. "Okay, but we get the follow-on mission."

Now it was his turn to pause. He said, "You guys are off cycle. You don't even have a team. Retro's retiring, Veep's attending SOTIC, and Knuckles is on a training billet for Carly."

I said, "They don't call it SOTIC anymore. It's just the SF Sniper Course now."

Kurt said, "Whatever. I'm sure that was a bullet on some officer's OER."

I said, "What's Blood doing?"

"Some liaison work with OGA."

"Well, there you go. That's my team."

5

★ ★ ★

I watched Retro throw the dice, holding a spit cup and arranging a huge dip of Copenhagen in his mouth with his tongue. I said, "At least he's getting in his craps time. He can't bitch about the mission now."

Knuckles said nothing. I looked at him and poked the blister. "What's going on with you and Carly?"

He said, "Nothing. I should be going on this mission. You've never left me behind."

I looked him in the eyes, the mission taking a back seat. He turned away. I said, "You've never shirked on a commitment before. Remember that time in Bosnia? When you were supposed to leave, but you refused because you feared for a source of ours? The Council ordered you out, and you stayed. You have a commitment to Carly. What's changed?"

He bluntly said, "We broke up."

I leaned back, taking that in. He'd spent so much energy getting her a shot at selection because of their relationship, and now they didn't have one. I knew it had to hurt. I said, "Does she still want to do it?"

Glumly, he nodded. "Yeah. She does."

"What was the breakup? Something bad?"

"No. We just . . . sort of decided. It wasn't bad."

I looked at Jennifer across the hall, waiting near the reception counter for our trigger. She was reading a magazine, oblivious to the conversation.

I said, "You can't do that, Knuckles. You made a promise. Carly deserves it. She bled for us."

He looked up, and I saw that he knew I was right. He said, "Yeah, I get it. You think I should train her? Knowing what you know about her? You had questions before."

I laughed and said, "So now you're questioning her capability because you're no longer in the sack with her? You brought this on yourself. And, yes, I think she's capable. Any team showing an interest in her?"

Kurt had already decided that—*if* Carly succeeded—she wouldn't be coming to my team. For one, there was no reason to stack a single team with the unique capabilities a female might bring. For another, he wasn't keen on the fraternization. He allowed it with Jennifer and me because we were civilians, and he honestly couldn't do anything about it. Knuckles, being active-duty Navy, was a different story.

"Yeah. Johnny's team. Axe likes her. He's seen Jennifer and wants that in the mix. But she's not Jennifer."

"Nobody is Jennifer. Train her ass to the best of your ability. This is just an Alpha mission. If you don't do it, Jennifer will lose trust in you. And that means something on this team."

He nodded reluctantly, and my earpiece came alive with Retro's voice. "How long can I play? I'm pretty sure I've destroyed every key card within ten feet of me."

Retro had a device that generated an enormous electromagnetic field around him. In essence, he was carrying a giant magnet in his pocket, which would wipe any hotel key that came within his web. Two feet to the right of him was the Bulgarian, Stanko, his iPad mini on the rail as he gambled.

Kurt had given us what he knew about the Bulgarian, most of which was useless, but one tidbit stood out: Like Retro, he was fond of playing craps. It had been a simple matter to find Tyler's booth—learning his company had the unimaginative name ParaBellum—and follow Stanko for the short time it took him to begin gambling. From there, I'd set my plan in motion, with Retro now on board when he learned all he had to do was roll the dice. Well, until he had to do something embarrassing. Which was why he was calling.

I said, "Next time you get the dice. Play to your heart's content until then."

I heard, "That's three players. Is the Taskforce going to pay for the bets?"

"No fucking way. Force it now, if you want."

I heard, "I knew you were too cheap. I should have left this team a long time ago."

I laughed and said, "I thought you were winning."

"I was. Not now."

Seven minutes later, through Retro's microphone, I heard, "New shooter, new shooter." Then Retro himself saying, "Okay, here you go. One roll, and then he's off to his room."

Off the net, I said, "Knuckles, get ready."

"You sure about this? When I get in the elevator with him, I'm done, forever."

"Yeah, I know. Sorry. But you're doing your part for America."

He scowled, and we both looked at Retro's table. He rolled once, got what he wanted, and jumped up and down, spilling his vile cup of spit onto Stanko's shirt. Immediately, there was an altercation, with shouting and threats. Retro handled it well, backing off and offering chips as a placating measure. Stanko took them, then stalked off, heading to the elevator.

I looked at Knuckles and said, "Showtime."

He nodded and left, walking behind Stanko.

Ordinarily, we could have used the Taskforce to figure out this guy's room. A seamless little hack that would prevent the ridiculous play I had just put in motion. In this case, because the entire mission wasn't sanctioned by the Oversight Council, Kurt had refused to give me the assets I'd need to do that, stating that I had my team and that was it. I'd been aggravated about that but knew better than to push.

I either accepted the mission or I didn't. We'd just needed to find another way to determine his room, and the easiest way was to get him to go there, so we could follow him.

I watched Knuckles get in the elevator with Stanko, the only two to do so, and knew Knuckles was pissed. No way would he be able to do anything against this target again. Not after riding up an elevator with him.

I remained still, sipping my club soda and waiting on the call. It came in two minutes. "Passed by him. He's in room 703."

A minute later, "His key card failed. He's on the way back down."

I said, "Roger that. Jennifer, you got the ball. Give us a time hack."

She said, "Roger all."

Retro came over to my table and said, "You done with me? I'd like to get back some of what I lost in the name of the Taskforce."

"Yeah. I'm done until tonight. I'll need you then."

Retro walked and talked like a Neanderthal, but underneath, he was a little bit of a computer geek. Honestly, beyond the loss of his friendship, that was going to be the biggest blow to my team. When he was gone, I'd have to find a replacement on the tech side. But I already had an idea about who that would be—the millennial currently in SF sniper school.

I said, "You sure that gadget you brought will work?"

Retro had given Knuckles what looked like a standard iPad charging cord, one with the small brick at the end. Instead of Apple-approved electronics, inside the brick was a man-in-the-middle device that would allow us to digitally drain everything in the iPad through its lightning port. When Stanko plugged it in to charge, we'd start sucking it dry.

He said, "Yeah, it'll work. I tested it on my own iPad. It's set for the Venetian Wi-Fi network, and I can access the website that downloads the data from anywhere."

Jennifer came on the net. "Ivan's at reception."

We always gave targets a nickname, just to keep them straight in case there was more than one, because using real names on an open net was a nonstarter. Ivan seemed to fit here.

I said, "Roger . . . break, break . . . Knuckles, you in the room?"

"Yeah, I am, but we've got a problem. He's got the iPad cord going straight into a USB outlet from the hotel. There's a bank of them on the desk. He's not using the AC adapter."

Retro said, "He'll have to use it sooner or later. We don't get the info right now, we'll get it eventually."

I said, "It'll join any Wi-Fi hotspot?"

Retro sagged back, realizing his mistake. He said, "No. Not if it's password protected. That needs to be loaded in advance."

Jennifer came on. "He's done. He's got his new key card."

Shit.

"Knuckles, Knuckles, abort. Get out. We need to regroup on a different course of action."

Retro stood up, saying, "Well, that was worth it. Can I get back to the table?"

I rubbed my forehead and said, "Yeah. We're done here."

I watched Ivan return to the elevators, still wiping a napkin on Retro's stain, and called Knuckles. "He's on the way up. You clear?"

"No. I'm taking a look around. The desk has some paperwork on it."

"Abort. I don't want to risk him knowing we were in there. This is low-hanging fruit. We'll try something else tomorrow."

I heard nothing, prompting me to say, "Knuckles, you copy?"

He came back, "We won't be trying anything tomorrow. I have a paper itinerary here for a flight. He's headed out of town."

"Where?"

"Tel Aviv, Israel."

"What time is the flight?"

"He's leaving Las Vegas in the morning, and Tyler Malloy is on the same itinerary. I'm out of the room."

The first thing that popped into my mind was, *Mission accomplished.*

Jennifer came on: "Tel Aviv? What's there?"

Knuckles said, "Shoshana, for one. Now I'm glad I'm no good for future work."

6

★ ★ ★

Aaron Bergmann's inner being felt the light begin to coalesce around him, the kaleidoscope of insane nightmares receding into the darkness. Slowly, his brain gained traction, like a man at the bottom of a lake looking up at the illumination from the surface, the image blurred, but better than the darkness. His conscious mind swam, getting closer and closer, until instinct took over, and he willed himself to stop, just below the surface.

He cracked his eyes open slightly, hearing talking nearby. He found he was flex-tied to a chair, which in turn was bolted to the floor. He felt a wave of nausea and fought through to understand where he was without allowing those who held him to realize he was awake.

And then he remembered.

There had been six men, all African natives, and they had attacked with wild abandon. He remembered shattering the jaw of the first, then pulling Alex free—*Alexandra! Where was she?*—only to be attacked by another.

He had been clobbered in the back of the skull with something hard, taking him to his knees, and had covered his head. He remembered the man to the right driving a boot into his face, and him catching it, then launching upright, holding the foot. He twisted, causing the man's leg to contort around the knee, and he slammed his elbow down into the tangle of nerves embedded in the man's thigh, then flipped him on his back.

Panting, he whirled, seeing Alex cowering next to the wrecked vehicle. He screamed, "Run. Run now!" He saw her take off down the dilapidated brick walkway, then turned back to the fight, thinking one thing: *Hold them off. Focus on me. Give her the time.*

Four men came at him, unskilled in fighting, but the odds alone guaranteed failure. Remarkably, they didn't resort to knives or other weapons, attempting to subdue him through blunt force, and he realized *he* was the prize. Which gave him an advantage, as he had no such restraint.

One man charged him, swinging his arms and bellowing. Aaron rotated, punching the man in the head as he came by, then trapping his elbow and whirling him in a tight circle, using his energy to fling him back into the others, breaking through the pileup. He leapt over the roof of the wrecked vehicle, running to the nearest door of the dilapidated building. He kicked it open, entered, then rotated around, using the doorframe as a funnel to prevent all four from attacking him at the same time.

They remained on the other side, confused at his tactic, unsure of who was going to be the first in. Aaron's only thought was that the longer he held their attention, the farther away Alex could get.

The biggest one decided to penetrate and came in like a bull. Aaron waited until he was past the doorframe, then launched at him, using his skill in Krav Maga. He hammered the man up close with his elbows, tearing skin in a flurry of blows, finishing by slamming the man's head into the doorframe and dropping him in the narrow space. One more obstacle to reach him.

Breathing heavily, he watched the men outside, now pacing and cursing. For the first time, he looked for escape behind him, seeing a factory of decrepit equipment and floorboards soiled from the homeless. He faced a choice: If he turned to run, he'd allow them through his protective channel without knowing if he could get out. If he didn't, they'd eventually find a way in behind him. They had learned from the big man. They wouldn't make that mistake again, and he was sure they were looking to penetrate the building in other ways.

They knew the terrain, and he did not.

He heard glass break to his left, beyond the room he was in, and realized they were coming. He decided on a feint.

He ran away from the doorway, apparently showing panic and giving the men outside a reason to attack. He buttonhooked to the left in the gloom, watching them pour in trying to find him, silhouetted by the light from the door. He waited until they passed and then ran out the door behind them, hitting the street at full speed.

He sprinted toward the tourist area of the Orlando Towers, seeing the remaining crowds still trickling to the parking lot. He felt hope, even as he heard the men spill out behind him. He knew they couldn't do anything once he was within the embrace of the tourists.

He saw an end to the row of buildings, and the expanse of the adventure playground in front of him, and redoubled his efforts. Sprinting forward with renewed energy, prematurely going through in his mind how he would contact his neophyte assistant, he cleared the final building and was clotheslined by the forearm of the blond man from the table meeting. He hammered the ground hard and rolled to his knees, trying to regain his lost momentum, but he couldn't. The man pushed him into the dirt with a hand on his neck and said, "Don't fight me."

Aaron did anyway, although it did no good. He was immediately surrounded by the other Africans, all attacking, burying him in bodies. The blond brought out a needle and shoved it into his thigh, saying, "Stop struggling. I have no reason to hurt you."

That was the last thing he remembered, and now he was tied to a chair in a room somewhere in South Africa. Or maybe not.

He heard, "What do you want to do?"

Then, in a heavy native African accent: "Give him to me. I can make him disappear."

Aaron recognized the next voice. It was the blond man who'd captured him, which probably meant the African accent was the man from the tape. The one called General Mosebo. The blond said, "And the girl?"

"I can make her disappear too."

Aaron mentally sagged. *So they have Alex.*

"How? She's Israeli. As is he. You can't make them 'disappear' without causing them to hunt us. You don't want to fuck with Israel, trust me."

From the general, Aaron heard, "Why? Their country is no bigger than mine."

"Have you never heard of the Wrath of God operations?"

"No. Should I have?"

Aaron heard laughter; then the blond man said, "Yes. You say their country is no bigger than yours, but when's the last time Lesotho traveled the world assassinating terrorists? Trust me, if you want to play with matches, you should at least read about a few barn fires."

Aaron racked his brain, trying to find an anchor as to why he was being held, but came up short. *Lesotho . . . Lesotho. What do they have to do with anything?*

The thick accent repeated, "Give them to me. I can make them disappear. Israel won't find them in my land."

Another man began talking, using a language Aaron didn't recognize and most certainly didn't understand. It wasn't the clicks and glottal stops of the Xhosa language, and wasn't Zulu, the predominant native language spoken in South Africa. The revelation increased his unease.

The conversation stopped, and the general said, "We can get him to a secret place. We can hide him until we decide what to do. Either way, we need to get him out of Durban. Out of South Africa."

Durban. That was at least six hours by road from Johannesburg. How long had he been out?

A new voice said, "What about the partner? The one the girl told us about? The one in Israel? She needs to be taken care of as well."

The blond voice said, "Yes. She will. But we can use her for leverage."

Shoshana. They know about Shoshana. What has Alex told them?

Before he could analyze the new information, the door to his room opened. He closed his eyes and let his head loll down. He heard, "How long are those drugs supposed to work?"

"Depends. There are a lot of factors, like if he just ate, or his muscle mass, or whether he was dehydrated, or—"

"Don't give me that doctor bullshit. Give me an answer."

Aaron heard the blond man speak. "He's awake."

The footsteps approached, and Aaron remained still. The doctor said, "He's not awake, but he will be. Given his body mass, he should have been out for twenty-four hours. Anytime now. The girl is a different story."

The blond said, "He's awake. He's fucking with us."

Aaron felt a fist curl into his hair and his head jerked upright. He opened his eyes, knowing the subterfuge was done.

The blond said, "Everyone out of the room. Now."

Aaron watched the scrum leave, remaining mute. The blond turned to him and said, "My name is Johan, and I've been tasked to find out why you're following us. Look, I don't like getting rough. I honestly don't. Please make this easy on me. Just tell me what you're doing here, and why."

Aaron spoke the truth, knowing that Alex had probably given up everything she knew. "I was sent to prevent embarrassment to Israel. They are afraid of nefarious diamond dealing. Afraid of a stain on the diamond exchange. That's all."

Johan nodded, then said, "I wouldn't expect you to tell the truth right up front. I'd believe you, except you happened to focus on me in Soweto, and I have nothing to do with the diamond exchange." He shook his head and said, "Too bad. You stepped into a world of shit."

He let go of Aaron's head, saying, "I'll let your partner live, if you just tell me how much Israel knows about our plans."

Aaron said, "Where is Alexandra?"

"She's here. I've already interrogated Alex. She's a nobody. Clearly untrained. Someone duped by the state of Israel and now regretting it. Her death will be on your hands."

He turned and gave Aaron the full force of his gaze, an unsettling stab. Aaron realized he was looking into the eyes of a man who had killed. Many, many times.

"But that's not the partner I'm talking about. I mean your *real* partner. The one in Israel. You tell me what you know, and I'll let *her* live."

Aaron heard the words and for the first time felt a sliver of hope. Left unsaid was Aaron's fate, but that mattered little. Since the moment of his capture, Aaron knew there was no chance of the Mossad helping. No rescue was forthcoming, and it had weighed heavily on his psyche, most notably because he felt responsible for Alexandra.

He was nothing but a contractor, hired precisely to prevent Mossad fingerprints on the operation in question. He was a piece of tissue the Mossad used to blow its nose and, once soiled, easy to toss aside. But his partner in Israel was something altogether different. She cared about him.

And she was a force unlike any this man had ever confronted.

Aaron said, "I have told you what I know, which is nothing. I have no idea what's going on here. I'm just a contractor hired by the diamond exchange to make sure their reputation is not sullied. That's all. Alexandra is even less. I brought her solely because of her knowledge of the exchange. Let her go. Leave us be. I won't tell anyone what's occurred. There is no reason whatsoever to involve my partner in Israel."

Johan withdrew a set of knuckle rings, a small, two-finger version of brass knuckles. With a sad expression on his face, the disgust of what he was forced to do apparently real, he said, "I'll know what you know soon enough. And you've just killed your partner. Our reach is long, and I must ensure our operation is contained."

Aaron steeled himself, knowing he would have to trade in order to be rescued, and the currency in question was pain. He had to force them to hunt in Israel.

The man in front of him had no idea of what he was threatening when he mentioned Aaron's partner. He thought he understood pain. Understood death. And he probably did, on an earthly plane. But Shoshana was made of something entirely different.

She was a supernatural predator who caused fear even in Aaron. Going after her would guarantee a response, if he could remain alive long enough to see it. Shoshana would unleash her skills only if she deemed the reason worthy, and, unfortunately for these men, harming him would trigger a reaction unlike anything they had ever seen.

Because he had the honor of being deemed worthy.

Shoshana kept her eyelids shut and rolled over, but she knew it was no use. She felt the light coming in through the window and succumbed to it. She opened her eyes. For a second, she was disoriented, not recognizing the room. Then she remembered: She was in a hotel in Haifa. By herself.

For the first time in a long while, she'd allowed herself to sleep until she rolled out of bed naturally, but she'd still awakened at the first light of dawn.

She threw off her covers and padded to the dresser, reaching for her cell phone. There were no missed calls. That wasn't unusual, given the nature of their work, but last night she'd had a bad feeling, and not in a normal, ephemeral way that most people get. It was visceral, and she had learned long ago to trust in her instincts.

She had a connection to the world around her that she couldn't explain, but she knew it existed. And it had saved her life on more than one occasion.

This feeling was different, though, in that it was tinged with something else besides danger. Was it jealousy? Was that it?

She had no way of knowing, because she'd never experienced that emotion in her entire life, until she'd seen Alexandra with Aaron.

Shoshana's history, like much of the history of Israel, had been one of hardship. Her ancestors had fled Europe to escape the slaughter of the Holocaust, only to meet the same end at the hands of a new breed of killer. Her grandfather had been murdered in the Munich Olympics massacre, sacrificing his life in a futile attempt to stop the Black September terrorists. She had been told of his heroic acts from the moment she could understand Hebrew, and then, when she was only ten, her parents were blown apart by a Hamas suicide bomber.

An only child, she had become an orphan—an orphan with a mission. She had served her mandatory time in the IDF military but wasn't satisfied. She'd gravitated to the Mossad and was invited to join, where she'd learned more things about killing than she'd ever learned about flying helicopters. The Mossad saw quickly that she held a talent for their world, and they used it, until it warped her.

And then she'd found Aaron.

She'd been thrown onto his team by the command, against the wishes of Aaron's teammates. Her last team had branded her a coward at best, and a traitor at worst, solely because she wouldn't kill an innocent man. A Palestinian she'd been forced to sleep with to set him up for the hit. She'd seen something in him, and not in a trusting, storybook way. She'd *really* seen something in his aura. Something nobody else apparently could. And she'd learned she was cursed with a gift.

Aaron had ignored the baggage and taken her on his team, when nobody else in Mossad would touch her, and she'd returned the favor by saving his life on an operation in Argentina mere weeks later—when nobody else would help. They had clicked.

For the first time in her bloody existence, she had connected with another human being. It had taken time, to be sure, with her unable to even understand the difference between simple respect and love, but eventually, they had both reached it.

She thought.

She had seen Aaron look at Alexandra when he'd first met her for the mission brief, surprised at her attractiveness. It had infuriated and confused her. Her entire universe of sexual experience had been sleeping with targets she was marking for a kill. Until she'd met Aaron, she'd never made love. Had never competed for a man in her entire life—had never even entertained the notion—and now she wondered if she was fighting for not only the man but also the single human on earth who understood her.

It had been disconcerting, and she wondered about the missing phone calls. Was it the mission? Or something else?

She looked at herself in the mirror, hoping to see what she knew wasn't there. And she was rewarded with exactly what her subconscious mind realized: She wasn't conventionally attractive. But she'd never cared about that before.

She made no attempt to wear makeup and had the body of a fifteen-year-old boy. It was nothing but muscle and sinew, without womanly curves. No bust and no hips; her shape couldn't compete with Alexandra's voluptuous assets, with the exception of her face. Thin and aquiline, it would have played well on the fashion runways of Milan, if only her body had decided to cooperate, but she understood none of that.

The pretty girls of her youth were crowned beauty queens and hailed but eventually faded to the background, making way for the next generation, as they all do with the onslaught of age. Shoshana had not. She became an elite killer, scaring even the ones who commanded her. She was an anomaly unlike anything the Mossad had ever seen. She could penetrate any defense, using an uncanny ability to read the opposition, and could kill without remorse. She was the perfect weapon. Right up until she decided she no longer wanted to be a weapon.

Looking in the mirror, she failed to see past the reflection, to what Aaron saw. What connected them. She'd seen his reaction to Alexandra and knew she wasn't even in the same league as her, and it made her question.

Was the feeling last night because of that? Or was it real? Was Aaron in danger, or was her relationship?

She was startled by her phone vibrating, and she snatched it up, looking at the screen. She saw a gobbledygook number—something that was clearly masked—and felt dread. It was the Mossad.

She answered in a hesitant voice, "Hello?"

"Hey, Carrie, it's Pike. I'm in town."

She heard the stupid callsign the Americans had given her and suppressed a grin, her earlier angst forgotten. Pike Logan was the last person she expected to hear from but exactly what she needed. He was all about the mission and would chastise her for her failing emotions.

He aggravated her to no end, usually bringing her to the point of wanting to slice his carotid arteries just to get him to shut up, but she never did, because when she looked into his eyes and read his soul, she saw he was just as tortured as she was. And just as good at killing. Once upon a time, he had crawled out of the abyss, finding Jennifer and a new life. She wanted to do the same.

"What on earth are you doing calling me? Don't tell me you want a tax receipt for that last mission. I can't help it if you are in trouble with your IRS."

She hadn't seen Jennifer and Pike since the wedding, and truth be told, she missed them. Missed teasing Pike, especially.

He said, "Naw, it's nothing like that. We're in town, helping out with some UNESCO work on that Caesarea site, and thought we could have dinner."

"Caesarea? Are you toying with me?"

Besides being a UNESCO World Heritage site, Caesarea also happened to be the name of the section in the Mossad that conducted covert action and was the organization that Shoshana had belonged to before she and Aaron went freelance.

"No, no, it's Caesarea for real. I was told not to even contact you, if you know what I mean, but I can't come to Tel Aviv without having a beer with you and Aaron."

She knew exactly what he meant. He and his partner, Jennifer, owned a company called Grolier Recovery Services, which ostensibly did archaeological work around the world but in reality allowed the United States to penetrate hostile states to put some threat into the ground. Mentioning Caesarea and saying he wasn't supposed to contact her told volumes: He was here on a mission, and it was outside the purview of the Mossad.

And the fact that he had told her that—knowing she would connect the dots—spoke volumes as well. He trusted her.

She didn't return the favor, giving a half-truth. "I'd like that, but you picked the worst week, dummy. We're up at the Dan Carmel in Haifa on a little vacation."

"The much-talked-about honeymoon? Aaron finally agreed?"

"Yes." *Well, he agreed until the mission came down.*

Aaron had already booked and paid for the hotel and had planned on surprising her with the getaway—and he had. Only now, instead of a happy event, it had been an afterthought as he was headed out the door with Alexandra. She'd decided to come up on her own.

Pike said, "Well, how far is Haifa? It can't be more than a couple of hours. How about we finish up here and meet you guys there?"

Quicker than she wanted, she said, "No, no. We're committed up here. We have something planned every day." She wasn't sure if she was protecting the fact that Aaron was active on a mission or protecting herself from embarrassment when they found out she was up here alone.

He said, "You have to eat, don't you? And Jennifer's dying to see Shoshana in married life. She's pretty sure you've killed Aaron and stuffed him in a hole somewhere."

Shoshana laughed and said, "Jennifer, or you?"

"Well, okay. Me."

"I figured. How long are you here for?"

"Probably a week."

Aaron should be back before then.

"Okay, let me talk to Aaron. Give us a couple of days and maybe we can break free."

8

I hung up the phone just as Jennifer exited the bathroom, wearing a bathrobe and padding around barefoot, running a brush through her hair. She said, "So, was she surprised?"

I said, "She was surprised." I glanced out the window of our hotel room, seeing the shoreline of Tel Aviv but running through Shoshana's call.

Jennifer stopped her brushing, saying, "But?"

I turned back to her and said, "But it was strange. She was strange. She doesn't want to see us."

"What? Seriously?"

"Well, she's with Aaron in Haifa, at some hotel called Dan Carmel. She didn't seem too interested in our visit."

Jennifer perked up at that, saying, "They're together at a hotel in Haifa? Is this the honeymoon?"

"That's what she said. But I don't know."

Shoshana was one of the strangest women—hell, humans—I'd ever met. When we'd first collided, I'd tried to kill her, believing she was responsible for the death of one of my men. I had failed. Later on, we'd crossed paths again, and she'd proven to be one of the most lethal operators I've ever met. She manifested some sort of weird animal vibe, like a dog that growled when a rapist entered a room. She saw things in the soul and could penetrate a man's intentions just by being in his presence. Truth be told, it was a little scary. I poked fun at her on the surface, but I'd learned it was real.

She'd had no social skills to speak of when we first met and had taken what I considered an unhealthy interest in my relationship with Jennifer, as if she was learning how a man and woman interacted, almost like an alien life-form. Aaron suffered through it, coaxing her along, or so I'd thought. He was the yang to her yin, and they clicked no less than Jennifer and I—on some weird astral plane. Eventually, they'd left the Mossad and set up their own private security firm, but I was pretty sure all of their money still came from that intelligence agency.

They'd married about six months ago in Jerusalem, and we'd been at the wedding, which, of course, since Shoshana was involved, turned into a damn fiasco. Jennifer had asked where they were taking their honeymoon, and Shoshana had latched on to that, having no idea such a thing existed. Aaron had rolled his eyes, but Shoshana was insistent, and it looked like she'd finally convinced him, six months later.

Jennifer said, "Well, maybe it's better to leave them alone. We don't want to do a repeat of the wedding."

Which was an understatement. I said, "I'm with you, but something was off. She wasn't Shoshana."

Jennifer threw a towel at me and said, "Quit reading into things. Let them have their fun. We have a mission here."

I grinned and said, "Thank God Kurt broke Brett free. Otherwise, we'd never get any sleep."

She went back into the bathroom, saying, "I'm not sure how he's helping us sleep."

I shouted, "What's that mean? I gave him the early shift."

She poked her head out and said, "Really? He gets the shift at six in the morning, and you still wake me up?"

"You didn't mind that at six A.M."

She smiled and said, "No. But it didn't add to my sleep."

I grinned and said, "We all have to sacrifice."

She raised an eyebrow, but I knew she wasn't going to push it. She said, "What's his status, anyway?"

"Still in the lobby. Waiting."

Our turnaround from Las Vegas had been immediate, with Knuckles and Retro heading back to DC, and Jennifer and me flying straight out to Tel Aviv. Knuckles had tried to argue one more time, saying he could man the TOC or something else not involving surveillance, but Kurt had overridden that decision.

We'd met Brett Thorpe at JFK, and, as expected, he was ready with a wry response after getting pulled from his liaison job. He'd held up his ticket and said, "Kurt told me to catch this flight. I asked why, and all he said was 'Pike Logan.' I saw the location as Israel, heard your name, and knew they were punishing the black man."

Brett was a short fireplug of a man, about five foot six and solid muscle. He'd been a Recon Marine in a prior life but had spent ten years inside the CIA's Special Activities Division before he was recruited to the Taskforce. At first, I'd been extremely skeptical of him—because he was CIA and we all belong to tribes—but he'd proven himself on a mission in Lebanon, with both his skill and his sense of humor, and I'd moved heaven and earth to get him on my team.

Kurt said I was stacking the deck, which, of course, was true, but he'd allowed it. Brett's comment was accurate enough, in that he'd stand out as an African American in Israel, but his skills overcame any doubt I had about him being able to operate. He was one of the best I'd ever seen.

I'd said, "Well, you weren't my first choice, but you know the push for diversity. I was only allowed one white boy, which meant me. With you and Jennifer, the team's a perfect example of what the world should be."

He'd laughed and said, "What's our cover?"

"Working it now."

During the twelve-hour flight, our cover story had been built, complete with official recognition from unwitting agencies within the United Nations. Ostensibly, we were going to make an assessment of the ongoing excavations at Caesarea, an ancient port just north of Tel Aviv designated a World Heritage site. Explorations had found extensive further archeological structures still buried, and we were going to help facilitate the bureaucracy of the UN in the work, using Jennifer's arcane knowledge of everything that was as old as dirt. When we'd found out through the Gogo inflight Wi-Fi, she'd literally clapped her hands. I told her not to get too excited. Chances were we would never set foot on the grounds.

We'd landed, met the UN folks at the US embassy, and coordinated for future meetings—which was how all of that shit always worked. None of those people could ever simply say what was needed. It was always one meeting after another, with me wanting to punch the people in the room. Jennifer, of course, tried valiantly to tie us into a trip to the site, knowing we would have to go if we said we would. They had said, "Of course. But first we must determine the parameters of how you can help us decide what we're going to do next." Basically, they were saying, *Not so fast. We get paid by the day. Let's drag this out a little bit.*

She'd been aggravated, but it gave us time to set our real mission in motion. For this one, we had the full backing of the Oversight Council, so we had all the tech and reach-back capability we needed. We knew the room the target was in and had reserved a room in the same hotel—the Hilton on the coast of Tel Aviv. What we didn't know was what the guy was up to, which was why I had been sent for the Alpha mission.

To start unraveling that thread, I'd placed Brett in the lobby early, drinking coffee and waiting on the target or his Bulgarian thug to exit the elevator.

9

★ ★ ★

Jennifer dropped the robe, put on her bra, and began pulling on a pair of jeans. Innocently, as if she cared only about the mission, she said, "I think we should go to Caesarea if this doesn't pan out in the next few hours. I mean, we're supposedly getting paid by the United States to do that. We could leave Brett here."

I laughed and said, "We're getting paid by the United States to figure out what that asshole is up to."

She slid her arms into a blouse and said, "Cover, Pike. We have to maintain our cover. We can't do anything over here without protection. You're the one who taught me that."

I said, "Okay, okay. I get it. You want to go look at pottery shards. We'll do it. I promise."

Jennifer's first love was archeology, and she was perennially aggravated that our cover never let her actually see the sites we were supposedly supporting. She'd earned at least one trip to a site.

She slid her feet into a pair of Salomon hikers and said, "You promise? We don't do it today and you know it's not happening."

I said, "Yeah, okay. After we flesh out what's going on. I'll take you there myself."

She sighed and said, "We're in the land of the Bible, with more history per square mile than anyplace on earth. And I'm not going to see any of that, am I?"

"No, no. You will. I promise."

Our computer dinged, and she went to it. She took one look at the screen and said, "Liar."

I ran to the computer and saw, *Pair's on the move. Just came to the lobby. They're getting coffee. Get your ass down here.*

I typed back, *On the way. Stage the vehicles,* then looked at Jennifer with chagrin. I said, "Sorry. I can't predict this stuff."

She threw her bag over her shoulder and said, "Yeah, yeah. Story of my life."

I said, "I really didn't plan this. Come on."

She held the door open, a little wicked grin on her face, saying, "Well, this just jacks it up another carat."

Lately, she'd started keeping a tally of my perceived transgressions. The score was in the currency of precious stones. Didn't do the dishes on my turn, making her wash a plate? That's an eighth of a carat. Our mangy, diabolically evil cat taking a shit on the floor because I didn't change out the litter box? A quarter. Deploy for an archeological site and not get to see it? A full carat.

I had no idea if she was kidding or not, and didn't want to even broach the fact that she was talking about a diamond. That had all sorts of subliminal connotations.

I grabbed our backpack of tech gear, both of us racing out. We reached the lobby and saw our targets crossing it, each carrying a paper cup of coffee. We ignored them, heading straight to the revolving door exit.

Getting outside, I saw Brett down the circular drive at a pullout, leaning on a vehicle. We got to him, and he tossed me a key fob, saying, "I'm getting reimbursed for the valet tip."

I clicked the door locks and said, "Easy day. You take a car as singleton. Jennifer and I have the other one. You got your earpiece running?"

"Yeah."

I clicked mine and said, "Test, test."

I heard him next to me, then in my ear: "I got you."

I said, "Okay, today's just exploratory. Let's see where they go, what they do. Get us an angle on what's going on. Remember, it might be nothing at all."

Brett slid into the seat of his car and said, "Somehow, you'll manage to turn nothing into high adventure."

I grinned and said, "We can only hope—but remember, it's Alpha only. The high adventure will come later, when we prove this guy's an asshole."

I saw Tyler Malloy exit with his sidekick from Bulgaria and took a closer look at him. As much as I wanted it to be true, he was not a pussy. Dressed in 5.11 pants, a Columbia shirt, and a Mountain Hardwear fleece jacket, he looked just like any other military contractor on the planet, but he was no longer a gunslinger and had no reason to dress like one. He was now an international arms dealer, and the fact that he refused to dress the part in his new position told me volumes.

He was about six-two and carried some weight, and not in a bad way. He hadn't left the Marines and dived into Mickey D's and Pop-Tarts. He'd clearly stayed in shape, and, of course, he maintained the operator beard, which I found ridiculous, because he was never an operator. But obviously, he thought he was.

They entered a Crown Vic limo and passed us, and we picked up the follow, Brett leading. They went through the intersection at the main road of HaYarkon, passing by the British embassy, and we hung with them a few cars back. They made no left or right turns, so the surveillance effort was pretty simple. Eventually, we entered Ramat Gan, a city/suburb east of Tel Aviv. We wound around for a few minutes, the channelized nature of the roads giving me confidence that we wouldn't be tagged as following.

Abruptly, the Crown Vic stopped outside of some mall area with four tall buildings jutting into the sky. Brett passed the drop-off, going deep and saying, "Diamond exchange."

I pulled up short with Jennifer and said, "What's that?"

"Just what I said. It's the Israeli diamond exchange. And it's locked down tight."

Jennifer had already been working her tablet and said, "It's one of the biggest diamond exchanges in the world. It rivals Antwerp."

She poked and prodded her tablet a bit more, then said, "It has some serious security. We aren't getting in there."

Shit.

I watched the two exit, and enter the front doors of the exchange. I waited a beat, then said, "Stage here. Let's see what happens."

Within two minutes, I saw the target we called Ivan exit. He stood on the steps for a minute, then waved over the limo.

Decision time.

I said, "Got Ivan out front now. Blood, I want you to stay on the building. We're going to take the trailer and see where it leads us."

Brett said, "Only if you quit using that callsign."

Everyone in the Taskforce had a callsign, and usually for something they did that wasn't stellar. I'd anointed him with the callsign "Blood," and he despised it.

I said, "No promises. Ivan's in the limo. We're rolling."

10

★ ★ ★

Tyler Malloy told the hired car to wait on them, then bounded up the stairs to the entrance of the diamond exchange, Stanko Petrov right behind him. He opened the door and said, "That fucker had better be down here to let us in."

Stanko said, "He'd be a fool not to."

Tyler moved into the foyer, seeing a security setup that looked like a cross between a top secret SCIF and a TSA airport screening. Metal detectors, thumbprint scanners, and six-foot rotating turnstile doors made of bars. Out front was a long desk staffed by men behind bulletproof glass. They looked at him expectantly, and he was brought up short. He glanced around, seeing nobody in the foyer who wasn't engaged, then approached one of the windows.

He said, "I'm supposed to meet a man named Eli Cohen. He works here."

The guard said, "I'm sorry, sir. I have no way to contact him. There are hundreds of diamond merchants, and they arrange the visits. I just process the application through."

Tyler cursed and turned away from the window. Stanko pulled his sleeve and pointed at a man coming through the metal turnstile. He was short, about five-five, with a mop of gray hair and a drooping mustache; his head was on a swivel, looking left and right.

Tyler locked eyes with him, and he came scurrying over. "Tyler Malloy?"

"Yes."

He stuck out his hand, saying, "I'm Eli Cohen. Sorry. I got held up. Let's get you inside so we can talk."

He glanced at Stanko, then said, "Is he with you?"

"Yes."

Tyler did the introductions, explaining who Stanko was and where he was from, and Eli said, "Nice to meet you, but you cannot come inside."

Tyler said, "Why not?"

"He's Bulgarian. I had no advance notice. He'll need a background check, and they won't do it while we wait. I'm sorry, but it's actually to our advantage."

"What do you mean?"

He glanced at the security window, making sure they were out of earshot, then said, "Our friends from South Africa are here. There's been a complication."

"What kind of complication?"

"There was someone watching the meeting, and he possibly heard what we were doing. He has a partner here. They came to take care of the problem."

"What the fuck? We're already compromised?"

"I don't want to talk out here. Just have your friend go meet them to see what they're up to. It would be better for all."

Tyler was about to tell the man to kiss his ass when Stanko touched his arm and said, "I can do that. No harm in listening." Meaning, *Don't throw this away because you're insulted.*

Tyler nodded, and Eli gave him an address to a restaurant in Jaffa, just south of Tel Aviv. Stanko left, and Tyler said, "Okay, get me into your office, because I definitely have some questions."

Eli approached the security window, showed his badge, and said a few words in Hebrew. He turned to Tyler and said, "Passport, please." Tyler switched places with him and surrendered his passport. He answered a few questions, placed his thumb on a fingerprint capture device, then had his photo taken. Two minutes later, he was given a new badge.

Eli led him to the security checkpoint, where he basically repeated the procedure, emptying his pockets for X-ray, passing across his badge, and placing his thumb on a fingerprint reader. Tyler followed Eli through the metal detector, and the guard manning it pointed at his cell phone, saying, "No pictures."

Tyler nodded, actually impressed at the security. Walking to the elevator, he said, "Is there some giant vault in this place, like Fort Knox?"

"No. Every company on the exchange has its own safe. The security is tight because at any given moment, people are wandering around here with millions of dollars' worth of diamonds."

Two men in yarmulkes came by, both pulling black roll-aboard luggage.

Eli pointed and said, "Those two aren't dragging their clothes from a plane flight. The bags are full of diamonds."

Crossing the foyer toward the elevators, he pointed to the left, toward a sunken open area full of desks, saying, "That's the trading floor. Rough stones on one side, polished on the other. Biggest exchange in the world."

"I thought Antwerp was bigger."

"So they say. Either way, we're the most respected. Our word is our bond."

The elevator closed, and they began to rise to the third floor. Tyler said, "If this is such a respected institution, why are you doing what you're doing?"

Eli said, "Respect doesn't pay the bills."

They exited the elevator and traveled down a sterile hallway, stopping at a simple metal office door. Eli unlocked it, and inside was a small, opulent showroom, complete with chandelier, oak walls lined with jewelry, cherrywood oval table, and Victorian chairs. In the back, past the showroom, were a couple of offices, one manned, one empty.

Eli closed the doors and said, "The truth of the matter is that the Israeli diamond exchange is under assault from a thousand different points. Child cutters in India, blood diamonds, wholesalers who have turned our business into a box store, and outsourcing to the third world; it's becoming fragmented. Israel used to be the epicenter of the diamond world. It's not anymore. People who've worked the exchange for generations are getting out—and not because they want to. That's not going to happen to me."

"What do you mean? How is the project in Lesotho going to help with that?"

"Lesotho produces the largest gem-quality diamonds in the world, but De Beers owns all the mines. Currently, the government only owns thirty percent of the production, but they're opening two new mines, which will be owned by the Kingdom of Lesotho, not De Beers. And, if we succeed, that government will be amenable to me. No middleman. Just me."

Tyler nodded, now understanding the *why* of his business deal here. Ordinarily, he didn't care one way or the other what happened with his weapons, but this time, he was betting on the come—providing his services without a concrete payout—so it was good to see the state of play.

"So, you put in Makalo Lenatha as prime minister, and he repays you with favorable diamond concessions, is that it?"

"Yes. In a nutshell. The current prime minister is no babe in the woods. He has enough corruption charges against him to sink the *Titanic*. He's just skilled in deflecting attention. We remove him, provide the evidence, and Lenatha, as the deputy prime minister, steps in. An easy coup."

"What if General Mosebo decides he'd rather be in charge? He's the one who controls the monopoly of violence. He's got the LDF Special Forces on his side. Which is being charitable in the description of that unit."

"He's on board, and those men are going to be the bulwark of the mission. All he wants is to remain as the head of the Lesotho Defence Force. The prime minister has demanded he retire, and he doesn't want to. Lenatha has told him that if he'll play ball, he can remain in charge of the LDF. That's all he wants. The prime minister was stupid to force the general's hand."

Tyler slowly nodded, then said, "What about the opposition party? The ones who stormed the streets last year?"

Eli snapped his head to him, and Tyler said, "You didn't think I'd get involved without a little bit of research, did you? What about the do-gooder party that everyone loves? The one that everyone wants in power? What if they come into play? It won't be a bloodless coup. It'll be a bloodbath. Can you withstand that on the evening news?"

Eli sat heavily in a chair and said, "Mosebo has taken care of their leader. They are no longer a force."

Tyler toyed with a necklace on the wall, his back to Eli. He said, "Taken care of him."

Eli said, "None of this is clean. Don't tell me you've grown a conscience."

Tyler turned around and said, "I'm just judging success, because whatever happens, I want to get paid." He bored his eyes into Eli and said, "And you've not given me a whit of confidence that you can do that."

11

★ ★ ★

Eli Cohen leaned back in his chair and waved an arm, saying, "You'll be paid. If not in what you want, I'll do it in cash."

"I don't want cash. I can get *cash* anywhere, with much, much less risk. I want the triggers. You said you could do that, and if you're telling me my alternative is a cash payment, I'm out."

"I can get them."

"How? You've never said. Are they Israeli? Are you stealing them from here, or what?"

"No." Eli sighed, then said, "Okay, I'll tell you something I'd hoped to keep hidden. Before I was a diamond merchant, before I followed in my father's footsteps, I was in LEKEM. You know it?"

"No. Never heard of it."

"We were the intelligence agency tasked with gleaning nuclear secrets for the Israeli nuclear weapons program. We traveled far and wide, stealing whatever industrial secrets we could to build our capability, sometimes by subterfuge, and other times with witting partners."

"The United States?"

"Maybe. Maybe not. Anyway, when we were done, we helped South Africa with Project Circle—the development of *their* atomic bomb. We were successful. They built six of them. In 1989, with apartheid ripping the country apart, the president, de Klerk, gave them up. He dismantled them. The bombs no longer exist, but your triggers do."

"And how can you get them?"

"I told you, I was LEKEM. My contacts remain. I can get them, I promise."

"I need the actual Krytron triggers. Not some bullshit. I need the real deal."

"I understand." Eli turned his chair and faced Tyler head-on. "I must ask, if you don't mind, who you intend to sell those triggers to. They are incredibly hard to manufacture, with tolerances that very few technologically sophisticated states can produce. Which means you aren't selling them to the West. They could make their own."

"Don't worry about that. I have a buyer. I don't ask about your diamond crap, you don't ask about my sales."

"But you did ask about my 'diamond crap.' Tell me it isn't Iran."

Tyler chuckled, then said, "It isn't Iran."

Eli nodded, saying, "Good. There are steps I won't take."

Tyler said, "Don't get your hopes up just yet. I haven't agreed to help. I still don't know what you want."

Eli went to his office, came back, and passed a sheet of paper across the table. He said, "This is what they need."

Tyler looked at the first line and said, "An aircraft with crew? HALO rigs? You want me to do more than just supply armament?"

"You said you could."

Tyler placed the paper on the desk and said, "Who are these guys?"

"It's a company called Pamwe Chete. The CEO is Colonel Lloyd Armstrong. He was a Rhodesian Selous Scout. You've heard of them?"

Tyler nodded, saying, "Yeah. I've heard of them. Guys who used to penetrate denied areas acting as the enemy guerrillas during Rhodesia's civil war. Pure balls."

"Yes. That's correct. When Rhodesia fell, he joined the South African Defence Force, in the Reconnaissance Commandos. He has extensive experience in this type of work. He's an expert."

Tyler nodded and said, "Okay, it sounds like you've got a force that isn't a clownfest, but what was the complication you mentioned earlier?"

Eli rubbed his face, glanced out the window, then said, "It appears we've been breached."

Tyler was floored. "Breached? What the fuck are you talking about?"

"There was a man in Soweto. He was following our team, and we captured him."

"And? What did he say?" Tyler knew beyond a shadow of a doubt that the men who'd captured him wouldn't be squeamish in the questioning, and the detainee would have talked.

"He held out for a long time. So long that the team feels he really didn't know anything. He had no knowledge of our operation and was apparently sent because of some shady dealings here, in the diamond exchange."

"You mean shady dealings with *you*?"

Eli snapped upright and said, "No. My name was never mentioned. Ever."

"Well, he was either following the contractors or he was following your man. Since he was talking about the diamond exchange, it seems pretty simple why he was there."

"It wasn't me, per se. He was there on some fishing expedition. We're not even sure he was from the Israeli government. I think it's some investigation that's much bigger than just my company, but we don't know for sure. We're not sure of anything except he has no knowledge of our coup."

"So he's dead?"

"No. Johan—the man who captured him from our team—feels it's better to keep him alive. As leverage."

"Leverage for what?"

"In case we're wrong."

"Well, that's fucking great. You believe you've been compromised, so you're keeping him as a bargaining chip? Why the hell should I continue?"

Eli grinned and said, "Because you want the triggers."

Tyler pulled back a chair and finally sat down. He said, "What's the team doing here? Who's Stanko meeting?"

"The man has a partner. She might raise an alarm if he doesn't contact her. We believe she's his control. She is expendable. He's only good as leverage as long as it's unknown he's captured. They're here to clean that up."

"He's working for someone higher than just one partner. Someone's paying him. Eventually, they'll know."

"Yes, but not before we've accomplished our mission. We aren't keeping him for a month."

Tyler played with a pen on the desk, spinning it in his hands. He finally nodded, saying, "Stanko is good at this sort of thing. He's the best at cutting leaks."

Eli smiled, relieved to have Tyler on board, thinking of the profits he would realize with his new diamond tenders. He stood up and held out his hand. When Tyler shook it, he said, "*Mazal u'bracha.*"

Tyler let go, saying, "What's that mean?"

"It's the traditional way of the diamond market. It means the deal is sealed and I stake my honor on its completion."

Eli said it with pride, not giving a thought to the fact that much more than his honor was at stake. He would learn that soon.

Pike pulled in behind the Crown Vic, two cars back, and said, "Give me a read. What's he doing?"

Looking at the tablet in her lap, a satellite feed of a moving map of Tel Aviv scrolling on the screen, Jennifer said, "He's definitely not going back to the hotel. He's headed south, toward Jaffa."

"Okay, that's good. He's got a mission."

"Or he's going shopping in the flea market."

Pike turned off the primary highway, still three cars back, and began winding through the surface streets. He said, "What flea market?"

Jennifer looked up from her tablet and said, "Do you really not do any mission prep before you travel?"

"Well, I packed the tech kit Creed gave me. And I dug out Shoshana and Aaron's phone numbers. Does that count?"

"No. It doesn't. Jaffa has a flea market that spans city blocks. People go there to shop."

Pike spun through another intersection and said, "That fucker isn't shopping for souvenirs. Trust me. What else is in Jaffa?"

Chagrined, Jennifer said, "You should really do some research before we fly."

"I'll do it tonight. Give me a prediction."

She thought a moment, then said, "He's either going to the port or he's going to the old city. He's meeting someone, and that someone isn't his demographic. He's trying to blend in, and he needs an area that has a hodgepodge of people, where they're used to seeing a melting pot and the crowd will be eclectic. Somewhere he won't have to explain why he's there."

"Why Jaffa and not Tel Aviv?"

"Tel Aviv is a city, with all that implies. It's a nineteenth-twentieth-century construct, with areas spliced out like the diamond district. Tel Aviv looks big, but the four square blocks you work in include everyone doing your business. Fashion district, diamond district, industrial section, it's like every other city on earth. Jaffa is different. It's one of the oldest ports in the world, if not *the* oldest. It's literally where Jonah put to sea in the Old Testament, before he was swallowed by the whale. Now it's full of art galleries and tourists. It's the place to do a meeting if you were getting together with someone unlike you."

She saw Pike consider what she'd told him. He said, "Not bad, little Jedi."

She said, "It's not rocket science, Rain Man. If you'd do your due diligence in mission prep, we wouldn't be having this conversation."

He flicked his eyes to her and let a grin slip out. "That's why I have you."

She grinned back and said, "Thank God for that."

They hit a traffic circle with a clock tower on the far side, and Jennifer said, "This is the outskirts of the old fortress walls of Jaffa. If I'm right, he'll be getting out soon."

The area was packed, the cars all slowed to five miles an hour dodging the pedestrians. Pike said, "Shit, no parking around here. If he ditches, you're going foxtrot behind him."

She packed the tablet and nodded, now into the mission. But not enough to keep her from educating Pike on a little history. They inched forward, and she said, "See that building? The one with the bars?"

"Yeah."

"That's where they kept Eichmann after they captured him. And that facade over there—the one that looks like the front of a building with nothing behind it? That's where the Irgun blew up a car bomb fighting the British mandate."

Pike scrunched his eyes and said, "Jesus, how much reading did you do?"

The Crown Vic pulled over, and Jennifer saw the passenger door open. She leaned in and kissed Pike on the cheek, saying, "Enough to know that Jesus wasn't ever here. And that I'd like to explore after this is done."

He smiled and said, "Okay, okay. I get it. Don't lose him."

She grinned and said, "Promises, promises," then leapt out, hearing Pike say, "Make sure your phone beacon is on. I'll be there shortly."

Following Ivan ended up being surprisingly easy, with the crowds from all over the world allowing her to blend in seamlessly. His choice of location helped her as much as him. He went straight past the clock tower, walking by the old city gate, and then cut in, headed to the port.

He went uphill, entering a park full of tourists out to enjoy the brisk winter air, and she paused, texting Pike.

You find parking?

She saw the bubbles on her phone, then: *Yeah. On the way.*

She texted, *He's in a park. I have him, but if he meets in here, I can't get close.*

She received, *I see you on my phone. Stay on him.*

She darted across the street and entered the park behind him, the concrete paths winding upward. Ivan gave no indication he was doing anything other than heading to a destination, and he clearly knew the terrain. He'd been here before.

He crossed over a bridge full of tourists, all touching a sign of the zodiac and gazing out to the ocean. She passed a placard proclaiming the WISHING BRIDGE and held back, letting him get to the other side. When he did, she darted across, wondering if she should slap her hands on the Virgo plate and throw out a plea for a successful mission. Or maybe a wish to explore this town when she wasn't carrying a weapon and following a killer.

She saw the symbol of Virgo and almost stopped, but a passel of schoolkids was around it, all chattering. She kept going, thinking she probably could have used that chance to put a hex on Pike to get off his ass with their relationship.

Where did that come from?

The thought came to her completely unbidden. She banished it and jogged a bit to catch up with her target, focusing on the mission.

Ivan left the park and entered the old city, an ancient citadel of stone that looked like something out of *Robin Hood*. It was peppered with small artisan shops selling jewelry and other things, and Jennifer could smell the history and felt a longing to slow down to enjoy it.

But that wouldn't happen on this day. Ivan began winding through the narrow alleys, skipping down the steps two at a time and glancing at his watch.

He's late. Which would make her surveillance harder, because one person moving fast was normal. Two, spaced apart, was definitely something people would notice.

She lost him at the bottom of a curving line of stairs and sprinted to catch up, spilling out onto a promenade of the ancient port of Jaffa, fishermen still working their trade like they had for a millennium. She pulled up short and glanced left and right, seeing tourists from the world over enjoying the setting.

Damn it.

She had to make a choice. Left or right. She decided left, toward the old port warehouses that now held restaurants and shops. Right was nothing but the promenade and would be looping back the way he'd come.

She moved at a rapid clip, scanning each café and shop. She had almost reached the end and was about to turn around when she caught her target talking to a hostess. She glanced at the sign outside the restaurant, THE OLD MAN AND THE SEA. She pulled up short, turning to the port and allowing him to enter.

The restaurant had an outdoor area that was enclosed in plastic to protect against the winter weather. Inside she could see a bustling enclave full of tourists.

Perfect.

She watched the hostess lead him inside, going right. Jennifer texted Pike her location, then approached when the hostess returned.

"Table for two? My husband is late, but I'd like to get out of the wind now, if that's okay."

The hostess smiled and said, "So you don't want to sit outside, I take it?"

She pointed toward the right, saying, "No, I think that little nook over there would be perfect."

13

Sitting at a small four-top table crammed into what looked originally to be a tool-storage area in the age of sails, Jennifer placed her back to the rough wall and inventoried the target table. Including Ivan, there were five men, all Caucasian.

When he'd approached, the four had stood up and introduced themselves, so she knew it was an initial meeting. Ivan was dressed in slacks and a jacket, looking like a businessman. The four he met looked more like adventure travelers, with loose-fitting shirts, cargo pants, and hiking boots. Given Ivan's position in ParaBellum, she was sure they were military contractors. But from where? And why were they here in Israel? Was Tyler brokering a deal with the Israelis for some type of armament? If so, why was Ivan just now meeting them? If they were here at the behest of ParaBellum, wouldn't he have brought known employees? And the biggest question: What did the diamond exchange have to do with anything?

She was brought out of her thoughts by Pike sliding onto the bench next to her, breathing slightly heavily. She said, "Need some more gym time?"

He said, "I went the wrong way down one of those damn alleys. I had to make up ground. That place is a maze, and dead reckoning using your GPS beacon wasn't the best idea."

He pulled his knapsack to his lap and opened it, saying, "What do we have?"

She told him what she knew, and he said, "Penetration options?"

"Haven't seen anything specific, but I'm sure they all have phones."

She watched him pull out what looked like a typical smartphone, but with a small antenna jutting out of the side. He booted up the device, saw a myriad of different apps, then set it on the table. He began dialing his real smartphone, saying, "Creed's going to have to walk me through this. I'll waste the entire meeting trying to get it to work."

She stopped him and said, "Let me talk to Creed. You scare him."

He passed across his phone with a grin, saying, "You mean he has a crush on you."

Bartholomew Creedwater was a computer network operations guy, which—like saying a loan shark was an alternative financing expert—was a polite title for what he really did. He was a hacker, and he was good at his trade. He'd worked with their team on a number of occasions, aggravating Pike with his clear attraction to Jennifer, but Pike recognized talent when he saw it, and Creed always seemed to work extra hard when Jennifer asked. He'd been dedicated to their team for this mission, acting as standby reach-back access for any technical capability that was required.

Jennifer put in a Bluetooth earpiece so it wouldn't look like she was talking on two different cell phones and waited for the call to be answered. She eventually heard a tentative voice: "Hello? Pike?"

She said, "It's Jennifer. We're on a target and need some help with penetration."

The voice turned almost giddy. "Hi, Jennifer! Tell me what you have. I'll get in. Can you access a USB port? Plug in one of my thumb drives?"

"It's not a computer. We're looking at a table, five guys having a meeting, all probably with cell phones."

"That's it? Do you have a number?"

Pike snapped his fingers and pointed. She said, "Stand by," and watched another man approach the table. An Orthodox Jew wearing a yarmulke and sporting *payot* curls. One of the contractors stood up and shook his hand, pointing at an empty seat.

This just got interesting.

Pike rotated his finger, telling her to speed things up. She nodded, and into the phone said, "I don't have a number, but I have the Pwnie phone out and operational. You said this thing could penetrate everything, Wi-Fi, Bluetooth, cellular. Everything."

She heard tapping on a keyboard, then, "It can, but I have to have a root. I can't just magically make shit happen. That's Hollywood." There was a pause, then, "Okay, I have you on the network. And you have a bazillion phones, wherever you are. I need to neck it down, and I can't do that here. It's why *you* guys go inside. If I could do it, we wouldn't need you. Give me something."

Pike said, "The damn meeting's going to end. Jesus. Can't Creed get us something?"

Jennifer shook her head, saying into the earpiece, "What phones do you see? Is there a block of them? One with a Bulgarian country code? Something like that?"

More tapping, then, "No Bulgarian country codes, but strangely, a few from South Africa. A smattering of Americans, some German, but most from Israel."

Jennifer saw Pike lean forward and knew he'd seen something. She waited, hearing, "You still there?"

"Yeah. Hang on." She looked at Pike and said, "What do you have?"

"One of those wannabe commandos is wearing an Apple watch. Ask if that's any help."

She said, "We have a target with an Apple watch. Is that any help?"

"No. Come on. You think I can type in 'Apple watch' and then get access to whoever you're looking at?"

Now aggravated, Jennifer snapped, "No, but doesn't that access a cell phone? Can't that neck things down? It's not like there are fifty of them in here."

She heard him come back sounding like a whimpering puppy. "Jennifer, I'm trying to help, but . . . wait, you might be onto something." Jennifer winked at Pike. Creed continued. "Can you get within thirty meters of the guy? If you can, I can use the Pwnie phone for a man-in-the-middle attack. Nobody wears an Apple watch as a timepiece. His Bluetooth will be tethered. That's the whole point."

Pike said, "Apple is leaving. Heading to the men's room."

Jennifer nodded at Pike, then said into the earpiece, "Creed, he's going to the bathroom. The women's room is right next door. Can you get a read through the wall?"

"Yeah, if it's only a single wall, the Pwnie will access it."

"Stand by."

She stood, and off the phone said, "Creed thinks he can penetrate with that guy's watch, but I have to get within thirty meters. I'm going to the bathroom."

Pike nodded and said, "Don't get burned. Let him in first. This isn't ending today."

She placed her hands on the table and leaned over, getting face-to-face, saying, "You told me I was a Jedi last mission. You can't keep giving me instructions. It's unseemly."

She waited to see if he would take the bait, and he did. Just like she knew he would. He leaned forward and kissed her, then, because he was Pike, didn't let it go. He said, "There are many more levels of Jedi to get to mine."

She stood up and said, "He-man woman-hater crap."

He laughed, and she sauntered off. It was a little bit of fun, but the point of the exchange was to solidify to anyone watching that they were, in fact, a couple. If something happened in the next few minutes, she didn't want the analysis later to report that a couple had entered and then spent the entire time staring at a table of five.

She threaded her way through the restaurant, keeping Apple in front of her. When he disappeared into the men's room, she accessed the ladies' room, finding it empty. She whispered, "I'm in. What do you have?"

Creed said, "I have a thread. A Bluetooth stream. You sure it's his?"

"Hell no, but we're in the back of the restaurant, and my room is empty. Do you have more than one?"

"No."

"It's his. Get your man-in-the-middle jihad on."

She heard the keyboard tapping and him saying, "You're a little more forceful today. You don't usually talk to me like that."

She said, "It's the stress. Sorry." What she thought was, *Pike is rubbing off on me.* She wasn't sure if that was good or bad.

He said, "I got it. I'm in. What do you want? His contacts, email, what?"

"We want to turn that watch into a microphone. We want to hear what happens when he returns."

"Easy breezy."

She said, "You're still the best, Creed."

She could almost feel the blush through the phone line. He said, "Anything for you guys. You're my favorite team."

Meaning *she* was his favorite. She grinned, thinking about the time Pike almost cracked Creed's head open in the Bahamas. *Favorite team. Yeah, right.*

She went back to the table, saying, "Can we get real-time?"

"No. The Pwnie just gets access. The feed will come to me, but I'll get it to you as soon as I can."

She sat down, winked at Pike, and said, "Sounds good. Thanks for the help."

She disconnected and told Pike the state of play. He said, "Well then, I guess we can get a couple of real drinks, since we're not going to be able to react to anything that's said."

They watched Apple sit back down, hoping the watch microphone was good enough to pick up what was being discussed. Three minutes later, their optimism plummeted, and not because of the technology. The meeting broke up. Pike watched them paying the bill and said, "I hope they laid out their evil plan at the last moment. What a waste."

She saw him bring out his phone, and he said, "Brett." He called and found that Tyler had left the diamond exchange and gone straight back to the hotel. She watched the party leave and said, "You want to stay on him?"

The waitress brought over their Bacardi and Cokes, and he said, "No. Our heat state is bad enough. He's headed back to the hotel."

She grinned and said, "Never waste a drink. Taskforce motto."

He raised his glass and said, "There's a reason for that. You might not get another one."

14

★ ★ ★

We finished our drinks, just making small talk, giving our target table time to disperse to wherever they were going. The last thing I wanted was to bump into one of them accidentally out on the street because we left too early, and it was really bad form to waste a drink. If I didn't know we were on a mission, it would have been a pretty good day on vacation. Jennifer evidently felt more like the latter, because she set her empty glass down and said, "Let's go explore the old city."

I stood up, throwing enough shekels to cover the bill, and Jennifer said, "I want to talk."

Which, of course, immediately turned our relaxing time into some sort of trap. I said, "Fine by me," and we set out, winding through the alleys and wasting the afternoon in art galleries. Okay, I thought it was a waste. Jennifer enjoyed it, which, because I knew we were never getting to Caesarea, would probably get me some points.

We exited the old city next to some sort of weird hanging orange trees—literally orange trees that were suspended in the air by wires—with me still waiting on the "talk," when she finally said, "You think Aaron and Shoshana will make it?"

I said, "What do you mean? Their company is obviously going strong. In today's world, there's a significant market for their talent, and a lot of shitheads who claim it. They measure up."

"That's not what I meant. I mean the marriage."

Holy shit. Where is this going?

I said, "They're just weird enough to stay together."

She looked at me, and I saw she knew I was dodging. I said, "They're connected on a level that few people are. It'll be fine."

We broke out into the main thoroughfare with the clock tower, and before she could say anything else, I said, "That worked out. Our car is a block over."

She started to say something, and I speed walked forward, getting away from the conversation. She caught up, and my phone rang. Creed, saving me by the bell.

He said, "I have the transcript, but it's not a lot of help. Whatever substantive info they shared happened before we accessed the Apple watch."

I said, "About what I figured. Did you send it?"

We crossed through the fabled flea market, although I don't know why anyone would call it "fabled," since it looked like every other flea market on earth. You were more likely to find a sculpture built out of wine bottles than a piece of the Ten Commandments.

Creed said, "I'll send it in a second. Typing final now. We had to do some work on the audio to get a clear readout."

We found the parking lot and our car, and I hung up. To Jennifer, I said, "Transcript is on the way."

She nodded, entering the vehicle. In short order, we were headed up the coast to the Hilton. In blessed silence.

We drove out of Jaffa and entered the outskirts of Tel Aviv, me pretending to fight the traffic to stay away from the conversation. But Jennifer was having none of it.

She said, "If they're so connected, what are we?"

I drove past the old Jaffa train station, now an eclectic outdoor mall, and said, "I have no idea what you're talking about."

She looked at me and said, "Yes, you do."

I gripped the steering wheel hard, and the sensation brought me back to Guatemala, when I'd first met Jennifer—and wanted to choke her. We'd been together going on seven years now, and I knew sooner or later a conversation like this would happen. I liked where we were but could recognize Jennifer getting antsy.

I said, "What do you want out of this?"

She slid her hand into mine and said, "Nothing. I mean, I'm just trying to sort out where we stand. Are we in a relationship because I'm an Operator in the Taskforce? Or are we in a relationship and I happen to also be in the Taskforce? If I left, would we still have what we have?"

I said nothing. After a two-minute silence, she said, "Pike? It's a fair question."

I said, "Is that what this is about? You want to leave the Taskforce?"

"No, no. Not at all. It's just a question." She looked out the window for a moment, then said, "Aaron and Shoshana recognized what they had and committed to it."

Uh-oh.

I said, "Shoshana wouldn't recognize a relationship if it came up and bit her in the ass. She's crazy. Don't you remember the wedding?"

"I remember it, but that wasn't Shoshana's doing. That was just outside circumstances. I didn't see *you* running away from the sound of the guns."

I said, "I acted defensively. Shoshana did not. She's fanatical. She'd do anything for Aaron, slaughtering whatever gets in her way. That's her idea of a relationship."

"Seems I remember someone else doing the same at one point in time. For me."

Jennifer was talking about Guatemala, when I had, in fact, turned into a sociopathic killing machine to get her out of the grasp of a drug cartel. I hated it when she used stone-cold logic and was absolutely confused as to where this conversation was going. As I'm sure she intended. It was a gift only women had.

My blessed Taskforce phone pinged with a message. I said, "Check my cell. I think Creed's message just came in."

She unlocked the phone as I pulled into the underground parking garage for the Hilton. I shut the car off and said, "Well?"

She passed the phone and said, "It's not much for our mission, but it *is* interesting."

I read:

UNSUB 1 (Clear Israeli accent): *. . . I don't have a location yet. I expect to have it by tomorrow.*

UNSUB 2 (Undetermined accent. Possibly South African): *How hard can it be? We gave you a full name and address. We just want a pinpoint from a local and some atmospherics.*

UNSUB 1: *I have that address, but your target isn't there. I think I know where she's located, but I want to confirm.*

UNSUB 2: *We've paid a great deal of money for this information. You're not getting any more, if this is some scheme to up the ante.*

UNSUB 1: *I know, and honestly, it gives me pause as to why. I'm digging around trying to find the target, and I'm hearing things. Things about the Mossad. You said this was a private conflict. A corporate fight. I don't mess with the Mossad.*

UNSUB 3 (Another possible South African): *It* is *a private thing. The target may have worked with the Mossad in the past, maybe, but I know that's not happening now. Just get us a location. You came highly recommended. Don't cause a blow to your reputation because of some rumors.*

Pause in the conversation. Unintelligible cross talk.

UNSUB 1: *Okay. Let's meet again tomorrow morning. You know the Tel Aviv Marina?*

UNSUB 2: *Yes.*

UNSUB 1: *There's a restaurant inside, near the water, called Fortuna del Mar. I'll meet you there at nine thirty tomorrow morning, right when it opens.*

The rest was just pleasantries and good-byes. I tapped the phone against my leg, thinking. Jennifer said, "I don't see what any of this has to do with an American arms dealer or the Taskforce mission profile."

"Me either. I'm considering passing this off."

"To who?"

"Shoshana and Aaron. The mention of Mossad is enough to inform them. If they want to play, they can. If not, then we did what we could. I don't feel right sitting on the information while we refocus on Tyler."

"You can't give them Taskforce intel. We weren't even supposed to tell them we were here."

I pulled out my phone, saying, "Screw all that NOFORN stuff. Sometimes our intelligence restrictions end up hurting more than protecting."

Jennifer just shook her head. Shoshana's phone rang out, going to voice mail. I hung up, saying, "No answer."

I dialed Aaron's number. It went straight to voice mail, no ringing at all.

I set the phone down, and Jennifer said, "No answer with him, either?"

"No. It didn't even ring."

She smiled and said, "Maybe they're doing honeymoon stuff."

I opened the car door and said, "Maybe, but it doesn't feel right. Aaron's the type who would answer that phone midthrust. He certainly wouldn't turn it off."

She got out, saying, "Quit being a worrywart. That's my job."

I laughed and said, "Okay, okay. You're right. He's probably trying to keep Shoshana from devouring him."

Aaron heard the rustling in the darkness and knew they were coming for him. He was in no shape to fight, having already suffered a brutal interrogation at the hands of Johan. Even if he was in perfect condition, there were too many to win against, but he would make it painful. Make it much, much more expensive than the watch on his wrist.

Mentally, he had already made the choice. He would fight to kill from the first blow. He knew that a pathetic attempt at an escalation based on their actions would only lead to an inevitable outcome. Having lived in a world of violence that few on earth could understand, he knew where this was going, and no restraint on his part would alter the trajectory he was now on.

Once he was overpowered, they'd beat him unmercifully. Punish him for his insolence. The only thing he had going for him was his propensity for violence, and he intended to use that to his fullest advantage. He knew he wouldn't be killed outright, even as he planned to kill those who attacked him. But his death would be real all the same. He wasn't going to risk catching HIV in some prison hospital. If they even bothered to take him to one.

He'd initially wondered why they left him with his Rolex when they took everything else, including his shoes in exchange for nasty-smelling tire sandals. Once he got into his cell with twenty other prisoners, it had become clear. It was to be payment for the block commander.

Most of the guards were okay, just bored with their jobs. Some were even nice, giving him additional rice for the extra seventy pounds he had on him compared to the other prisoners, who'd clearly been locked in the dark for a long, long time. The block commander, however, was different. He was a sadistic son of a bitch who ran the prison like a little kingdom, granting favors for payment, even if the favor was simply not getting pounded with his baton. He was tall and thuggish, skin as black as coal, with deep-set eyes in a stretched face; Aaron called him Lurch. It seemed the respite from his punishment in Durban had been the proverbial jumping from the frying pan into the fire.

The interrogation had lasted most of the night. When Johan finally tired of the questioning, Aaron had been thrown into the back of a dented Toyota 4Runner, his hands and feet flex-tied together. He'd lain still, taking stock of his condition. Johan had been clinical in his beating, taking care not to do any permanent damage, but Aaron still felt the pain in the soles of his feet and had trouble seeing from the swelling around his eyes.

Still, he surmised he would live, and he was sure he'd given them enough to want to hunt Shoshana, feeding on their mistaken belief that she was his control and had to be contained as well.

His thoughts turned to Alex, wondering what had befallen her. His biggest fear was precisely that they'd surmised she was nothing more than she professed—an employee at the diamond exchange—and thus expendable. To prevent that, he'd debated sprinkling her with a little bit of intrigue during his interrogation, but he couldn't bring himself to do so. Giving them the idea that she had lied—that she was hiding something—was asking for her to undergo the savage pain he was experiencing, and he simply didn't have that in him.

Now the decision tore at him. Maybe he should have. She'd have been tortured—most likely sexually—but she'd be alive. The second-guessing and recriminations were pinging back and forth in his brain, like a handful of rubber balls, when he was rewarded with the one bright spot over the last twenty-four hours: Alex was unceremoniously thrown into the back with him.

Relieved to see she appeared unharmed, he whispered, "How are you? Okay?"

When she saw him, her lips trembled and her eyes began to water. Clearly, his condition wasn't that reassuring. She said, "Oh God, what have they done to you?"

"Nothing. It looks worse than it is. It was a necessary evil to get us out of here. How are you?"

"Get us out? How is you getting beat on helping? Are they going to do that to me?"

He realized she was on the verge of breaking—but also that she hadn't been touched. Yet. He said, "Keep calm. We're alive because they want us to be. We're useful, as long as we aren't a liability to them. You need to be strong, because if they feel you're incapable of following orders—if you curl into a ball and just quit—they'll kill you. Understand?"

She nodded, then slid her hands forward, touching a bruise on his cheek. She said, "We're truly screwed, aren't we? You can tell me. Be honest."

He smiled, the expression turning to a grimace when the smile reached his split lips. He said, "No, we're not screwed. At least not totally. What we are is alive, and we need to keep ourselves that way, because there's someone coming for us."

She said, "The Mossad?"

They heard the car doors open and close, and they remained silent. Someone lifted the back hatch and threw a section of carpet over them, hiding them from view, then slammed the hatch closed. The SUV began moving, and Aaron whispered, "Not the Mossad. My partner. Shoshana."

Alex looked deflated at the answer. "What on earth can she do all by herself against this? She doesn't even know we've been taken."

Aaron said, "She will soon. Have some faith, because believe me, she does. Hopefully I've set in motion something that will force her to track us. And she will not quit. Ever."

Alex began to softly weep, saying, "They'll just kill her, like they're going to do to us."

Aaron said, "They'll try, but they won't be able to."

Alex wiped her nose and said, "How can you say that? They caught *you*. They'll kill her. She doesn't even know they're coming."

Aaron took the barb and let it slide. He said, "Look at me."

She did. He locked eyes with her and said, "You are *my* responsibility. You *will* come home. Stay alive. Whatever it takes. They'll probably separate us when we stop, but don't give up hope. Shoshana *will* come for me. She'll come for the both of us."

Wanting some spark of hope, Alex said, "She can't stop them. Even you couldn't. What can she do?"

Aaron held her hands and said, "She'll come. And when she does, she'll be bringing enough friends to ensure success."

"What friends? Who?"

"I honestly don't know. But I trust her. And you should too. Keep the faith."

That had been twelve long hours ago, and now that he was facing a cell full of hostile prisoners, Aaron wasn't nearly as sure as he had been in the back of the SUV.

He had an iron faith in Shoshana and knew she would unravel what had happened to him, but that would take time. He'd naïvely thought he'd just sit as a hostage until Shoshana arrived, but that was not to be the case.

If he wanted to leave the prison alive, he would have to fight to stay that way. He watched the waning rays of the sun out of their lone window and knew that when it hit the horizon, the waiting would be done. They were coming, and there was nothing he could do to stop it.

16

★ ★ ★

The morning air was a little bit chilly, but not unbearably so. Still, it required a jacket to knock off the edge. I'd never been to Israel in the winter, and honestly, I was surprised at how cold it was. I guess that made me an ignorant American. I mean, it was the Middle East, wasn't it? Should be hot. The sad thing is I'd spent a winter or two in Iraq and definitely knew that place got cold.

Watching the people walking on the promenade, you'd have thought it was the Antarctic, with women dressed in full-on parkas complete with fur-lined hoods, and men wearing Michelin Man puffy jackets. They clearly didn't like the cold weather any more than Jennifer did.

She was curled up tight next to me, snuggling in to get away from the wind. Our surveillance position was a bench situated on a bluff high above the walking/biking promenade that ran adjacent to the Mediterranean, at a spit of green space called Independence Park. The location did make the weather worse, as the breeze was heavier up here than it would be down on the promenade itself, but the position gave us an optimum view of the exits out of the Tel Aviv Marina, and I had to cover all bases with only three surveillance bodies.

Last night we'd kept tabs on our targets—Tyler and Ivan—and all they'd done was have dinner at a sushi restaurant in the lobby of the hotel. That wouldn't have been much to speak of, except one of the South Africans had joined them. Unfortunately, not the one with the Apple watch. So now we had Tyler himself complicit in whatever the South Africans were doing, which, when I'd reported back to Kurt Hale, was enough to warrant surveillance on the meeting we knew was occurring this morning.

Since I was going to use Brett in the morning, Jennifer and I had left the hotel last night and sauntered the five hundred meters down the promenade to the marina. We'd found the restaurant—a unique place right next to the water, with inside and outside sections, complete with a folk singer—and had ordered dinner. From there, we'd both gone to the "bathroom," which happened to be located outside the restaurant in the marina proper, which allowed us to identify all the choke points for the next day's surveillance. Mission complete, we'd had some more vacation time, enjoying the music. Honestly, I wanted to enjoy it, but I was dreading another round of "What are we doing with our lives?" Luckily, Jennifer could smell my angst and settled for the extra downtime. We'd gone to bed without any drama.

We'd gotten up bright and early and had been in position for an hour, with the wind chill starting to bite. I pulled out a set of small binoculars and scanned the entrance to the marina while Jennifer cowered under my arm looking for some warmth, like a cat seeking to escape the snow. She said, "This is bullshit. You should have told me to pack a coat."

I said, "It's the Middle East. With global warming, I thought it would be a hundred degrees."

She punched me and said, "Liar."

I said, "Got an Orthodox Jew entering, but he's not our guy."

She perked up. I relayed to Brett, and he said, "Still no sign of our targets."

Five seconds later, he said, "He's inside, looking around. I think he's the contact."

We waited a bit, and I saw two other men walk down the small access to the marina. One of them was Apple Watch. I called, "Two targets inbound, neither from our primary deck. It's the guys from Jaffa, but Apple Watch is in the mix. Get ready to record."

"I'm set. Pwnie phone is ready to go. Creed is online."

"Roger all."

From there, I was helpless to affect anything, just sitting in the cold waiting on some report. It was the worst part about surveillance. We sat in the wind for another twenty minutes, and then I saw the Orthodox Jew leave. I waited on the readout of the meeting from Creed, but nothing came. One minute went by, then two. The Jew was sauntering slowly down the promenade, about to be lost from sight, and I still had no report. I called Creed and said, "Get me something. I don't need it clean. I need it now."

Creed said, "Pike, we have to eliminate audio errors. The wind is huge, they were outside, and a lot is lost in that. We need to work it to get you the transcript."

I snarled, "He's walking away. Get me what you have right fucking now. I need to know if I should focus on him."

I heard nothing, then, "The only thing I can break out right now is a hotel in Haifa. The Dan Carmel. I have no idea why that was mentioned. Most of the conversation is lost in the wind noise. If you'd give me some time, I can figure it out."

The Dan Carmel? That's where Shoshana is.

I hung up the phone and slapped it onto my thigh, my mind racing. The action caused Jennifer to jolt upright. She said, "What?"

"I don't know. I think they're after Shoshana."

"*What?*"

I stood up, calling Brett, "Blood, Blood, I'm taking that Jew down. Be prepared for backup."

He said, "Come again? I'm with the targets right now. They're having breakfast. I'm still recording."

Shit.

"Okay, okay, you stay on them. We're going hunting."

"Pike, we don't have Omega authority. You can't kill or capture here."

I stood up, my eyes on the Orthodox Jew, saying, "I can't take him with me, but I can certainly take him down."

He said, "Why? What's going on?"

"I don't know, but I think I do."

"What the hell does that mean?"

"Gotta go. I need to use my phone. Remain in place. Get what you can. We'll see you back in the room."

I clicked off, and Jennifer said, "What's gotten into you?"

I dialed up Shoshana yet again and got voice mail, yet again. I cursed and started jogging down the path to the promenade, Jennifer right behind me. She said, "What are we doing?"

I said, "They mentioned they were hunting a person who might have worked for the Mossad, and one of them said it was a 'she.' They had the address, but the target wasn't there. They had to locate the target, and it's at the same hotel that Shoshana is in."

I saw our target and slowed to a walk, saying, "I think they're hunting her."

Jennifer looked at me like I was from a distant planet and said, "How on earth did you get Shoshana out of those tidbits? Pike, that's crazy."

"Yeah, maybe, but we'll know soon enough."

We reached the promenade, and I saw the target walking up it, about a hundred meters away. She said, "What do you mean?"

"I'm going to wring that guy out."

"*What?*"

I stopped and looked at her. "Look, I can't explain it, but I'm right. I know I am. I can feel it. I just need to confirm."

She scrunched her eyes and said, "You sound like Shoshana."

That brought me up short. I said, "Stop it. I'm not saying I'm some empath. I'm saying the evidence is there."

She saw the guy getting away and started walking, saying, "There is no evidence. You have two sentences."

I said, "So, you want out?"

We saw the guy mount some stairs, moving toward the surface streets of Tel Aviv. She picked up her pace, closing the distance to the staircase, but said nothing. We rounded the turn, now headed back the way we'd come, going up the stairs. He was already lost from sight.

I said, "Jennifer, I'll do this alone."

She turned to me and said, "No. I can't have you execute something heinous. You'll probably lose it and kill him."

She started taking the stairs two at a time, and I followed, saying, "What the fuck are you talking about?"

She kept striding forward, saying, "Whenever you get around Shoshana, you devolve into what you once were. It's like you guys compete to see who can be the most sociopathic. I've seen it, and I'm not allowing it to happen here."

I jogged behind her, saying, "That's not what's happening. She's in danger. I can feel it."

We reached the top, and she sighed, saying, "I know. I believe you."

Confused, I said, "*Now* you believe me?"

She smiled and said, "I *always* believe you. Shoshana is right. You are like her in some ways. I just don't want to see the other side of her come out in you."

I swiveled my head left and right, looking for the target. I said, "You have such little faith."

She did the same thing, saying, "Best predictor of future performance is past performance. And I've seen your past performance."

Before I could answer, she said, "There. Going toward the parking garage."

We were on an open deck that was decrepit, looking like its heyday had been in the eighties, the area falling into disrepair. I saw the target headed to a structure that was empty, with a FOR LEASE sign in every window. It looked like an entertainment center that had gone bankrupt, with crumbling concrete and graffiti left behind.

It didn't take long to assess my options. This place was perfect. I said, "We take him here. Before he gets to the street."

She nodded, agreeing. She said, "Let's do it. But don't kill him."

We waited until he disappeared into the shadows of the abandoned structure, then sprinted forward. We entered the dark, the concrete strewn with detritus, and I held up a hand, listening. I heard the footsteps to my right and slid forward. He was now shuffling through the gloom. I heard him inadvertently kick some trash, and I sprinted forward, running past an open area full of pillars and balconies that might have been pretty cool in the day but now looked like a set for *Planet of the Apes*. I heard the traffic of the street below, and I knew I had to get him before he reached it.

I caught a glimpse of him through the pillars and then saw a spiral staircase headed down. He was almost to it. He was going to make it to the street and prevent me from taking him down. I improvised. I shouted, "Hey! Help me."

He heard the words and whipped around, trying to find the source. To Jennifer, I said, "Lie down, now."

She did. I said, "Help me! My wife has collapsed! Help me!"

He paused, looking at the stairwell, then at us. He made up his mind, running back to our location, Jennifer prostrate on the ground and me kneeling over her.

He said, "What happened?"

I said, "Nothing," then exploded upward, throwing a wicked uppercut that lifted him off his feet. Jennifer leapt up, and I said, "Cover the rear."

She did.

I turned my focus to the target and said, "Who were you chasing? Who did you give to the men at the restaurant?"

He struggled to ascertain what I'd said, my earlier blow clouding his head. I slapped his cheek and said, "Answer me."

He covered his face and said, "What are you talking about? Why are you attacking me?"

I jerked his hands apart and began searching. I found a slip of paper with a name, and I saw I was right.

Shoshana Weinberg, room 747, Dan Carmel, Haifa. Reservation for seven days.

I became incensed, batting the guy's head back and forth. "Why are you hunting her? Why did they want this?"

He waved his hands around, trying to prevent my strikes, whimpering. He said, "It's a drug thing. She's causing issues with that organization. They aren't going to hurt her. Just scare her. I promise."

That really set me off. *Fucking liar.* I started punching, hard, snapping his head back. I felt his nose break, and Jennifer sprang back to us, grabbing my arm and shouting, "Don't!"

I calmed down and returned to the target. "I want the truth, or you're fucking dead. Why. Are. You. Hunting. Her."

Through the slobber of snot and blood, he said, "I told you. Don't kill me. All I do is find them. I don't do anything else. I get paid to find people. You should talk to the drug guys."

And I realized he thought he was speaking the truth. I said, "Where's your phone?"

He pulled it out, saying, "Take it, take it."

I did, then said, "Show me the number of the man you met in the restaurant."

"I don't know him. I've never seen him before."

"*Show* me."

He did, and I noted it. I then said, "Show me the number of your partner. The one who sent you here."

He scrolled through the call list and pointed again.

I pulled his wallet out of his pocket, thumbed through it, then stood up, towering over him. I said, "You leave here, and never mention a thing to anyone. You did your mission, and it was uneventful. You understand?"

He nodded, hope flooding through him.

I said, "If I find out you've spoken to your crew, if I see they've been warned, I'll come back and carve you up. You understand?"

He nodded his head hard enough to cause bloody snot to fling off, saying, "Yes, yes, yes."

I squatted down again, getting close to his face. I tapped his head with his wallet and said, "If I have any trouble in the next few days, I'll know why. And I'll hunt you. Trust me, you think you can find people, but you have never met anyone like me."

He sagged back and said, "I won't talk. I promise."

I stood up and said, "You picked the wrong girl to chase. If she were here, you'd get a lot worse than this."

And I hammered my boot straight between his legs, hard enough to lift him an inch off the ground. He screamed and rolled into a ball.

Jennifer jumped at me, jerking my shoulder back and shouting, "What the hell are you doing?"

I said, "Making a point. Come on. We don't have a lot of time."

Shoshana heard the knock on the door and thought about just not answering. Aaron had scheduled and paid for an in-house masseuse, and it was supposed to be a double, with her lying right next to him. Now it seemed a little bit of an obscene indulgence. She'd never had a massage in her life, and doing it alone was not what she wanted. Even as she knew Aaron would want it for her.

She went to the door and looked through the peephole, seeing a lithe woman and a portable table. The woman turned toward her door and knocked again, and she felt the heat. Saw red.

Shoshana snapped back from the peephole, confused by the feeling. She'd had nightmares every night she'd lain down to sleep, and now she was reading this woman as a threat. But she *couldn't* be. Aaron had scheduled her. Aaron had planned this.

What is going on with me?

It was the girl. Alexandra. She was clouding Shoshana's judgment. For the first time, Shoshana doubted her own instincts.

Aaron hadn't contacted her since she'd been at the hotel, and neither had the Mossad. But she'd had two calls from Pike. She'd heard the phone ring, saw the strange number, and refused to answer. If it were the Mossad, they'd leave a message. She didn't get one, which meant it was Pike. And he kept calling.

She was too embarrassed to answer the phone and admit she was here by herself. He'd tell Jennifer what had happened, and she couldn't take the pity. Her "honeymoon" was a sham, and her lie would expose a truth like lancing a boil full of pus: She didn't have what they had.

She decided to banish such thoughts and continue with her "vacation." Like Aaron would have wanted. She opened the door. The woman entered, told her the parameters of the massage, and then asked her to disrobe while she set up the table. Smiling the entire time, she made Shoshana feel ridiculous about her earlier instincts.

Shoshana went to the bedroom of her suite and closed the door. She dropped her jeans and pulled off her blouse, wondering if she was supposed to take off her underwear. She poked her head out and asked, and the masseuse told her yes, all she would need was a towel. The masseuse smiled, and the red returned. Shoshana closed the door again, forcing the feeling away.

She removed her bra and panties and wrapped herself in a large bath towel. She looked at herself in the mirror, sighed, and opened the door.

The first thing she saw was the masseuse casually leaning against the wall, hands behind her back, entirely relaxed—but her aura radiated danger like a neon sign in Shoshana's brain. The next was a man appearing from the kitchen alcove, a suppressed pistol in his hand.

Before she could react, she felt the suppressor of another pistol seat against the side of her head. She slowly turned and saw another man, his finger to his lips. He said, "No shouting."

He expected her to become instantly compliant, because of both the pistol and the fact that she was wearing nothing but a towel, the setup designed specifically to make her feel vulnerable.

It failed miserably in its task.

Shoshana snapped her head down, clearing the barrel, and rotated her left arm over the gun hand of the intruder, trapping the pistol. Simultaneously, she slammed a palm strike into the man's face hard enough to shatter his nose. He screamed, and she jerked the pistol free, then slipped behind him, the towel falling down.

She took aim at the other man while using the first as a shield. He leapt forward, looking for a shot, the barrel of his pistol waving all over the place in an attempt to hit her without harming his partner.

She had no such restrictions. She tracked his movement and pulled the trigger, hitting him twice in the chest and dropping him to the floor. She jumped backward, then lashed out in a front kick, pushing the second man away from her. He hit his knees, then stood up, turning around with his arms held high, his face streaming blood from his ruined nose. "No, no, no, wait—"

She lined up the front sight on the red coming from his nose, a liquid bull's-eye, and pulled the trigger. His head snapped back, and he collapsed in a heap. She stalked forward, doing nothing to cover her bare flesh. She put another round in the head of the first man, then closed on the masseuse.

She was crouched on the floor, her arms over her head. When she looked up, seeing Shoshana, naked and holding a pistol, her eyes sprang comically wide.

She said, "They paid me to let them in. They said it was a prank. They didn't say they were going to hurt you. Please."

Shoshana shot her in the forehead. She watched her slump to the ground, then stood up, checking through the peephole. Sure enough, there were two more men providing rear security down the hall near the entrance to the elevator.

She ran back to the bedroom, throwing on her clothes. She knew she had only seconds before the men outside grew curious at the lack of activity in her suite.

She went to the sliding door and opened it, looking down from the balcony. She was on the seventh floor, but it looked like she could go from balcony to balcony and reach the ground. It was a hard climb, and not without enormous risk, but she'd seen Jennifer tackle much worse.

But she's a monkey.

She shoved her newfound pistol into her pants and circled over the railing, mentally attempting to channel Jennifer's skills.

19

I saw the Dan Carmel hotel above me, on the top of Mount Carmel, and realized I'd somehow missed the turn that would take me up there. I was one road down the slope from it, next to something called the Louis Promenade. I cursed and pulled into a tourist bus parking area for a garden of some sort, making sure Brett was behind me. I saw him pull into my bumper, and I pointed up the hill.

I glanced to my left and said, "Wow. Take a look at that."

Falling below us, in leveled terraces down the side of Mount Carmel, was a manicured landscape that was so perfect it almost looked fake, like a computer rendition of what man could never achieve on his own. Stairs, trees, and flowers all seamlessly blended together, providing a lush path to the bottom of the hill.

Jennifer leaned over me and said, "That's the Baha'i Gardens here in Haifa. Glad you ignored the GPS."

Our GPS had been woefully inadequate since we'd arrived, with map data that was clearly older than the roads around Tel Aviv. After a few screwups, with us being on streets the GPS didn't recognize, I'd ceased using it, which Jennifer thought was ridiculous.

She'd said, "Most of these roads were built before Moses smashed the tablets. I think we can trust the GPS for ninety percent of what's here." I, being smarter than any computer, had disagreed. And now I was parked in a tourist bus stop trying to read my map.

Jennifer said, "The gardens were just deemed a UNESCO heritage site. Maybe we should go check it out. You know, before we get in a gunfight and have to flee."

I ran my finger down the map, finding my location and considering her request. Maybe we would, once I'd confirmed Shoshana was okay, since I'd already tortured Jennifer once today.

We'd come up the coast highway, and in so doing, we'd literally driven right by the Caesarea archeological site, with Jennifer longingly looking out the window, like a child in a car seat pulling away from home for the first time. She'd turned away from the site and glowered at me. I'd simply shrugged.

It had taken about an hour and a half to get here, and we'd burned another thirty minutes before that doing initial planning and a map reconnaissance. Brett was bemused at the whole thing, but, because he was Brett, he rolled right into the mission. Left behind was the fact that we had no sanction to do anything here. We were now using US government assets to protect a foreign target, potentially causing an international incident with no tangible tie to United States security. That's how the Taskforce would portray it. I'd simply say it was no different than taking up for a friend in a bar fight.

A little chagrined at Jennifer's comment about the gardens and her attitude toward Shoshana's and Aaron's well-being, I looked up from the map and said, "Looks like we need to backtrack to that last traffic circle."

Jennifer saw my face and said, "Hey, come on. I was just teasing about the gardens."

I put the car in gear and said, "I know."

I looked behind me, getting Brett's eye, and rotated my finger in the air, telling him we were doing a U-turn. Jennifer slapped a hand to my wrist and squeezed, saying, "Pike, that car up the hill. Apple Watch is in it."

I whipped my head forward, and as sure as shit, he was sitting in the passenger seat of an SUV, another man behind the wheel. I called Brett, saying, "We got Apple to our front. I'm going to do a U-turn and head to the hotel. I want you to remain here and keep eyes on. Let me know what he does."

He said, "Black SUV?"

"That's him."

"Got it. Call when you've got the precious cargo secure."

"Roger that."

I pulled to the right, then put the car in reverse, starting a three-point turn. I had my head facing to the rear when Jennifer said, "Pike, Pike, the SUV is getting antsy. Two guys in the back are digging through backpacks, and Apple is shouting into a phone."

No sooner had she said that than a figure came flying over the stone wall of the Louis Promenade, hitting the street hard enough to land on a knee, one hand breaking the fall. I saw a pistol in the waistband, and the figure stood up, looking right at me.

It was Shoshana. She locked eyes with me and snarled, then took off down the street, running toward the gardens. *What the hell?*

The SUV jumped into the road, racing down the asphalt straight at Shoshana. He was going to hit her. Kill her right here.

I jammed our car into drive, bolting forward and shouting, "Seat belts, seat belts! Hang on!"

Shoshana leapt onto the sidewalk, and the SUV attempted to follow, now fewer than ten feet behind her. I jammed the accelerator to the floor and braced for impact. My rental slammed into the front quarter panel of the SUV, the impact flinging us both sideways, glass from the shattered headlights spraying the road. I saw Shoshana enter the gardens and begin leaping down the stairs; then she was lost from view. I got on the radio and shouted, "Blood, Blood, get on Shoshana!"

He said, "Easy day." I saw his door open, and he sprinted across the road. I heard, "ROE?"

I opened my own door, saying, "Protect the asset. Lethal force authorized."

Apple exited, cursing and yelling. I walked across the road, seeing the two in the back also get out. He pointed into the gardens and they took off; then he turned to me. I held up my hands and said, "Sorry about that. I lost control. I spilled my coffee."

He said, "You dumb motherfucker." He saw the crowd gathering around the accident and said, "It's okay." Not wanting to get enmeshed with any authority figures, he retreated back to his SUV and drove away.

I ran back to my own car, saying, "Blood, you've got two on foot behind you."

He said, "I got 'em. Shoshana's running straight down the hill. She's about to enter a gaggle of tourists. A big gaggle."

"Keep her in sight, but don't close on her."

Brett was one of the fastest men I'd ever met. There wasn't any way Shoshana would outrun him. He was a little bit of a freak on foot.

"That'll be easy. But why? I thought I was protecting her."

"She looked at me when she came over the wall. She's in death mode. I don't know why, but don't push it with her. She'll kill you."

"Well, that's fucking great."

20

Shoshana reached the crowd and immediately snaked her way to the middle, making sure her shirt covered the pistol at her back. There were about forty tourists, all on one of the free scheduled tours, and with any luck, she could use them as cover all the way down to the traffic circle at Ben Gurion Street.

The crowd moved forward slowly, and she kept her head on a swivel, looking for anything out of the ordinary—single men or couples paying too much attention to her and not enough to the splendor of the gardens.

She tried to make sense of what had just happened but came up blank. She had no known current enemies and had done only one operation in the last year for the Mossad, and that had turned out okay, with her eliminating the one man who would be a suspect here. He was dead, and his boss was currently in an American prison.

There was only one connection she could come up with, and it scared her to her core: For whatever reason, the Americans wanted her. Probably wanted Aaron too, but she was lucky he was out of the country. It was why Pike was here with a team, supposedly just wanting to come visit. When she'd said no, his plan of suckering them into a trap had fallen through. He'd clearly kept calling in an attempt to salvage that course of action, and when it had proven fruitless, he'd come in hard.

The realization was crushing to her. She'd been lied to and manipulated her entire life and had only just now begun to find some semblance of normalcy, and that had first come with her trust in Pike and Jennifer. He could have killed her once, and he hadn't. And now he had used that trust against her.

But Jennifer would never do that. It's not in her makeup.

Was it? What if Pike had told her some monstrous lie? Would she believe him over what she knew about Shoshana?

She was unsure but certainly not willing to test it. Pike was the one man she'd ever encountered who measured up to her skill. Not even Aaron could do what he did. She'd seen him operate, and he was an apex predator. A wrecking machine that had an uncanny talent for succeeding, even with the odds stacked against him. If Pike was hunting her—even here, in her home country of Israel—she was in trouble.

Brett watched Shoshana blend in to the tourist crowd and thought, *Good girl.* He located the two men from the SUV, then held up until they passed him, Brett pretending to gaze at the splendor of the gardens falling down toward the Haifa harbor. When they were down the slope in front of him, he picked up the follow, seeing the tour group approaching the Shrine of the Bab, a large temple that housed the founder of the Babi faith—the forerunner of the Baha'i religion. He saw the men split up, with one speed walking to the left, getting ahead of the tour group.

Going to attempt a blocking position.

He was the threat. Shoshana would walk right into him. She'd see the man to the rear, he was sure, but since she was focused on the rear, she'd miss the one to her front. Ignoring any looks that came his way, he began running, taking the steps of the slope three at a time and eating up the ground. He circled left, getting off the stairs and into the gardens themselves. He saw his target fifty meters away, going down a stone stairway next to the shrine. Brett cut back to the center, entering the stairwell and skipping down the stone, not worried about the man looking at him, because he was a complete unknown. He'd done this many, many times, and he would use his race as deflection. The target would see him—a black man in Israel—and never assume he was a threat. He would *have* to be a tourist, simply because he stood out too much to be of any use as an intelligence asset.

The man turned at his approach, his hand snaking to his waist. Brett said, "The gardens are amazing. I never thought I'd see something like this."

The man relaxed and said, "It's truly a wonder, but I've lost my wife." He chuckled and said, "She disappeared somewhere up top."

Brett said, "I know how that is. Where you from?"

With some irritation, the man said, "South Africa. Now, if you don't mind, I have to find my wife." Brett nodded but stayed a step behind him.

Brett said, "Hey, you ever seen the Batman movies? Where that guy appears out of nowhere and crushes the bad man?"

Confused, the target said, "What? No, I don't watch those movies. Sorry, but your American films are stupid. Please leave me alone."

He turned away again, presenting Brett with his back. Brett saw a peculiar lump and realized he was wearing a plate hanger. Level III body armor. Brett glanced to his rear and saw they were alone. He snapped forward, looping his arm around the man's neck and kicking the back of his knee. The man struggled for a second, then Brett lowered him to the ground, unconscious.

He whispered, "You should watch them, dumbass."

Shoshana stuck with the tour group as they approached the Shrine of the Bab, its golden dome towering above the terrain of the gardens. The tourists began to spread out, viewing the expansive garden next to the temple and entering the shrine itself.

She found herself alone and circled quickly to the right of the temple, searching for the entrance and a place to hide until the tour continued its march. She went down a flight of stone steps and found herself in a cul-de-sac of sculptured shrubs, looking like a set from a Dr. Seuss movie, the bushes turning the area into a makeshift maze not unlike a Christmas tree lot. About forty feet in diameter, it was ringed by a nine-foot wall of stone. A good place to hide until the tour moved on, but not what she wanted, as there was no escape route other than the stairs.

She turned to leave, and the stone in front of her smacked her face with spall. She immediately flung herself backward, rolling over her back onto her feet. Someone had fired at her, and now she was trapped.

She had to get out, immediately. Pike would be attacking soon, and he would be coming in hard. He knew what she was capable of and would want to overwhelm her. She ran toward the wall and leapt up, missing the top and falling back down. She heard footsteps pounding down the stairs and ducked behind one of the shrubs, peering through the foliage. One man reached the bottom, a pistol held to the front. She didn't recognize him from Pike's team. She breathed through an open mouth, her own pistol at the ready, waiting for him to conduct a systematic search, hoping to slip into a place he'd cleared and get back up the stairs while he continued.

She watched him and learned that wasn't going to happen. His technique wasn't methodical, with him slowly walking through the area behind the barrel of his weapon. Instead, he began moving in a rapid, practiced manner, attempting to flush her out while providing a shifting target to hit.

He was skilled.

She crouched and began backpedaling, stopping when her back was to the wall. She turned and looked up, considering another attempt but knowing she'd be highlighted for him to take a shot at her.

The searcher came one row over, racing down it, his weapon sweeping left and right. She took aim and fired a double tap. And missed.

The man oriented on the sound of her suppressor, without any physical fear of her shots, coming straight through the shrubs with his gun in a high two-handed grip. As soon as he cleared them, she fired, hitting him in the chest. Her weapon locked open on an empty magazine, and the round rocked him back, staggering him. Then he kept coming.

Body armor. Shit.

He brought his weapon to bear, and she screamed, throwing the pistol at his head and launching herself at him. He instinctively ducked the projectile and returned to aim, but she was on him like a cyclone.

She grabbed his wrists with both hands, controlling the pistol, and planted her right leg behind his knee. Teeth bared, she surged forward with her entire weight, flipping him over her leg and slamming him to the earth. On the way down he fired one, two, three times, the bullets snapping by her brow. He hit the ground hard, and she landed on his stomach with her knees, punching the body armor and knocking the wind out of him with a visible grunt.

She torqued his weapon to the ground, slamming it into a rock and breaking his hold, the pistol bouncing away. He sprang up on his knees, swinging at her head with a wild blow. She blocked it and rotated to his back, locking her legs around his waist. She grabbed the top of the plate carrier through his shirt and yanked down, hearing the Velcro holding it in place tear slightly, enough to send the ceramic front plate into his throat and causing him to gargle.

He staggered upright, rising like a zombie with her on his back, wildly swinging his arms to get her off. She tucked her head and dug in, cinching her legs and using the weight of her body as leverage on the armor. His breathing began to rasp, and she let up lightly, then slammed down again, feeling the Velcro rip free under his arms and giving her the leverage she needed. He fell to his knees, no longer attempting to attack her but now trying to fight the armor.

She leapt off him, lined up, and threw a spinning kick with all the force in her hip, whipping her foot around hard enough to crunch his cheek. He fell like he'd been hit with a cinder block.

She grabbed his pistol and sprinted back up the stairs, the barrel leading the way. She reached the top and saw no threat. She stuffed the pistol behind her back and began running down the stairs toward the traffic circle below, no longer caring about the cover of the tourists.

She crossed the garden bridge over Abbas Street and kept going, ignoring the views and focusing on the finish. She finally reached the traffic circle and found the iron gate to it closed. She began climbing, with the tourists on the other side taking pictures up the slope, amazed at her actions.

She flung herself over and began running down the street, thinking of escape. Thinking of where she could go.

She saw a bus stop ahead of her and recognized the line to Acre. *Better than nothing. A clean break.*

She ran on board and paid the fare, then sank down into her seat, breathing heavily and thinking about her predicament. The bus began to pull away, with her mind working furiously over her next steps.

Because of it, she missed the Orthodox Jew who entered behind her. And the fact that he was talking on a cell phone.

I reached the traffic circle at the base of the gardens and pulled up short, letting the tour buses go around and around for their pictures. I clicked into the radio. "Blood, we're finally at the bottom. What's the status?"

"I got one bad guy down, but Shoshana did her own damage. I got cops all over the place."

"What happened?"

"I'm up for ideas. I took the guy that went long. He was setting up for an ambush, so I took him out. She did something. I don't know what, but whatever it was, it was complete. They've got an ambulance here, and it's not for my guy. All I did was choke him out. No permanent damage."

"Where is she?"

"I tracked her to the traffic circle at the base of the gardens, and she boarded a bus going to Acre. I couldn't follow, obviously. You were right. She's on the warpath."

I said, "Okay, okay. So she's good? She's free?"

"Yeah, she's free from here, but I don't know what assets are against her. If you're asking if I was successful in protecting her, I'll tell you that I was here. *Here.* I don't know about anything else."

Shit. Brett had worked operations like this for a decade. He was putting a little frosting on the turd with that answer. He had gotten her clear from the gardens, but he didn't think that was the end. I gave him our location and waited on him to arrive.

Why won't she fucking answer her damn phone?

Jennifer said, "What now?"

"I don't know. She's in the wind, and she's being chased by a team.

Apple Watch is still out there, and he was just security in a car. We know they had a team that went up, and there's no way Shoshana eliminated them all. If she had, she would've walked out the front door instead of jumping in front of us."

Jennifer said, "Why do you think she looked at us that way? She wanted to shoot us."

"I don't know. I've thought about that . . . I don't know."

Jennifer toyed with a napkin between our seats, then said, "I think I do. She thinks you're after her."

"*What?* That's fucking crazy. All I did was ask for dinner."

"Don't get mad . . . but she *is* a little off. I think she saw you and made a connection to something that isn't there."

"What about all that empath shit, where she can see a threat? The thing you think is real? Why would she look at *me* as a threat?"

Jennifer exhaled and said, "Good question. I don't know."

I said, "I do. Because she's fucking crazy. Jesus. I should have never called."

Jennifer looked at me with a side-eye and said, "Really? Your call caused this? So you completely ignored all Taskforce protocols to go running up here to protect her? Ignoring our main target? Quit it."

I sighed and said, "Okay. I'm worried about her. That look wasn't right. She wanted to shoot me, for real. I saw it. She bolted not because she was deciding whether she should or not. Just that she didn't have the time to waste."

"I know. And it's also irrelevant. This is like trying to save a tiger in the water. We want to help, but the tiger thinks we mean harm. In the end, you have to rescue the tiger, no matter how much it claws."

Brett came up, slapping the window. I popped the locks, and he slid into the back. He said, "Okay, she did some serious damage. The guy she took out looks like he's been through a meat grinder. He's on the way to the hospital—alive—but I'm surprised she didn't kill him."

"And your guy?"

"He's probably slinking back to the base right now, coming up with a story of how he was blindsided by Batman."

I put the car into drive and pulled away. Jennifer said, "What now?"

"I guess head on back to Tel Aviv and try to at least accomplish our mission. It's going to be hard enough explaining this detour to Kurt. We gave her a day. Maybe more."

Jennifer sat up straight in her seat and said, "Are you kidding me? We did this today but didn't solve the problem."

The words were music to my ears. I said, "So you want to continue flagrantly ignoring our mission, which, by the way, is paying our salary, to go chase that nutcase?"

Brett's head went back and forth between us, but I knew he didn't care. He just liked watching the fight. Even though he didn't realize there wasn't one.

Jennifer became incensed, saying, "Okay, I made a joke about the gardens today. But there's no way I'm leaving Shoshana out on her own with a team of assassins hunting her. A *team,* I might add, that's tied to our mission. What the hell has come over you? You're always the first to tip over the applecart."

Brett started laughing, now in on the joke. She turned to him and snapped, "You think this is *funny*? You think her getting killed is humor?"

He said, "I think Pike was looking for a solution, not a fight."

She looked at me, and I grinned. She smacked my shoulder and said, "Why do you do that stuff? Just agree with me. I'm always right."

I passed through a traffic light and said, "Yeah, that's true. But we still have no leverage. No anchor to tug on."

She sat in the car, tapping her fingers on the dash, and I knew her mind was working a thousand miles a second. I, honestly, had no idea what to do next. And I'd done the thousand-miles-a-second routine. I was willing to see what her brain could come up with.

She finally said, "Okay, we know she's being hunted, right?"

"Yep."

"And we know that they're good at what they do. They've managed to plan an operation against her using both native assets and transnational killers. They have some talent, and they have some money behind them. They won't stop because of what happened today, and we probably didn't short out their ability to succeed."

I said, "Okay, that's reassuring. So, we have no idea how to find Shoshana, but they do, and they're going to kill her. Great."

"That's not true. We know at least three of the players that are hunting her, right?"

"Who?"

"Apple Watch, the Orthodox Jew, and the man he met at the marina restaurant."

"Yeah . . . I guess that's right. You mean we have their cell phone numbers?"

"Yes. Exactly. And we know Shoshana is going to Acre, and that's only thirty minutes away."

"Wait, we know she got on a bus that *goes* to Acre. We have no idea if she's riding it the whole way."

Jennifer pursed her lips, not liking the logic, and said, "Okay, we know she's on the bus, and we know the location it ends at."

"So?"

"So, if these fucks are so good at their job, they'll find her. All we need to do is find them."

I sat in silence for a moment, just letting the car glide forward. It was pure genius. I glanced into the rearview mirror, catching Brett's eyes. He said, "You screwed up bringing her on board. You're no longer the smartest person in the room."

Jennifer perked up at the comment, looking like Marisa Tomei at the courtroom scene of *My Cousin Vinny.* If she'd put her hands on the dash and shrugged, it would have been a fait accompli.

I said, "Dial up Creed. Get us a geolocation of those numbers."

22

★ ★ ★

Shoshana waited until the bus reached the apex of its route, stopping outside the old citadel of Acre. A crusader castle that was jam-packed with tourists, it bled into the Turkish Bazaar, a maze that would allow her to disappear. She knew of a youth hostel deep in its embrace that would be completely outside of the scope of anyone searching for her. Even Pike. She exited after everyone else, glancing left and right, not realizing she'd already had a bull's-eye placed on her head.

She hit the street and glided through the tourists, moving swiftly into the citadel and ignoring the pleas of those outside begging for money. She raced through the exhibit, searching for the exit on the far side, the one that would let her into the Turkish Bazaar. She was growing more and more paranoid.

Pike had an ability like hers, she was sure. He could *see* where she went. Could *feel* her weakness. He was coming, and she was dead. Given all her missions in the Mossad, she came as close as she ever had to total panic.

And it was precisely because she'd found a reason to live. Before, if she'd have died, it was just something that happened. And might actually release her from the trials the Mossad had put her through. Now? She had a *reason* to live. And if that meant killing Pike Logan, she'd do it. But she didn't think she could. He would win. She'd seen it.

She exited the walls of the crusader museum and followed the signs for the bazaar, an ancient Turkish market buried in the narrow stone alleys outside the castle. It was once the primary market for the locals—and still was to a certain extent—but it now catered to tourists as well, selling more souvenirs than spice. She went down an alley, looking for the hostel she remembered, something backpackers used, with no outward signs of availability. A place that was found through word of mouth in Internet chat rooms vice any advertising.

She broke through the alley and found herself in the market, stalls left and right selling everything from candy to leather goods. She continued forward, her head swiveling, sliding through the mass of humanity, looking for a threat.

She went deeper, and the street signs went from Hebrew to Arabic. She believed she was in far enough to be secure. No way would anyone but an Israeli be able to find her here.

She began to relax, blending in with the throngs of tourists out to see a "real" market, even as the shop owners catered to their whim of what "real" meant, doing whatever it took to get a sale.

She felt her stomach growl and realized she hadn't eaten since she'd awoken. She'd been going on adrenaline and fear for hours. She saw a shawarma stall and went to it. She bought a meal of lamb and slid in behind the stove to eat it on a chipped picnic table.

She devoured the food, feeling more comfortable about where she stood. She considered contacting Aaron. She hadn't before because of the mission, waiting on him to call her, but this had obviously changed things. Her phone was still in the hotel, and she'd have to think a bit about how to get back there. She was sure she could. Pike might have surveillance on it, but odds were, he knew she wouldn't return. He wouldn't waste time on that.

She took a bite, gazing across the concourse, and froze. She saw Jennifer coming through an alley, the light from the outside silhouetting her in the gloom of the market. At first she thought she was wrong. Because it couldn't be. But it was. And behind her was Pike.

Her world collapsed. It was unreal. There was no way they could have found her. And yet here he was.

She lowered herself, putting the food on her plate and withdrawing her pistol. She mentally prepared to kill those she loved. A necessary evil.

She saw Jennifer looking at a device in her hands, trying to orient it. Which was confusing. They were tracking her through electronic means? No way. She'd left her phone in the hotel. She had nothing on her that could be tracked. Nothing.

It took a moment for the truth to settle. *They're tracking someone else.*

They came across the food court, trying to look like a couple on a date, but she saw the adrenaline in Pike's face. He was on the hunt. But for whom?

She slid backward, keeping low, leaving her food behind. She turned, about to sprint out of the area, when she heard a commotion behind her. She whipped around and saw that Pike had an Orthodox Jew on the fetid stone floor, torqueing his arm in a manner it wasn't meant to go, jamming the man's face into the offal from a millennium of travelers. She slid forward, hiding behind the table.

She heard, "Where is Shoshana? How many men are in here looking for her?"

The man said, "No one! I swear. I just called them. They're on the way, but they aren't here."

Pike slid down to his level, gave him the full heat of his gaze, and hissed, "If she's hurt, you're going to feel pain you have never imagined."

The words sank in, and it was a revelation. A mishmash of emotions that she'd never expected to feel. It righted everything she'd known for the last four days. All the fear and trepidation she'd felt fell away like the chrysalis of a butterfly.

Pike *was* pure. And her instincts had been right.

She saw Pike crank the man's arm back and heard the wail. She stood up, providing a view of her body. Jennifer saw her and slapped a hand on Pike's shoulder.

Shoshana said, "I'm over here. Right here."

Pike released the guy on the ground and stood up. He said, "You want to take his place? Because I'm about to do the same to you. At least he has a phone that he actually answers."

She gave a brilliant smile, showing her teeth, the relief flooding through her. She said, "You're just sweet on me."

23

★ ★ ★

Aaron heard the men stir on the far side of the cell and knew the time was coming close. When they'd arrived last night—after twelve hours of riding under the carpet in the back of the SUV—their captors had separated Alex from Aaron and tossed him into a room with little light, the only illumination coming from a cracked window high on the wall. He was surrounded by prisoners who flitted about like roaches, all seeking to escape attention from the guards. He was the only Caucasian in the place. He hoped the fact that they'd separated Alex meant they at least understood what would happen to her if she were to be incarcerated with him.

The prison was a decrepit cinder-block structure, without even bars or individual cells. All the men were thrown together, which made rest difficult. At least getting locked up alone would have meant enough security to sleep.

He'd learned early that these prisoners were different from what would be expected. They weren't here for petty street crimes. They were imprisoned for something else. Some wore the tattered remnants of military and police uniforms. Others clung to the remains of business suits. And they were tribal. The uniform crowd kept to themselves, and they seemed to want to curry favor with the guards by abusing other inmates, as if their actions had an impact on how long they would remain.

The ones in civilian clothes were different. Special. As a class, they weren't overtly abused, and the uniformed prisoners seemed to defer to them. From what Aaron could see, their punishment came at the hands of the guards, with restricted movement in the prison and less food.

Aaron belonged to a third class—the one of victim. A minority of the prisoners belonged to neither tribe, and they were the ones whom the uniformed prisoners preyed upon, to the delight of the actual guards. Tonight it was Aaron's turn.

Aaron had taken the farthest pallet from the door, putting his back to the wall and stretching out his shackled legs, waiting for nightfall. Waiting on the darkness.

Now he listened to the rustling and feigned sleep. There was enough light in the gloom to make out shapes, and he could see the guard outside the cell room, faintly illuminated by a single bulb. That would be the trigger.

He mentally began rehearsing how many he could remove before he went down. Breathing long and slow, he prepared for the fight.

He saw the guard get off his stool and wander down the hall. He felt the adrenaline surge.

Showtime.

No sooner had the guard disappeared than seven men stood up, walking slowly toward him, attempting to maintain silence. The leader was in the front, and that's whom Aaron would take first.

He waited until the first row of four was standing above him, then reached out and snatched the ankles of the leader. With a roar, he powered up, ripping the man off his feet and slamming his head into the concrete floor.

The other men actually leapt back at his yell and the violence, momentarily confused. Aaron used the stitch, the small bit of precious time. Keeping the corner to his back, he shuffled forward, his arms cracking out with the speed of a whip, his fists connecting with the first three men, a startlingly rapid attack.

They did whatever it took to get out of range, scrambling back and exposing the second row of three. The surprise gone, these were ready, circling to the left and right and bouncing on their feet, their shackle chains ringing on the concrete. They came in at the same time.

Aaron tucked, placing his elbows against his head to absorb the blows, knowing the prisoner chains on their ankles would prevent knees and kicks. He was hammered above his ears repeatedly, the punches doing little damage. He waited for an opening, then shot an uppercut almost from the ground, lifting one of the men off his feet, teeth twinkling in the twilight as they spewed out of his shattered face.

Aaron turned to the other two, only to find himself now facing all five. They closed in for the kill. Aaron raised his fists. The men circled, laughing at his predicament, sure in their numbers, not realizing what they faced.

Aaron was a grinder. A pounder. He'd spent close to twenty years learning how to destroy men with his hands alone, and after all that time, he'd learned to play to his strengths. He was no Jackie Chan, doing fancy kung fu maneuvers. His power lay in his fists, in a stand-up slugfest. While the shackles were stifling the men's ability to use kicks, they did nothing to Aaron's fighting effort. He could take a punch. Take a great many punches. And he could return them with a force few could withstand.

He kept the corner to his back and waded in, swinging his fists in jackhammer blows. His punches glanced off two of them, then connected solidly with one, dropping him like a puppet with the strings cut. He continued, tucked in and low, bobbing and weaving, blocking fists and snapping heads.

In frustration, one of the men did what Aaron feared most: He screamed and jumped inside Aaron's range, wrapping his arms around Aaron's waist.

Before Aaron could get free the remaining men jumped on him, causing them all to crash to the ground in a heap. Aaron brought his legs up and circled the chains from his shackles around a neck, launching his legs back out and jerking the man off him.

He tucked his head as the remaining three began to beat him, knowing his time was running out. He wrapped one arm around his skull and snapped out with the other one, popping a man hard enough to split his lips. He whipped his feet out, spreading his legs wide, hearing the man in chains gargle. He grabbed the throat of the man above him. Holding him in a death grip, he leaned back until the man's head was against the wall, then punched him in the forehead, causing his skull to ricochet. He focused on the final man, grabbing a thatch of hair like he was pulling weeds and drawing his arm back like a piston.

Before he could swing, a dozen flashlights split the darkness, and shouted orders filled the air. The guards poured in, ostensibly to save him from getting beaten to death. They ran in with a choreographed charade, batons out, only to halt, the yelling fading away. He found himself facing Lurch, looking confused and astonished at the carnage.

Lurch began screaming in Sesotho, and Aaron tossed the remaining conscious prisoner away, then untangled himself from the man still in his chains.

One of the guards checked the prisoner Aaron had choked, then rattled off something, causing two guards to flee the room.

Lurch's face split into a smile. He squatted down until he was level with Aaron.

"Bad, bad mistake, Jew. I don't know why you were in here to begin with"—he turned and used his baton to poke the body of the man Aaron had choked with his chains—"but now it's murder. And there is a specific punishment for that."

He raised his baton, and a voice from the back of the room floated out. "Leave him be."

A tall prisoner, gaunt, wearing the remnants of slacks and a suit jacket, came forward. His coffee-colored skin was stretched taut, with pronounced cheekbones and so little body fat one could trace the pulse in the veins of his neck, but he held himself as if he weren't in prison.

Lurch said, "This doesn't concern you."

"I decide what concerns me. Leave him be."

Lurch began rapidly shouting in the Sesotho language, but the man remained unmoved. Lurch pointed his baton at the man, glared at Aaron, then flicked his head at the guards. They left the room, with Lurch giving one last stare, a beam of pure hatred.

The man held out his hand, helping Aaron to his feet. He said, "My name is Thomas Naboni. You're not the usual type we get in here."

He laughed at his joke.

Unsure of what had just happened, Aaron said, "Thank you."

Thomas smiled, his teeth gleaming white and in perfect condition, a stark contrast to the rest of his appearance. He said, "When a man helps another out of free will, it says something of his character."

Still confused, Aaron thought he was referring to himself. "Yes, and I appreciate it."

Thomas said, "I'm talking about you. As hungry as you must be, you gave your food to another."

The guards had brought their meager rations earlier in the day, and one of the suit prisoners had been refused food. A stick of a man who was clearly starving. The others of that clan had shared their portions, and Aaron had kicked in, solely because the man looked on the verge of death.

A half cup of soiled rice saved my life?

Remembering the deference the guards had paid him, Aaron said, "I only did what I thought was right. Who are you?"

Thomas waved the question off and said, "Doing what is right is why you are alive now. The better question is why you are in here at all. What is your crime?"

Aaron said, "I'm a mistake. I've done nothing."

Thomas laughed and said, "Like us all. Like us all."

24

★ ★ ★

Like everyone else on the aircraft, Johan van Rensburg stared intently out the window, waiting on the land to reveal itself below the weather they were in. The aircraft circled, one wing held low, lining up with the small national airfield of Lesotho, Africa. Unlike the rest of the passengers, either tourists anxious to see the exotic land for the first time, or natives to whom air travel was a luxury rarely experienced, Johan was looking for something specific.

The aircraft broke through the low-hanging clouds, and the land burst forth below them, a rugged pictorial straight out of *National Geographic,* with high plateaus jutting out of the lush greenery like a setting from *Jurassic Park*.

While the tourists and locals took in the splendor, Johan looked more clinically. He didn't care about the beauty. He cared about a drop zone. A location where he could insert the team that would be close enough to the capital city of Maseru for his operation yet far enough away to not be noticed. A DZ that didn't require a hard slog to a rendezvous with transport. Because he'd need the men fresh.

Once they hit the ground, they'd be in motion for forty-eight hours straight, and every bit of energy he could conserve on the front end would pay dividends on the back. He knew, from experience.

Johan had perpetrated violence in many, many different countries inside Africa, but this would be the first time he did so in his own homeland. Well, not really his homeland, but close enough.

He had been born and raised in South Africa, a country that had fought between Dutch and British parentage for a century in various civil wars, until the country abandoned both, declaring outright independence. Then, as if it couldn't stand to be without an enemy, the country began to fight itself, with the colonial masters now pitted against the native population. What had once been seen as a sidenote in the colonial era, as the Dutch Boers took on the British military, became the main event. The politics of apartheid eventually consumed the state.

Johan came of age at the end of the white-rule era and the beginning of one man, one vote. A newly minted member of the famed South African Reconnaissance Commandos—the Recces—he served in 5 Recce on the small teams, doing external work in the border wars, a vicious, guttural fight that nobody else on the planet even knew existed. He learned there were no winners. Only survivors. After risking his life alongside black tribal members—men who were now his brothers—he came home from a final tour only to find his unit disbanded.

There was a new South Africa, and it was all about majority rule and dismantling anything that smacked of the elite apartheid state.

He'd left at that point, anxious about the fire consuming the country he called home. He had a unique skill, and a talent for using it that had been forged in combat. He'd plied that skill all over the continent, working with whomever would hire him, but as he did, his view of the world began to harden. He'd once been a member of an organization that held honor above all. Now honor was secondary to money.

He'd signed on with Executive Outcomes, Sandline International, and a few other outfits, fighting from Angola to Sierra Leone on behalf of everyone from De Beers Diamonds to national governments, and he'd seen that his talent could do both good and bad. Initially, the work had been pure, with a chain of command that understood the continent and a body of men who grasped war at the visceral level—but the taint of the mercenary hung large over them, eventually forcing the various companies out of business even as the African countries that had hired them praised their contributions.

After that, things had not been so clean, with him working solely for monetary gain with little in the way of moral restraint. He didn't mind a coup here and there—hell, the entire continent was a mess of intrigue—but he began to have misgivings.

When he looked in the mirror, he preferred to see someone who righted the wrongs of the world with the barrel of a gun, not someone who killed for money. In his heart, he knew that was nothing more than a myth. He'd seen enough evil to know he wasn't pure.

Once, long ago, he'd helped a warlord achieve success, and then he'd watched the man order the massacre of an entire village, solely because he believed—against all evidence—that the village had been against him. Johan had done nothing. He'd let the slaughter happen, and in so doing had become complicit in the deaths.

To this day, he would lie awake at night hearing the screams, knowing he could have stopped it. To be sure, it wasn't his fault. He wasn't in charge. But he *did* have a rifle in his hand. And had failed to use it to prevent the massacre.

In time, he'd become somewhat of an anomaly in the cloistered world of mercenaries on the continent. Most of the hires would do whatever was asked, cloaking their activities inside the parameters of the job. He was different. Among the major players in Africa, he was known as the Lily Boy. A purist who didn't understand the dirt required under the nails to accomplish the mission.

Johan didn't care. As he'd recently shown in his interrogation of the Jew, a little dirt never bothered him, if it was necessary. It was the mission alone that mattered to him. It didn't have to be noble, but it couldn't be outright evil.

Their aircraft came into final approach, and off in the distance he saw a large escarpment with a single dirt road snaking to the top. The terrain was flat and isolated, without any structures that he could see. It was his drop zone. Johan mentally recorded the flight path, judging where the radar arrays would be aimed to track the approaches of civilian aircraft, wanting to avoid them when they came in on an aircraft that most certainly wasn't going to land. He didn't worry about military systems. He knew Lesotho had no air defense systems to speak of. Such a thing would be absurd, as their borders were protected by South Africa.

Like the Italian microstates of the Holy See and the Republic of San Marino, Lesotho was an island in the middle of another country, completely surrounded. While Lesotho claimed sovereignty, it knew its hold on power was at the behest of the surrounding state—in this case, South Africa.

Lesotho was a mountainous land, its entire history a fight for survival, with the country founded by a tribe seeking refuge from the more martial Zulu clans. Climbing high into the mountains, the Basotho tribe had built a kingdom in rugged terrain that was just too hard to attack. The first king, Moshoeshoe I, had proven adept at the skills of both fighting and diplomacy and had guaranteed the kingdom's survival by engendering the protection of the British.

When South Africa had declared independence from the United Kingdom, so had Lesotho. And it had lived ever since as a sovereign state, surrounded completely by the country of South Africa in a strangely symbiotic relationship.

Its primary export was water, drawn from the dams in the highlands, and its primary customer was South Africa, making the country of Lesotho a strategic resource that irrevocably altered its ability to forge its own destiny. No matter what happened in the small kingdom, South Africa was inexorably tied to the outcome.

The last bit of unrest in Lesotho had caused a proactive response from the surrounding state. Ostensibly to stop the bloodshed, South Africa had deployed troops in a peacekeeping role, and it would have been seen as a true gesture of goodwill, except that the troops deployed to the dams that controlled the water into South Africa, letting the blood flow as long as the water did. The implication from that deployment was clear: Lesotho could pretend to be sovereign but only so long as it was peaceful.

Besides water, Lesotho had one other blessing—or curse, depending on whom you asked: The mountains produced some of the largest gem-quality diamonds on earth. The kimberlite mines of Lesotho did little to help the poverty of the average Basotho tribe member, but they were why Johan's skills had been brought in.

Lesotho had had a number of coups in its history, some bloodier than others, but none that relied on the help of an outside element. Johan's job would be to topple the government as rapidly as possible, using a martial skill that the troops in Lesotho could only dream of. His boss's job would be to placate the South African high command.

Johan wasn't privy to the details—that wasn't his job—but he believed Colonel Armstrong was using his contacts in South Africa to keep them at bay. He didn't know for sure, and in fact didn't want to know, but he understood that as long as the coup was relatively bloodless and swift, South Africa would stay away. If it turned into a street fight, South Africa was coming in just as they had before, and Colonel Armstrong's plan would fail.

The small aircraft hit the tarmac and rolled up to the lone gate of the Moshoeshoe I International Airport, a little bit of a misnomer because the only flights that came in were from Johannesburg. Looking more like an airfield at an island resort than the sole international airport for an entire country, the limited infrastructure made Johan smile.

It was a good sign.

Johan turned on his phone as he waited for the passengers to deplane, seeing a string of text messages appear, all demanding he call. He wondered what had happened in Tel Aviv, but he certainly couldn't talk on the aircraft.

Eventually, he walked down the airstairs and across the chipped tarmac. He entered the airport—a one-story brick building with only two rooms, one for departures and one for arrivals—and waited on his luggage. Through the window he watched a single man open the small cargo hold of the aircraft and begin transferring the bags by hand, without the benefit of a conveyor belt. He knew it would be a while.

He retreated to the corner of the room and dialed his phone, the text messages beckoning him, becoming more than he could ignore. In short order, he learned the disaster of the attempt to eliminate the partner of the man they'd captured. And it was total. Not only had three of his men been killed, but the woman was still on the loose.

Who in the fuck was she?

There was no way she could have escaped his team without help. *No way*. So, what now?

Maybe they'd misread the man they'd caught. Maybe he *was* Mossad. But that made no sense. Their contact in the diamond exchange—who would know—said he wasn't.

Either way, it was a disaster. And all the more reason to keep the man they'd caught alive. They'd need to hand him over after the coup to defuse any response. The last thing Johan needed was another private military organization hunting his ass down because he'd killed one of their own. Especially one from Israel.

He said, "What's your assessment?"

"Johan, she killed three of my men. Three trained men. That's not luck. That's skill. Something else is in play here."

"Any indications of Mossad efforts? Any at all?"

"No. The man inside the diamond exchange used to be in intelligence, and he assures us that the effort earlier in Joburg was just a stab in the dark. According to him, nobody in Israel cares."

"Then why are three men dead?"

He heard nothing for a moment, then, "You want my honest answer?"

"Yes."

"The woman we went after wasn't his control. I don't know what she is, but she wasn't some meek desk worker waiting on his contact report. She's a fucking killer. And she had help. One of my guys was incapacitated by a black man."

"African?"

"No. The man he took out said he spoke English with an American accent."

What the fuck? American?

"So should we continue? Is this team a threat?"

"Honestly, I don't even know if it *was* a team. We tracked her to her hotel, and she was alone. I don't know where that guy came from or where he went after. He did nothing to help her when she was under attack."

Johan took that in, then thought for a moment. He came up with nothing to ask. He said, "Give me your gut instinct on this."

"The mission takes priority. We gave her a scare, and she's on the run. We lost track of both her and the black man, but they have no idea what's going on. She might try to decipher our plan, but it won't be in Lesotho. If anything, she'll show up in Joburg hunting her partner's last location, which is *our* terrain, and we can kill her at our leisure."

Johan's voice grew hard. "A 'scare,' Andy? It cost the lives of three men. Three men I needed. I'm not so sure *you* are not to blame."

Johan heard nothing for a moment, then pure venom. "You fuck. I don't know why you've been brought on board, but the dead are *my* men. *My* men. Don't question me on my operations. The police here are going batshit. We don't have the cover to continue hunting her here even if we wanted to. We need to bail."

Johan backed off. The men on the team were all Special Forces—most from South Africa—but Johan had been long gone from that world, having spent close to a decade working for the United States in Jordan, so much so that he no longer knew who was worthy or not on the continent. The team was much younger than him, and outside of his orbit of personal connections. All he had was Colonel Armstrong, a man he knew by reputation, and someone who had lived what he had. Armstrong had built the team, and if he said they were good, then they were.

Johan said, "Okay, okay. I'm in Lesotho now. I need you to get to Cape Town anyway. Check out the shipment. I've identified the drop zone, but I need you to check the goods to make sure. Colonel Armstrong is there now, and he has the contact information."

"I can do that."

"Then, go. Get to Cape Town. Get out of the heat of Tel Aviv. Make sure that American arms dealer hasn't screwed us."

He heard, "Will do," then hung up.

Johan put his phone away, realizing he'd become engrossed in the conversation, and worried that someone had overheard. He surreptitiously glanced around, but nobody was near him.

He saw a porter manhandle a cart full of luggage inside and recognized his bag in the middle. He waited on the man to finish unloading, found his luggage, and prepared to exit, only to be surprised that he had to place the bag on an X-ray machine for customs. That was stricter than the routine of any country he'd entered in the last two years. He did so, with some trepidation, because he had something to hide.

The customs officer behind the screen pinged on an item, and Johan knew what it was. The beacon he was to emplace on the drop zone. As the official opened his luggage, Johan began developing a story on the fly to explain the device.

The official pulled out a square container a little fatter than a box of tissues, asking, "What is this?"

Johan inwardly sighed in relief. He'd also brought with him a quadcopter unmanned aerial vehicle for the reconnaissance he was about to conduct, something that was much easier to explain.

"A drone. You know, a flying camera? I take pictures with it. I'm a photographer, and I want to get some landscape shots of your waterfalls."

"Show me."

Johan pulled open the Velcro top and withdrew a DJI Mavic Pro, the four lift propellers collapsed into the body. He unfolded them, then pretended to have it zoom left and right, saying, "I fly it and it takes pictures."

The customs official smiled and said, "Put away, put away."

In short order, Johan was on his way, but that one encounter told him all he needed to know about trying to bring in a team overtly. They'd considered it, because they were sure that they could bring a howitzer into the country without any question, but it turned out—as it had on every other mission he'd done—that his choice to conduct a recon early had been prudent.

He had two days to figure out how to take down an entire country, and he was sure he could. He'd done it before, and in lands far more complicated than Lesotho. What he was unsure about was the woman in Israel. Admittedly, she was a small pinprick. A nothing in the greater plan they had in play. But she had proven lethal, and that was worrying.

I heard a knock on the door and knew it wasn't the maids. I looked at Jennifer and said, "Here we go. Get ready for the shit show."

She said, "You can talk her off the ledge."

I turned to the door and said, "I don't think so. The ledge has become about an inch wide."

I opened the door, seeing Shoshana outside it, her face determined. I said, "You're a little early for lunch."

She brushed past me, saying, "I don't want lunch. What did your vaunted Taskforce say?"

I let her storm into our decidedly small room without complaint. I knew she was on the verge of going berserk because of some stupid theory about Aaron, and she was still a little embarrassed about the whole "honeymoon" lie. I escaped to our tiny bathroom, letting Jennifer handle her for a minute.

We'd spent about thirty seconds inside the Turkish Bazaar before bundling up Shoshana and fleeing Acre. She'd wanted to question the guy I'd knocked to the ground, but I already knew he would be worthless for information—and that she probably wanted to inflict pain more than gather intel. I had no idea how many men were on the team we'd interdicted and had no intention of finding out. After an all-too-brief reunion, where she'd immediately turned into a slaughter monster wanting to kill the guy, we hit the road, me practically dragging her to our car.

Once on the highway, with Shoshana muttering expletives, I'd asked her where to go. She began to take me to task for making her leave, and I told her to back off, a little miffed at the lack of gratitude. Seeing the fireworks building, Jennifer had interjected, and, of course, that had been enough.

It aggravated the shit out of me, but those two had some secret connection, and it was enough to calm the little demon down. I'd asked her where we should go to lie low, and Shoshana had pulled a hotel out of thin air, giving me directions, but first demanded we go back to her hotel room.

That was ridiculous, and we started to build up into a fight again. Once again, like a mother separating two irate siblings, Jennifer stepped in, first asking Shoshana why it was necessary, to which she said she needed her clothes, her phone, and any other identifiable things in the room. In pure Shoshana fashion, she'd checked in under an alias and wanted to sterilize the site to protect herself.

Which was a point, I guess.

Jennifer then asked me why not, to which I basically exploded that it was idiotic to return to a room full of dead bodies from an assassination team that was still chasing us. The thought spoke for itself. Except Shoshana said now was the best time to return—before the bodies were found and after the team was left in disarray.

Which was another good point.

I reluctantly agreed to at least conduct a recce to see if it was possible, stating that if there was any chance of compromise, we were out of there. Of course, we'd slipped in and out without issue, and Shoshana had gloated with a *told you so* look.

I'd asked her where we were supposed to go now, and she gave me directions to the hotel. It was one near Ben Gurion Airport, and I'd asked why there. She told me the reasons—and they made sense.

Called the Sadot—or "fields" in Hebrew—it was a small boutique establishment situated in a medical complex. It was the closest hotel to Ben Gurion, just twenty minutes to the terminal and, more important, sat behind a guarded gate. Only patients and hotel residents were allowed to pass, and with the security posture of Israel, it was a layer of protection we could use. The rooms were microscopic, but the location was outside anything that my team or Shoshana had touched. It would do.

We'd conducted a detailed hot wash of what had occurred, with Shoshana pinging back and forth between emotions, like she was short-circuiting. Eventually, she'd calmed down enough to tell us about Aaron and the busted "honeymoon," only now she was convinced that the entire event was some sort of indicator that Aaron was in trouble.

She'd called him, but the phone rang out to voice mail, just like it had when I'd tried earlier, and I could see the tension rising in her. She would remain on the leash only so long.

She'd wanted to fly straight to Johannesburg and rip that town apart looking for Aaron, but I'd convinced her to let me leverage the Taskforce. I'd sent everything I had—a complete situation report, license plate numbers, descriptions of the men, the phone numbers we had, and the strange nexus between my target, the hit team, and the diamond exchange. Kurt had told me to give him eight to ten hours. Now that time was up, and Shoshana wanted answers.

Through the bathroom door, I heard Jennifer say, "Kurt hasn't called back yet. Give it time."

Shoshana went to classic Shoshana. "Fuck that. We're sitting here *wasting* time. We know those operators were from South Africa, and Aaron's last known location was Johannesburg. That little sexpot from the diamond exchange probably set him up."

I heard the words from inside the bathroom and immediately perked up. Earlier, I'd asked Shoshana what Aaron was doing, and she, of course, refused to tell me anything beyond the fact that he was operational. It wasn't upsetting, because beyond telling her we'd crossed paths with the guys hunting her, I'd also refused to say anything about what *I* was doing. We'd both reverted to our operational security, and my mission—while obviously tied in with her somehow—had been outside the scope of what she needed to know.

But that comment was too much. I opened the door and saw her facing Jennifer with her hands on her hips.

I said, "What sexpot from the diamond exchange?"

She realized she'd slipped up and said, "Nothing. He took a girl from the diamond exchange with him. It's why I stayed behind. She had the knowledge he needed."

"Do you know who she worked for?"

"Pike, I can't talk about it."

After all we'd done for her, completely outside of our mandate—to include putting my team in jeopardy—the answer aggravated me. The stonewalling was too much.

I said, "Right, Carrie. It's all *secret*. You know, we might have solved this a little earlier if you'd bothered to answer your phone for a dinner date. But I forgot, you were on your 'honeymoon.'" I said the word while using my fingers to make air quotes.

She turned red, balled her fists up, and I thought for a fleeting moment she was going to attack. Instead, she started to brush past me, and I swear I thought I saw her eyes water. But that was impossible. Carrie didn't cry.

Jennifer, having the intuition that I was lacking, gave me a look of pure venom. I realized using the callsign she'd earned on another mission—because she was borderline psychotic—and disparaging her relationship with Aaron had hit a lot harder than I had intended. But how could I know that Shoshana actually had feelings?

She'd never had before.

Jennifer grabbed Shoshana's arm, preventing her from leaving. Shoshana started to jerk it free, and I held up my hands, saying, "Whoa, Shoshana. Wait."

She said, "Fuck you." To Jennifer, "Let go of my arm, Koko. I mean it."

Jennifer did, and before I could stop her, she said, "Shoshana, our target went into the diamond exchange. We couldn't follow, but the coincidence is too much."

That brought Shoshana up short. She looked at me, then went back to Jennifer. Jennifer said, "What was Aaron doing?"

"What were *you* doing? Tell me who you were following."

I said, "Carrie, cut the shit. You want to solve this, you work with us, not the other way around."

Jennifer looked alarmed at my tone, but I knew I was on solid ground now. No disparagement. Pure mission. Shoshana would understand that. She glared at me, and I said, "I apologize for what I said before."

That worked the opposite of what I wanted, like she was hiding the fact that it even mattered. She tensed up, her muscles vibrating, and said, "I don't need this. I'll save Aaron myself."

She tried to go past me, and I blocked her. She said, "Get the fuck out of the way, Nephilim. I don't want to harm you."

I looked into her eyes, getting her to read me. Knowing she would. I said, "I want to *help* you. Help Aaron. Like I did yesterday. Don't treat me as the enemy. I didn't mean what I said. I would never hurt you on purpose."

She tensed up, and I refused to raise my arms, even though every single fiber of my being wanted to protect myself from her inevitable attack. I felt her weird glow float over me, and then she sagged back against our small desk.

Whew.

I had won.

27

★ ★ ★

Shoshana said, "I don't know what he was doing. He got the mission and determined I wasn't viable to help. It was tied into the diamond exchange, but it wasn't anything violent. He was doing something to prevent the embarrassment of the state. Nothing more. It was an economic mission, not national security. Someone in the exchange was doing something that would cause repercussions to the exchange's honor code and reputation."

I said, "Do you know who it was? I mean, inside the exchange?"

She perked up, saying, "No, but I can find out. I'll contact our control at Mossad. They'll know."

I shook my head. "You can't do that. Think about it. Why are you asking? Because someone attacked you? And how did you get away? Because of an unsanctioned US mission on Israeli soil? That's not happening."

She snarled, "Fuck your Taskforce. If it means saving Aaron, you'll have to take the repercussions. You don't like it, get on a plane right now. You'll be out of the country before anyone can react."

Jennifer was taken aback at the ferocity. She said, "Wait a minute, you'd throw us to the wolves, after Pike disobeyed orders to save you?"

Shoshana looked at her, then nodded, saying, "Yes. Would you not do the same for Nephilim?"

Jennifer gave no answer, and Shoshana said, "Of course you would. You can hate me if you want, but Aaron means more to me than your emotions or your organization. I need to leave. I need to contact the Mossad for the man Aaron was sent to investigate."

She looked at me and said, "Don't fight me, Nephilim. Let me go."

I stepped aside and said, "Sure. Head on over to Aaron's control. See what you get."

She hesitated, and I continued. "Why wasn't the Mossad used on this? If it was so important? Why use a contractor?"

She said, "Because they wanted a cutout. It's standard operating procedure. You know that."

"And why is it standard procedure?"

She said nothing. I said, "Because they *wanted* a cutout. You just said that. Why the cutout?"

She just looked at me. I said, "Shoshana?"

She said, "Because they didn't want any official Mossad hand on the problem."

I nodded. "Think about what you just said. If something went wrong, they could disavow any official Israeli response, correct?"

She didn't answer, and so I continued, driving home the knife. "If Aaron is in danger, why are you finding out about this because of an attack on you? Why didn't the Mossad contact you after he disappeared?"

She remained mute, and I said, "You *know* why. Just as I do. Because they used him as they intended. He was a throwaway, and when things went bad, they did just that."

She said, "No. They will help. They are Israeli."

I grabbed her arms in my hands and leaned into her face, aggravated at her naïveté. Knowing it was nothing more than hope. Shocked, Jennifer leapt forward. I flicked my head to her and snapped, "Back off."

She did, unsure of what was about to occur. Jennifer knew, beyond any doubt, no matter what happened, that I would move heaven and earth to do whatever was required to help her. Because of that, she assumed that the organization we worked for would do the same. She was wrong—and Shoshana alone understood that. More so than me. I knew her history.

I returned to Shoshana and locked eyes with her. She made no move to resist. I said, "They *will not* help. They put Aaron into play precisely so they could cut him free. If you go to them, if you make a stink, they'll react, no doubt. But it might not be the way you envision. They might cut him off completely. Cause him to be killed."

She half-heartedly struggled to get free, saying, "They would never do that."

I said, "You mean like they didn't with you?"

She stopped moving and looked at me, and I felt the weird glow. I said, "I understand loyalty. I understand a unit's mission. But some things supersede that, and you know it. *We* are those things, damn it. *We* mean more than the Mossad. Jennifer and me. And *you*."

She sagged, no longer offering any resistance. She said, "Okay, Nephilim. Okay. What next?"

I said, "Let the Taskforce do its work. Let's get a thread instead of hauling off half-assed. Aaron is tied in to our mission. I don't know why, but let's use what we have. You can't get anything out of the Mossad, but you have us. *Use* that."

I dropped my arms from her, and she looked at Jennifer, then back to me. She said, "You mean that?"

"I do. And I know *you* know that. So cut the shit."

She tried to hide a smile, then said, "I thought you didn't believe in me."

"I don't, but I know *you* do."

Like a light switch had turned off, she became feral again, saying, "Don't make fun of me." I saw it and put the reaction in my back pocket. However good she was operationally, she had turned a corner with Aaron being gone. She was no longer on an even keel. It was something to remember.

Jennifer stepped in, saying, "Shoshana, come on . . ."

Shoshana looked like she was willing to take the fight even to Jennifer. I had seen enough.

I said, "Carrie—" and she glared at me. I repeated, "*Carrie,* we're on your side. We showed that yesterday. Let the Taskforce do its work."

The computer on our desk began bleating. It was our VPN chirping, along with a download from the Taskforce. The invisible hand of the United States was at work, and its reach was vast.

I said, "There you go. They're calling now. Let me talk to the Taskforce, and then decide if you want to go off half-cocked on your quest for Aaron."

She said, "Do you really want to help me, or are you just preventing me from screwing up your mission?"

Jennifer said, "You know better than that."

She nodded, then said, "Okay, but make no mistake, my mission is Aaron, and if our paths diverge—if your mission comes crossways with mine—I'll do whatever it takes to save him."

I punched the accept button on the computer, saying, "Yeah, yeah. Shut up. I can't have the Taskforce know you're in the room."

Before the screen cleared, she touched my shoulder. I looked at her and saw nothing but death. She said, "Nephilim. I mean that. Don't cross me. If it comes to it, I will do to you what you would do to me to save Jennifer."

Jennifer looked confused at the statement. Shoshana's eyes were as cold as stone in a river. I knew she was serious because her statement was true. I *would* do what she said, if the roles were reversed.

I reached up and softly touched her cheek. "It will never come to that. Ever."

She was shocked at the gesture, but I meant it. She smiled, a little bit of the feral still there, and I said, "Get away from the fucking screen."

She backed off, and I leaned in to hear what the Taskforce had found.

Johan poured a drink from the hotel minibar, waiting on the stored video footage from the Mavic Pro to download. It was an amazing system, designed and innovated by market demands, and as such, was a technological feat that the slovenly procurement system of any military simply could not produce. By the time they had something like the Mavic, the Mavic would be in edition number twelve. Maybe that edition would work data at exponential speeds, but the Mavic he had was still transferring the video to his MacBook at a decidedly mundane rate.

After landing, Johan had spent eight long hours driving around Maseru, pinpointing and recording the grid of the locations the team would need to neutralize. Weak links in the chain and specific points of failure that were the underpinnings of the entire government.

It would seem ridiculous for a force of fewer than a hundred to attempt such a thing, but unlike other countries with multiple centers of gravity—such as the United States—Lesotho had essentially one: the capital city of Maseru.

All power radiated out from there, with every other village being simply a satellite that rotated around the host. Cut the weak links inside Maseru and the rest of the country would fall in line. Do it right and they wouldn't even be aware of a change until it was already a fait accompli.

The prime minister's residence and parliament were first, of course, but those were the no-brainers. Others were less obvious but just as critical, such as the lone Lesotho television and radio station and the sole Internet provider. Stop the flow of information and stop anyone from even knowing a coup was in progress.

In addition to the levers of information and government, he had to prevent the engagement of the one martial arm the prime minister commanded, the Maseru police, and that meant the police headquarters building. Johan couldn't attack all the stations in the city, but he could prevent the central command from issuing orders—which would be critical.

While General Mosebo would guarantee no military would respond, the police were another story, as the prime minister had made a concerted effort over the last year to co-opt them—precisely because he feared General Mosebo's growing power base within the Lesotho Defence Force.

Finally, Johan had to pinpoint the location of no-fire zones—areas that would remain neutral and stay out of the fight, unless Johan's men carelessly provoked them. Top of this list was the US embassy. He knew that the US ambassador was currently backing the prime minister in his spat to have General Mosebo removed from the head of the LDF, and that backing had teeth, with millions in aid money being used as a bargaining chip. This had led to most of the parliament siding with the prime minister—and had left Mosebo out in the cold. The embassy would sit out the violence, hiding in their enclosure, but only if they didn't feel threatened. If they did, Johan's men might be facing a battalion of Marines, ostensibly to protect the embassy but more likely to project American influence. The key was not to give them an excuse.

Other countries' embassies were marked as well, but only because they could cause issues with the consolidation of power. They had no force projection capability, but they most certainly could withhold recognizing the new government, acting in a tiff because some of Mosebo's men had dropped an errant mortar into their compound.

After he'd finished getting the grids to all the locations, he'd come back to his hotel and loaded the destinations into the Mavic Pro. Attaching his smartphone to the controller, he'd taken it out on his balcony and then sent the drone flying.

The thing was a marvel of technology that beat any military system he'd ever worked with. With a thirty-minute flight time, a seven-kilometer range, software-driven obstacle avoidance, and a high-resolution, gimbal-stabilized camera, he could cover every target he'd located on the ground from his hotel balcony, getting video that would be more useful for assault planning than the top secret satellite images he'd used in the past.

He'd had to swap batteries twice, but eventually he had a bird's-eye view of every target, to complement his on-the-ground reconnaissance. He was satisfied with the work and was about to contact the team in Cape Town to learn their progress, when he heard a knock on the door to his hotel room.

He closed the computer, glancing at the gear strewn around his bed, thinking of hiding it. He went to the door first. He regretted it the moment he put his eye to the peephole.

Outside were three thugs, tall and meaty, with close-cropped Afros. And they weren't in any type of uniform. They weren't maintenance or hotel staff. Which meant they had the wrong door. Or he was in trouble.

Through the door, he said, "Can I help you?"

He heard, "Mr. van Rensburg?"

Shit. Johan glanced back, wishing he'd taken the time to sterilize his room. The drone was on the bed, with the computer attached to it by a USB cable. Next to the window was the drop zone beacon, working through its software and GPS signal.

No time to stall, idiot. Why did you ask the question? In intelligence, it was always the little things that caught you. Complacency. Something he'd taken advantage of with the Israeli not two days before. And now he was guilty.

He thought about running to the bed and furiously cleaning what he had, but he wouldn't be able to hide the systems in a place they wouldn't find with a minimal search. Even if he could, they might have a key, and if they did, they'd come in only to find him shoving everything under the bed.

He said, "Yes? Can I help you?"

"Open the door. We have some questions."

He paused, then said, "Pardon me?"

"Open the door. We're from Lesotho security, and we have some questions related to your safety. Please. We mean no harm. We can do it right here in the hallway."

Lesotho security? What the hell does that mean?

"I'm sorry. I'm not in the habit of opening the door to strangers in a foreign land. Let me call the front desk."

He put his eye to the peephole and saw the lead Neanderthal grin. He heard, "Do it. We'll wait."

Shit. They're real. There was no way they'd bluff this far. They'd already talked to the front desk and had cowed whoever was there.

He heard, "Johan? You still there?"

Thinking furiously, he said, "Yes. I'm here."

"This won't take a moment. The longer you stall us, the more we fear for your safety."

What a fucking lie.

He made his decision. *Get in the hallway and close the door.* Let them talk to him out there. Don't let them in the room. If he couldn't defuse what they had in mind then he was screwed anyway.

If they demanded to go in the room, he, in turn, would demand hotel personnel accompany them. Which should at least give them pause.

He flung open the door and pushed past them, jerking it closed. He said, "What on earth are you talking about? Why are you here?"

They circled him, and one, taller than the others, leaned in and said, "Are you Johan van Rensburg?"

"Yes. You know that. What's this about?"

"It's about your nonstandard travel today. It's about your work for the Americans."

Americans? What the hell?

It wasn't lost on him that it was the second time he'd heard that word in the last two days. America cared as much about Africa as it did for a nose hair that had grown too long. And yet, he'd had an American interdict his team in Tel Aviv, and now he had a bunch of thugs accusing him of the same.

He said, "I'm not American. I'm South African."

"Passport?"

He handed it over, now sure he was in the clear. Whatever the Americans were up to here, it had nothing to do with him.

The brute took it, then said, "Follow me."

Johan said, "Wait, what? I'm not going anywhere."

The man held up his passport and said, "Yes, you are, if you want to get this back."

Johan was now sure that they were from the Lesotho police and he'd been tracked somehow. And if they suspected anything, they'd confirm it with the evidence in his room. He needed to prevent that. They hadn't asked for his key, which was a plus. If he refused, they might. He was sure he could win a battle of wits alone at police headquarters, but he couldn't if they confronted him with his equipment.

Johan said, "Okay, okay, what do you want to talk about? We could do it at the bar."

"Not the bar. We have a place that's secure. Someplace you'll be safe."

Johan saw his face and knew it had nothing to do with being safe and everything to do with controlling the environment. The easy answer would be, *No, let's do it right here, in my room,* but that was a nonstarter. So far, they'd made no move to open his door. *Go? Or not?*

He decided to go. They had thought he was American, and when he'd proved he wasn't, it had altered their calculation. They had an order, which was to bring him in for questioning, and they'd execute that order even if their information was wrong.

He'd talk to the man calling the shots. Once that guy saw his passport, he'd be cut free.

He said, "Okay, but I can't stay long. I have a dinner reservation upstairs. Are you going to let me make that?"

"Yes. Of course. We only want to protect you."

Right.

They left the hotel, Johan sandwiched in the back of an SUV between two thugs who never smiled. They wound around the city streets and then headed into the country. The drive began to confuse him. If they were police, he should have traveled to their headquarters—a location he now knew intimately.

They didn't. They pulled onto a dirt track outside an eight-foot-tall barbwire fence, and Johan recognized the location. Set against the backdrop of a high ridgeline, it was the Makoanyane Military Base. The location of the headquarters of General Mosebo's Special Forces Company. The very people his men were training outside of Cape Town.

What the hell?

29

★ ★ ★

They drove through the gate, the soldier manning it looking intently at Johan—probably the only white man he'd seen today—and then wound around a dirt track, weaving between concrete buildings. They stopped outside of a U-shaped structure set off on its own, surrounded by woods, the wings made of cinder blocks and crumbling. The driver parked, and the thug on the left exited the vehicle, waving him to get out. He did so and was immediately flanked by the other men, one on each side and one in the back.

They led him toward the south wing, the portico crumbling with age, and into a space that looked like a classroom. The walls were covered with sheets, hiding what was behind them, but he could make out an insignia: the 505th Intelligence Battalion. The intelligence organization for the Lesotho Special Forces Company. General Mosebo's private spy organization.

He had little time to reflect on that, because in front of him were three men seated behind a table. On the other side of the table was a single chair.

So they'd staged this. They'd set up this little interrogation facility in the time they'd driven here. Which told him volumes. One, they weren't an element that habitually did questioning, because if they had been, they wouldn't have taken the time to turn a classroom into an interrogation facility. They would have just taken him straight into a cell with iron rings and blood on the wall.

Two, they weren't that switched on, because the cloth on the wall did little to hide what was behind it. Clearly, it was a little bit of amateur hour, which explained why they hadn't searched his room. Even so, he had to tread lightly, because there was no way he could let on what he was doing here. They worked for General Mosebo, but that meant little. Mosebo wouldn't lift a finger to help him. The men in the room had no idea of the plans in motion, and if they learned it from Johan, Mosebo would deny it, hanging him out to dry. Literally. Not an entertaining thought.

The one in the center, a tall, reedlike man, said, "Take a seat, please."

Johan did. One of the thugs who brought him in began pacing behind him, causing him to want to look over his shoulder. *Intimidation.*

The man on the right had his passport and was flipping through it. Johan said, "What's this about?"

The man on the left stared at him, trying to look aggressive. He had almost no neck, a bald head, and deep-set eyes. Johan tried to look suitably intimidated, but the man reminded him of a frog. He spoke, and his English was so bad Johan could barely understand it.

"You are an American spy." At the end of the statement, he snorted, an odd, out-of-place utterance.

Johan didn't have to feign shock, because it was the last thing he expected. He said, "What the hell are you talking about? I'm from South Africa. I'm a photographer. I only came here to take pictures of your landscape. The Maletsunyane Falls and the highlands."

The man on the right slapped the table hard and said, "You lie. Look right here."

He held up Johan's passport and pointed. "An H-1 visa for the United States. You work for them."

Johan could not believe his bad luck. These men hated the United States for backing the prime minister in his fight against General Mosebo, and he was here to help them get exactly what they wanted, but they were blinded by their paranoia. The irony wasn't lost on him that his presence was, in fact, a good reason to be paranoid. Or that because he'd worked as a security contractor for a duplicitous asshole in the United States, he was now suspected of being a spy. He'd ended up killing that man, but he couldn't say that here.

Wait—that's a mistake. I did have a visa to work in the US, but I slaughtered my boss because he was helping terrorists. Don't tell anyone. It's our secret.

Probably wouldn't go over too well.

Johan said, "Yes, I worked in America. I work all over the world. How does that make me a spy?"

The man on the left said, "You know who has you, don't you?" He finished the question with the odd snort, like ending a sentence triggered some visceral phlegm reaction.

Johan said, "Uhhh . . . no, I don't. I have no idea why I'm here. I was told Lesotho was very beautiful, but that's not what I'm seeing now."

The tall reed in the center said, "You are working with American Special Forces. We know they have a team here. We know they are at the embassy right now."

What in the hell? The damn Americans. The news filled Johan with not a small amount of worry, if only because their fear was rooted in something concrete, thus making it harder to dissuade them from their chosen conspiracy. He was sure it was nothing more than a security assessment team provided by the US Special Operations Command to do a routine check, but with the paranoia shown here, that mattered little. They'd probably do the same if a USAID team came in delivering wheat.

The frog on the left said, "We know they landed today, and now we want to know why."

Johan thought, *You know because the damn embassy* told *you they'd be coming.* But he couldn't show any familiarity with soldiers or embassies. He simply said, "I'm just a photographer. I didn't fly in with any American team. I flew in from Johannesburg by way of Durban."

The frog said, "If you're a photographer, where are your cameras?" *Snort.*

What is up with that guy?

He ignored the quirk because the question put him in a bind. He couldn't lead them back to the hotel or he'd be spending the next few years in some rotten hole once they saw what he'd done. But not saying anything would look just as suspicious.

Time to shift tactics. He became belligerent, raising his voice, against training protocols. "My cameras are in my hotel room. Where *you* snatched me up." He pointed to the man circling behind his chair and shouted, "I offered to show those idiots who brought me here, but they had no interest!"

That answer seemed to rock them back a bit, giving him hope. Time was not on his side. Sooner or later, they'd wonder why he hadn't asked for the South African embassy's help—which was something he most definitely couldn't do.

He stood up, snarling, "I've had about enough of this shit. Stupid talk of spies and Americans. I'm a South African citizen, here to help your tourism industry, and you treat me like a criminal!"

The man pacing behind his chair stepped forward and punched him in the kidney, bringing him to his knees in an explosion of pain. He feigned being hurt much worse than he was, thinking, *Okay, that didn't work. Looks like you're fighting your way out.*

He had no idea how he'd get out of the camp but was thinking only of one step at a time. He crawled on his knees, hacking spittle like he was incapacitated, searching for the man who'd punched him. He was the one who worried him the most. The hired gun. Not the officers behind the table. Take that guy out and the rest would be easy.

His eyes aimed at the floor, he saw the boots of the man, just outside of striking range. Still crouching and feigning injury, he shuffled forward on his knees and coiled his legs.

He heard, "Stop this!"

He turned, and a new man had entered the room. From the reactions of the others, Johan could tell he outranked them all.

The man said, "What is going on here?"

Like you don't know. Johan was sure he'd been listening next door, and the violence had been more than he was willing to sanction.

Johan waited and saw the expression of the frog go from bewilderment to anger. The frog said nothing, but it was enough for Johan to realize he was right. Whoever the man was, he knew exactly what was happening, and Frog wasn't too happy about being thrown under the bus.

The reed in the center rattled off a bunch of sentences in Sesotho, and the man answered. After a back-and-forth, the center man left the room and the commander took his spot. At that point, Johan knew his gambit had worked. The roughing up of him, with no evidence, had spooked the commander, and now he was going to play nice.

This he did, apologizing for the "inconvenience."

Johan said, "So that's it? I'm free to go?"

"Yes, but you understand why this happened, correct?"

"Fuck no."

The words came out as a slap, and the commander leaned back. He said, "The Americans are against the LDF. They want Lesotho defenseless. They have relentlessly persecuted our commanding general—and your own country has shown no inclination to help, leading those in power to wonder just what South Africa wants."

Johan started to say something, the unwinding conspiracy theories becoming ridiculous—not least because he was living the very conspiracy on behalf of the man talking—when the commander held up his hand, saying, "I know, I know, you're just a photographer. A man who knows nothing of such things but apparently travels all over our capital city without a camera today, stopping at some decidedly strange spots."

Johan remained quiet, sensing the endgame and not wanting to screw it up. First rule of interrogation: If the interrogator wants to talk, let him.

He continued. "If, by any chance, you bump into the US ambassador on your sightseeing trips, you might tell him how we feel. Let him know that Lesotho will not tolerate American interference. We don't fear Special Forces. We have our own—and as I'm sure you've now seen, they're just as good."

Johan kept his opinion to himself, realizing that this man truly thought he was a spy and was giving him a message to take back to the US embassy. The lunacy of the entire situation made him wonder about the general they were supporting. If Mosebo was half as crazy as these men, he probably deserved to go.

The commander smiled and handed back Johan's passport. He said, "Can you relay that, if you get the chance?"

"Yes, of course. But I've told you—"

"Yes, yes, I know. You're just a photographer."

A man entered the room with a digital SLR and a piece of paper with handwriting on it. The commander said, "You don't mind if we use our own, do you?"

The man handed the paper to Johan, and he saw it was his name and passport number. He was instructed to place it under his chin, like a common criminal, and the man took several photos. When he'd left the room, the commander said, "Balim, take him back to his hotel."

To Johan he said, "But rest assured, we'll be watching. Johan the Photographer."

Johan nodded and followed Balim out the door. On the silent drive back he reflected on two things: One, these men were nowhere near as good as Colonel Armstrong thought they were. The cream of their intelligence crop not only never searched his room, they didn't even make him empty out his pockets. It didn't bode well for General Mosebo's troops, whom they were currently training. And two, there was a United States Special Forces team on the ground, which made the no-fire box of the US embassy critical. In no way did he want them involved. This had to be clean, Lesotho against Lesotho. Any fight drawing in the Americans would be a mess of the first order.

Balim pulled into his hotel drive-through and put the vehicle in park, not saying a word. Johan exited and for the first time felt the sweat under his shirt.

For as amateurish as the interrogation had been, it had still been harrowing and had come close to leading to mission failure. He went up to his room and realized the reconnaissance he'd been sent to do had accomplished exponentially more than he had expected, but he needed to get out. Now.

No way was he going to ply his cover tomorrow, driving around taking pictures of waterfalls. The only pictures he'd get would be on the mountainous plateau, when he emplaced the beacon for the drop. After that, he intended to be on the first plane smoking out of the country.

The next time he'd see Lesotho would be under a parachute canopy, and the three in that room had better hope they didn't end up in his gunsight.

30

Knuckles saw the phone in the team room blink and answered, hearing, "He's here. Just walked in."

He said, "Thanks," hung up, then jogged down to the second floor toward Kurt Hale's office. He knocked, and Kurt looked up, a phone to his ear. Kurt said, "Never mind, he's in my doorway."

Kurt hung up and said, "What, you have a beacon on my ass or something?"

Knuckles grinned and said, "No, sir, I just knew you wanted me here. You still serious about taking me to the Oversight Council meeting?"

"Yeah. I'm serious. George is on leave, and I need someone to keep me company." Kurt smiled and said, "I can't do these meetings by myself."

George Wolffe was the deputy commander of the Taskforce and the natural choice to take to an Oversight Council meeting. Knuckles—an Operator—was not. And he knew it.

He said, "What about Blaine? Where's he?"

Blaine Alexander was the Omega chief. The man who called the shots when an operation was executed to put someone's head on a spike. Once a lieutenant colonel in the Army, he'd controlled every single hit that Knuckles had been on under Taskforce authority. He'd retired from the military and taken a contracting job with the Taskforce. Which is to say he was doing the same thing he'd done on active duty.

The Taskforce was weird that way. It was a digital machine in the world of the analog government. But it didn't explain why Knuckles was going to an Oversight Council meeting.

Kurt said, "Blaine's busy on a project." Kurt looked at him and said, "You afraid of going?"

"No. Hell no. Just wondering, is all."

Kurt said, "Well, quit it. There aren't any surprises with me."

Knuckles heard the words and wanted to laugh, wondering if Kurt actually believed them. Behind his back, Kurt Hale was called Yoda, and that was for a reason. He never gave an explanation for doing anything and always confounded those around him, right up until he was proven correct. There was a purpose behind Knuckles's attending the Oversight Council meeting, but, maddeningly, Kurt wouldn't say what that was. Knuckles had lived with that for the last seven years he'd been in the Taskforce, and, while it was aggravating, he'd never complained. Because at the end of the day, it usually meant he'd get to put a terrorist down.

Kurt exited the office and Knuckles followed. He said, "Hey, sir, just out of curiosity, why me?"

Walking toward the elevator, Kurt said, "You heard the VTC yesterday with Pike, correct?"

"Yeah. Of course. Pike's got a thread, but we have no idea what it is."

"No, I mean did you *hear* the VTC?"

Okay, Yoda, I'll be your Skywalker.

He said, "Yes, sir? What do you mean?"

Kurt pressed the button for the elevator, then turned to Knuckles. He said, "How's it going with Carly? How's the training?"

The shift of the conversation was pure Hale. Knuckles wanted to punch the wall at the change of subject, but he knew Kurt had a reason. He said, "It's going."

Nothing more, letting Kurt know he didn't appreciate the shift.

The doors opened, and Kurt said, "You know there are a lot of guys hoping she'll fail."

Knuckles said, "She won't."

Kurt looked at him and said, "You sure about that? Because from what I'm hearing, you'd just as soon she did."

Knuckles bristled and said, "She'll do just fine. She's switched on, and she's got a natural talent. When I'm done with her, she'll smoke most of those assholes talking."

Kurt laughed and said, "Touchy, touchy."

"I'm just sick of the bedroom talk. She's working her ass off, and it's because of her, not me."

The door opened, and Kurt said, "That's why you're in the elevator with me. I need to know."

And Knuckles realized that Kurt was doing a pulse check of his organization. Wanting to assess where the real level was.

Knuckles said, "Sir, she's good. Better than good."

"And you have no issue with that? Since you're no longer . . ."

They exited into the parking garage, and Knuckles said, "Come on, sir, can't she just be judged on her damn skill? Does she have to be 'the girl who dated an Operator'?"

Kurt said, "No. Not at all. My point was, can she work in the Taskforce with you, the guy who used to ball her?"

Knuckles was incredulous. "Did you really just say that? *Sir?*"

Kurt stopped and faced him. He said, "Yes, I did. I don't give a shit about political correctness. I care about killing terrorists. And I need to know if this is going to be a problem. Because if it is, she's got no chance at selection. I need to hear it."

Knuckles sighed, then said, "You know, I'd like to tell you you're right and she needs to go. I really would. But, truth be told, she's good. I'll be straight up—I don't want her in the Taskforce. She's headstrong and she's got no off switch. But that's just me talking from a failed relationship. If that hadn't happened, I'd tell you she's better than about half the people in this building."

They reached Kurt's car, Kurt circling to the driver's door and Knuckles waiting on the passenger side. Kurt unlocked the doors, and Knuckles said, "She'll do just fine."

Kurt said, "Are you willing to keep training her?"

Knuckles opened the door and said, "Are you kidding? Of course. No way is she going to fail. My name is on that chit."

They settled into the seats, and Kurt said, "You mean that?"

"Yes. Look, sir, we parted ways, but make no mistake, she's talented. I can see it. Pike can see it. Jennifer can see it. I'm not just making it up, and while I don't like the way things ended with us, I do appreciate skill. She's got it."

Kurt put the car in drive and said, "Does she have enough training to do drills on her own for a while?"

"What's that mean?"

He said, "Nothing."

They drove the rest of the way in silence, passing by the monuments of Washington, DC. They rolled into the access point for the Old Executive Office Building and, after showing identification, were waved through. Kurt parked, and they walked up the steps to the building. Kurt said, "You ever been to one of these before?"

"No. I'm not sure why I'm here right now."

Kurt laughed and said, "It'll become obvious later. We'll enter, you'll go to the back of the room, and I'll brief. Clear?"

Knuckles said, "Yeah. Clear." What he thought was, *Clear as mud.*

Kurt said, "Just answer what I ask, when the time comes."

They approached the scrum of people attempting to enter the secure room, and Knuckles said, "What the hell does that mean?"

Kurt shook his head, telling him no more talking. Fuming, Knuckles waited in line, then passed over his cell phone, went through a metal detector, and took a seat at the back of the room, watching the most influential bodies in the United States government gather around and talk as if they were out for a midmorning tea. It was surreal. The same people he saw discussing death and destruction on Sunday shows were now chatting as if they were deciding where to get brunch. He realized they were, in fact, just people. But powerful, nonetheless.

The Oversight Council had been designed by Kurt Hale and the previous administration to control Taskforce activities. While the Taskforce operated outside the bounds of the US Constitution, Kurt had known they needed a check, lest they turn into something vile.

President Hannister had inherited the Taskforce after the death of the previous president, and he had a choice: Disband the unit or embrace it. Initially, he'd been leaning toward disbanding it because he'd seen in past operations the threat the unit posed to the fabric of a democracy, but then he'd learned—the hard way—the good it could do. It wasn't hyperbole to say that the Taskforce had prevented World War III, and Hannister had been the president when it happened. It was the deciding vote to embrace the unit.

The Council was the sole body that oversaw Taskforce activities. Comprised of thirteen people both inside and outside the government, it was a Faustian bargain for those who chose to embrace the responsibility. Get read on to the Taskforce, and gain the ability to be in a secret circle that few on earth knew existed. But to do so meant agreeing to an illegal organization that could cause any member to go to jail for a long, long time.

Knuckles wondered how many in the room did it out of patriotism, or simply out of a junior high *I'm in on a secret* bullshit. Hard to tell, but that was the way of the US government.

All would proclaim patriotism, but only a few could look in the mirror and say it wasn't because of ego.

31

No sooner had Knuckles taken a seat at the back than the entire room stood up. President Hannister had entered.

Knuckles stood like everyone else, but after seeing the people chatting before, he couldn't get past the feeling that this whole thing was show, with none of the folks on the Council assimilating the true seriousness of what was being discussed.

President Hannister said, "Good to see you, Kurt. I've only got about thirty minutes to hide in my schedule, so let's get to it."

Kurt started his slideshow, going through the various operations, and received no pushback. Knuckles's eyes were glazing over, until Kurt reached South Africa.

He gave the current assessment and then said, "I'd like to continue with the operation. I know it's weak, but Tyler Malloy is doing something bad, and there's not a lot of risk here. I can't prove a clear and present danger, but Malloy's trying to get a tool that will be harmful to United States interests."

Knuckles inwardly chuckled. "Trying to get a tool" was far removed from "acquiring nuclear triggers that are impossible to get."

Then the national security advisor spoke, and he realized that the crowd wasn't nearly as out of tune as they appeared to be on the Sunday talk shows.

"Kurt, your mandate ends with sanctioned terrorist groups. This guy is a US citizen, and, yeah, he might be doing something bad, but it's not your problem set. I was against granting you Alpha authority for Tel Aviv to begin with. No way will I agree to further actions in South Africa."

"Sir, I understand, on the surface, but the man I'm following is working with terrorists. Yes, he's an American citizen, but he's also a threat. Do we want to chase the triggers *after* they're released, simply because they ended up in the hands of a terrorist group we're sanctioned to interdict? That makes no sense."

Amanda Kroft, the newly minted secretary of state, voiced her opinion. "And letting you run amok is the answer? How many disparate 'threats' in the future will you find that you need to interdict? How far up the food chain do we hunt? This man is an arms dealer. Scum, yes, but *legal* scum. Maybe you think we should start hunting the head of Northrop Grumman? Where does it end?"

Knuckles was taken aback at the ferocity of the comments. The new secretary of state was pretty attractive, in a cougar sort of way, and he'd thought she would be on their side by her appearance, because he was a little bit of a man-whore at heart. He had no idea of the cesspool Kurt waded through on a daily basis to give him the authority to operate. It was an eye-opener.

President Hannister held up a hand, and the room grew quiet. He said, "Kurt, do you really feel this is necessary? Do you truly think hunting this man with the Taskforce is in our best interests?"

"Yes. I do. He's got something very bad at his core. I admit I don't know what he's up to, but I do know if he gets those triggers, he's going to cause problems."

Amanda said, "Problems how?"

Kurt looked at her and said, "Problems like a lot of dead people, and a response from the United States that'll cost billions of dollars. It won't happen tomorrow. It's not a ticking time bomb like the movies, but it's real nonetheless. He gets those triggers and he'll sell them to the highest bidder, and whoever buys them will not have our interests at heart."

She leaned back and said, "So says the man with a hammer. Everything is a nail."

Knuckles saw Kurt smile at her, not the least bit offended. He said, "Ma'am, sometimes there are actual nails in the world. And I admit I'm the hammer."

Knuckles watched the stare-down. She said, "Okay, Kurt. Convince me."

He said, "Knuckles, how many men have you killed?"

Knuckles was brought up short at the utterance of his callsign. He said, "Sir?"

The entire room rotated around to look at him.

Kurt said, "How many men have you killed?"

"Sir, I don't know. I don't keep a count."

Kurt smiled, then said, "Yes. I guess that was a poor framing of the question. How many men have you killed that could have been prevented?"

Knuckles now knew why he was in the room. And he believed in the question. He said, "Almost every single damn one."

The secretary of state looked at him, and he locked eyes with her. She said, "Who are you?"

Knuckles said, "Well, ma'am, I'm not the killer man. I'm the killer man's son. But I do the killing until the killer man comes."

Her face scrunched in confusion, and Kurt said, "He's a Taskforce Operator. He works for you. And what he's telling you is that preventing terrorism is much better than reacting to it."

Knuckles nodded, keeping the eye of the secretary of state, and not because of the current fight. *She's a little hottie.* She brushed her hair aside, and he saw she had no ring on her hand. *Hmmm . . .*

She maintained eye contact for longer than necessary, then broke it. He knew it was because of his stare. She said, "Okay, Kurt, what are you asking for here?"

Knuckles realized they'd won and then wondered if Kurt had brought him here solely for that exchange. *Surely he wouldn't do that. I'm an Operator. Not a piece of meat. He didn't just do that . . .*

Kurt said, "All I want is Alpha authority to continue to South Africa. From the data Pike sent, we have a thread of a phone that was used in Tel Aviv. It's now in Cape Town. All I want to do is what we did in Tel Aviv. Just explore. We won't do anything overt."

Alexander Palmer, the national security advisor, laughed and said, "You just briefed us on a damn fiasco in Tel Aviv. What part of that was 'just exploring'?"

"Sir, we wouldn't have this thread if Pike hadn't intercepted the men hunting Shoshana. He took the initiative, and now we are where we are. I don't know the intersection, but I do know it's worth exploring."

Palmer said, "None of that had anything to do with Tyler Malloy. None. It was all about Pike's misguided loyalty and willingness to ignore orders. You just said he lost the actual thread of Tyler by chasing after these other guys."

"I disagree. Tyler's chief of security met them in Jaffa, just before they began hunting Shoshana. I admit, conducting the operation in support of Shoshana caused Pike to lose contact with Tyler, but he had to make a choice, and he determined a clear and present danger that was tied into what Tyler was doing. He opted to focus on the threat, but there's a connection. I just need to find it."

Surprisingly, Amanda Kroft said, "I'm inclined to let them continue." And she glanced at Knuckles when she said it.

Knuckles thought, *I cannot believe Kurt did that.*

President Hannister said, "I am as well. Palmer, put it to a vote."

He did, and Knuckles watched the lethal authority of the United States vote in favor of continued action, all because of his eye contact.

The meeting broke up, and he rejoined Kurt on the way out the door. When they were out of earshot, he said, "Tell me you didn't just prostitute me."

Kurt laughed and said, "You ever bend over backward for a pretty face?"

Knuckles glared at him, and Kurt said, "Oh no. Not you. Never. Well, I have. And *you* have a pretty face. Sorry if it's a role reversal, but I met Amanda at her in-brief. She's a holy terror, but she's got a soft spot for the military. I saw it in action. She really likes the military, which is a first for a SECSTATE. And you look like an Abercrombie & Fitch model. Sorry. Not sorry."

Knuckles said, "That is the most sexist, bullshit thing I've ever heard."

They reached the car, and Kurt said, "Yeah, except it worked. Look, she's good people. She's still finding her way, and I knew she'd fight this just to prove she wasn't a wallflower. I had to defeat that, and I used you. It worked."

They entered the car, and Kurt put it in drive. He said, "Don't get all pissy about it. Christ, *I'm* the one dealing with integrating females."

Knuckles looked out the window, then said, "I guess that's all I'm good for now. Integrating females, or getting them to vote your way."

Kurt laughed and said, "No. That's not all you're good for. There's a reason I wanted you to see that meeting. And it's because of Pike."

"Yeah, how's that?"

"Pike is on to something. He doesn't know what it is, and neither do I. But he's peeling something rotten. I put him on that thread, and he's unwinding it."

Knuckles waited for more, and when none came, he said, "Okay, so what? That's par for the course. And I don't even play golf."

Kurt looked at him and said, "Shoshana was in that room during the VTC yesterday. I know it, and you know it. No matter what I said today, the original mission is gone in Pike's mind. That's what I meant when I asked you if you'd really listened."

Knuckles nodded, feeling out of his depth. Wondering if this was what Pike went through every time he talked to Kurt. He said, "And what does that mean?"

"It means I need you to keep Pike on track. I don't know what the fuck Shoshana's up to, but whatever it is, Pike will see it through. Those two are connected."

"And how am I going to help?"

"Pike's going to go on the warpath. I know him. It'll happen sooner or later, and he'll need some shooters. He'll ask for you."

Knuckles couldn't believe the 3-D chess moves Kurt was making. And he honestly didn't like the implications. He said, "Sir . . . I'm not deploying to trick Pike. I'm not sure what this conversation is about, but I can't do that."

He locked eyes with Kurt, afraid of the anger, but said, "I can't."

Kurt pulled into the underground garage, passing a sign for Blaisdell Consulting, the cover organization for the Taskforce. He threw the car into park and said, "I would never ask you to do such a thing. That's not what I meant."

He sat still for a minute, then turned and said, "Pike is doing what we all would. It's why I sent him on this, but sometimes what's pure isn't . . . pure."

Knuckles said, "That's bullshit. And you know it."

Kurt smiled and said, "Yes. I do. Pike's going to solve this problem, but he needs someone to keep him in balance."

Knuckles barked a laugh, trying to gain a foothold on what Kurt wanted and failing. He said, "Yeah, he'll solve it. No doubt. What makes you think he'll need shooters? It's just an Alpha operation."

Kurt said, "We have a sanctioned mission from the Oversight Council, which is to prevent the selling of nuclear triggers to terrorists. Pike knows that, but he also has a sweet spot for Shoshana. And she's a fucking cyclone."

He turned to Knuckles and said, "Pike is pure, and so are you. Aaron is gone, but he's at the heart of this thing. Shoshana doesn't care about nuclear triggers. All she wants is Aaron back home—and he might be dead already. Whatever the truth is, it's going to twist Shoshana until she explodes. Pike'll see it happening, and he'll be torn between his mission and her. He'll defer to her. Defer to hunting for Aaron. I know him. He can't do otherwise. Your job will be to get him back on the path of our mission."

He turned the car off, looking out the windshield, lost in thought. He glanced back at Knuckles and said, "Trust me, Pike's going to want some shooters. And I'm sending you."

32

★ ★ ★

Aaron took his bowl of rancid rice and retreated to the corner of the cell, putting his back against the wall, surrounded by the suit clan. Since the fight the night before, he'd taken to eating with them at every meal. They had some sort of protected status in the jail, and he could use all the help he could get. As usual, he committed half of his meager rations to the pot for those who were being punished by the guards. A small price to pay for the benefits he was gaining.

Thomas Naboni took his bowl and sat next to him. He ate in silence for a moment, waiting on the guards to leave. When they did, he passed a piece of torn paper to Aaron.

Aaron opened it, seeing a note from Alex. It was succinct: *I'm okay. Your friend has ensured that happens. Don't worry about me. But don't leave me when you go.*

Beside the sentence was a smiley face. That was all, but it said much more than it seemed. One, it relieved the enormous worry he'd had about her condition. If she had the ability to actually write down a smiley face, she was doing okay. Two, the note told him that she still trusted him to get her out. Still believed in his James Bond, Mossad, nonexistent miracle ability. It gave him pain, but he *would* get her out. Sooner or later.

Aaron nodded, then said, "Thank you. This means a great deal to me."

Thomas said, "She is being strong. Trust me, her incarceration is not easy. All I did was prevent any assaults against her. It would be better for you to confess to whatever you've done and get her out of here. She won't last."

Aaron said, "I've done nothing. I mean that. We were abducted in Johannesburg, drugged, then driven to Durban. I was tortured there, and now I'm here."

Thomas leaned his head back, looking suspicious. He said, "You weren't captured here? In Maseru?"

"I don't even know where Maseru is."

Thomas took in the words, then said, "But you're *here,* in *this* prison."

"What the fuck does that mean?"

There was a commotion outside the door to their cell room, and Aaron saw the guard become agitated, snapping to attention. Everyone began vibrating and chattering. A man entered, and Aaron recognized him as the African at the meeting in Johannesburg. Lieutenant General Jonathan Mosebo.

Thomas fell back at his entrance, scurrying away, his star wilting under the sun of the general. Aaron saw true fear on his face.

The general advanced on Aaron, ignoring all else in the cell. He reached him, and Aaron put down his bowl of rice, sitting cross-legged and saying not a word.

Mosebo said, "So you've survived. I wouldn't have expected it."

Aaron remained mute.

Mosebo bent over, and the guard known as Lurch circled behind Aaron. Mosebo cupped his chin and said, "I want to know what you're doing with the Americans."

Aaron said, "I have no idea what you're talking about."

Lurch hammered him at the top of the neck, right where the skull met the spine, eliciting a scream. Aaron fell forward onto his face, and Lurch grabbed him, jerking him upright. Panting in the pain, Aaron said, "I don't know anything about any Americans. I don't even know where I am."

Mosebo slapped him, not hard, but enough to telegraph that worse was coming. He said, "There is a United States Special Forces team here. I want to know why. They claim it's just security assistance for the embassy. Did you call them?"

Aaron laughed and said, "How? How would I do that? And if I did, why am I still here?"

Mosebo's face contorted into a rage, and Aaron realized he was paranoid. Truly paranoid crazy, looking for the bogeyman everywhere—even in this cell that he owned. Before he could get punched again, Aaron blurted out, "I don't even know who *you* are. I have no idea why I'm here. I'm nothing but a diamond merchant."

The comment took the heat off the boiling water. Mosebo nodded, then said, "I want to know why you were in Johannesburg."

"I told the South African in Durban. The one who questioned me. I gave him all my answers. Ask him. He knows I'm nothing important."

Mosebo squatted down, getting face-to-face. "I don't trust that man either. He tells me to keep you alive, and I wonder why, if you're not important. It would be much easier to bury you under a bridge, but he won't allow it. Who *are* you?"

Realizing his life was on the line, Aaron showed fear, blubbering like the corporate whore he was supposed to be. Through his weeping, he said, "I promise, I know nothing. I'm a nobody. A nobody."

In a pique, Mosebo lashed a hand forward, cuffing Aaron in the head. He said, "Maybe your little friend will provide some answers."

Aaron's face snapped up, locking eyes with Mosebo, and he saw the man inwardly shrink at the murder in his eyes, the violence held just below the surface. It was nothing overt, but Aaron realized he'd made a mistake. Mosebo had gained a glimpse into Aaron's true self.

Mosebo regained his composure from the show of fear and leveraged the weakness in Aaron's response.

He said, "You will tell me who you are. Or I'll take it out on her. I'll be back." He cuffed Aaron's head again and said, "You understand?"

Aaron looked at him and nodded, but he could still see the fear in

Mosebo's eyes. He hadn't meant to let slip who he was, what he was capable of, but he had, and it had bought him time. How much, he didn't know.

Lurch kicked him in the kidney, knocking him forward, and they left the cell. Gradually, the men inside began to stir. Thomas came forward, looking at his face and saying, "Did they harm you?"

"No. Nothing worse than I've felt before."

Thomas said, "Who are you? For real."

"I'm a nobody. I keep telling everyone that."

Thomas sat back on his heels and said, "You are a liar; that much is plain."

Aaron sighed and said, "I'm a nobody *here*. I have no idea who that guy is or why I'm locked up." He looked at Thomas and said, "Who are *you*? As long as we're being all honest."

Thomas looked toward the door, making sure the guards were out of earshot, then said, "I'm a nobody as well. *Here*."

"What does that mean?"

Thomas crossed his legs, settling in. He said, "You're not some insignificant person. Somewhere, you're a somebody. And I need a somebody. Your friend said, 'Don't leave me when you go.' Why would she say that?"

"She places faith in me. She truly is nothing in this game, and she's my responsibility. I told you that before. We're trapped in a design not of our making."

Thomas looked at him for a moment, then said, "I believe that to be true. But it's not the full story. General Mosebo has only visited this prison twice before, and each time, it was for me."

He raised his shirt, showing jagged scars across his belly.

Aaron saw the damage and said nothing. Thomas said, "I know why that is. I had something to give him, which I did not."

He dropped his shirt and said, "But I don't know why he would come for you."

Aaron shook his head and said, "I honestly don't know why either. I have nothing. I've *done* nothing. I'm not a threat to him."

Thomas smiled and said, "Yes, you are. You may not realize it, but you are. And I could use a threat."

Aaron barked out a laugh and said, "The only threat I am, you saw last night. I can fight, but that does little good in here."

Thomas smiled again, his teeth as white as snow in the darkness. "But you have friends, don't you? You have connections beyond what you've shown. A government, perhaps?"

Aaron sighed, thinking of the Mossad and the lack of help he was so close to achieving. He said, "No. I have no government willing to free me here."

Disappointed, Thomas said, "So you're not being sought? Nobody is trying to help you?"

Aaron glanced at him, then looked away, but once again, his eyes gave away the answer. Thomas saw the hope leaking out and said, "You have someone? Someone's coming to find you, yes? Not a government? That's good too. That's okay. Who is he?"

Aaron said nothing. Thomas said, "He can help us both. You have a secret, and so do I."

Aaron let the words settle, understanding he now had an ally.

He said, "It's a she. And yes. She's coming. When she does, you want to be on my side, I promise."

33

Shoshana watched the car pull into the roundabout in front of the Victoria & Alfred Hotel, then saw her target exit. She took a left into a tourist car park and pulled into a spot that gave her a view of the entrance. Before committing, she wanted to know if he was entering the hotel or going deeper into the famed V&A waterfront of Cape Town, South Africa.

Originally constructed as a simple stopover point for Dutch East India Company ships traveling to India and the Far East, it had transformed in the modern era into a tourist promenade, with everything from a giant aquarium to a Ferris wheel that looked like a miniature London Eye. Even though it was becoming overrun with pedestrian walkways, shops, and restaurants, it was still a working port, and Shoshana hoped her target was doing something other than getting a beer.

In truth, she was a tad bit aggravated at the slow-moving surveillance effort and wanted nothing more than to corner her target and rip off his head, spilling out the secrets that he held. But she couldn't, because Pike had demanded they *develop* the situation. She feared the delay was putting Aaron in danger.

She'd lost the ability to sleep at night, worried beyond measure about what was happening to her touchstone. Her gateway to normalcy. She didn't realize it, but her fear of losing Aaron was driving her to become exactly what she was trying so hard to leave behind. A monster that shouldn't walk the earth.

She saw the target bypass the entrance to the hotel, moving deeper into the waterfront. She exited the car, taking up a loose follow, keeping his blond head in sight in the distance and wondering why his mission even mattered, whatever it was. There was nothing in Cape Town for her. Yeah, the man they called Apple Watch might be doing something heinous, but who cared what the Taskforce thought? He was a bad man like a bazillion other folks in the world. Divining his evil plot wouldn't get her Aaron. Only skinning him alive would do that. She was regretting volunteering for this task. She should have followed the black man.

In Tel Aviv, they'd learned that the Taskforce had identified Apple Watch's iPhone in Cape Town, South Africa, at a hotel in the old Muslim section of Bo-Kaap. They'd done a hasty site survey via online tools and then had flown to the bottom of Africa to interdict the target. The flight route had been circuitous, forcing them first to go to Europe before traveling back down to the edge of the earth in South Africa, and the time lost had eaten at Shoshana.

She'd become incensed when Pike had developed a surveillance plan on the hotel but no follow-on takedown. No planning for exfiltration with the target, no interrogators, no requests for support assets whatsoever.

She'd eventually interrupted the operations order, saying, "I see a lot of sneak-and-peek crap to set this guy up, but nothing about taking him down. When are we doing that? We're wasting time with this tiptoe stuff."

The room had gone quiet, all eyes on Pike. In a measured tone, he'd said, "Shoshana, we don't have authority to do that. Not yet, anyway. We have to build the target package and then get approval."

She heard the words and felt betrayed, her earlier fears coming home. They didn't care about Aaron. They cared only about themselves. She'd snapped to her feet and said, "I told you I wouldn't stand for any bullshit. That man knows where Aaron is, and I'll take him down by myself if I have to."

Pike shook his head, saying, "And then what?"

"And then I wring him out. Find Aaron."

She'd glared at him, then Jennifer, and started to walk to the hotel door. Pike had said, "What if he doesn't know where Aaron is?"

She stopped, the anger flaring out, saying, "Then I move on to the next one."

Pike said, "What next one? We don't have a next one yet. And what happens when our target set realizes you've hit him? You think they'll just continue like business as usual? Or shift? Perhaps move Aaron to a new location. Or kill him."

She balled her fists and let out a guttural animal sound, something from deep within her soul. She knew he was right, and that fact was eating her from the inside out. She wanted to *fight*. She was like a wolf caught in a bear trap, ripping its limbs to get free, the action itself doing more damage than the trap, but continuing to thrash in a frenzy nonetheless.

She tamped down her instinctual fear, managing to stop her internal struggle. Pike nodded, seeing the change. In a gentle tone he said, "Shoshana, sit down, please."

She did, and he finished the OPORD detailing trigger and bumper locations. He ended by saying, "Remember, Apple is our only key, and today is just development. We record every thread and then explore those threads. *That's* the mission." He looked at Shoshana and said, "Can you do that?"

She nodded firmly, and he said, "Good. Let's get cracking."

They'd traveled to their designated surveillance bumper locations around the hotel, with Brett on the trigger position inside and Shoshana on the least likely egress the target would use—the one away from the city center. It aggravated her, but she understood why.

Two hours later, sitting in her rental car parked on Wale Street outside a traditional Cape Malay curry restaurant, she heard the trigger call.

"All elements, all elements, this is Blood. Apple is leaving the hotel foxtrot, intending right on Wale Street."

Shoshana perked up at the call. *Foxtrot* meant he was on foot, no vehicle. *Intending* meant Blood thought he was taking a right on Wale Street, not a left. Which meant he was coming to her.

She said, "This is Carrie. I copy."

Pike and Jennifer, in the other two bumper positions, did the same, and she saw Apple Watch coming up the hill. She said, "Carrie has the eye, still foxtrot."

She'd wait until he passed her before exiting her vehicle, just in case. He didn't. He stopped at the corner, across the intersection from her position, and a car pulled up, heading the other way. He got in the passenger seat, and she put her car in drive.

She called the team, gave them a description of the car and the direction of travel, and then passed Pike headed the other way. She grinned. She was now the only one who could follow in the short term.

They wove through the city until they hit Long Street, the target taking a right. Shoshana followed two cars back, immediately hit a throng of pedestrians, and grew afraid of a break in contact.

"Pike, this is Carrie. Apple is on Long Street, and this looks like the barhopping, boozing area. Nothing but pubs and restaurants, with backpackers and locals all over the street. I might lose him."

Jennifer came on. "Carrie, this is Koko. I've got visor two blocks up." Meaning she was ahead of the target. Shoshana slowed her urgency through the crowds. She heard Jennifer come back on. "Pike, Carrie's right. This avenue looks a lot like Bourbon Street."

"Got it. No issues now, but it's something to remember if we have to do night ops here. Brett's parallel to the north, and I'm to the south. Target's not getting out without us picking him up."

Shoshana saw the target car pull over next to a two-story building with a hotel on top and a bar on the bottom. Apple left the vehicle, and the car rolled on. She called, "He's foxtrot now. I'm passing. It's the Long Street Hotel, some type of social club on the bottom."

She rolled through the intersection, seeing Apple enter, and called, "I'm off."

34

★ ★ ★

Johan passed by the Cape Town South African history museum, entering the expanse of green known as the Company's Garden. Once a plot of land that grew the food for the Dutch East India Company outpost, it had been preserved as a park that spanned hectares of terrain, running right next to the Houses of Parliament of South Africa. It was a crowded place with all manner of people, both rich and poor, black and white, and was a good location to conduct a meeting that wouldn't draw attention. Especially since both he and the man he was meeting were wanted by South Africa for disobeying the '98 Regulation of Foreign Military Assistance Act.

Birthed because of the rampant mercenary activity in the nineties, with less-than-stellar men working for charlatan organizations that built their false pedigrees on the backs of the success of professionals like Johan, it was a law that caused him to tread lightly in his homeland.

He wandered through the gardens, watching the kids play with soccer balls, taking paths that would channelize anyone following him without appearing as if he was doing anything overt. The winding trails and thick vegetation provided a ready-made surveillance-detection route and were the reason he'd picked this garden to meet the colonel.

Walking on a path that wound through the trees all by itself, he approached a group of teenagers and saw one of them stand up. His skin coal black, wearing worn Nike sweats and shoes that were untied, he had the vacant stare of a person feeling no pain but looking to apply some.

Johan passed him by, and the group stood up, following. *Shit.* Exactly what he didn't need. The entire point of choosing this location was to sniff out anyone following, not get a police response because of an altercation. The teens were searching for easy prey, and he was simply looking to remain invisible.

He turned abruptly, and they all stopped short. Five of them, all stoned. He looked the leader in the eyes and realized there was no reasoning with them. Nike Sweats was panting, sweat rolling off his face, pupils dilated. He didn't care about the police or anything else. He cared about the kill. Strangely, Johan understood.

Johan said, "You want to make some money?"

Taken aback, Nike Sweats said, "Yeah . . . how? What you talking about?"

"You leave me alone, and I'll pay you five hundred rand."

Nike Sweats smiled and said, "You got five hundred, maybe you got more. Maybe I'll take it."

Johan took two steps toward him, closing into his personal space and pulling out a folding knife. He flicked it open and brought it blade-first into the man's groin. He said, "You want to make the money, or lose your nuts?"

Nike Sweats was frozen in place. The others became agitated, not sure of what to do. They'd never been on the receiving end of a hunt.

Johan sawed the blade, splitting the cloth of the sweats. He looked at them and said, "He can't speak. You guys want to make some money?"

One of them nodded, saying, "Yeah, yeah. We'll take the rand. And you can have his balls."

The others laughed, and Johan pulled the knife away. He withdrew his wallet, pulled out several notes, and threw them on the ground. He looked at Nike Sweats and said, "Not everyone is prey around here."

He turned and walked away, hearing them scamper on the ground for the money.

Johan was incensed. He had a mission, and it was almost short-circuited by a bunch of random losers. *Should have fucking gutted them.* But he knew he wouldn't even if he could. They were just a by-product of the poverty that abounded in Cape Town, and they would end up dying an early death by someone else's hand. Not his.

Johan continued on the path until it reentered the main promenade, a statue of the famed politician Cecil Rhodes towering over the pavestones, the outside of the monument now cloaked in protest placards accusing him of all manner of evil. An indication of the new face of South Africa.

He went by it, threading through the woods until he saw a coffee shop with outdoor tables sprinkled along the garden path. He entered the patio and saw Colonel Lloyd Armstrong sitting under an umbrella, two steaming cups of coffee on the table. He was wearing chinos and a short-sleeve business shirt, his eyes hidden behind a pair of Ray-Ban aviator sunglasses. The attire did nothing to hide his prior profession.

A hulking man with his hair cut close to the scalp, he looked like a cartoon version of a lion tamer, right down to the cigar he was smoking. Nobody would mistake him for a banker, regardless of what he was wearing.

Johan slid into the seat next to him, hoping for a surprise. He was disappointed. Armstrong said, "Why didn't you just kill those fucks?"

Taken aback, Johan said, "Good to see you too, sir. What fucks?"

Armstrong raised his coffee mug and pointed with it. Johan turned and saw the drug-addled group following along his path. Armstrong said, "What did you do, pay them to leave you alone?"

Johan smiled and said, "Yeah, I did. I'm going to claim it as an expense."

Armstrong laughed and said, "Always the one to avoid conflict." He turned serious, saying, "But that's not what happened in Lesotho. I got the SITREP. What's the true story?"

Johan told him everything that had occurred, giving an assessment that wasn't included in his clinical report. He detailed the atmospherics of Maseru and the impact of the US Special Forces team's arrival, ending with his assessment of General Mosebo's troops.

"They aren't that good. In fact, they're shit. You told me earlier that they were some of the best on the continent, but that's not what I saw. How is the training going? Am I wrong?"

"No. They aren't as good as we were told, but they aren't completely raw recruits. They can work an AK, and they understand basic fire and maneuver. We're just honing some edges. The first two packages are already back home. We're finishing up with the last one."

"Did you break them out by ability, instead of by LDF assignments? Because some areas are going to need more skill than others."

"Yes. They know they'll get separated. They just don't know how yet. I was waiting on you for that."

Johan leaned back, making sure nobody was within earshot. He said, "I'll have a complete report by tonight, but basically, we'll have four stop-groups. The easy ones will be the parliament building itself and the television and radio station. The tough ones will be the police headquarters and the prime minister's residence. The police will be a firefight, so we'll need to go in hard. The prime minister's residence will be the same. It's hardened, gated, and he has a robust protective detail, but unlike the police headquarters, it's a much more delicate mission. We can't just kill everyone. We'll have to make sure he remains alive."

Armstrong said, "I'll need specifics on force sizes, weapons, and contingencies."

Johan took a sip of his coffee before answering, then said, "You'll get it tonight, but basically, in order of skill, the best fighters go to the residence, second best to the headquarters, and the rest to the television and radio station. The least skilled simply take over the parliament building. It'll be closed at night, with a skeleton security-guard force. It's purely symbolic."

Armstrong took a sip of his coffee, and Johan said, "One thing we can't do is cause the Americans to interfere."

"We won't. We work this quickly and they won't have a reason to."

Johan said, "There's something else that concerns me. The Israeli."

"What about him?"

"We went after his partner, and we were eviscerated. She had a team working with her. And the team included Americans."

Armstrong waved his hand in the air, washing away the worry. He said, "I got the report from Andy. I understand it was a mess, but I don't assess it as having an impact on our operation. We went after her—a mistake, no doubt—but my contacts in Israel say there have been no repercussions. We stuck our hand into the flame and got burned. Nobody is looking into it beyond a police response. Nobody is looking for outside influences."

Johan said, "Nobody but her."

"What's that matter? She's a single slash. She can't do anything."

"She had help from someone. One of the team says it was the United States."

Colonel Armstrong barked a laugh and said, "No, let's be precise. He said he was choked out by an *American*. Big difference. I have Americans on *this* team. They're everywhere, and they have the skill forged from combat. The continent hasn't seen this level of American involvement since the end of the Vietnam War."

Johan said, "So you're not concerned? We're dealing with a diamond merchant who's also former Israeli intelligence, and when we try to cauterize a leak, we get annihilated. By the partner of the man we now hold. How much do you know about the background of the diamond dealer? Is he telling the truth?"

Armstrong took a sip of his coffee, then said, "He was a member of the LEKEM. It was an Israeli intelligence organization designed to ferret out nuclear secrets. Their whole purpose was industrial espionage in their quest for the bomb. And they were good at it."

"Why does that matter? Some old gray dick from Israeli intelligence is supposed to be a guy I trust? Who do you know inside South African intelligence that you trust now? Nobody, that's who."

Armstrong said, "He isn't South African. Israel is different. Because of his placement, and the sensitivity of the activities back in the day, he has plenty of contacts inside Israeli intelligence. They still call on him from time to time. Shit, he was the guy who helped us build our own bomb."

Johan sat up. "What's that mean?"

Armstrong put out his cigar and said, "You were young, but you remember when we gave up our nuclear weapons at the end of apartheid?"

Johan laughed and said, "Yeah. We were the great saviors. The first to voluntarily relinquish our nuclear weapons. You and I both know why that happened."

Armstrong nodded and said, "Because we were afraid of who was going to take over after apartheid ended. Afraid of loose nukes. But that's not the point. Getting the nukes is where our Israeli contact comes in. He—using LEKEM assets—is the one who gave us the technology. Project Circle."

Shoshana continued slowly down Long Street, keeping an eye on the front door of the club in her rearview mirror, then heard, "This is Koko. I've got a parking spot. I'm foxtrot one block up."

Pike said, "Koko, your target. Get in there. Blood, Blood, what's your status?"

"One street over. Parking now."

"Prep a Dragontooth. He's meeting someone, and I want a beacon on that fucker. Break, break—Carrie, keep on the target car. Let me know where it goes."

In spite of the fact that she was now out of the action, Shoshana smiled. Pike was working the problem better than most. She checked her rearview mirror, saw the vehicle coming, then said, "I'm on him."

She followed the car down Long Street, watched it turn into a paid lot, and went past before pulling to the side of the road, wishing like hell she was in the hotel. Pike had planned it perfectly, keeping her out of the action. Keeping her from doing anything of substance.

Thirty minutes later, she was grinning again. Jennifer had said that Apple Watch had met a black man inside the bar and had been passed a key. From there, her target car had circled around and picked him up, and she was the only thing in play, as everyone else was on foot.

She'd followed the car to the V&A wharf and had decided to stick with Apple, letting the car go free. Someone else could track it. If they could get here quickly enough.

She trotted across the street, passing the lobby of the ritzy V&A Hotel and a host of taxis and tour cars, seeing the blond head disappear into the crowd.

She followed him through the tourists, passing beer gardens and restaurants, then hit the water of the harbor. He took a right, headed toward a pedestrian bridge that crossed a concrete canal of water leading to a marina. Before he reached it, a light started flashing, and a man prevented anyone from crossing. Shoshana looked into the harbor, saw a sailboat approaching, and realized the single footbridge was a miniature drawbridge. It began to swing away, letting the boat through, and she was stuck on the same side with her target.

She went to the breakwater, watching a mother and two kids feed the seagulls. She took a seat on a bench, trying to remain invisible.

She kept her eyes on the target and received a call from Pike. "Carrie, Carrie, what's the situation? Last call was a dismount at the wharf. Give me a lock-on."

Afraid he was about to pull her off, she said, "Crossing the footbridge. No clear direction or purpose. I'm still good. Heat state is ice."

"Don't fuck with me, Carrie."

The bridge took an agonizingly long time to transfer back. She said, "I'm not, Nephilim. Have some trust."

He said, "We're at the wharf. We're coming. Just keep him in sight and rotate out when I call."

The light went off, and the pedestrians began to cross. She followed the target, saying, "Okay. As long as I'm not forced into something before you get here."

She heard him panting on the radio, clearly running his ass off. "Don't . . . You . . . Do . . . A . . . Fucking . . . Thing."

The target passed the famed clock tower of the wharf, right in front of the gateway ferry to Robben Island, the location of the desolate block of granite on which Nelson Mandela had been imprisoned for most of his adult life. He reached the lower level of a two-story mall and walked in with a purpose.

It was a shallow opening, with few people. If she entered at his intrusion point, she would be burned. If she didn't, he would accomplish whatever he was doing inside.

But he was boxed inside the mall. And she needed more manpower to continue the surveillance. She couldn't do it alone, as much as she wanted to.

Every fiber of her being told her to follow, Aaron at the forefront of her mind, begging the target to give her reason to interdict him. But she did not. She deferred to the team. She called Pike, told him the status, and rolled off, going to the right of the building to a set of stairs next to a garish Ripley's Believe It or Not! attraction. She went up them and then took a seat on a bench, waiting on the cavalry to penetrate the mall.

She heard, "We can't get across. The pedestrian bridge is rotating for a boat."

No sooner had that come across than the target exited right in front of her, moving to a placard on a wall, pretending to study it while glancing at the door.

The realization hit her immediately, along with how lucky she had been.

Surveillance-detection route.

He'd entered the mall solely to pick out anyone following, taking the escalators to the second floor, then rapidly exiting. Anyone who did the same would clearly be on him. And she'd beaten his game, all because she wanted to prove to Pike she wasn't a lone wolf.

She smiled and clicked her radio. "He's back on the street, and I'm on him."

"Shoshana, back off. Your heat state has got to be molten by now."

She said nothing, letting the target go by her, not moving at all as long as she had him in sight. He walked about a hundred meters, leaving the tourist area and entering the working port. He took a left at a jetty full of warehouses, and she stood. She walked for about thirty meters, making sure he wasn't doing more countersurveillance work, then sprinted to the corner of the warehouses.

She heard, "Shoshana, we're coming across. Give me a damn status."

She pulled up short, then stuck her head around the corner. She saw the target seventy meters away, unlocking a door on the row of warehouses, then disappearing inside.

She said, "I've got him. He's on the jetty past the tourist area. He's inside some shipping warehouse, but I can't get close."

Pike said, "Pull off. We'll meet you at the clock tower."

She saw the target appear again, closing the door. She said, "He's out. He's out. He's headed back my way. I'm off."

She slipped around to the other side of the jetty, where the boats docked and unloaded. She ignored the looks of the hard men on the dock, waiting on the target to pass. When he did, she called Pike, telling him Apple was on the way and running right into him, and that he had control.

"What are you going to do?"

"Check out that warehouse."

She slunk down the jetty, trying to look like she belonged, dodging forklifts and staring eyes. She reached the door she'd seen Apple exit, glanced left and right, then turned the handle. It refused to move.

Shit.

She considered picking the lock, but one look at the activity around her and she knew that would be a nonstarter. She studied the lockset and then had an idea. It was a six-pin restricted-key cylinder built by the Swedish lockmaker Assa Abloy. Something she knew about from her work in Israel. She took a knee, set her cell-phone camera on macro, and took a frontal shot of the keyhole.

If Pike's vaunted Taskforce didn't have the ability to do anything with the photo, she knew a group that did.

36

The mention of Project Circle only increased Johan's unease about the mission. He'd been deceived plenty of times in the past, all to get him to ply his skills. The last man who'd done it was the American he'd worked for a year ago. The one who'd given him his H-1B visa, which had caused the Lesotho security men to spike. That American had caused the death of many, many innocents and had attempted to use Johan to cover up his transgressions. Johan had unfortunately done so before learning the truth, and then had slaughtered the man in his office, leaving his broken body as a warning to others.

What does South Africa's nuclear program have to do with Lesotho?

"So this guy, our mundane contact in the diamond exchange, was intimately involved in our development of nuclear weapons?"

"Yes."

"And that doesn't give you concerns about what happened in Tel Aviv?"

"No. It gives me confidence. He would know if it was anything more than bad luck and unforeseen skill."

Johan nodded, saying nothing. Armstrong said, "What's going through your mind?"

"It just sounds more complicated than a simple coup in Lesotho. More in play here."

Armstrong leaned over the table, getting eye to eye. He said, "It *is* more complicated, but not for you. You do your mission, and don't worry about the rest. That's my problem."

Johan nodded, now wishing he had two fingers of scotch instead of coffee. He said, "Who's taking over in Lesotho? Why are we being hired?"

"The diamond merchant hired us for the oldest reason on earth—money. As for who's taking over, it's nothing but more of the same from all over the continent. Someone wants power. The prime minister is as corrupt as a rusty nail. His deputy will assume the position, with General Mosebo remaining as the true power as the head of the LDF, and the king will remain the king. It's nothing you haven't seen before. A transfer from one asshole to another."

"And the country? What will happen when we're successful?"

Armstrong looked at him with true mirth and said, "Seriously? Don't tell me Lily Boy is now concerned with the local population."

Johan glanced away and said, "I've seen bad go to worse." He turned back to Colonel Armstrong. "And so have you."

Armstrong slapped his shoulder and said, "Don't worry about it here. The government will function just like it did. All we're doing is replacing one man with another."

Johan nodded, then said, "What about the man we captured? The Israeli?"

"What about him?"

"I wanted to keep him alive for bargaining in case something went wrong, but given this information, I think it's a risk. I say we smoke him."

Armstrong considered, toying with his cup. He said, "No. We leave him in Mosebo's hands. Right now, we're cut from him. If things go well, we'll let Mosebo deal with him. If they go wrong, we still have a bargaining chip with the Israelis."

Johan glared at him and said, "I thought the Israelis didn't matter."

Armstrong slapped a hand on the table in irritation, causing the coffee cups to jump. Johan didn't react, keeping his stare. Armstrong said, "Just do what I ask. You're hired for a single mission. A tactical mission. Get me the plan, and execute."

Johan nodded, took a sip of his coffee, and said, "Okay, sir. I can do that. How are we looking for armament?"

A couple took a seat at the table next to theirs, and Armstrong rose, saying, "Come. Follow me back to my car."

They left the restaurant's patio and circled around the statue of Cecil Rhodes, seeing the gang from earlier lying in the grass like a pack of mongrel dogs.

They entered a secluded path on the edge of the wood line, and Armstrong said, "Andy just went to get the key for the warehouse. He'll report back, but I don't see any hiccups."

Johan said, "Who's he getting the key from? Who else is involved?"

"It's the same guy who got us the safe house in Durban. He works for the man providing the weapons and equipment."

Johan glanced at the colonel but said nothing. Armstrong said, "What?"

"Do you trust this American?"

"He's done what he's said he'd do so far."

Johan broke a stick off a tree and tossed it. He said, "I don't like working with him. What's he gaining? Why's he involved? Money makes people do strange things."

Armstrong said, "He's not getting money."

"What, then?"

"Don't worry about it. That's my problem."

"Come on, sir, what's he getting out of this?"

Armstrong stopped on the trail, looked at Johan, and said, "He's getting something from my connections in the South African Defence Force. Something that they no longer need but he can use."

"You have the SANDF involved in this? How?"

"I had to get the SANDF involved precisely to prevent them from invading Lesotho because of our coup. They're worried about the interruption of the flow of water. I'm working with the army headquarters, just letting them know what we're doing and assuring them that that won't happen. Using my connections to prevent mission failure. The American is greasing the skids with money."

Johan nodded, saying, "Okay, sir, that makes sense, but I wish you'd include me on the overarching plans."

Armstrong chuckled and said, "Johan, you're good, but you're only a tool. Let me worry about the bigger picture. You just execute your plan. That's all you're being paid for, and all you need to worry about."

Johan bit out, "Fine, but my *tactical* operation is predicated on your *strategic* decisions. You didn't answer the question. What is the American getting from them?"

Armstrong sighed and said, "Look, Johan, not everything is black-and-white like you want. Sometimes we have to do what we don't like, but if it'll alleviate your angst, I'm meeting him tonight. Why don't you come as well? Feel him out. Get some confidence in the mission."

Johan said nothing for a moment, then, "Okay. Where?"

"The old castle. The ceremonial guard out there is actually active-duty army recruits. There's a SANDF recruiting station in the back." Armstrong laughed and said, "My SANDF contact didn't want to be seen with me on the streets. Imagine that."

There was a rustling in the brush, and the mongrel pack of youths appeared, led by Nike Sweats. Armstrong became quiet, waiting on them to pass. When they didn't, he said, "What the fuck do you kaffirs want?"

Nike Sweats nodded at Johan and said, "He knows, old man."

Johan said, "I paid you. I've already paid."

"Yes. You have. But he hasn't."

Johan said, "You remember what I said earlier? That not everyone is prey? You're looking at it right now."

Nike Sweats said, "Yeah, I heard you. I just didn't believe it." The men circled around them, and Johan knew they were committed, but he still believed there was a way out. He looked at Armstrong and saw the violence beginning to build just below the surface. He said, "Sir, don't."

Nike Sweats and one other closed in tight, the rest remaining in a loose circle, sure of their numbers. Armstrong shook his head and said, "Lily Boy, like I said, sometimes we do things we don't like. Distasteful things."

He curled his knuckles into a flat ledge and lashed out, his fist striking as fast as the head of a snake, spearing into Nike Sweats's throat. Johan heard a hoarse bark, and the man dropped to the ground, rolling and attempting to scream. All that came out was a guttural moan.

Armstrong turned to the man next to him. The boy brought his hands up in a pathetic attempt at defense, and Armstrong grabbed the lead one, twisting his hand backward and locking up the joint. Armstrong looked into his eyes and said, "Jump, kaffir," then rotated the wrist in a circle, against the way it was designed.

The boy felt the pain like an electric current and literally leapt off his feet to stop it. Armstrong rotated forward and down, and the boy flipped over, hammering the ground on his back. Armstrong let go of his wrist and slammed his fists into the man's face, once, twice, three times. Johan saw his head snap back, bouncing off the gravel, and his eyes roll in his head.

Armstrong stood, turned to the remaining youths, and said, "You fucks want to die today, keep pushing."

They ran, exploding away like confetti out of a popped balloon.

Johan said, "That wasn't necessary."

Armstrong said, "Bullshit it wasn't. There was a time those kaffirs wouldn't have dared to even approach. I saw it in Rhodesia, and I see it here. They need to learn who's the boss. Something you failed to show them."

Johan simply nodded, but he saw another side of the man he worked for.

And he didn't like it.

37

★ ★ ★

I heard the rapid knocking, turned back to the computer, and said, "Creed, someone's banging on my door. I'll call you back." I disconnected, blacked out the camera, and went to the peephole of our door. I saw Shoshana, showing up forty minutes early. It was starting to become a trend.

I let her in, and she immediately started looking around for Jennifer. Since our room doubled as our tactical operations center, or TOC, I always rented a suite, which meant Shoshana couldn't see everything from the doorway.

Sometimes it pays to be in charge.

She said, "Where's Jennifer?"

I mimicked her voice, "Oh, hi, Pike. Sorry I'm early. I'm sure you didn't have anything going on."

She started to move to the bedroom, saying, "I want to talk to her. I won't interrupt whatever you're doing."

"You already have."

She turned back to me, and I said, "She's in the shower. Thanks for showing up."

She scrunched her eyebrows, her little Vulcan brain running through the parameters of my statement. Finally, I saw them clear, along with a tinge of embarrassment. Honestly, doing that to her was like telling jokes to an alien. *But, I still don't understand why a chicken is even near a road. Please explain . . .*

She flicked her eyes to the bedroom, then back at me. She said, "You were going to . . ."

I laughed and said, "No, Carrie. Jennifer *is* in the shower, but that's it. I was on the line with the Taskforce. I disconnected before answering the door."

"You talked to Creed? Can he use my photo?"

"I was actually on the VPN with him when you so rudely interrupted. He got the photo, but more importantly, the audio we got from Apple Watch at the Long Street Hotel wasn't nearly as good as we had before."

Apparently, Apple Watch had gone all operator starting to operate, because he'd switched the Apple watch for a Casio G-Shock, which meant Creed could get audio only from his phone, crammed in a pocket. Which meant everything we heard sounded like a bad celebrity recording from the back of a Lincoln. Creed was working the audio to see what he could get.

Shoshana said, "That beacon you put on the other guy is still working. We have his hotel."

The black man who had passed Apple Watch a key had wandered about for a bit, then gone back to the Long Street Hotel. We had a location of his room and real-time GPS tracking of him, but he was not a priority. At least not to me.

I said, "And?"

She flashed her teeth in a grin that wasn't a grin. It was more like watching a wolf smile. "And let me have a crack at him. I won't need Creed to do any audio work."

I changed the subject. "Creed says he can do anything the Mossad can. He's building us code for the key. All we have to do is find a 3-D printer."

"Does he know what he's doing? Or is he starting from scratch?"

"No, he actually knew about your process. Apparently, it's been kicking around in the US as well. Don't worry."

Shoshana had come back with high-resolution cell-phone pictures of a keyway for a lock on the warehouse Apple had visited, and she had asked if the Taskforce could build a key from it. Of course I'd said no, because who the hell can build a key from just looking at the keyhole?

Turns out, the Mossad, that's who. The lockset used a restricted key, meaning the key blank itself—besides the traditional teeth—had cutouts in the spine that fit the metal in the cylinder, like sliding a piece into a jigsaw puzzle. The purpose was to prevent the key from being duplicated. The only people who would have access to those unique blanks were locksmiths who had an arrangement with the lock manufacturer. It was a method to prevent someone from stealing the key and making a copy at the local hardware store. Unfortunately for the lockmaker, all of those various cuts in the spine of the key showed up in the picture, not unlike a picture of a child's 3-D puzzle, where he or she has to match up squares, triangles, and circles—only now the picture was much more complicated. It was a good security tool, but once you had a key blank that would actually fit into the cylinder, it was easy business to develop a bump key to defeat the lock.

I said, "Can you work a bump key? Since this is your big idea?"

"Why? You can't?"

Jennifer came out in a hotel bathrobe and slippers, her hair in a towel. She saw Shoshana and looked at the clock on the wall. I said, "Jennifer, you're okay. Carrie's early."

Jennifer took the towel off her head, working it in her hair. She said, "What's up? Something new?"

Shoshana said, "No, I just wanted to know if Nephilim, here, could get the Taskforce to do what we can."

I said, "Shoshana says we can't build the bump key. I was just asking her if she could use it."

Jennifer said, "Can't be that hard. A bump key is a bump key."

A so-called bump key was nothing more than a key blank with teeth set to engage the pins in a lock. In an ordinary lock, the varying degrees of the cuts were what told the lock to open. In a restricted lock, there was the additional level of the convoluted key blank. In both cases, the pin-tumbler lock worked the same way and had a similar vulnerability—pure force. The bump key worked with shock, in that you inserted it into the cylinder and then gave it a light bump, with the force of the blow driving all the pins to the shear position. If you maintained tension on the key, in effect, it caused the cylinder to unlock. You didn't need to know the exact position of the cuts, because force drove them where they were supposed to be.

Shoshana said, "The problem is the keyhole. It was complicated, which is why I suggested the technique we use."

I said, "Let me get Creed back on the line."

I thought about having Shoshana leave the room, but hell, Kurt knew she was here. It was stupid to keep playing high school games. The VPN connected, and Creed came on, saying, "Pike, seriously, I've been sitting here for ten minutes. I have better things to do."

"Sorry about that. I got held up with a crazy woman."

He said, "Shoshana? Was that who it was?"

He said it like a teenager in high school asking about the prom queen. Creed was a good guy, but his crush on Jennifer was truly annoying, and now his curiosity was piqued by the exotic Israeli, whom he'd yet to see. I was sure he thought she was a woman with the rack of a Penthouse Pet and the suave banter of a female James Bond. I didn't have the heart to put her on the screen.

I said, "Yeah, but she's gone now. She's got concerns about the data you're going to send. She thinks the Mossad has this perfected and you're just guessing."

On the screen, Creed laughed. "Yeah, they're waaaay ahead of us. Shit, this was all developed by civilians here in the US. The damn program we modified came out of MIT. There isn't any supersecret crap here."

I saw Shoshana glower and raised a finger off the screen.

Creed brought up a PowerPoint slide showing a lock cylinder and said, "The attack in question is an Ikon SK6. It's pretty sophisticated as far as the chamber goes. You see it looks like a *Z*. That's no issue with the 3-D printer. The problem is that the third pin is made to false set if not enough force is used. What that means is that it won't be a quick bump. You might have to work it a bit, not unlike picking the thing with tools. I've sent the data to your Grolier email. All you have to do is use a flash drive to load it into a 3-D printer."

"So this thing isn't going to be the easy fix? I don't want to do the work if it's asking for a fiasco."

"No, it'll work. It's just that it might take more than one bump. Don't worry, the Mossad doesn't have anything better. I'm getting sick of hearing about them, like they're a gift to the intelligence world. I earn my keep just fine."

Shoshana had heard enough and leaned into the screen, giving Creed a full view of the Israeli. She snarled, "Nobody asked for your opinion. Just send the fucking data. We'll do the rest."

I saw Creed recoil, and I pushed her bodily out of the way of the camera. Creed said, "Who the hell was that?"

I said, "Your fantasy. She loves you."

He said, "*That* was Shoshana?"

38

★ ★ ★

Shoshana retreated and began pacing the room. I snapped my fingers at Jennifer, telling her to get Shoshana under control. Her body passed by the camera, and Creed said, "Was that Jennifer? In a bathrobe?"

I put my hand to my eyes and squeezed. I said, "Creed, what did you find from the audio?"

He said, "You got a headache or something? Was that Jennifer? I want to say hello."

I cut him off. "Creed. The audio."

Truculent, he said, "The only thing we got was that there is a meeting tonight at nine, at someplace called either the castle of hope or the castle of probate. We think it's a nickname for something having to do with law enforcement."

"That's all you got, out of the entire conversation?"

"Pike, his phone was in his pocket. I'm not even sure the readout we have is right. The only thing we could positively identify was the word 'castle' and the time."

"Who's he meeting?"

"We have no idea."

"Jesus, man. What good are you?"

"I'm good enough to get you a key blank for the warehouse."

"This meeting is happening tonight?"

"As far as we can tell. Look, we did a search, and there's a police station that's got a history of doing shady things. It's nicknamed the 'hope's last probate' or something to that effect in Afrikaans. We think that's where he's headed tonight."

"Where is it?"

"In a district that's full of crime. One of the old townships near the airport. It fits."

"That is fucking bullshit. That's the best the Taskforce could come up with?"

"Pike, we only had the two words."

"You know these guys are planning for something, right? They're tied in to our target, who's one of the biggest small-arms dealers in the United States. No way they'd meet at a police station in the ghetto. Those words you caught mean something, and we need to find out what."

Creed looked hurt and said, "Pike, I'm the computer guy. I can get you the key blank. I can get you the penetration of a phone, but I can't tell you what it means."

I leaned back, knowing I was beating up the wrong man. I said, "Yeah, I get it, Creed. Sorry. That was uncalled for."

He brightened, and Jennifer, from the back of the room, said, "I found it."

I said, "What?"

"It's the Castle of Good Hope. A fixture in town. It's the epicenter of Cape Town history. Where the whole place started."

I looked at Creed on the computer and saw he was no help. To her, I said, "What's there?"

"Uhhhh . . . it's a tourist attraction. It was the original fortification for Cape Town. It closes at four."

I turned away from the computer and said, "So these guys are going to do a meeting at a closed tourist attraction at night? What the fuck? That's no better than the police station."

Shoshana glowered at my tone, then moved behind Jennifer, putting a hand on her shoulder. Jennifer kept typing, but all I could see was the hand. It was an intimate gesture.

There was a time in our past when we were sure Shoshana was a lesbian, not least because she clearly enjoyed annoying me by flirting with Jennifer, but that theory was supposedly destroyed by Aaron.

And I realized she wasn't bound by such a definition. She was Shoshana, and she didn't understand the distinction. She gave her love stingily, but when she did, it was total, and woe betide those who attempted to harm the ones she'd granted access to her vault.

Thank God she was sweet on me.

Jennifer finished typing and turned to me triumphantly. She said, "It's the castle."

"How do you know?"

"There's a South African National Defence Force base at the back of it. They're going there because they're meeting South African military. Whatever these guys are doing, it's tied into the South Africans."

In the span of six seconds, I went through everything I knew about our operation, and what she said made absolute sense. Tyler was doing something with *South Africa*. And we didn't have a second to waste. The meeting was happening in less than two hours.

Before I could even issue an order, someone else knocked on the door. Shoshana went to it and let in Brett. He saw everyone there and said, "Am I late? I thought this meeting was at seven."

I said, "You're not late. Well, not from my time schedule. We're all late now. Jennifer, bring up a map of that castle." I looked into the computer and said to Creed, "You sent the key data?"

Creed said, "Yeah. You got it."

I turned to Shoshana and said, "Find a 3-D printing place around here. Get us that key. Probably can't do anything tonight, but at least find out where we can go tomorrow."

To Jennifer I said, "Get us a complete layout of that castle. Find me penetration points, surveillance locations, everything."

Brett said, "What the fuck did I miss?"

I said, "Go prep some kit. I don't want to rely on computer-hacking shit. Give me something that can hear from a distance. Old-school stuff."

He said, "What's going on?"

"We've got a surveillance mission at nine tonight. We have about thirty minutes before we need to roll. Get back here in fifteen, and I'll have an OPORD done."

He left without another word. Which is why he was on my team.

Shoshana, on the other hand, said, "I'm not doing bullshit support work. I'm going with you."

I turned to her and said, "No, you're not. Get the key made. It's a team effort."

I saw the anger flare, and she said, "Those fucks know where Aaron is! I'm not going to break into some warehouse." She advanced on me, and I grabbed her arms before she could do something she'd regret.

She looked into my eyes and said, "I'm *not*."

She quit fighting, and I looked into her eyes, just to make sure she wasn't tricking me. She wasn't. I let her go, and she said, "You told me we'd find Aaron. You promised. I can't keep doing this. All we do is Taskforce crap. Aaron is in *trouble*."

She said the last word with so much pain it caused me to flinch. She was right, and I knew it. But I also knew I didn't have the authority to do anything else. I had what I had, and I'd use that to help her, but I couldn't just go ripping into everyone like she wanted, because it would destroy my mission. Possibly destroy the ability to prevent more deaths than just Aaron's.

I said, "Shoshana. Give me the night. Just give me this night. We have no idea where Aaron is, and I might find that out. Please. I'm asking."

She said, "We have the black man from the meeting today. I can go to him. I can find out what he knows."

I said, "No. No, you can't. We don't know his connections, and I'm not sanctioned for that. And you don't even know where he's located."

She said, "I do. I have your Taskforce phone, and I see the beacon. Pike, he's no threat. He's a nobody. And I'm not Taskforce. I'm freelance. Nobody can blame you if I interdict."

I'd voiced the question for a reason. She was thinking exactly like me, but I couldn't ask out loud if she could find the guy, like I wanted her to execute something, but I had to make sure. Just in case.

In the room, I said, "You want me to take that phone back? Do I need to worry about you?"

She pursed her lips, then shook her head, resigned to my decision. I said, "Okay. Just get the key so we can see what's in that warehouse. Let us work tonight."

Shoshana said, "You didn't lie to me, did you? About Aaron? You would never lie to me, would you?"

I said, "No, Shoshana. And you know it."

She glanced at Jennifer again, as if she wanted to ask her the question but wasn't sure of the answer.

She said, "Outside of Aaron, you two are the only thing in this world I trust. The only ones who have ever understood me. You are *me*. Please tell me that that's enough."

I didn't know what to say. She'd never been vulnerable before. She was so full of violence that hearing the words was as strange as seeing a lion exposing its belly for a man with a knife. But I couldn't promise what I couldn't deliver.

I said, "You have our support. Let us exploit tonight. We can talk about the future tomorrow."

She wanted to believe we were infallible, but she understood all I could promise was to help. I couldn't guarantee success. She nodded and went to the door. She opened it and said, "I feel like I'm doing nothing. I'm letting Aaron die."

I said, "Get the key. That warehouse may hold the information we need."

She nodded glumly, and I said, "And keep an eye on that beacon."

She said, "Why?"

"Because I said to. But just keep an eye until I say otherwise."

She let the wolf smile slip out, her true essence coming back. She said, "Thank you, Nephilim."

And she left the room.

Jennifer said, "What was that about?"

I said, "Nothing. We have a mission to plan."

39

★ ★ ★

Throwing shallow pools of light with a harsh downward slant, the vapor lamps gave too many shadows for Jennifer or me to recognize anybody who arrived at the front of the castle. Though the lighting wasn't conducive for identification of Apple—now Casio—Watch, we knew the time he was supposed to show, so we had something to go on. Not that we could see the entrance anyway, since we were hidden off to the side in the dark, waiting on Brett to give us the signal to climb.

Outside of the thirty-foot circle of light at each lamp, the rest of the terrain was pure black. While I ordinarily liked being the one to make the trigger decision on an operation, pulling myself out of control was a conscious choice. Here, I couldn't positively trigger *and* execute. I needed some help, which was why I delegated to Brett. We had a lot of technology—like night vision goggles—that could supposedly solve every problem, but at the end of the day, sometimes old-school, man-on-the-street was the way to go.

I called, "Blood, we're set. You got eyes on?"

"Yeah. I'm good for the short term. Not sure how long I can stay. I've had a couple of cops look at me."

I'd placed Brett across the street, in the old square from the original heart of the eighteenth-century community, adjacent to the Cape Town city hall. Once a parade field celebrating the life of the town, it had become nothing more than an acre of pavement used as a flea market. At the end of apartheid it had been a ghetto-strewn mess, but since then, there had been a lot of cleanup. It was now a location for street vendors to sell their goods—and also a place for panhandlers.

Brett had been tasked with assuming the position of a homeless squatter, of which there were plenty, but it wasn't a sure thing the authorities would let him remain. Technically, it was illegal, and the police ran them out on a daily basis, but because the panhandlers kept coming back, I figured it wasn't a bad decision. Nobody returned to a place where the punishment was more than they were willing to endure.

I said, "Any movement?"

"None. Castle is clean. You're good to go. Koko, break a leg."

She grimaced at me in the dark and said, "That's not what I want to hear."

Although it had a moat and was made of stone, the castle was not a traditional one in the European or Hollywood sense, with tall spires and an imposing drawbridge. It was created more as a defensive fortification than for living. Built in the seventeenth century, it was shaped in a square, with four bastions that jutted out of the corners and an iron-gated entrance. It had been the home of the Dutch East India Company's initial outpost for the ships plying their wares farther on, and, like most of the settlements expanding out of Europe, it had nothing to do with exploration for exploration's sake and everything to do with the whims of the corporation.

After making friends with the natives, the company had decided to form an outpost on the southernmost point of Africa. Knowing how precarious its position was, the Dutch had outlawed any effort to enslave the local population, choosing instead to co-opt them, a decision that would pay dividends for years, right up until the slavery was exposed not in outright ownership but in political negligence. The true slaves were brought in from Malaysia, a decision that would prove just one more bit of trouble for the eventual melting pot of modern-day South Africa.

During its entire existence, the castle had never fired a shot in anger, nor had a shot been fired against it. In the modern day, it was a tourist attraction, but its history prevented an easy penetration for surveillance.

Because it was a defensive fortification, it was impossible to sneak through a back door. It had none. It had one entrance, and that was on a winding path that crossed the moat, threading through a gate topped by stone lions. Something the tourists loved, but not great for sneaking in. Which led me to post up in the tourist parking lot on the side and let Brett give me atmospherics on the surrounding threat.

I looked at Jennifer and said, "You ready to go?"

Her eyes were glistening like they always did when I asked her to do something remotely insane. She glanced up the wall and said, "Yeah. I'm good."

I grinned and said, "Okay, spider monkey, get up top."

Before she was an actual Operator in the Taskforce, Jennifer had made the mistake of showing me a skill that was very hard to teach. It relied on talent. She'd once been a contender for Cirque du Soleil and had an acrobatic ability that few could match, which meant she could climb like a squirrel over just about any obstacle.

Don't get me wrong, I could get to the top of the castle just as easy, but I had to carry our kit up there, so she'd do the initial climb and give me a helping hand with a grapple hook and a knotted rope.

Okay, that's not exactly true. She could outclimb me on any given day. I was pretty sure she could slither up plate glass with nothing but spit on her hands. But I *did* have to bring up the gear.

She went to the corner of the bastion, felt the rough stone, searching for purchase, then began climbing. She made it look effortless. She got up about eight feet and turned to look down. She said, "Catch me if I fall?"

Which was something she always said, like it was an affirmation of her worth. I grinned, knowing she couldn't see it in the darkness, and said, "Always."

I heard a couple of scrapes and then saw her shadow racing up the stone like a gecko. Four minutes later, the rope tumbled down. I clicked my earpiece and said, "Blood, we're in. Going up now. Keep eyes out for Apple Watch."

"Roger all. I'm moving now. Cops are circling, but I still have view of the entrance."

I grabbed the rope and started climbing, saying, "Don't get compromised. You're our exfil. Whatever you do, don't get arrested."

He'd dropped us off at the tourist bus parking across the moat on the northern side, underneath the shadow of Table Mountain, and we'd walked in to our climb point, away from the entrance. If he was interdicted, and we were compromised, we'd be running back to the hotel on foot.

He said, "Don't worry about it. Worse comes to worst, you can use that privilege you have. Especially here, but I'm blending in just fine with the rest of the brothers."

Which was a poke in the eye to me for using his race to accomplish the mission. He hated that shit, but we both knew I understood his skills.

I reached the top, and Jennifer held out a hand, hauling me up over the edge. I rolled over the parapet and whispered, "Anything?"

She said, "No."

I pointed at my eyes, then lowered my night vision goggles. She did the same, and then we crouched for a minute, getting the sights, sounds, and smells of the battlefield. All was quiet. I mentally pulled up the map of the castle as I scanned, trying to determine what was different—because it was *always* different.

The castle was laid out in a square, split in half by a single partition in the middle. The actual living, functioning parts of it were in the walls themselves, with a courtyard in the front half and a pool and smaller courtyard in the back half.

We were kneeling on the grass-covered roof of the southeast bastion, overlooking the front courtyard, next to a mortar position that was created to defend the castle from an attack that never came.

I surveyed the area under my NODs, looking for a vantage point.

In the back of the courtyard, along the wall that split the castle in half, was an ornate portico fronted by the statues of famous native tribal leaders who'd fought the encroachment on their terrain. It was the governor's quarters of the historical commander of the garrison, and the location of the meeting tonight.

At least I hoped it was, because it was the closest clue Creed could come up with.

40

Back in the hotel, we'd spent thirty minutes designing a surveillance strategy for the meeting and had learned that it wasn't going to be easy. The castle sprawled across acres of terrain, with museums, displays, jail cells, and offices spread throughout. They could be meeting anywhere, and that wasn't even including the SANDF base in the rear. It was like getting tasked to pull surveillance on a meeting in the Pentagon and knowing only the address of the building.

Creed had come back online saying he thought he'd necked down the location of the meeting. The Taskforce had managed to clarify one bit of the audio exchange at the hotel, wading through the white noise. They'd identified the words "governor" and "museum," which, juxtaposed with what we knew about the castle, could only be the old governor's residence.

I'd given the orders, and Brett had brought down a unique piece of kit to help us penetrate the meeting: a clandestine laser microphone.

We had to hear what was being said in the room and didn't have the time to sneak in and place microphones, but the laser would do the work for us. When someone speaks in a room, the noise is transmitted throughout, and when it hits a window, the window vibrates ever so slightly. Our laser microphone would detect the vibration, and when we captured the return, we could translate the light into sound. Yeah, I know, it sounds like Luke Skywalker magic, but it's real.

I looked at my watch, tossed my rucksack to my feet, and said, "Break out the kit. We've only got about twenty minutes to figure out the angle."

Jennifer started digging into the pack, pulling out the laser and receiver, while I continued scanning with my NODs, trying to find the IR cameras that I knew were there. From our initial reconnaissance, we'd determined that the cameras were at ground level, where the tourists wandered. I hoped that was correct, because if we were caught in them, we'd get a security response.

She pulled out a small tripod and what looked like a digital SLR camera. Designed to hide what it truly was—which mattered not a whit here—it had both a visible aiming laser and the infrared reading one. She looked across the courtyard and said, "I can hit it from here, but you'll have to be on the other side to catch the pitch."

I looked down the wall we were on and said, "I don't think so. You hit it from here and that laser's going off into space. Let's tighten it up."

The angle of reflection was exactly like hitting a bank shot on a pool table—the larger the angle of the shot, the wider the bounce off the bumper. In this case, I wanted to make sure the bounce off the bumper would be something I could catch. We slithered across the roof until we reached a small tower jutting out of the masonry. I looked at the angle again and said, "I think this'll work. Set it up."

She mounted the "camera" to the tripod and initiated the visible laser. She aimed it at the governor's residence, and I saw the splash on the brick above the French doors. She worked the tripod until the beam was hitting one of the windows. I looked at the angle of the bounce back and said, "I can catch that. Hope this is worth the effort. See you soon."

I moved down the wall to the spot I thought would be the catch area, then clicked my earpiece. "Send me a visible."

Right as I said it, I saw a security guard appear in the courtyard below. I crouched and said, "Stand by, stand by, stand by."

Through my earpiece I heard, "I see him."

The guard completed a lap, then disappeared through the wall to the back courtyard. I hit the timer on my watch to get a sense of the schedule, then said, "Send it."

I heard, "Roger," then saw the splash, and in short order, I had the receiver catching the glow on my own tripod. I said, "We're set.

Switch to infrared," then attached the octopus of cords between the receiver and the digital recording device.

Why they made the transmitter look like a camera when the rest of the kit looked like it came from NASA was beyond me.

Down in the courtyard, I saw the lower-level door of the governor's residence open, and three men stepped out onto the portico. Two I didn't recognize, but one was Tyler Malloy. *Jackpot.* "Koko, Koko, you seeing what I am?"

"Roger. Got him."

One of the men—not Tyler—began walking across the courtyard, and my earpiece came alive. "Pike, this is Blood. Apple Watch and an unknown are walking across the moat now, heading to the front entrance."

"Roger, I copy. We've got jackpot on the meeting site. You have visibility of the entrance?"

"Yeah, but just that. Once they pass the gate, it goes dark. Break, break—lost contact. They're inside."

No sooner had he said that than the three men appeared beneath my feet, walking in the scattered illumination of the vapor lamps. They passed directly underneath one, then stopped to discuss something. A bolt of adrenaline went through me, the same feeling one gets from a near-miss car accident—the pounding heart and the fight-or-flight response.

They left the pool of light, and I brought up my NODs, seeing the same thing I thought I had, but I wanted confirmation. I said, "Koko, Koko, take a look at the unknown from the parking lot. Anything stand out?"

I waited, tracking the man all the way to the portico. They entered, and I saw them climb the stairwell for the second floor. Jennifer came back on.

"No way. Is that Johan?"

41

★ ★ ★

Johan followed Andy through the iron portcullis, seeing Colonel Armstrong coming across the grass in the gloom of the sporadic lighting. Through the courtyard, on an ornate portico, he saw two more men.

They met just inside the gate, shook hands, walked a bit, then Armstrong stopped, saying, "Before we go inside, a few things. Andy, did everything check out?"

"Yeah. It's fine. Everything we asked for is there. Ammo, explosives, grenades, rifles, it's all there."

"Communications?"

"Thales PRC-148 MBITR radios. Looks like US military surplus, but they function."

"Parachutes?"

"Twenty MC-4 ram-air free-fall rigs. They're used. Probably old US military stock as well, but they look good. We can get a rigger to check them out, right?"

"Probably. We'll have to ask that man on the porch."

Armstrong turned to Johan and said, "The man on the right is Tyler Malloy, the American providing our equipment and transport. The one you were concerned about."

Johan nodded, saying, "So now I have to trust the American to certify a parachute he sold us? No, thanks."

"No. That would be from the man on the left. Just call him Colonel Smith."

"He's South African military?"

"Yes."

"From where? What's his background?"

"Not your concern. In fact, don't even broach it. He's taking a considerable risk just meeting us. Look, you wanted to come feel out the American—Tyler—so I let you. Don't say a word during the meeting besides the initial pleasantries. Let me handle everything else."

Armstrong turned to Andy and said, "You'll address any needs we have with the equipment, but it doesn't sound like much."

Andy nodded, and Armstrong looked to Johan one more time. "No Lily Boy stuff here, okay?"

"Yes, sir."

They approached the porch, and Johan sized up Tyler Malloy. He was not what Johan had expected. He had a hard look, like the men Johan hired, not like the suit-and-tie set who usually worked Tyler's end of the street. Johan shook hands, and, as expected, Tyler's grip overcompensated. Johan returned it with a smile.

Colonel "Smith" looked like every other high command he'd ever served. Civilian clothes that didn't fit right and a little bit of a stick up his butt. He had a pinched face with a pencil mustache that was bordering on Hitler territory. He didn't even bother to shake hands, apparently wanting to get out of the light before anyone noticed them standing together. They marched inside, then went upstairs, stopping in a room filled with paintings. A museum of some sort. In the center were a couch and three chairs circling an ornate coffee table.

Johan and Andy got the couch; the rest went to the chairs. Tyler said, "So, did you check out the equipment? Does it meet your requirements?"

Armstrong said, "We had a couple of questions, but, yes, it appears to. Andy?"

Andy leaned forward and said, "What's the pedigree of the HALO rigs you got us?"

"From US Army Special Operations Command. Excess after they adopted the RA-1 system. Don't worry, they aren't junk. USASOC wouldn't let them go out for garage sale if they posed a life-support risk. Any that were even close to posing a hazard due to wear and tear were destroyed."

Johan spoke. "And we should just trust you on that? Last thing I want is to have my lines all snap with dry rot."

Armstrong shot Johan a look, and Tyler said, "I don't provide faulty equipment. I only provide what I would use myself."

"So you know how to operate a free-fall parachute?"

He asked the question on purpose, wanting to gain some insight into Tyler's background beyond his personal appearance. Tyler turned red, giving Johan a partial answer. Armstrong cut off the conversation before it grew more heated, saying, "Colonel Smith, would it be possible to get a certified rigger to give the parachutes the once-over? Out at our training facility?"

Smith nodded and said, "I can do that. But it's going to cost you. I'm already hanging my ass out here."

Armstrong said, "I can talk to my employer. I'm sure he won't mind."

Smith said, "What's your timeline? How soon?"

"We're emptying the warehouse in the morning. We'll take the equipment to the training site, zero our weapons, shake out the comms gear, do a practice jump with the rigs, and then be ready. We're finishing up the final training package with the natives right now, so say within three days."

Smith said, "I can make that happen."

Tyler said, "So, sounds like we're tracking. Let's talk pay."

Armstrong said, "Colonel Smith?"

He said, "I've got them. I can transfer them at any time."

In a measured tone, Johan interrupted, saying, "No offense, but not all of us are *tracking*. My big question is the aircraft. We have our hands on the equipment, but it's useless without the infiltration platform. I'm going to need pilots who know something about a parachute drop, and Mr. Malloy's not giving me a lot of confidence in that area."

Colonel Armstrong frowned, his expression showing the displeasure boiling underneath his words. He said, "Johan, let me worry about that."

Tyler leaned in and said, "You have a problem with me, Johan?"

Johan returned his stare, his cold blue eyes not flinching. He said, "Yes, a little bit."

Tyler said, "Have I let you down yet? Did you have any trouble smuggling the Israeli? Or interrogating him?"

Johan saw the anger build and was a smidge amused. Tyler stabbed a finger in his face and said, "That was *my* safe house. I took the risk. It's *my* warehouse on the waterfront. More risk. So far, I'm the *only* one who has stake in this game, so back the fuck off."

Armstrong glared at Johan, his message clear. Johan retreated, but he didn't want to. Tyler aggravated him with his attitude, with his fake-ass operator beard, and by pretending to be some personal badass while he did nothing but sell weapons to anyone who would purchase them. Johan leaned back but left his eyes on Tyler. Tyler looked away first.

Focusing on Colonel Armstrong, Tyler said, "Enough with the questions. My work is done. All that remains is my pay. And you haven't given me any indication that you can produce."

Armstrong said, "Mr. Smith was involved with Project Circle. He has the access, and he can deliver."

Smith looked shocked at the admission. He stammered, "I . . . I wasn't involved . . . but I'm now in charge of the repository of the project . . . I don't think we should talk about such things here."

Tyler glared at him and said, "I want my payment now."

Armstrong raised a finger, a civilized gesture that got the attention of all involved. He said, "No, no. Your work isn't done until you land that plane back on South African soil, and we're on it."

Incensed, Tyler said, "That wasn't the agreement with Cohen. That was *not* the agreement. If this thing fails it is not my fault. I get paid either way."

"I agree with that, with one caveat: If it fails, me and my men are still flying out. I won't hold you accountable for what happens on the ground, but I can't possibly throw away my security by paying you now. What's to stop you from just flying your ass somewhere else? Even if it's successful? We cannot be on the ground while they consolidate power. We dismantle, and they clean up. We were never there."

"That was not the agreement."

"It's the agreement now. You want those triggers, you follow through. If I make it back to South African soil, you get them. It's that simple."

Aggravation bleeding through, Tyler said, "Okay, okay. So you're satisfied with the merchandise?"

Armstrong glanced at Andy. He nodded, and Armstrong said, "Yes. I am."

Tyler stood up hard enough to knock his chair over. Clearly displeased, he said, "This is not how I do business. I make an agreement, and I get paid."

He looked at Colonel Armstrong and said, "Believe me, you don't want to mess with my business. I have friends you don't want to meet."

Hearing the words, Johan stood as well, giving Tyler the heat of his stare. He said, "Don't give me a threat. Give me a promise."

Tyler's eyes went back and forth between the men, confused. Johan cleared it up for him. "If you're not on that airfield, I'll gut you alive. And that's a promise. Bring your friends if you want. I'll gut them too."

Tyler glared at Armstrong, then at Johan. He stormed out of the room without a word.

Nobody said anything for a moment; then Colonel Smith rubbed his face, clearly distressed at how the conversation had deteriorated and how he was now involved. He tried to bring it back to his world. The military one.

He said, "Lloyd, speaking of failure, if you don't secure that place quickly—if anyone else becomes involved—you know I can't stop what's coming. South Africa won't sit on the sidelines if America or some other country is stopping a bloodbath."

Armstrong said, “I know. I know. Don’t worry about that. You’ll be protected.”

A SANDF member in uniform entered the room, startling Colonel Smith. The sentry said, “Sir, you told me to alert you about any activity.”

Colonel Smith said, “Yes?”

“Well, it’s nothing big, but we have some suspected trespassers outside the gate. American tourists, apparently. I didn’t want to disturb your meeting, but you said to tell you if we heard anything . . .”

Johan thought one thing: *Americans. Again.*

42

★ ★ ★

I'd been sitting up top for five minutes, monitoring . . . well, monitoring nothing, really. I was just hoping the laser was actually recording something, and reflecting on the fact that Johan van Rensburg was somehow wrapped up in this mess, when Brett came on. "Pike, Pike, I've got eyes on Carrie."

What. The. Hell.

I turned toward the square two hundred meters away but of course couldn't see anything. "What's she doing?"

"I have no idea. She's just leaning against a palm tree, staring at the castle."

Why is she here? I said, "Carrie, Carrie, you on the net?" I heard nothing. "Carrie, Carrie, damn it, if you're on the net, you'd better answer."

Nothing.

Brett said, "You want me to go interdict her?"

"No. She's already pinpointed you, I promise. She knows where you are. I don't know what she's doing, but don't spook her."

I saw a flash of light off to my left and crouched down, thinking, *What now?*

It was a security guard coming up the stairwell on the far bastion. *Jesus Christ. What the hell is he doing up here?*

Hiding in the shadow of an old outcropping of brick, I watched him in my NODs. He went around the bastion, flashing his light here and there, occasionally lost from view before reappearing.

And then he began threading through the ancient defenses toward me. *Shit.*

I looked at the receiver, seeing it in the green of my NODs.

Decision time. Break it down and hide, or hope he just goes past? The equipment was really hard to see, and even if he found it, it looked like some weather device. Breaking it down now would mean losing the conversation. But if he *was* out looking as protection for the meeting, we'd be in trouble, because he wouldn't let it go.

He came up the stairs from the mortar casement in the bastion, entering my level, and I made a decision. I raced to my equipment, saying, "Koko, Koko, I have a guard headed our way. Break down the laser and get out of sight. Let him go by, and we'll reconnect."

I expected some questions, but all I got was, "Roger that."

Brett came on: "Pike, Koko. You need exfil?"

"Not yet, but get ready. If he does a lap and keeps going, we'll get back in play."

"That's risky."

"I can't get by him now anyway. My only chance is to let him miss me."

"How are you going to do that?"

Good question.

I collapsed my tripod and shoved the whole thing against the wall, scuffing grass and dirt over it, watching the light bobbing toward me, thankful that he couldn't see anything outside of the scope of the beam.

That was the primary problem with using a flashlight—you lost all night vision because you were staring into the glow—but it didn't help me if he shined it on my body. There was nothing to camouflage me like I had used on the tripod. Jennifer had mortar pits, casement walls, and the captain's tower in her position on the bastion. I just had about a thirty-foot-wide path of grass that was the roof of the front of the castle.

I said, "I honestly don't know."

"Well, that's about what I would expect from you. Moving to the car. Good luck."

There was a wrought iron railing on both sides of the wall to prevent tourists from splashing their brains onto the pavement below, and I decided to just hang from it, but now I had a choice: drop inside the castle, or outside? Inside would put me in view of the meeting, but outside would allow everyone in the square to possibly see the crazy man hanging.

The flashlight advanced, and I chose outside. At least if I fell—and I didn't break a leg—I could run away.

I flipped over the side and hung there holding my breath. I heard Brett come on. "Pike, Pike, is that you? Are you kidding me?"

I said nothing, seeing the light bobbing by. Brett then said, "The good news is, I'm in the car. The bad news is, Shoshana's seen you. She's moving toward the castle."

Damn it.

I wanted to scream, *Stop that crazy bitch,* but I couldn't risk talking.

I hung there for what seemed like an eternity, then heard Jennifer whisper, "He's at my location. I'm secure. When he gets by, I'll call."

Which was enough to let me know I could talk and move. I climbed back over and said, "Blood, Blood, what's Carrie's status?"

"I lost her. I'm up the street, on the main drag that leads to the tourist parking lot, same place I dropped you off."

Damn that girl. The last thing I needed was her trying to penetrate the castle on some misguided mission to find Aaron.

Jennifer came on, and now she was talking so low I could barely hear her. "Pike, this is Koko. He's found the rope. He's looking at the rope."

We'd pulled our grapple hook and coiled the rope at the base of the wall, not wanting it to be seen hanging down from the outside, but I'd never considered it being seen from the top.

"What about you?"

"I'm good. He won't find me. I can move when he does. But he's got a radio."

Well, this just turned into a shit sandwich.

I started packing my receiver, knowing the mission was over. I said, "Take him out. Now."

"He's already used it."

Which meant removing him from the equation would only prove whatever suspicion he'd called when he was found. Whoever he'd radioed was on the way.

I shouldered my rucksack and began slinking toward her position, saying, "Blood, Blood, get ready for a hard exfil. Break, break—Koko, status?"

I heard nothing and took a knee, waiting. Finally, I heard two clicks, which meant she couldn't talk. I moved close enough to help if she needed it, then simply waited, my head wanting to explode from the silence. Thirty seconds passed, and then I saw the flashlight bounding along the adjacent wall, moving away. Koko came on, saying, "He's looking for us. He thinks we're deeper in, ahead of him."

I sprinted as fast as I could with my NODs on my head, finding Jennifer on a knee behind the captain's tower, holding her tripod and camera in her hands. I pulled off the NODs, dropped the ruck, and said, "Break it down. We're going."

She started working, and I called Brett. "Blood, we're coming over the wall. You ready?"

Getting compromised was one thing, but getting caught was something that absolutely couldn't happen.

He said, "I'm set at the original drop-off. You want me to come to you?"

The parking lot had a narrow bridge across the moat, and if he came in, it would be easy to prevent him from getting back out with a vehicle.

"No. Stay where you are. We'll come to you."

Jennifer stood up, handing me the ruck. I said, "Come on, let's go. You first."

She said, "I can't retrieve the rope if I go first."

She thought she was repeating in reverse what we'd done originally, with me using the rope, her tossing it to me, and then her climbing down the wall, but it was too late for that.

"We're both going to scale the wall. We use the rope now and they'll know we escaped. It stays just like he found it. Hopefully, we get away clean and it's just a mystery."

She said, "I can pull it up after you go."

"We don't have time for that shit. Every second counts. It'll take too long going one at a time."

She looked down the wall and said, "You sure you can do this?"

"Are you fucking kidding me? Don't get cocky. Get on the stone."

She grinned, her teeth glowing in the night, then flipped over the wall, holding the parapet with her hands while she sought purchase with her feet. She looked up at me and said, "I'll catch you when you fall," then began scampering down. I let her get a body length away and then followed.

I got about halfway down, still fourteen feet above the ground, and saw the lights of a cop car rolling down the road toward the moat. I moved faster, not wanting them to see us on the wall, and felt my foot slip.

I rapidly slid it left and right, looking for purchase, then felt my handhold going. I lost my grip and then was in free fall, sailing by Jennifer. I slammed into the ground on my side, getting the breath knocked out of me.

Jennifer dropped to the ground next to my body, scrambled to me, and leaned over as if she was going to hoist me to my feet. I knocked her hands out of the way from pure embarrassment, saying, "Get out of sight."

I rolled over, and we both ran to the edge of the moat. It had a seven-foot culvert of concrete, with the water far below. No way to slide down that and escape. We'd never make it out the other side without being seen. I briefly considered just hiding in the water for the night but knew that was ridiculous.

Jennifer said, "What's the plan?"

I said, "It's completely shot now. I thought you were going to catch me."

She looked at me like I'd grown a horn, and I grinned. She hit my shoulder, and I saw the cop car roll across the bridge.

I said, "Stand up. We're going to bluff our way out."

"Pike, how?"

I stood, saying, "How what? We're just a couple of tourists out on the night. There's nothing connecting us to the rope up there."

"Except for that damn backpack on you."

The headlights from the car blinded us, and I said, "Too late."

The light bar on the roof began flashing, and three people came out of the car, advancing warily. One said, "Come to us, please. Hands in the open."

Raising my hands in the air, I said, "Whoa, whoa. What's up, Officer? We're just checking out the castle."

"It's closed now. What are you doing?"

"Just walking around."

"Come to me. I won't ask again."

We started walking toward them, and he shouted, "Hands! Let me see your hands."

We both raised our hands high, and I heard his partner call into his mic, "Couple of Americans. We're checking them out."

We stopped five feet away, and I reached into my pocket. The cop shouted, "Hands!"

I said, "I'm just getting my passport . . . Calm down."

I withdrew my fingers from the pocket, holding my passport in the air. His partner said, "What's on your back?"

And I knew we weren't going to get out. *Damn suicide bombers making everyone jumpy.* They would find the laser mic, the NODs, and everything else. I triggered my radio and said, "Blood, we need some help."

Cop One said, "What?"

And then he hit the ground face-first like someone had tied a rope to his legs and jerked out with a pickup truck. His partners whirled at the motion, and something came across the hood of the car, like a wraith in a horror movie. A movie I'd seen before.

I saw the form engulf one cop, and I launched on the last guy, sweeping his legs out from under him and hammering his skull. He bounced on the ground and, surprisingly, tried to fight back. I blocked his blows, cradled his head, and choked him out. He relaxed like a toy doll, unconscious, and I turned to the other fight.

I saw the dark angel over the cop, blotting out the light, him struggling and the wraith winning. He thrashed for a second, then grew still.

The form rose, and Shoshana said, "Why am I always saving your ass?"

I stood up over my cop and hissed, "What the hell are you doing here?"

Surprised at my tone, she said, "Huh? I got the key. I was just sitting around. I thought I could help."

Aggravated, I bit out, "And you don't bother to get on the radio?"

Jennifer slapped me on the shoulder and started speed walking past the police car, saying, "Hey, we need to go. Pike's happy for the help."

Shoshana glared at me, then began jogging to catch up with Jennifer, saying, "Doesn't sound like it to me."

The sentence hung in the air, and I knew we'd just crossed the Rubicon. The words on the tape were damning, and not in a way that would help my mission.

Shocked, unable to believe what she'd heard, Shoshana looked at me and said, "Play it again."

I said, "Shoshana—"

She cut me off, saying, "Play it *again*."

I rewound the digital recorder by twenty seconds and hesitated, not wanting to set off the grenade. She glared at me and said, "Play the damn tape."

I hit the button.

It was the last bit of recording we had obtained before we had to break down our laser microphone and flee like a couple of shoplifters at Macy's.

And it was brutal in its simplicity.

You have a problem with me, Johan? Have I let you down yet? Did you have any trouble smuggling the Israeli? Or interrogating him?

Shoshana hissed, growing dark, and the recording continued. *That was* my *safe house. I took the risk. It's* my *warehouse on the waterfront. More risk. So far, I'm the* only *one who has stake in this game, so back the fuck off.*

The true revelation was that Tyler was neck-deep in whatever mess was going on, but all Shoshana heard was a single word: Israeli.

She turned to me and said, "They have Aaron. That *fuck* you called a friend has Aaron." She looked at me with more pain than hatred. Pain at my perceived disloyalty because I'd told her I knew who Johan was.

The room grew tense, with Jennifer staring at the recorder and Brett surreptitiously putting a hand to the butt of the weapon on his hip. He understood the threat.

Shoshana flashed her eyes to me and said, "You call Johan a *friend,* and he's talking about interrogating Aaron?"

She stomped in a circle, fists clenched, looking at each of us in turn, and said, "I swear to God, if he's harmed, I will kill *every—single—one* of you."

And she meant it.

There was so much anger boiling forth I didn't think I could contain it. It was reaching critical mass. I stood up, my hands in the air, and said, "Shoshana, Johan isn't a friend. I never said that. He's just someone we've run across."

She slapped a wall, hard, growling like an animal and growing more incensed. She said, "Jennifer said you could have brought him down, but you did not. She said you saw something in him."

In a soothing voice, I said, "Hang on, hang on. You're reading into this."

She thrashed uncontrollably, like a child throwing a tantrum, then screamed, "Am I reading into him torturing my husband? My partner? My *world*? You fucking *knew* this guy, and he's the one that has my life!"

She grew still and said, "He has my life. And you knew it. You knew it all along."

Johan was a man I'd crossed in Morocco a year ago. He had been working for a sleazebag American defense contractor—a man who was trying to protect himself from being found complicit in terrorist attacks. Like 9/11.

Johan had done some bad things, but he'd realized he'd been duped and then had set about righting the wrongs. At the end of the day, he'd ended up helping to stop a catastrophic attack on US soil, but I was never sure of why he'd done it. He wasn't a friend, but he was someone I understood. Even given that, I'd kill him in a heartbeat if it meant getting Aaron back. Something Shoshana no longer believed.

I said, "We ran across each other on our last mission, but he's not a friend, and I had no idea he was here."

Her eyes lidded, and she said, "You fucking *liar.*"

And that was enough. I stood, my fists balled, and both Jennifer and Brett jumped up, realizing I was dropping into her world.

I leaned into her space, vibrating in anger. "You ungrateful bitch. I saved your fucking *life*. I would *give* my life for you. And you don't even *see* it."

She lashed out with a fist and caught my chin, a hard, snapping blow, throwing my head back. Jennifer jumped between us, but I knew it wasn't necessary. If she had wanted to harm me, she wouldn't have used a punch.

I rubbed my jaw and said, "You done?"

She gave another guttural moan and then drove her fist into the wall, punching through the Sheetrock.

I said, "Is the Mossad going to pay for that?"

She whirled back at me, and Jennifer ducked out of the way. I said, "Stop it. Now. It's getting a little old."

She wound up for more combat, then melted right in front of me, all the anger leaking out, leaving a scared child in its wake. She said, "Help me. Please. Pike. They have Aaron."

She had never asked for a single thing in her entire life, and her words gutted me, because there was nothing I could do to alleviate the pain.

I said, "We will, Shoshana. We *are*. We're trying to unravel the thread right now. Let us check out that warehouse. My target is Tyler, and I need evidence against him to continue. I need to see what's in that warehouse so I can give the Taskforce a plausible reason to continue. You made the key, and we'll use it."

Shoshana had proven more innovative than I would have thought, finding a hobby shop with a 3-D printer in the time we'd left her. She'd loaded the flash drive into it and had a plastic key created, using the photo she'd taken and the program from the Taskforce. The hobby shop hadn't cared what she was doing, as long as she paid.

I saw the dark angel begin to bloom, and she said, "Screw the warehouse. Let's go get that fucker Johan. *He* knows where Aaron is."

I said, "We can't do that. We still work inside a construct. Aaron isn't here, in Cape Town. We aren't going to save him by running amok. We're going to save him by working the problem."

I knew it was bullshit, and the statement itself disgusted me, but I couldn't have her interdict our only thread.

She shook her head and said, "That's just more words. We can't wait for that. We need to wrap up the people at that meeting. If not Johan, take out Tyler."

"Tyler won't give us Aaron. He's a braggart. And he's my main target. You heard them talk about payment. That wasn't money. That was something else. The Taskforce thinks it knows what that is, but they need to be sure. If I want to continue, I need to build a pattern of activity against him. Not take him out without sanction. All that'll do is get me pulled and Aaron dead."

She snatched her purse from the table and said, "I'm not waiting. I told you what would happen when your mission crossed over mine. I'll do it alone."

She started stalking toward the door and I said, "You still have my Taskforce phone?"

She whirled around, digging into her purse and saying, "You want it back? Fine." She tossed it onto the table next to the door. "Take the damn thing. I don't need it."

I said, "I didn't ask because I wanted it back. I asked because you never fucking use it. Although I'd like you to."

She stopped but said nothing, waiting.

I forged ahead. "The guys are talking about a HALO jump and training natives. This problem has gotten bigger than the initial mission. I have to see what's going on. I'm required to develop the target."

She said, "And you think America will care about some criminal activity in South Africa? When it doesn't have anything to do with terrorism? Why would they let you continue?"

I said, "Let us check out the warehouse, and let me worry about selling it."

She looked like she was going to attack me again. I held up a hand and said, "Why don't you go locate our beacon? Instead of peeling Johan or Tyler apart, go take a look at the guy from the meeting, as someone not affiliated with the Taskforce."

It took a second for my words to penetrate her head. When they did, I saw the dark angel blossom, and it was scary. Her eyes bored into mine, and everyone in the room ceased to exist except for me and her.

She said, "You mean that, Nephilim?"

Jennifer half rose from her chair, understanding what I was doing. Before she could stop it, I said, "Yes. For Aaron."

I walked over to the table, picked up the Taskforce phone, and handed it to her, saying, "Blood, text her the picture of the target you took inside the Long Street Hotel."

He did as he was asked. She turned without a word and left.

The room was silent for a moment; then Jennifer said, "Jesus, Pike, she's going to kill that guy."

I leaned against the counter, my hand tapping it unconsciously, wondering if I'd done wrong. I said, "Yeah, she might, but we've got nothing else to go on, and the Taskforce won't give us sanction, no matter what we find in that warehouse. We won't see any evidence of nuclear triggers. All we have right now is the mention of a payment."

She said, "Pike, we don't work like this. We can't let her do this."

I locked eyes with her and said, "Aaron's worth it. No matter what."

She looked at Brett, and he nodded, saying, "If it were me, I'd want you on my side. Fuck the Oversight Council."

44

★ ★ ★

Aaron took his small bowl of rice and scuttled out of kicking range of the guards, settling in next to Thomas. Thomas looked at him with a little bit of admonishment, and Aaron knew why. Although he was starving, he knew the price.

He duckwalked over to the communal bowl and kicked in his share of rice, then came back to the wall.

Thomas said, "You don't have to do that, you know."

Like Aaron had a choice.

He chuckled and said, "I know. If I want to die, I can eat that rice."

Thomas's face grew stern, irritated at the suggestion. He said, "You do what you want, when you want. I don't ask anything of you."

Aaron said, "Yes, you do."

Thomas put his bowl on the ground, glanced to make sure the guards were out of earshot, and said, "Who are you? Really?"

The question brought a stab of regret. It had been two days since General Mosebo had visited, and Aaron knew his time was drawing to a close. The clock was ticking faster and faster. Sooner or later Mosebo would return, and when he did, Aaron would be faced with a choice. Sacrifice his life in defense of Alex, or simply let them have their way with her.

He didn't like the options, because he was sure that no matter what happened, they would have their way with her. He would just be dead.

He'd given up hope on Shoshana. Not that he didn't think she was searching for him, but she had nothing to go on. His mind refused to think of the inevitable: They'd killed her. That simply wasn't possible. Still, in a small recess of his soul, the thought grew. And with it, a desire for vengeance.

If that was true, then he had no reason to pretend or cover anything he was doing with the Mossad. His loyalty worked as an ingrained thing, but there was a limit. If what he loved had been killed, and the Mossad could have prevented it, then they'd forfeit the right to his soul. He could take the pain and blood for himself—hell, he'd signed up for it—but if they'd stood by while Shoshana had been hurt, then they'd reap what they sowed.

But he still had a problem: Alex was being held and he had no means to get her out, unless he went full-on crazy, trying to escape. He might not make it, but the action might be heinous enough to draw a press crew, even in this backwater. They would probably kill him, but if it was reported in the news, the world would be different. It might get her an out.

Thomas saw his change in demeanor and repeated, "Who are you?"

Aaron said, "I'm the man who's going to get out of here."

Thomas scoffed and said, "You still don't know where you are, do you? There is no 'out of here.' We're inside the military base of the Lesotho Special Forces. You get out of this prison and you still have to escape the base. It won't happen."

Aaron said, "Maybe not, but I can promise one thing: I'll get out of this prison. That I know I can do. You asked who I am; I'll return the favor. Who are you?"

Thomas smiled and said, "I'm like you. No reason to be here."

Aaron dropped his bowl and said, "Apparently so. Look, I don't have the energy to continue with this dance. My name is Aaron Bergmann. I was hired to find out about illegal diamond trades. I got caught up in something much bigger. That's my story. What's yours?"

Thomas set his chipped bowl on the ground and said, "I'm a political prisoner."

Aaron felt a wisp of a smile starting to form, and Thomas held up a hand, saying, "I know that's what you would expect me to say, but it's true. I was threatening the lifeblood of the politicians here, and I was removed. To this hellhole."

Aaron leaned forward and said, "Don't hand me that shit. Lesotho isn't Sierra Leone. It's stable, and has been that way for years."

Thomas smiled and said, "It's stable because of our natural resources. Resources that are being exploited at the expense of the people."

Aaron rolled his eyes, and Thomas chuckled. "Yes, I guess I do sound a bit like Che Guevara. But it's true."

Aaron heard his statement and was intrigued. He said, "How do you know about Che Guevara?"

"I was never meant to be a politician here. I was destined for greater things. I left home at the age of twenty-one to attend the University of Chicago, on a USAID scholarship. I earned my bachelor's and master's in economics, and then my PhD in international relations from Georgetown. I had my sights set on the world stage, not Lesotho. I had no intention of coming home."

Thomas gazed at the wall, lost in thought. Aaron said, "So why did you?"

Thomas shook his head, remembering. Perhaps regretting. He said, "My nephew left school at the age of fifteen. He enrolled in one of the local initiation schools, and he died. It was a tragedy. A mess."

"Initiation school? You mean he left to learn a trade?"

"No. There is a Basotho tradition from a long time ago where the young men leave the villages and head into the mountains for months, learning to be men of the tribe. In the old days, it was just a tribal tradition. In the modern day, it's all about money, sanctioned by the government of Lesotho. It had died out in my generation, only being conducted in the extreme rural areas. After the fall of white rule in South Africa, it regained prominence. Then, with the introduction of AIDS, it became something of a rite of passage that held more than simply becoming a man. My nephew was attending one of these so-called schools and died in the mountains. They refused to bring him to medical care because the initiation rites are extremely secret. If he'd have lived until the school was over, he could have seen a doctor. He did not."

Aaron said, "What are these rites about? Hazing? Beatings?"

"No, not at all. That's not what killed him. Truthfully, most of the schools are based on tribal instructions about taking care of family, tribal traditions, and that sort of thing, but one thing they do is circumcise the members. Since HIV has become so prevalent, the population has a misguided notion that circumcision will prevent infection, which is another thing driving the enrollment to these schools. A tribal healer does it with Lord knows what. My nephew bled out."

Thomas looked at him with an embarrassed grin. Aaron said nothing. No words came to mind.

Thomas waited a bit and, when no derision surfaced, said, "So I came home to help the family, then to fight the schools, trying to get some laws in place to ensure the safety of the men—boys—participating. One thing led to another, and I was running for office."

His eyes glowed, and Aaron saw the true believer come to the fore. "This country has so much going for it, and yet the government steals it all, allowing the population to live in squalor. One in ten houses has freshwater, because we send all of it to South Africa. The dams block the flow, for Johannesburg's use, and the villagers still use buckets in a muddy creek. We have mines that produce the biggest gem-quality diamonds on earth, and all that profit goes to private companies outside of Lesotho. We have nothing to show for our richness, unless you count being the highest per capita nation on earth infected with HIV."

Thomas had worked himself into a little bit of a frenzy, his voice rising with the crescendo of an itinerant preacher. He realized the mistake and quieted down.

He said, "You asked me how I got here, and it's pretty simple. I seemed to resonate with the population when I was fighting against the initiation schools. One thing led to another, and I was running for parliament. And I was popular. This was before I understood what running for the government meant. You were either on the inside or you were an ineffectual flea. I became neither, which made me a problem. General Mosebo was the solution. He worked with the prime minister to get me removed from the equation."

Aaron nodded, but something didn't ring true. Against his better instincts, given the man and his brood were keeping him alive, he broached it. "So why are you still breathing? Why not just kill you and bury you in a cesspool somewhere?"

Thomas smiled and said, "I honestly don't know. I'd like to think it's because I have too much power, even in here, but I know that's not true. They could make me disappear completely, permanently, so why keep me alive? I mean, my family has no idea where I am. I wasn't arrested on charges, there was no publicity, so why keep me alive?"

He turned to the lone window and said, "I think it's because they fear me. The people love me, even as they don't know why, and because of it, the government fears making me a martyr. I'm like the Count of Monte Cristo, or the Man in the Iron Mask. Someone they should have killed years ago but did not."

Aaron smiled at the references, which a simple criminal from the country of Lesotho would never have heard of. Clearly, the man was what he professed.

Thomas returned to Aaron and said, "I think of those pieces of literature daily, fantasizing about them. Someday, the government will regret not killing me, just like the men in those books. And then you showed up."

Aaron said, "So? Why do I matter?"

Thomas smiled, his teeth gleaming in the darkness.

"Because, Mr. Death, you're going to make the fantasy real."

Tyler barged into the small lobby of his hotel, his head still full of steam from the meeting at the castle. He was brought up short seeing Stanko Petrov sitting in the lobby. The security man rose at his entrance, meeting him at the bank of elevators.

He said, "You don't look pleased."

"That fuck Armstrong isn't paying until after the mission."

"That wasn't the deal. You gave them the arms, you should get payment."

Tyler said, "They seem to think once we're paid, we won't have any incentive to continue with the transportation agreements."

He punched the elevator button with a grim smile and said, "Truthfully, they have a point. If that operation turns into a mess, there's no way I'd risk my aircraft going back in. Now I have no choice. Hassan is not going to be pleased."

"You still want me to take care of the loose ends? Or wait?"

"No, go ahead. They don't matter anymore, but remember, no signs of violence."

"That's not an issue. The warehouse guy wants to be paid in drugs. I'm meeting him now. He'll get a blissful sleep."

The elevator opened, and Tyler put his hand on the door to keep it from closing. "What about the Durban contact?"

"I'll figure it out. He may not be a threat, but if he is, I can fly out there tomorrow. He's looking to get paid as well, so it's not like he'll run from me."

"Okay. I gotta Skype meeting with Hassan. Might as well give him the bad news."

"Will he still pay? We've put in significant time and money for this little adventure."

Tyler entered the elevator and removed his hand, saying, "We'll see." The door closed, and he rode alone to the seventh floor. He entered his room, opened his laptop, then opened the Skype app, dialing a grayed-out contact called Raghead Number One. The Skype bubble gave its distinctive bleeping, but nobody answered. Tyler looked at his watch and disconnected, seeing he was a few minutes early for their preplanned meeting.

He stood, fixed himself a scotch from the minibar, then tried again. This time the screen cleared, revealing an Arabic man with a clean-shaven bald head and a neatly trimmed beard. Tyler smiled and said, "Hassan. Good to see you."

"And you too, my brother. Give me some good news."

"Before that, tell me you've followed procedures. You're not on any local Wi-Fi in Beirut, right?"

"No, no. I'm on the resistance's phone system. It's secure."

Tyler had met Hassan Kantar in Bulgaria, long ago. He was one of the many Syrian recruits the CIA brought over to train on small-unit tactics, before being inserted back into the cauldron that was the Syrian revolution. Along with others, Tyler had instructed him on the AK-47 and the RPG-7, back when he was fresh out of the Marines and still doing the grunt-level work.

They had somewhat bonded, because Hassan's English was better than that of the rest of the recruits, and because the Syrian was so inquisitive. He spent every lunch and dinner break sitting down with Tyler, asking all manner of questions about the program, how they would be used, and whom they would be fighting—the Syrian regime or ISIS.

It was a touchy subject from the beginning, and Tyler had been instructed to avoid it, sticking strictly to the tactical training. The US position was that the men would fight ISIS, but the recruits they'd found most definitely hated the Syrian regime more.

It turned out, there was a reason for all the questions. The CIA had finally gotten around to vetting Hassan, and they'd discovered he was Lebanese, not Syrian, and worse than that, he was suspected Hezbollah—the Lebanese terrorist force that was fighting alongside the Syrian regime. He most definitely wasn't a "rebel."

Hassan was unceremoniously whisked out of Bulgaria and quietly flown back to Syria. The CIA program had been under relentless attack in Congress because of its lack of mission focus and, ironically, poor vetting procedures. There was no way they would let it be known that they'd allowed a potential Hezbollah spy into the training program.

Eventually, Tyler had formed his alliance with Stanko and had left the grunt work behind, becoming the primary supplier of arms and ammunition to the Syrian rebel train-and-equip program. From those beginnings, he'd tentatively branched out, and his first foreign sale not involving the United States was to Lebanon, a small purchase of magazines and ammunition. He was surprised during the negotiations to find his old "friend" Hassan Kantar involved. They'd rekindled their relationship, him for the inroads into the lucrative Lebanon arms market, and Hassan for . . . well, Tyler never looked too closely at that.

Tyler turned down the volume of his laptop and said, "You're positive the connection is secure?"

"Yes, yes. Hezbollah built their own communications architecture to prevent the Zionists from penetrating it. And we've gutted the United States' ability to monitor in this country."

In 2011, Hezbollah counterintelligence had managed to penetrate CIA operations and over a span of months had not only publicly named US national clandestine agents on broadcast television but captured, tortured, and killed the entire indigenous network the CIA had built. It was a fait accompli, but even so, Tyler wondered if Hassan was being too complacent.

He said, "Two thousand eleven was a long time ago. They haven't been sitting still."

He saw Hassan wave his hand, the action appearing jerky due to the poor Skype connection. Tyler heard, "We are fine. Tell me, do you have good news?"

Here we go, thought Tyler. The problem was that, for whatever reason, Hassan had demanded a deadline. He wanted the triggers sooner, or not at all.

Tyler said, "The good news is, my contact does have the product. The bad news is, I'm going to be delayed in delivery."

Hassan frowned and said, "How much of a delay?"

"Possibly a week. Possibly more."

Hassan shook his head and said, "That is not good. Not good at all."

"Why? Who cares if the delivery is delayed? What's the rush? Project Circle has been dead for years. You can wait a little bit longer."

Tyler and Hassan's relationship had culminated with this deal. One hundred Krytron nuclear triggers smuggled from South Africa's Project Circle by way of Israel, to which Hassan was willing to pay one million a trigger.

Tyler wasn't stupid. He knew that Hezbollah was completely controlled, trained, and funded by Iran, but he simply followed the mantra "See no evil, hear no evil." Had he done a modicum of research, he would have learned that the Joint Comprehensive Plan of Action against Iran's nuclear ambitions had proceeded on pace, but it had done nothing to lessen Iran's cravings to become a nuclear power. The JCPOA had inspections set to occur soon, which would complicate the transfer, but that was far removed from Tyler's radar.

After all, he needed to be able to tell Cohen with a straight face that he wasn't delivering nuclear weapons components to the avowed enemy of Israel.

Hassan said, "You were supposed to deliver two weeks ago. I gave you the original deadline, and you missed it. Now you're going to miss another?"

"Hassan, it's not like we're talking AK ammo here. These triggers aren't growing on trees. It took longer than I thought."

Hassan tapped the table, then said, "Can you deliver worldwide? Bringing them that late to Lebanon may be problematic."

Tyler said, "Where?"

"I don't know. I'll have to confer with my superiors. Perhaps Afghanistan. Or Iraq. Maybe Turkey."

It wasn't lost on Tyler that all three countries shared a border with Iran. He said, "I can, physically, but I don't own the infrastructure on the ground. That was your job in Lebanon."

Meaning, he was carrying nuclear weapons components, something that the average customs official would most definitely have an interest in.

Hassan waved a hand again and said, "Let me worry about that. Call me in a week with an update. It might be possible to deliver them here, depending on how late you are."

Tyler disconnected, thinking about the ramifications. This ultimate deal was getting harder and harder to execute. Then he thought about the payout.

It would be worth it.

46

★ ★ ★

Shoshana wound her way down Long Street, the stop-and-go traffic causing her to consider abandoning a plan for a drive-by of the hotel first. The street was packed with cars fighting the partygoers, all rowdy and some drunk, the bars and balconies full of patrons shouting and laughing. In between the revelers, like sharks swimming among an unwitting school of fish, she spotted several seedy characters. Furtive, feral teenagers advertising their purpose like a neon sign to Shoshana. Pickpockets. Or worse.

She saw the hotel one block up, then an alley to the left. She took it, driving right up against a trash bin, close enough to the wall of the alley that the passenger door wouldn't open.

She sat for a minute, mentally tallying where she was in relation to the hotel. She figured she had about a hundred meters. She checked her Taskforce phone, first confirming the beacon was still in place, then flipping to the picture Brett had sent, memorizing it.

She left her purse, not wanting the aggravation of protecting it, but took a small strip of leather with two wooden toggles on each end, and a folding blade. She shoved the purse under the driver's seat and exited, running into a teenager in the dim light, high on something. He smiled at her and held out his hand, asking for money. She said, "You want to make a night's wages?"

He nodded dumbly. She said, "Watch this car for thirty minutes. When I return, I'll pay you. Don't let anyone mess with it."

He nodded like a puppy, saying, "Thirty minutes?"

"Maybe sooner."

She walked away, entering the flow of people on the street. She stayed on the south side of the street, passing by the Long Street

Hotel, assessing it for atmospherics. The bottom floor was a bar, which was par for the course on Long Street, the patrons spilling out onto the pavement, which would make her job easier. The noise alone would camouflage her intentions.

She was out for information on Aaron, and she would get that currency any way she could. In the end, the man in the room owned his own fate. She wouldn't kill him, unless she found him complicit. If he had anything to do with Aaron's disappearance, he would suffer the consequences. All that remained was how painful it would be.

She went fifty meters past the hotel, then jogged across the street. She began walking the other way and reached the side entrance to the hotel, a stairwell leading to the second floor, away from the crowds of the bars.

She pulled out her phone, checking the Taskforce beacon. She knew the hotel had only twelve rooms, all on the second floor, which would eliminate any three-dimensional problems finding the correct room. She saw the target was in the back, away from Long Street. She turned into the stairwell and saw a Caucasian man at the top of the landing. Talking to her target.

I pulled the car into the same parking lot on the waterfront we'd used earlier in the day, saying, "Everybody good with the plan?"

Brett chuckled and said, "Yeah, but I'm not sure Koko, here, can pretend to be on a date with you. Might want to switch to the angry girlfriend ruse."

I looked at her and said, "You're good. Right?"

Jennifer was still a little miffed that I'd let Shoshana go by herself to interrogate the hotel contact. She claimed it was because she was convinced Shoshana was going to torture and kill the guy—something she couldn't tolerate—but underneath, I could tell, she was worried for Shoshana's safety. Which was a little bit odd, considering Shoshana's skill, but Jennifer had always been protective of her.

She said, "We should have done one, then the other. Check him out, then hit the warehouse. Four on one is better than one on one. She's walking alone now."

I said, "Jennifer, we have no sanction. She's not Taskforce. Let her work the problem. We've got sanction for continued Alpha, which means the warehouse. That's it."

She opened the door and said, "Like that's ever stopped you."

I exited and said, "What, now you want to go off half-cocked?"

She said, "I want to protect the team. Period."

"You mean Aaron."

"Yes. We need to find him, for her. You're putting Shoshana in danger, and I don't mean her body." She glanced at Brett, then hissed, "You're putting what she *wants to be* in danger."

I said, "You aren't going to change who Shoshana is, and she's in no danger."

Before she could answer, I cut off the conversation, saying, "Brett, we're going to get a beer at that corner bar right before the draw-bridge. Give you time to check out the area. We'll go slow; you go fast."

The plan was pretty simple. Brett would penetrate the dock area, giving us real-time intelligence on what was there, and early warning. We'd walk up and use Shoshana's key. We'd be in and out in thirty seconds, documenting what we found for the Taskforce.

Easy breezy.

Brett speed walked across the street, blending in to the crowds out for the nightlife. Jennifer and I took our time, walking slowly, hand in hand. We reached the waterfront and the bar, taking stools out front. We ordered a beer and glass of water each, knowing we'd drink the water and leave the beer. It was a travesty, but I had a personal rule about screwing over waitstaff just because we were on a mission.

Jennifer said, "You sure Shoshana will be okay?"

"What do you mean by 'okay'? She won't get hurt, of that I'm sure."

"I mean . . . she's on the edge. We saw that in Haifa. She's not right, here. If she kills someone in cold blood, because she's hell-bent on finding Aaron, it'll take her back."

"Back where? She's a killer. It's what she does."

"It's what she *did*. We need to find Aaron *our* way. Show her she doesn't have to be a beast."

I leaned over and took her hands. "Jennifer, you can't save every stray dog. Carrie is Carrie. She is what she is."

"So you are what you are?"

"Yes. Precisely. That's my point."

"But you aren't what you *were*."

That was dirty pool, pulling in my past with the implication that I was just one more stray dog she'd saved. Which, unfortunately for my argument, happened to be true.

"Jennifer, we may be too late to do anything about Aaron."

She nodded, knowing what I was saying was true but not wanting to address it. She said, "Shoshana wants to talk to me. She said so. When you were out of the room."

I asked, "About what?"

Jennifer balled up a napkin and tossed it at me. I batted it away, and she said, "About Aaron. Relationships. About not killing for a living. And how you keep throwing her back into that life, like a damn pimp."

I said, "Hey, that's not fair . . . ," and my earpiece came alive. "Pike, Pike, this is Blood. It's clear. One guard, but he's making a lap. You got a ten-minute window."

47

★ ★ ★

Shoshana immediately backed away from the stairwell, before the men could focus on her. She retreated to the bar that occupied the first floor, bumping up to a table on the outside patio and waiting for them to pass.

A man slapped his hand on her shoulder, causing her to whirl around. He said, "Hey, sheila, you looking for a drink?"

Two things went through her mind: One, he was Australian; two, he provided the perfect cover. She reverted back to her time in the Gaza Strip, when she hunted men with her body. She said, "I'd love one. Scotch, straight up."

The man left, and she was accosted by two others, both friends of his. She engaged them in conversation but kept an eye out, off the porch to the alley. She saw her target pass by and moved to follow. One of the friends said, "Where are you going? He hasn't even brought the drink back."

She said, "I'm sorry. You guys have it."

The other, clearly drunk, said, "That's fucking bullshit, you slash. You can't get him to buy you a drink and then just toss off."

She saw the targets getting away and apologized again. The drunk blocked her escape, incensed. She grabbed him by the crotch and the throat, slamming him into the wall, saying, "Don't fuck with me."

She stared into his eyes, and he wilted. She dropped him to the floor and threw some money on the table. She exited the bar, the Australians lamely shouting insults her way, but none followed.

The street was crammed with people, and she'd lost sight of her target. She brought out the Taskforce phone and saw the beacon still inside the hotel room. He'd left it behind.

Damn.

She started threading through the crowd, moving with an economy of motion she'd learned in the markets of the West Bank. She broke through a gaggle and saw the Caucasian and her target entering a car. She focused on the vehicle, fusing the model, color, and every dent into her brain, then immediately reversed course, running flat out back the way she'd come, back to her car.

She rounded the corner to the alley and saw the high teenager sitting on the hood. Just like she'd asked. She smiled, unlocking the door. The teenager said, "Hey, it's only been about ten minutes. You promised pay for thirty."

She dug her purse out from under the seat, pulled out a wad of rand that would last for a week, and threw it into the street, saying, "You did good work."

He scrambled to pick up the money, and she reversed the car, whipping it hard enough to catch him with the front quarter panel. He flipped over the hood, hitting the ground on the far side. She rolled down the window, shouting, "You okay?"

He stood up, holding the wad of cash and smiling. "I guess that was for the last twenty minutes."

She rolled out of the alley, forcing her way into the traffic of Long Street and ignoring the honking.

She couldn't make any headway on the two-lane road and prayed the target car was stuck in the same mess. She beat the steering wheel, working into a rage that would consume anyone who approached, when the target car passed her going the other way.

She looked as it trailed by, moving ten miles an hour, her target in the passenger seat, oblivious to the death that was in the opposite lane. When it was past, she cut across the traffic, causing screaming and honking. She pulled into an alley, did a three-point turn, and began following, now four cars behind.

They made a left and rights, leaving the nightlife and passing through the colorful Bo-Kaap neighborhood, the narrow alleys bringing her back to the West Bank, and then eventually they started going uphill on a switchback road, leaving all traffic behind.

She made a hairpin turn and realized they were headed to Signal Hill, an old naval fortification from the time of sails.

The road was a skinny two-lane affair, with houses on the lower part of the slope to her right and rocky hillside to her left. If the target car stopped anywhere on it, she would be forced to continue, as she had no plausible reason to do the same.

She decided to back off, letting the car get far enough ahead that all she could make out was the glow of the headlights in the darkness. When she lost the glow, she advanced until she made contact again, driving with only her parking lights.

She followed this rule for the next few minutes, starting and stopping, until she crested a small rise. She saw the headlights and pulled over to the side of the road just as they disappeared again. She began moving forward slowly, like she had before, but the lights didn't reappear. She fought the urge to switch on her own headlights, allowing her to drive at speed, when she realized that the car had stopped next to a patch of shanties built onto a level plot of ground on the high side of the hill, behind a chain link fence. Constructed of plywood, discarded tin, and whatever else could be scrounged, it was a mini-slum with a plume of smoke coming from somewhere in the back.

She pulled over to the side of the road, seeing the dim outline of the car. She wondered about the stop, going back and forth on whether it was worth a penetration. Wondering if this was the endgame and whether it was time to turn on her skills.

She inched forward in her car for another hundred meters, then killed the engine, just watching. Waiting to see what happened.

Eventually, the Caucasian returned to the car, followed by two locals. The moonlight was too low to determine if either was her target. The car started, headlights flared, and it drove another couple of hundred meters before stopping again.

She pulled out her phone and brought up a map. The icon of her location pulsed less than two hundred meters from the Noon Gun, where tourists came to watch a cannon fire exactly at noon every day, a vestige of the signals given before everyone had a quartz watch or cell phone.

She slipped out of her vehicle, deciding to go on foot. She went into the shadow of the woods, steering clear of the shantytown, hearing laughter and shouting from within. She reached the edge of the Noon Gun park, seeing a decrepit naval fortification in the moonlight. Old armories built into the dirt, concrete bastions from World War II, and slashes in the earth clad in cement, designed for men to scurry about loading the weapons that no longer existed.

She held up, turning her ear to the wind. She heard a fleeting voice, lost as quickly as a wisp of smoke. She crouched in the darkness, cocking her head. She heard it again. She advanced forward, reaching the crest and seeing the entire Table Bay spilled before her down the mountain, a spectacular view.

She ignored it, focusing on finding her target. But there was nothing.

She waited, closing her eyes and focusing on her hearing, shutting out all other senses.

She heard one more scrap of words, tangled in the wind. She slinked forward, getting closer and closer to the noise, until she was crawling on a concrete platform that overlooked a sunken walkway between decrepit gun positions, the cement split with weeds. She saw a light and flattened on the ground like a snake.

She heard a noise and began slithering forward. She reached the edge and peeked over. In the pit, she saw the Caucasian, along with the two black men. She recognized one as her target.

The Caucasian said, "Here's what you want. You and your buddy."

He held something in his hand, and she saw the first black man extend his arm. The Caucasian said, "Before you get paid, who have you told about what we're doing? Who knows about the warehouse?"

"Nobody, man. You asked for the warehouse, and that's all I did."

"You saw the contents. I know you did, and that was a mistake. Not your mistake, but it was a mistake either way. Did you tell anyone?"

"Nobody. I don't tell nobody."

The other man said, "Hey, what the hell are you guys doing? Let's get the juice going. I don't got long. I got to get back."

The Caucasian said, "Just a minute. One more minute."

Shoshana realized by his accent that he wasn't American. He was from somewhere else. Eastern Europe?

The man from the shantytown said, "Fuck that, bruh. I sold you the shit. The discount was that I get some. Let's use it."

"I paid you. Wait a minute."

The man rolled over and said, "I'm not waiting." He reached for the box between them, and the Caucasian pinned his hand to the concrete, saying, "That's not for you. It's for us."

Shoshana's target said, "What the fuck you doin', man?"

The Caucasian reached up with his giant paw, placed it against the drug dealer's head, and slammed it into the concrete. The man screamed and rolled away, holding his skull. The target jerked upright, now afraid, saying, "Whoa, whoa, man, no reason to get violent."

The Caucasian said, "Sit down. Now."

The man did. The Caucasian said, "I need to know. Who did you tell about the shipment?"

"Nobody. I told you, I didn't tell nobody."

The target's brow began to leak sweat, and the Caucasian broke open the box between them. Shoshana saw a needle. She thought he was about to threaten the man but then saw his eyes open wide in anticipation. The Caucasian said, "You want to taste this? Yes?"

"Yes. Please. I did what you asked. You owe me payment."

"Tell me who you talked to, you dumb fuck."

"I told you. I only talked to the guy in Durban. The one who helped with the Israeli? He's cool. Come on, man. He's cool. You know that."

Shoshana felt a bolt of electricity go through her. It was all she could do not to leap down into the pit.

The Caucasian said, "Yeah, he's cool. I'm going to see him tomorrow anyway. Hold out your arm."

The target did, and the Caucasian injected the dope into his veins, watching the man's eyes. He relaxed, sagging into the concrete, and the Caucasian turned to the other. He said, "Your turn."

The dope seller, still holding his head in pain, realized he was in trouble. But not nearly quick enough to prevent the outcome. He tried to stand, but the Caucasian caught him, flipping him over onto his stomach, the man's arms flailing about ineffectually. The Caucasian reached under his chin and snapped his neck like he was cleaning a chicken.

The target saw the action, now caught in the embrace of the drugs. He struggled upright, saying, "What you doing?"

The Caucasian said, "Ridding the world of vermin."

Stupidly, the target said, "What?"

The Caucasian sprinkled the grounds with drug paraphernalia, then said, "Enjoy your last high."

He spit on the ground, then jogged away, running up the stairs, taking them two at a time. Shoshana flattened, and he went by her without even realizing she existed. He disappeared, and she looked back over the wall. The black man mumbled, "What dat mean? What you doing?"

Shoshana realized he'd just killed the target with an overdose. She glanced back, making sure the man was gone, then leapt down into the pit. She checked the first man, finding him dead. She went to the second, seeing him sagging backward, his eyes lidded. She raised him up, and he sluggishly responded. She patted his face and said, "What man in Durban? Who is the man in Durban?"

"Wha . . . who are you . . ."

She slapped him, hard, saying, "Who is the man in Durban?"

"Eshan? My friend Eshan? He's my bruh . . . he's . . . ," and he passed out. Shoshana jerked him upright again, saying, "Don't go, motherfucker. Don't go. Who is Eshan? Wake the fuck up."

His eyes fluttered, and he fumbled at his waist, saying, "He's my bro . . . I call him . . . he knows me . . . we didn't do anything . . ."

She slapped his hand away, digging into a pocket and pulling out a cell phone. She powered it up, seeing a password screen. She held it in front of his face and saw he was slowly losing his grip on reality. She slapped his face again and said, "Open this. Show me Eshan."

He brightened for a moment, saying, "You'll get him here?" His words were so slurred she barely understood him.

She said, "Yes. Unlock the phone. I'll get him here."

He sat upright, a small bit of drool forming on his lips. He focused on the phone for a full ten seconds, Shoshana wanting to punch him in frustration. He finally tapped in a sequence of digits. They failed. She bit her lip and said, "Again. Do it again."

He did, and it failed again. She slapped his face and got a response. He jerked upright and said, "You fucking witch . . . you witch . . . ," and began to sag again. She grabbed his hair, shaking his head back and forth, and said, "Do it again."

He tried one more time, and the phone opened. She scrolled through the contacts and found someone named Eshan. She held it up to his face and said, "Is this Eshan from Durban?"

He said, "My bro Eshan . . . he knows I didn't do anything wrong."

She grabbed his shoulders and shook forcefully, saying, "Is this Eshan from Durban?"

His eyes rolled back into his head, and he was gone.

48

★ ★ ★

I tossed more rand than was required onto the table, and we left the bar, both beers still full.

Unfortunately.

I said, "Blood, we're headed your way. What's your location?"

"I'm sitting on the corner across the street from the turn down to the wharf. You'll have to pass by the wharf road, and you'll see me. I'm on some railway ties."

"Got it."

We went up the stairs past the mall, going by the cheesy Ripley's Believe It or Not! exhibit, then cleared the last of the tourist area. We walked past a parking lot, seeing a spit of land going out into the water, the sparse finger of terrain covered in warehouses, forklifts, and gantry cranes. We continued on and I heard a hiss.

I looked to my right and saw Brett curled up like a homeless derelict, in the shelter of an incredibly ugly concrete building.

I went to him, took a knee, and said, "No change?"

"No change. I timed the guy. He takes ten minutes to go down and come back. He starts on one side and returns on the other, and he just went down the front, so you've got about five minutes to get in and get out."

I nodded and said, "Other surveillance?"

"Four cameras, all on the corners. You leave here and go wide, you'll miss the one on this side. The other one already caught you walking up, though."

The warehouse in question was the second to the last on the finger of land jutting out into the harbor. There were six of them, and each had no internal security. The security apparatus was dedicated to the entire warehouse facility. The first camera didn't concern me, because it caught everyone walking on the quay. The second, on the other hand, would confirm the first, if looked at after the fact.

I said, "Jenn, you lock down the water side; Brett, you lock down the land side."

They both nodded, and I said, "Showtime, but remember that the easy missions are the ones that get screwed up. Treat this like we're taking out bin Laden."

We avoided the lens of the far-side camera, then closed in to the wharf, walking down it like we belonged, which we most certainly did not. Pretending to be on a date did no good here, and Jennifer knew it. She put her hand inside her purse, where I knew a nasty little stiletto resided, and I said, "No lethal here."

She said, "I know, but it's a pretty good intimidator."

We passed by the various warehouses and reached our target, a rolling door with a side entrance, a lone bulb illuminating the lock. I nodded at Jennifer, and she continued on, reaching the corner of the warehouse row and taking a knee.

I turned my attention to the lock, pulling out Shoshana's 3-D key, a bit of solidified plastic with a blob on one end sticking out from the blade. It looked like something a child had made dripping mud on a beach, but the end result mirrored the lock face. At least I knew it would pass through the keyset.

I inserted it slowly, not wanting to cause a jam. It went all the way in, the unique sleeve for the secure feature of the lock defeated. I felt it seat and glanced down the wharf, seeing Jennifer scanning the area. She flicked her eyes to me, and I nodded, letting her know we were game on.

I withdrew the key about an eighth of an inch, pulled a small rubber mallet from the cargo pocket of my pants, then tapped the key, twisting as soon as it seated. The lock refused to move.

I took a breath, slid the key out again, and tapped once more, this time harder. No result. I knew I wasn't hitting it hard enough, but I was worried about the strength of the key because it was really nothing more than layered plastic.

Brett came over my earpiece, saying, "Are you fucking with me? You've got less than three minutes to get inside. I *do not* want to go physical here."

I said, "I'm working the problem. The lock isn't releasing."

"Well, get it to release or back off. You've got two minutes and counting."

I hammered the key again, harder than I should have, and twisted. I felt the key break inside the lock but also felt the lock turn free. I said, "I'm in."

I entered the room, the darkness overpowering, but I could feel the space inside. I closed the door and pulled out a SureFire tactical flashlight. It blazed into existence, and I began stabbing the gloom with the sharp blade of light. I saw crate after crate of munitions, a veritable backlot on the set from an eighties action movie. I pulled out my phone and began recording, getting everything I saw in digits.

I cracked open one of the crates, seeing a Sig Sauer MCX assault rifle. A *true* assault rifle, with the ability to selective fire between full automatic and single shot. A weapon that was made to achieve dominance, and not in a cheap way. I took a picture of the serial number and went further, looking for anything that smacked of nuclear devices.

I found MC-4 parachutes, Belgian mini-grenades, door-breaching charges, and a ton of ammunition, but no indication that any of it had anything to do with nuclear weapons.

Like I expected.

I was about to tell the team I was coming out, when Jennifer came on: "Pike, Pike, this is Koko. There's a group of three headed your way."

I said, "To me? Coming to me?"

"I don't know, but I think you tripped an alarm. The key wasn't the only protection. They're moving with a purpose. They just passed me. You've got about thirty seconds to get out, but you can't come out the way you went in. Find another way, on the other side."

Holy shit.

I ran to the far side, the dockside, looking for an escape. I found another rollup gate but nothing that would give me easy access to the walkway outside. There was no regular door on the dock front. I said, "I got nothing in here. Can you interdict?"

Brett came on, saying, "I see them, and they're not out for a stroll. They're definitely on a mission."

I jerked the rollup door, getting no movement. It was locked tight, and even if it was the same key, mine was broken off inside the original door.

I heard the men outside the door and grabbed a steel support beam, shimmying up it and launching myself higher, into the rafters. I balanced on a beam, then slid to the rear, pinning myself against the wall.

They entered, flashlights spraying all over the place, but none up top. They wandered around a little bit, then began to leave. I heard one say something about a faulty alarm, and I hung tight, breathing a sigh of relief. Another said, "That jammed lock wasn't faulty. Something's going on. Someone was in here and might still be. Let's search it for real. Find the lights to this place."

Christ.

They stumbled around a bit, but nobody could seem to find the switch that would turn on the illumination. I knew they'd eventually locate me, with or without the overhead lights. I clicked my earpiece three times, the code for *in trouble, need help now.* Jennifer came back on, whispering, "I'm right outside. The walkway is clear. If I do something, it's got to be contained inside. You want me to penetrate?"

Brett said, "Stop, stop. Do nothing. There's a cop car next to me, and it's not a rent-a-cop one. It's real."

The men gave up on the light switch and began searching in earnest, all flashing their beams into every nook and cranny of the small warehouse, and occasionally shining them up. They went to the far side, and I took the moment to actually talk.

I whispered, "Koko, go to Blood. Get out of the blast radius."

"What about you?"

"Don't worry about me."

"What? No way. I'm coming in."

I hissed, "Get your fucking ass out of here, now."

She said, "What are you going to do?"

"Play a little *Splinter Cell*."

"What's that mean?"

Brett got it immediately. He said, "Koko, come to me. Exfil now."

She said, "I'm coming, I'm coming. What about Pike?"

The men came back toward my location, stabbing the darkness with their beams of light. I sized them up. There were three of them; two looked in shape, and one had a gut that was over his belt by about a foot. *Probably the guy in charge.*

On the net, Brett said, "He'll be just fine. You ever play the video game *Splinter Cell*?"

I heard her huffing as she ran. "What the hell are you talking about?"

The men came directly below me.

Brett said, "Trust me, Pike's better than Sam Fisher. If he called it, he'll be fine."

And I dropped from the ceiling, landing on top of Fat Man, driving him into the ground.

The other two whirled toward me, their lights flashing like laser beams, stabbing all over the place, trying to find the essence of the violence in their midst.

I snatched the light of the closest man before it highlighted me, seemingly out of thin air for the target who held it, and punched him straight in the throat, causing him to collapse, rolling on the floor and gasping with guttural spurts.

I turned to the other man, who was now whipping his light around like he was schizophrenic, desperately trying to find the threat. I trapped the hand holding it, letting him know he'd found the bogeyman, and he freaked out, thrashing like a madman. He swung a hard left, and I ducked under it, still holding his hand, his body rotating from the blow. I swung around, jerking his hand up behind his back, then launched forward, snapping the gristle in his shoulder and driving him into the ground. He screamed and hit the concrete, softening the fall with his forehead. He quit fighting.

I stood up, then checked each man, making sure they were breathing. The one I'd punched in the throat was rasping and rolling on the ground, but he'd live. The other two were out cold. I ran to the door, knelt down, and cracked it open, whispering, "I'm coming out. Am I clear?"

Brett said, "Clear. I say again, clear."

I exited, took one look around the wharf, then sprinted back to Brett's location, finding Jennifer with wide eyes, amazed I was walking free.

I said, "Time to go."

Brett started walking toward the pedestrian bridge, saying, "I guess that went okay."

I took Jennifer's hand, trying to blend in again, saying, "Sam Fisher would have been proud. All I was missing was a sticky cam."

Jennifer said, "How did you get out?"

I said, "Play the game."

49

★ ★ ★

We met back in my suite to convene a short war council prior to contacting the Taskforce. Earlier, before we'd penetrated the warehouse, I'd sent transcripts of the conversation at the castle, and Kurt had told me he'd wait at the office for a final report. It was closing in on four A.M. in Cape Town, which meant it was only nine P.M. in Washington. Kurt would definitely still be there.

I heard a knock on my door, and Jennifer let in Brett. He looked around and said, "Where's the psycho?"

"Still out. Haven't heard from her."

He pursed his lips but remained quiet. I said, "She's fine. She'll be back."

He said, "What are we going to tell Kurt? What's your preferred course of action?"

"I want to take that fucker down. They're training for a free-fall operation, and we just saw a stockpile of weapons in a warehouse secured by Tyler Malloy. There's some nefarious shit going on here."

"You know that's not going to be enough. 'Nefarious shit' doesn't rise to the level of Taskforce involvement. It's got to be related to terrorism, not to African shenanigans."

"Tyler's payment for all this is something bad, and he's going to sell that to someone who's not in America's best interests. They mentioned Project Circle."

Brett nodded and said, "Hey, I agree with you, and if I was still working for the CIA, I'd work an angle to take him out as a threat against US interests, but I'm now with the Taskforce, and we have limits. We do terrorism, not all-source threats."

I said, "Well, let's see what those limits are." I nodded to Jennifer and said, "Get us online with the Taskforce."

She manipulated the laptop; we heard a bunch of bleating and beeps and then saw some staff guy on the screen. Jennifer said, "Can you hear me?"

He said, "Yes. Go."

"This is Prometheus Pike. We have a scheduled contact with the CEO of Blaisdell Consulting."

He nodded and said, "I'm not sure he's here. He might be at dinner."

Jennifer said, "No dinner needed. We're secure."

He smiled and said, "Roger that. Stand by. I'll go find him."

That exchange was a dance to make sure we weren't under duress. If Jennifer had said, "Okay, well . . . call us back" or "How long should we wait?" or anything else, the guy would know she was calling with a gun to her head. "No dinner needed" was the response that released him.

We sat around, staring at the walls, waiting on him to find Kurt, and then heard a knock on the door. Brett went to it and then glanced back at me with a smile. He opened the door, and Shoshana entered, fired up. She was wired and blasting sparks.

She came right to me, held out a phone, and said, "We need to go to Durban. Today."

I said, "Whoa, whoa, what's up?"

"Some Eastern European guy assassinated the man I was going to question. Killed him with an overdose of heroin, but they talked beforehand. My target mentioned Aaron. His friend in Durban was the man who coordinated for the safe house Aaron was . . . was interrogated in."

She could barely say the final part. I glanced at the computer screen, but it was still blank. This was the worst time to talk to her, as I had seconds before I had to talk to Kurt. I said, "Okay, okay. We're on with the Taskforce here shortly."

"Pike, that guy is going to Durban to kill the contact. I don't know who that European is, but he's cleaning house. We're going to lose the thread."

I said, "What did this guy look like?" She described him, and I knew it was Stanko. Now Tyler was deeply, deeply involved in whatever was going on. He wasn't just providing arms. He was killing to protect the sale.

She held out the phone and said, "I have the contact's number. A man named Eshan. The European said he was going to meet him today. And that means he's going to kill him."

Which introduced a little bit of pressure. If it was real. I said, "Why do you believe that?"

"Because he killed the target I was after. Not only that, he killed the man who provided them the heroin. He murdered them both, then planted evidence around them to cause the police to look at a drug crime. It wasn't a snap decision. It was planned. He's going to kill the man in Durban, and when he does, we'll lose Aaron."

I nodded, absorbing the information. She walked to me and took my hand, forcing the phone into it. She said, "That's the guy's number. Get the Taskforce to track it. We need to beat him to the target."

I started to say something, knowing that tracking the phone wasn't in the cards, and she said, "Please. For me."

I squeezed her hand and said, "Shoshana, I'm with you. I am. But if I can get Omega for Tyler Malloy, we're at jackpot. Let me work Kurt instead of chasing a local thread. We squeeze Tyler's ass and we have it all."

She said, "If you get permission, if you do this, will you continue? Once you take Tyler down, you have no reason. The mission will be over."

The computer bleeped, and I heard, "Jennifer, good to see you. What did you find in the warehouse?"

She said, "I'll let Pike do the talking."

I ignored the discussion, focusing on Shoshana. I said, "Yes. I will, even if it means me doing it alone."

Jennifer scooted out of the seat, and I sat down, my game face on. Kurt said, "Well, from that expression, there must be some wicked shit going on. What's up?"

I knew I had to go full bore if I had any chance of getting authority. I said, "Sir, you got the transcript, right?"

"Yeah, but there's not a whole lot in it that would constitute Omega authority. We can pass the information to the appropriate law enforcement agencies, but it doesn't look like a Taskforce problem."

I said, "Sir, I just came back from the warehouse. It's full of top-notch weapons and explosives from all over the world. These guys are planning an invasion of something. They're going to assault somewhere on the African continent, and that's going to upend whatever US interests are involved."

"Pike, all we have is a transcript about weapons. Tyler sells weapons. It's like making a case that a mechanic is selling drugs because he's talking about repairing cars."

"Sir, come on! They talked about a HALO operation. They talked about training people. It was much more than a single sale of weapons."

"I hear you, but it's still not a Taskforce problem."

I said, "Hang on. I have a photo of one of the weapons. Can you track it?"

"Yeah, sure."

I transmitted the picture of the Sig MCX and said, "See where that thing was supposed to go, because I guarantee it wasn't here."

He said something to the man behind him, then returned to the screen. He said, "What do you want to do?"

"Take Tyler's ass out. He has information that might be pertinent."

He said, "Pertinent."

I said, "Yes, sir. Pertinent."

"Meaning he knows where Aaron is?"

Shoshana leapt out of her seat, and Jennifer just about tackled her to keep her offscreen. I said, "Why would you ask that?"

"Don't fuck with me, Pike. I know why you're pressing, and it isn't because of some threat to America."

I raised my voice, saying, "It's the same damn thing. Aaron was searching for something bad, and he found it. We were searching for something bad from a different angle, and *we* found it."

"So do you want to stop the bad or find Aaron?"

"I just gave you my answer. It's the same thing."

He said, "Pike, I'd really like to turn you loose, but I can't. I have to brief the Oversight Council tomorrow to get authority, and you have to *give* me something."

I said, "Sir, they mentioned Project Circle. Did you see that? It's the reason you put me on this wild-goose chase."

Honestly, before this adventure, I'd had no idea what Project Circle was, but after we'd heard the tape from the laser recording, I'd turned Jennifer loose on a computer.

He said, "Yeah, I did. And you did exactly what I wanted in Vegas. Look, you've accomplished your mission. You've cracked open that asshole's complicity. Now our job is over. It's not terrorism. It's State Department sanctions and FBI arrests. It's not Taskforce. Trust me, he's not going to get away with anything. Time to come home."

I said, "Sir, really? These guys are about to do something bad. Surely you can see that?"

He said, "My target is Tyler, and until you get me something I can use, he remains with Alpha authority. The rest isn't terrorism. The most I can do is feed your intelligence into the system."

I nodded, thinking. He said, "What's going through that bullet head?"

"You brief tomorrow, right?"

"Yeah."

"And we still have Alpha to explore? To find terrorism connections?"

He hesitated, then said, "Yeah, that's right. Why?"

"You remember that guy you made me follow in Las Vegas? The one without Oversight Council sanction?"

I said that for a reason, just in case he was going to tell me no. And by his expression, he knew it too.

"Yes. Stanko Petrov."

"He's headed to Durban tomorrow. I'd like to follow him to explore. Just see what he's doing."

He slit his eyes and said, "What's he up to?"

Innocently, I said, "I don't know. That's why I want to go. He's apparently meeting a local national up there, and I have that guy's number."

"What do you want from me?"

"I want NSA collection on that handset. Find out what he says and give me an anchor to continue Alpha."

He leaned back and said, "Pike, I don't know about that. There's a lot of friction around such a thing."

"Come on, sir, there aren't any 702 or FISA restrictions here. They can do it. We're not talking about infringing on anyone's rights. It's two foreigners talking about criminal shit on foreign soil. No Americans involved."

When the Taskforce had been created, it was done with the effort of streamlining our counterterrorism ability without duplicating other capabilities, and—because we were basically illegal—without the ability to start some Gestapo surveillance effort in the United

States. The end state was that the Taskforce was given authority to geolocate handset information through electronic signature but was forbidden from developing the ability to actively collect on what was said on those phones.

For that, we relied on the NSA, but in order to do that, we had to work through a labyrinth of cutouts to get the request into the beast in such a manner that they would collect without realizing who was requesting the information. Given all the misguided hysteria of collection on US persons with 702 and FISA, it had become a pain in the ass.

Kurt said, "But you're asking to circumvent FISA and 702 by default. Your immediate targets are foreign, but your actual target is American. I don't know if I can sell that. The Oversight Council will see right through it."

I leaned forward and played my trump card. "You don't have to go to the Oversight Council. They've already approved Alpha. All you have to do is get it in the system."

"But the problem remains. We're twisting the system to track an American."

I said, "Cut the crap, sir. I'm asking you to track this guy so I can crack open enough information to prevent an asshole American from getting nuclear triggers to sell to terrorists. You know it and I know it. I'm not going to start asking to listen in to Aunt Polly's phone conversations."

He exhaled, and I dropped the hammer. The one he should have never given me. "Sir, it's no different from tracking a guy in Las Vegas without Oversight Council sanction. What was it you said? 'But he's not American, so it's legal.' You knew that was bullshit when you ordered it. But you did it because you thought you were right. Don't go wrong now. It's the same fucker you had me track in Vegas. The same one. I'm on the thread. Let me get it done."

He sat for a moment, looking at the screen. His setup was a little more professional than mine. I could see him fully in his chair, but

I'm sure what he saw from his vantage point was a forehead and two glaring eyeballs.

He shook his head and said, "Is Shoshana there?"

She stood up again, and I flicked my hand behind my back. I said, "No? Why do you ask that?"

"Don't fuck with me, Pike. Don't twist what you're doing."

I said, "Because we don't do that, right? What happens in Vegas stays in Vegas."

"What's that mean?"

"You have a mission you can't get approved, you send me. I have a mission I can't get approved, I call you." I leaned back from the screen and said, "It's known as keeping America safe, and it's worked out pretty well. You trusted me in Vegas, and I'm trusting you now."

He laughed, a real thing that permeated the weak VPN connection.

We sat for a second, saying nothing, Shoshana as taut as a trip wire. He said, "Okay, Pike. I'll get your collection. Just this once."

I showed no emotion on my face, but inside, I was doing a happy dance. I said, "Thank you, sir."

He said, "Tell Shoshana she owes me."

I said, "What's that mean?"

He reached forward with his hand and said, "You know what I mean." And cut the feed.

I turned to the room, about to give out instructions, and Shoshana stood, vibrating like a piano wire. She said, "I won't forget this, Nephilim. Ever."

I chuckled and said, "Yeah, right up until I give you an order."

She walked to me, leaned over, and kissed my forehead, the action shocking the hell out of not only me but both Jennifer and Brett.

She drew her hand across my cheek and said, "No. I will *never* forget. My life is now yours."

She floated her weird gaze on me, and then she left the room.

It took a second to even realize she was gone, my mind focused on her disconcerting stare. I turned to Jennifer and said, "What the hell was that? What did she mean?"

Jennifer's mouth opened and closed, trying to find something to say. She settled with, "I don't know. Maybe she's truly sweet on you."

Brett said, "Better him than me, because she's flat-out scary."

51

At five hundred feet, Johan worked the toggles of his parachute, turning into the final upwind segment of his flight pattern. He maintained his distance from the parachute below him and saw the man behind him doing the same.

So far, the team Armstrong had built had shown martial skill in both individual abilities and team dynamics, and the aircrew Tyler had provided proved they could plan and execute a jump run. All in all, Johan was gaining confidence in the mission.

He saw the lead jumper touch down, and then, like dominoes, the ones behind him, until Johan was flaring his own chute. He hit the ground, ran off his speed, then rotated to collapse his chute, watching the remaining members of the team land, all within half of a football field. It would be a greater diameter at night but was still much smaller than the plateau where he'd placed the beacon.

He half-hitched the lines of his parachute, gathered the canopy, and walked to the trucks in the middle of the drop zone, finding Colonel Armstrong sitting on one of the trucks' beds.

Armstrong said, "Looked good."

Johan nodded, saying, "Yeah. Only two jumps and we're tracking fine. The men are experienced."

Armstrong smiled and said, "I told you not to worry."

Johan shucked his parachute harness, letting it fall to the ground. "We'll see tonight. You have the drivers, right?"

Tonight was to be a full dress rehearsal, using the same type of beacon he'd placed on the plateau and the very drivers who would meet them on the ground. They would simulate as much of the same conditions as they could, doing a blind drop that Johan had set up earlier in the day, briefing the pilots the same way he would for the infiltration, and testing whether the drivers could find the drop zone and recover the jumpers.

Armstrong said, "I have the lead driver. We'll have to substitute for the others."

"Sir, why? Jesus, you know how critical the infiltration is. I need them all here."

"There are issues getting them out of the military base. The drivers aren't just privates. I thought it better to get the team leaders here. General Mosebo wasn't willing to let every officer of his Special Forces leave. It would raise questions, and . . . he's fucking paranoid. You'll need to work with that."

"What's that mean?"

"He thinks everyone is out to get him. He doesn't trust his own men, so he definitely won't trust you."

"Fucking great."

"It won't matter. He's going to hide during the entire thing. He's not brave enough to take charge of the operation. You probably won't even see him until it's over. Anyway, a month ago he planned a cover trip for seven to 'visit South African Special Forces,' something that now looks natural and would be odd to change. I thought you'd want the six team leaders instead of splitting that in half with drivers."

Johan slowly nodded, then said, "Getting on the ground is critical. We fuck that up and nothing else matters."

"You'll have the lead driver. It'll work out."

Johan said, "I guess we'll see tonight."

"Have you decided on assignments for our guys?"

"Yeah. My team's taking the television station."

Armstrong squinted his eyes and said, "That's the easiest target. I figured you'd be on the prime minister. He's the center of gravity."

Johan said, "I need to be able to control the overall operation. It's centrally located to all the other objectives, and I won't get tied down in a gunfight. I can flex as a reserve if I need to. Someone's got to be the ground-force commander, and with you staying airborne, that leaves me."

Armstrong nodded and said, "Okay, okay. I wasn't implying anything. What did you give Andy?"

Johan smiled and said, "He's got the police station. Toughest target."

Armstrong nodded and said, "He'll like that. So you're prepared to go tomorrow night?"

"Barring some disaster at tonight's rehearsal, or something catastrophic at our planning session with the African SF guys, yeah, we will. Are we good on the safe house in Lesotho? I don't want to land and be asked where I want to go."

Armstrong laughed and said, "Yeah, we're good. Tyler got us a compound. Some bed-and-breakfast with five rooms. We own it all."

"A bed-and-breakfast? You're kidding me."

"No, it's some rustic place out near the king's residence. A village called Morija."

"The king? Are you serious? You're putting us near that sort of security?"

"He lives about seven kilometers away, in another town. It's through the mountains, and it's rustic. Trust me, there won't be a threat. It's better than a hotel in the city. At least you can plan, out in the mountains."

"What do we do if he tries to stop us? I don't mean tactically, like we run into his security. I mean strategically, like he comes out against us before we consolidate control. The people love him."

"He's not allowed to. It's in their constitution. The king can't interfere with the government. We saw that in 2014, with the half coup that started this whole mess. He sat on the sidelines the entire time, letting the ministers of parliament and the military sort it out. All he's going to want is peace, and he'll get it with your operation. In twenty-four hours it'll be over, and he'll stay at the residence the entire time, with his men on high alert to protect him. He's not going to venture out to stop anything, and when it's over, he'll see the writing on the wall. He'll state the coup was for the best, and something like 'why can't we just get along?' The people *do* love him, and that's going to work in our favor."

Johan said, "I hope you're right."

Armstrong said, "I am. I've put a lot of work into this."

Johan nodded, saying, "Tyler got the safe house? We couldn't get it on our own?"

"He was offering the total package, and he's operated on the continent quite a bit. Why would I want to sacrifice profits doing the work ourselves?"

"Because it means less chance of something getting fucked up, that's why. You trust him that much?"

"I trust his greed. He wants to get paid, and he won't screw anything up before that occurs."

"Yeah, you keep mentioning that he's fronting this whole thing, so what's he getting out of it? It's not money. Cohen's paying us flat cash, but he isn't for Tyler, or he wouldn't be donating all this shit for free."

Armstrong saw the men coming off the drop zone and said, "I told you, it's not your concern. Time to get busy. The Lesotho men are waiting in the barracks."

Before Johan could question him again, Armstrong shouted, "Andy, I saw that ass slide! Not what I remember from the Recces."

Andy jogged up and laughed, saying, "I wanted to get closest to the mark. Didn't work out."

He slapped Johan on the arm and said, "Still trying to beat this guy."

Armstrong smiled, saying, "Everyone's been trying to beat Johan for years."

Johan did not return the smile. He said, "But I always come out on top." He looked at Armstrong, thinking about his reluctance to discuss Tyler's payment. He didn't like being kept in the dark. It smacked of being used.

He said, "Don't I, Colonel?"

Armstrong hooded his eyes, and Johan turned to Andy, saying, "Load up the men. We've got some planning to do with the locals."

52

★ ★ ★

I was afraid the plastic chair I was in was going to break, which would definitely draw attention to me. That would be fine if I was trying to win some money on a reality television show, but it was decidedly the last thing I needed here. I hopped one chair over and scooted my bowl of gruel to me. Something called "bunny chow," it was basically a hollowed-out piece of bread full of bean curry and mutton. It looked as gross as hell but was actually pretty tasty.

I heard Brett on the radio: "Gaining a little weight there, commando?"

"No. The chair was split on one side. Anyone heavier than a five-year-old is risking an adventure."

Shoshana broke in: "Maybe you should skip the bowl of fat."

I said, "Enough about the food. Do we have three-sixty coverage of this place now?"

The café itself had no walls but was situated in the middle of the market, with tables and chairs like a food court in an American mall or airport.

Brett said, "I've got the entrance and the northern side."

Shoshana said, "Koko and I have the south blocked and can see clean through to the northern entrance."

I said, "Okay, I've got the west and can also see through to the east, so the surveillance is good. All that's open is an east exit."

Shoshana said, "You want Koko and me to split up?"

"No. Not with the threat readout Koko gave us. Stay in place together. Someone accosting either of you will only bring trouble. We'll sort it out with what we've got."

We'd caught a nine A.M. flight out of Cape Town to Durban, packing everything we had and hastily finding hotel rooms in the new city. We knew Stanko was flying as well but had no idea how. He could have beaten us using a private aircraft—which Tyler was more than able to pay for—or he could have ended up on our flight.

He wasn't, but with upward of seven flights a day, it could have been at any time.

We'd landed, rented a couple of Land Rovers, checked in to our hotel, and contacted the Taskforce—and they had news.

Stanko had talked to Eshan and had set up a meeting with him at four P.M. today, at a restaurant called the Queen Victoria Gourmet Café, in the heart of something called the Victoria Street Market.

The conversation was strained, even reading it in black-and-white from a transcript, with Eshan wanting a public meeting and Stanko demanding privacy. It told me Eshan wasn't as stupid as the other target Stanko had killed. This one knew the danger of working his side of the fence.

Stanko had threatened withholding payment, and Eshan had countered by questioning why he was afraid to meet publicly, which deflated Stanko's argument. There was no reason not to, if all you were going to do was pay for services rendered. Stanko had relented and said he was on the way, landing at three, which meant he left after us, because it was only a two-hour flight.

Jennifer had done her due diligence with research, something she was a little bit of a freak at, and had learned that the Victoria Street Market was an enormous rat warren of Indian immigrants selling everything from spices to African masks, all under one gigantic roof. It turned out that Durban had the largest Indian population of any city on earth—outside of India—and way back when, they'd built this market when they'd been excluded from the city center because of their heritage.

In the modern world it had blossomed into no less than nine different markets, spanning city blocks, at a place called Warwick

Junction, and had become both a local place to shop and a tourist stop—if you were in a group with a guide.

According to Jennifer, crime was rampant, and single females were easy prey. Jennifer said predators loved the place and it was routinely rated as unsafe, with pickpockets and worse prowling around, which was why I'd had Jennifer and Shoshana pair up.

Our females weren't, of course, easy prey, but I couldn't afford either of them becoming involved with teaching a pickpocket that his chosen choice of employment held significant risks, which meant I either paired them up with Brett and me, leaving me a team short, or I paired them together.

I opted for the latter, figuring Shoshana's glare would scare the hell out of anyone thinking of attempting anything.

We'd entered the market at 1530, giving us thirty minutes of leeway, and found it just as advertised: narrow alleys lined with stalls, all selling seemingly the same cheap-ass tourist knickknacks.

We'd split up, searching for the café, and Brett had found it, then vectored us in. Now I was eating a bowl of bunny food as we waited, checking out everyone who entered.

I'd almost finished my bread bowl when Brett came on, saying, "Ivan's in the net, I say again, Ivan's in the net. Northern entrance. Just went by me."

Stanko was the only target we had whom we could recognize, so he was key to locating the contact. I casually turned my head and saw him enter, still dressed uncomfortably like a shady businessman, although with that usual Eastern European "Boris" vibe. The only thing he needed to complete the vision was a fedora and an overcoat with the collar turned up.

He sat in the center of the café, not bothering to order anything from the counter, his head constantly swiveling around. Eventually, a man who had been at the café before we'd entered stood up, surprising me. An Indian guy, tall and thin, with a gangly walk that reminded me of a stork. I'd assumed the contact would be African.

He settled in to the table, and I clicked on the net, saying, "Target seated. Acknowledge."

I got a couple of "Rogers" and said, "Anyone with a camera angle?"

Jennifer said, "I got it. Clean view."

I kept my eye on the meeting, saying, "Okay, when this breaks up, we follow Mowgli. Let Ivan go."

Brett said, "This naming convention is becoming borderline inappropriate."

I said, "Well, we're in the business of being inappropriate."

I watched them talk, then saw the conversation get animated, with Mowgli leaning forward and waving his arms around. Clearly, he wasn't happy.

Shoshana came on, saying, "I think Ivan's trying to get him to leave. He didn't bring the money."

I said, "I think you're right. Get ready."

Eventually, Mowgli nodded, and Stanko leaned back, saying something. They both rose and left. To the fucking east.

I said, "Get on them. Get on them. I can't get there."

Shoshana said, "We have them. They're entering the market."

Brett said, "I'm one row over."

I stood and ran to the far side, saying, "He isn't going to pay; he's looking for a place to kill that guy. Don't give him any space."

I heard Shoshana say, "I've lost him. I've lost him," then: "Pike, this is Koko. I'm breaking off. Going parallel."

I said, "Roger that. Everyone, we're okay, we're okay. He isn't going to murder him in the mall."

Brett said, "Pike, there are plenty of places in here to kill the guy."

Which was true. I said, "Anyone have eyes on?"

I got nothing back.

53

★ ★ ★

Kurt Hale walked up the steps of the Old Executive Office Building with George Wolffe, his deputy commander. Fresh off of leave, Wolffe was wondering what shit storm he was entering. He said, "So, you've got Pike chasing a thread that has nothing to do with terrorism, but you think it does? Is that what you're going to brief?"

Kurt said, "Yep."

"And he's been freelancing all over Africa based on your actions in Las Vegas? Do I have that right?"

"Pretty much."

George said, "Why the hell do I *ever* go on leave? Every time I do, you dig us into a shit sandwich."

Kurt opened the door and smiled, saying, "This time, we have the intel community on our side."

"What does that mean?"

"It means I might just be right for once."

They walked to the room chosen for the Oversight Council meeting—which changed every single time they met, a product of being off the books—and turned in their cell phones. They entered a small conference room, seeing the usual suspects gathered around. Secretary of state, secretary of defense, director of the CIA, and all the other Oversight Council members.

They drew a small murmur when they entered, but nobody approached, not wanting to get tainted with whatever Kurt was going to brief. Talking beforehand might be construed as support. Better to just sit back and wait to see what happened.

Only one man made eye contact with Kurt: Kerry Bostwick, the head of the CIA. He simply nodded, which told Kurt all he needed to know.

Kurt took his seat, shuffling his papers in front of him while George took a seat in the back.

The light above the door flashed, saying it was unclear, and the president entered. The room rose, and he said, "Sit down." He turned to Kurt and said, "I hate to be a broken record, but we need to get this done quickly."

The one thing Kurt liked about President Hannister was that he made an effort to attend every single Oversight Council meeting, unlike his predecessor. The one thing he hated was that every time he did, he demanded the meeting be short because he was trying to cram it in between other state functions. President Warren—the man who'd created the Taskforce—understood the implications of action and attended only when he felt it necessary, which had caused heartburn with Kurt in the past when the Council devolved into a bunch of shouting. President Hannister had decided that he would attend every single one, but in so doing, he forced the meetings into a box that was smaller than necessary for the conversation.

Kurt wasn't sure which approach was better.

He stood and said, "If it's to be quick, then I'll cut to the meat. We need to get Omega authority for Tyler Malloy. He's about to gain nuclear triggers and sell them to a terrorist organization."

Kurt saw the room draw back, all but Kerry Bostwick, his ace in the hole.

President Hannister said, "Last time you briefed, you had a thread in Cape Town. Are you saying it's been proven by Taskforce activity?"

"No, sir. Not by Taskforce. We've continued Alpha—and are still pursuing the same—but we didn't get conclusive proof with our operations. We did, however, get proof from combining intelligence through all-source collection, and we believe the threat is real."

He flashed the first PowerPoint slide, showing the conversation Pike had obtained at the Castle of Good Hope. He said, "As you can see, at a meeting with Tyler Malloy, these men are discussing an assault of some kind. We don't know what the assault is, but we do know, from Pike's penetration of the warehouse, that it's real. They're going to attack something."

He flipped the slide and pointed at the transcript on the screen. "Tyler Malloy is aggravated about not getting paid, and the man in the room—Mr. Smith—describes that he was involved in Project Circle."

He turned back to the room and said, "Project Circle was the South African nuclear program. They built six bombs before they dismantled the entire program, and Tyler Malloy wants something from it."

Alexander Palmer said, "So, what, you want to take him out because of a conversation? It sounds to me like we should be alerting State about this crap, not conducting rendition operations on foreign soil."

Secretary of State Amanda Kroft said, "I'm game with that. We can stop this through diplomatic means. It would take one phone call."

Kurt said, "No, I don't think so. The man known as Mr. Smith is high up in the South African military. We don't know how far this goes. You alert them through diplomatic means and the whole thing falls apart. He'll get away."

She said, "But we stop it."

Kurt said, "For now. I want to stop it forever."

Palmer said, "But you have no proof of anything other than this recording. All you have is a mention of Project Circle. Hell, he could be getting paid in scrap iron for all we know."

Kurt said, "I would agree with you, but we've come upon some corroborating intelligence. Kerry, you want to weigh in?"

The room looked at the D/CIA, and he said, "Sir, in general collection of potential threats, we caught a conversation between Hassan Kantar and an unknown American. Hassan is a known member of Hezbollah, and he's in the pocket of Iran. He's also discussing Project Circle."

He passed around sheets of paper to the group, letting them digest the conversation. He said, "You'll see three key points: One, the UNSUB asks if he's secure, and Hassan talks about being on the 'resistance' communication net, which means Hezbollah. They created their own net after the 2006 war. Two, he has a timeline that's pretty succinct, which is unusual. Why would Lebanon care about a timeline if it were innocuous? They wouldn't, but Iran would. The next JCPOA inspections are due in the upcoming weeks, which is the only reason Hassan would care. Three, Hassan talks about the delay causing a transfer to a country other than Lebanon. A country bordering Iran."

He glanced around the room and said, "The bottom line is that Hassan is up to no good, and we believe he's working with Tyler."

Palmer said, "How do you know that? I mean, how do you know it's Tyler? The name is masked. Why even bring this here without concrete proof?"

Kerry said, "It's not masked. If I could unmask it, I would, but we don't know the far end. We only know he's American because of his voice. They caught this through a Skype conversation. We don't have a name; all we got was an IP address. It ended in Cape Town, South Africa, which is where Tyler was on the day this call was made. It's him."

The group took that in; then President Hannister spoke. "Kurt, what are you asking for here? What do you think is going on?"

Kurt said, "I think Tyler's doing something shitty on the African continent in conjunction with elements of the South African military, and he's getting paid with nuclear components from their Project Circle. In turn, he's going to sell them to Hezbollah, who will pass them to the Iranians. That's what I think."

Palmer said, "That's a bit of a stretch. You're connecting a lot of dots."

Kurt said, "Not really. We haven't collected any intel mentioning Project Circle in close to thirty years, and now we have two hits in the same week? One from a direct Taskforce operation, and another from NSA collection of a known Hezbollah terrorist? No, this isn't fishing. We knew going into this that Tyler Malloy was looking for nuclear triggers, and I think he's found them. Not only that, but he's going to sell them to terrorists in the sway of Iran."

Hannister nodded slowly, then said, "So what do you want?"

"I want Omega authority for Tyler. Let me round him up and bring him home."

Palmer said, "Wait, he's American."

"Sir, with all due respect, I'm sick of that excuse. He's a threat, plain and simple. All I'm talking about is capturing him. Not killing him in a drone strike, and we had no problem doing that with Anwar al-Awlaki."

Palmer looked at President Hannister, deferring to him. Hannister said, "Okay, say I do agree. Pike doesn't have a team there, and the flight alone is close to eighteen hours. How can he do this?"

Kurt cleared his throat, then said, "Well, sir, I've pre-positioned assets on the African continent. I've got the rest of his team working a logistics contract on our base in Djibouti, in the Horn of Africa."

Kurt saw Hannister's expression going cold, bordering on anger, and he quickly said, "Sir, I had to prepare for Pike finding something. They were nothing more than a reserve in case he got in trouble."

"So you weren't setting us up for your preferred course of action?"

Kurt said, "Sir, if I was, I still had to brief here today. They're cleaning the crap out of pipes on our base, working in the engineering section. I wouldn't have sent them to Pike without authority. You say no and they all come home."

Kroft, the secretary of state said, "Who is it?"

"Knuckles and Veep. You met Knuckles the other day. The guy with the long hair."

Kurt saw her memory click, and prayed.

Favorably, she said, "Yes, I remember him." Nothing more, but Kurt hoped it was enough.

Hannister said, "Okay, Kurt, I'll put it to a vote. Omega for this? As weak as it is?"

Ten minutes later, the meeting was breaking up, and George Wolffe sidled his way, saying, "That was close. One vote away from a no. I was surprised the SECSTATE said yes."

Kurt packed up his briefcase and said, "Yeah, I know. Thank the heavens for Knuckles."

Puzzled, George said, "What else did I miss on leave?"

Stanko and the man we called Mowgli had walked through our one blind spot to the east. When I heard no contact from my team, I said, "Okay, we've got a grid search. Start working it methodically, but keep pressing forward. They aren't going to circle around behind us. He left to the east for a reason."

Shoshana came on the net, saying, "The parking garage is to the east. Across the footbridge."

I said, "Who's closest?"

Jennifer said, "This is Koko. I am."

"Go. Get to the footbridge. It's a choke point. Everyone else, keep searching."

Brett said, "This is Blood. I have him, I have him. He's still walking east, and he's got Mowgli's arm in his."

"Where? Where are you?"

I glanced around and knew there was no way Brett could describe anything that would narrow our ability to find them in this maze. Brett said, "I lost visual in the market, but they're still moving east. That's all I can say. Everything looks the same."

Shoshana said, "Pike, Pike, we need to get ahead of them. I'm moving to the bridge."

I said, "Roger that," and began running, slapping hanging silk scarves and pushy vendors out of the way, jumping over produce and cheap souvenirs, the stall owners yelling at me as I passed.

Jennifer came on. "This is Koko. I've got them, I've got the eye. They're at the entrance to the walkway headed to the garage. Ivan is forcing him now."

Shoshana said, "Interdict! Take him out!"

"I can't. I'm on a vantage point for visual, but he's ahead of me. I didn't make it to the bridge." Then: "I lost contact. They're out of view."

"Did they enter the walkway?"

"I don't know. They looked like they intended to, but the walkway's got walls. I couldn't see what they did."

I ran by a stall and saw the footbridge to the far-side parking garage through the wood slats in the rear. I held up, realizing I'd have to run about a quarter mile through the maze to get to it. Or I could just plow through the stall. I did so, ignoring the screaming from the owner, bashing my way through his wares and entering another stall on the far side. I did the same to him, ignoring the products hurled at my back, and reached a maintenance walkway that led to the bridge. I started sprinting, saying, "I'm at the bridge, I'm at the bridge. Who's here with me?"

Shoshana said, "I'm close, I'm close."

Jennifer said, "I'm off. I can't interdict."

Brett said, "I'm three minutes out. I have a route."

Running flat out, I said, "Koko, break off. Get our car. Stage it outside the parking garage. Carrie, close on the target. Blood, lock us down on the bridge. Prevent anyone from interfering."

Brett said, "Got it. You think he's going to kill him in the garage?"

"Yeah, I do."

I reached the footbridge, seeing it was also lined with people selling tourist crap, this time music, with a bunch of stalls full of pirated CDs. I sprinted down it for about fifty meters, then held up, searching. I didn't see my target. But I did see Shoshana, moving with a purpose.

I clicked on. "Carrie, Carrie, do you have eyes on?"

"No. I'm on the bridge and moving to the garage."

Which brought up a decision. Were we ahead of them? Had they somehow slipped behind us? Should I stay here, providing choke point surveillance, and let her go forward, or back her up?

I heard, "Pike, Blood, I'm at the entrance to the bridge. I got nothing."

Which made my decision for me. I said, "Blood, close down the entrance. I'm halfway across and moving forward."

Shoshana said, "I got him, I got him. They're in the garage but not stopping. They're headed to the other side, to another market. The meat and fish one."

The damn place was so huge that there were markets all over the place, sprawling about like fungus. I said, "Okay, okay, stay on them. I'm right behind you."

I crossed the bridge, hit the parking garage, and said, "Carrie, I'm across. Give me a lock-on."

She said, "I'm on the far side of the garage, to the south. Toward the entrance to the meat market. Follow the signs."

I said, "Roger. Coming now."

I saw the arrows for the meat section of the market and began jogging. I got about fifty feet, then heard, "Pike, he's pulling him off-line. He's not going to the meat market. Mowgli's fighting him."

I picked up the pace, saying, "Give me an assessment."

I heard her come through the radio, breathing hard, running toward something, saying, "He picked a corner. Away from everything. He's going to kill our target."

I started sprinting, saying, "Carrie, be sure."

I heard, "I'm fucking sure."

I rounded the first row of cars, searching desperately, then caught movement out of the corner of my eye, away from the walkway, in a dark section of the garage.

It was Stanko, and he had a garrote around Mowgli's throat, the man on his knees, the wire ripping the life out of him. I started sprinting toward them and saw a shape spring onto the hood of a car and launch itself on the pair.

Shoshana.

She hit Stanko on his back, causing the wire to dig deeper. I ran as fast as I could, watching Stanko try to shake her off without the use of his hands.

Shoshana snarled, reached for his face, and plunged her fingers into his eyes, puncturing the orbs and causing him to scream. He released the wire and began thrashing. Mowgli sprang up and ran like a lightning bolt toward the new market.

I dove at him and missed. I rolled upright, flipping my head between his back and Shoshana's fight. I ran to Shoshana. She had Stanko on the ground, him keening like a wounded rabbit, thrashing about uncontrollably, Shoshana ripping him apart. I witnessed the dark angel in all its fury. The blood coating her wrists, she looked at me and hissed, "Catch the target."

I nodded, unsettled by the carnage. I turned and started running, calling Brett on the way. "Blood, Blood, cross the bridge. Go to the meat market. Target's on the loose."

I heard, "On the way."

I ran flat out, trying to find the man, entering another maze of stalls, but this one selling fresh fish and meat instead of African masks and tourist trinkets. I went down one aisle, then heard people shouting an aisle over, from some disturbance. I sprinted to the end and turned the corner, seeing Mowgli running ahead of me. I heard, "I'm across, in the market. Where do you need me?"

I thought, *Holy shit, that guy can run,* but said, "Come straight in. I've got him in sight, and he's slowing. He thinks he's safe. Koko, Koko, status?"

"I've got the Rover and I'm outside."

"Station at the entrance to the meat market."

"Where's that?"

"Fucking find it. Break, break—Carrie, Carrie, status?"

I got nothing and continued following our target.

He slowed to a fast walk, and I did the same. I heard, "Pike, this is Blood. I see you. I see you. Where do you want me?"

"Get ahead of him. One row over."

"Roger that."

I kept on the guy, and he slowed to a walk, breathing hard. I hung back, letting him think he was safe. He glanced to the rear and saw me, and his eyes went wide, convinced I was the bogeyman. Which, of course, I was.

He went batshit, sprinting flat out. I said, "Blood, Blood, I'm compromised. I'm compromised."

The target reached the turn to the nearest aisle, and a form launched itself across a freezer full of crab, hammering the guy at chest height and bringing him to the ground.

I ran up, the people around us all shouting and yelling, Brett on top of the guy as he thrashed on the ground. He punched him in the nose, and the kid screamed, rolling around on the floor protecting his face, his will to fight gone.

I reached them and held up my hands to the crowd, saying, "This man is a pickpocket. He's been stealing for weeks."

Surprisingly, the owners of the stalls began clapping, some trying to kick him. I smiled and said, "Thank you for your help. All we want is for the market to be a place people want to come to."

They cheered, and we hoisted the man to his feet, leading him to the exit.

On the radio, I said, "Koko, tell me you're out front."

"Right outside."

"Roger that. Carrie, Carrie, status?"

"I'll meet you out front."

I didn't want to ask her what had happened to Stanko and was just happy she would make exfil. I looked at Brett as we duckwalked the "perp" out of the market. He said, "If we make it out of here, it's going down in history."

I saw the entrance to the market and said, "Looks like we're making history."

Aaron heard the scurrying outside the makeshift toilet and waited for his signal. He got it, three seconds later. Two clanks of an aluminum cup from Thomas.

He ignored the overpowering odor and stood on the literal bucket of shit, sliding his hand against the walls until he was level with a square window. Well, "window" was a misnomer. It was just a hole in the wall, without any glass or bars.

It was currently too small for a human to fit through, but that was why Aaron was standing on the bucket. The building was cinder block, but the window had a ring of bricks around it, all mortared in a less-than-perfect manner. He began scraping the mortar between the bricks with the handle of a spoon. His purpose was to weaken the mortar so that, when the time came, he could create a hole large enough to escape through by smashing the bricks. And he needed to do it soon, because he had no idea how long the guards would allow the blanket they'd erected to remain.

Their toilet consisted of the stalwart bucket, and using it was enough of an embarrassment that Aaron had feigned erecting the blanket out of modesty, giving the men privacy. The guards hadn't taken it down, and the next day he'd raised it until it covered the opening of the window, then had pulled Thomas aside for a discussion.

Aaron was losing weight and, along with it, the ability to fight. If he was going to escape, he needed to do it earlier rather than later, because he knew getting out of the building was just the first step. But that first step was huge, which meant he needed help. At that night's meal, he'd sat next to Thomas and detailed his plan.

Thomas wasn't convinced, feeling the effort would bring on the ultimate punishment, which he'd thus far avoided. Aaron had pressed, saying, "Your fate is preordained. It's not happened yet, but it will. Do you think sitting here in this cell is getting you favor? They will kill you the minute they think they can. Maybe the reason you've lived this long is simply the fact that they haven't generated the courage. They will, eventually. I promise."

Thomas had said, "I thought you had a friend. Someone who would get us out."

Aaron shook his head and said, "She's out there, I know it, but we have to work for ourselves. Not waiting on some miracle. If she comes, she comes, but we need to plan as if she isn't."

Thomas had agreed, with the caveat that he wouldn't allow any of his tribe to help. They'd only provide early warning. That was good enough for Aaron, and he'd set to work. He'd been at it four times today and was close to getting the first brick weak enough to break free. His primary problem was that he wasn't sure if the uniformed tribe wouldn't see his handiwork and alert the guards to curry favor. Which meant not creating damage that could be found by them when they utilized the bucket. But that also meant that when he finally attacked the bricks he'd worked, he might not have weakened them enough.

A problem for another day. He wasn't near that end point yet. And so he scraped through the next brick's mortar, slowly but surely weakening it until he felt it could be broken free with force.

He pulled out a chunk of mortar and tossed it hard out of the window and into the forest, not wanting anyone passing by to find it, but he didn't worry too much about that. He'd studied what was beyond, and it was woods, with the foliage growing right up against the building, something that would help them escape.

He scraped again and then heard an incessant clanging. He stopped, dropping to the ground. He paused, heard nothing else, and was about to remount the bucket when he heard Lurch screaming in English.

"Where is the Jew? Where is he hiding?"

The sound of prisoners scrambling penetrated the blanket, the men retreating out of range of the sadistic guard's wrath. He pulled the blanket aside while pretending to draw up his pants.

Lurch said, "What is this? You don't feel like you can shit in public? Are we not good enough for you?"

Aaron remained silent. Lurch said, "You won't have to worry about your modesty anymore. My general is back home. We had a discussion about you, and I'm pleased to say that he's going to talk to you tomorrow. So prepare yourself."

Aaron knew that was pure psychology, designed to eat at him. Designed to get him prepared to tell the truth. The nightmares he would conjure in his mind from the threat were to soften him and get him to cave at the first act of violence, before they moved on to whatever he'd developed as a worst-case scenario in his mind. It was psychological warfare, and he'd been in such positions before. The statement was ham-handed. Amateur hour.

Aaron said, "Why hasn't he returned to question me yet? I've been telling all of you that I've done nothing wrong. I demand to speak to my embassy, right now."

An innocuous statement that would be expected from an innocent tourist, but it set Lurch off. He became visibly incensed, and Aaron realized he'd made a mistake. Lurch smacked him on the side of the head hard enough to drive him to the floor, screaming, "You do not make demands! You have no embassy here. You have *nothing*."

Lurch paced around, wanting to hurt Aaron, but something held him back. He returned to Aaron and snatched his head by the hair, jerking it upward. He said, "I was told not to harm you, so I won't. But that's just for today. Tomorrow night, you are *mine*. And I'm going to have your little bitch with me. Maybe I'll use her right in front of you, after I've had my way with *you*."

He flung Aaron to the dirt and stormed out. Thomas reached for Aaron's hand, helping him to his feet. "It's not good to antagonize them."

Aaron rubbed his head and said, "Yeah, I didn't know that before."

Thomas laughed, then turned serious. "You are in significant danger. I feel I must tell you that. General Mosebo is not a man to cross. There will be pain."

Aaron pursed his lips and said, "Or it might be a way out."

"What do you mean?"

"I'm not leaving here without Alexandra, and he's bringing her to the interrogation."

"How does that help?"

"Nothing. Forget I said it. Let's work on the window again. I'm close to creating a hole we can all get through."

Thomas saw the absolute conviction on his face and said, "You truly believe you are leaving here, don't you?"

Aaron smiled and said, "Yes, I am. And I'm bringing you with me. I promise."

I felt my phone vibrate but was afraid to leave Shoshana alone with the target. No telling what she would do. I looked at Jennifer, held up my cell, and glared at her. She nodded.

I exited, looked at the screen, and saw it was the Taskforce. I answered and heard, "Go secure. Calling back in two."

I did as the disembodied voice asked, and the phone rang again. I answered and heard, "Colonel Hale wants to do a VTC right now."

I said, "I'm in the middle of something. Tell him I can't do it. I don't even have a computer here. I'll call him back."

The guy on the other end said, "This is at the request of Colonel Hale. You'll do as you're told."

I grinned, knowing the guy on the other end of the line thought he had absolute power. He believed, because Colonel Hale had told him to call, that he was above the Operator, but he wasn't. I decided to screw with him. I said, "Who the fuck is this? Just so I know when I get back to DC."

I heard a spluttering, then, "I'm just relaying the message, man."

He'd turned human all of a sudden. I chuckled into the phone and said, "Hey, I'm just kidding. Tell Yoda I'll be up in twenty minutes. I'm really in the middle of something."

"Who's Yoda?"

"The man who you told me to call."

He said, "Uhh . . . Roger that . . . I didn't mean anything earlier."

I said, "Hey, don't take it personally. Tell Kurt I'll call back in twenty."

"Will do."

I hung up, patting myself on the back about solving the problems of the Taskforce, and then realized I had to talk to Yoda. Colonel Kurt Hale, and he was most definitely not going to let me continue.

But I was sort of locked in now.

We'd dragged the Indian contact to our Land Rover and had demanded he take us to the safe house where Aaron had been held. He'd done so, completely compliant, willing to answer any question we threw at him, maybe because we'd saved his damn life, but probably because he was a survivor.

We'd interrogated him and learned quite a bit, not the least of which was that he'd seen Aaron being hauled into the house, along with a female. That was enough to turn Shoshana insane. She wanted to skin the guy alive, not so much for further information—he was giving us whatever we asked—but because she was still in a bloodlust. She kept repeating that he was holding back, but I doubted it. Especially since she was standing in front of him with her wrists coated in blood and ocular fluid from the man she'd killed.

We knew that Aaron had been held in this very house. It was the closest we'd come, but he wasn't here now. The Indian told us that he'd been taken from here, along with the woman. Taken to Lesotho. Apparently, there had been a high-ranking member of the Lesotho military at the house, and he'd demanded to take them with him, to protect what they were doing.

There had been a fight about it, with some blond-headed South African saying it was a mistake to take him. He'd wanted to hold the man and woman here, then let them go, "after."

I knew it was Johan.

The Indian said that he'd lost the argument because what they were doing was too sensitive, and the man from Lesotho believed the captives were holding out on information. The blond had said he'd told all he would tell. He knew nothing.

Shoshana had asked, "How did he know that? Who did the questioning?"

The Indian had looked at her and said, "The blond man did. It wasn't pleasant."

And I knew that was Johan too.

Shoshana heard the words and snarled, spitting nonsense, not even able to get out a sentence. She wanted to eviscerate the Indian with her bare claws. Which she could do, as I'd just seen. I stepped in at that point, pulling Shoshana into a hallway, out of view of our target, saying, "Killing him won't do anything for Aaron."

She vibrated in front of me like a shaken soda can, waiting on someone to pop the top. I saw the signs, because I'd been there before. I said, "Stop it, right now. Calm down."

"He knows where Aaron is. He *knows*. He's just not telling us."

"He knows what he's seen. That's all. He's not part of the plan."

She curled her fingers into fists and snarled, "I'm going to fucking kill him. Right here, right now. If that's all he has in his head, then it's time to punish him."

She was on fire, like when she ripped Stanko apart. I grabbed her shoulders, and she began to fight back. I slammed her into the wall and said, "You want Aaron back? For real? Or do you just want to kill everyone, because you're Carrie?"

She quit fighting, saying, "I'm no longer Carrie. I don't like that callsign anymore. I'm not the Pumpkin King. I'm married now."

The comment made me want to punch the wall in frustration. I couldn't even keep up with her changes. I spluttered, "You just said you wanted to fucking *kill* him. Carrie fits perfectly. So does Pumpkin King, for that matter. Or maybe I should just settle for plain ol' crazy."

The Pumpkin King was a reference to what I'd called her in the past, when she'd first started having feelings for Aaron but wasn't sure how to attack it. She was just like the main character from that ridiculous Tim Burton movie *The Nightmare Before Christmas,* trying to be something she wasn't. It fit then, and she'd only gotten worse since. She was still trying to pretend she was something else, because she thought if she faked it hard enough, it would magically come true.

I said, "You *are* the Pumpkin King. That's not going to change, but it doesn't matter. You've succeeded."

She said, "What's that mean? *You* still think I'm a psycho." She glanced down at the ground and said, "They all do."

I drew back and said, "You never watched the movie, did you?"

"No. Why would I? You were just making fun of me."

I laughed and said, "Jesus Christ, woman, why do I use movie references if you won't even watch?"

She started to worm away from me, saying, "I've had enough of this."

I pushed her back into the corner and said, "Hang on. Stop."

She bristled, and I said, "You want to kill him because, when you peel back the layers, it's all you know. That's the Pumpkin King. But you don't need to lash out anymore. You said it yourself. You're married now."

She looked confused at the turn of the conversation, and honestly, I was just winging it. I was in an enemy safe house interrogating a known target and talking to a crazy woman to keep her from killing him. Someone I cared deeply about. This sort of shit wasn't taught in the Top Secret Leadership Techniques School we had.

I said, "You wanted to talk to Jennifer, and I know why. You're afraid that you're different from her. That you can't be like her because of what's in your heart. What you've done. You want her approval, as if that will change you, but you don't need it. She isn't better than you. Just different. You are what you are, and it's good. Aaron knows it. And that's all that matters."

She spit out, "Unless he's dead."

I said, "He's not. He's just not here."

She looked up at me, boring in with her weird glow, and said, "Do you really believe that? Or are you just trying to keep me from killing that man?"

I said, "I believe it."

She seemed surprised and said, "You really do?"

"I do. He's alive. He's Aaron. Honestly, I wasn't sure before, but when this guy told us he'd been brought here for interrogation, that upped the odds to about ninety percent. If he wasn't killed outright, then he's alive."

I saw the words give her strength, and she said, "Will you help me? When the Taskforce says to stop?"

Jennifer entered the hallway, blessedly interrupting. I said, "Who's on Mowgli?"

"Brett. He's fine. What's going on here?"

I said, "Nothing. We're just talking."

Jennifer became canny, saying, "About what?"

I said, "About not killing everyone we meet."

Jennifer said, "Unless they need it."

Shocked, expecting support, I flicked my head to her with a glare. I said, "Nobody's killing anyone here."

Jennifer said, "That's not what I meant. Some people need killing. Some people need something else."

She moved to Shoshana and said, "That man doesn't need killing, does he?"

Shoshana became subdued. She shook her head. Jennifer turned to me and said, "But Shoshana needs something else."

I sighed and said, "Okay. Okay. So we go to Lesotho. One more link in the chain."

Shoshana glowed at the words, then leaned in and whispered into Jennifer's ear. Jennifer looked at me and nodded. I said, "What was that all about?"

"She wants to go back in with Mowgli. To wring him dry. She thinks he's keeping something secret."

I looked at Shoshana, and she gazed right back at me. She said, "No vendetta. I saw something in him. He's lying about something."

"You saw something, huh? As in a Shoshana vision, or the Pumpkin King?"

"Shoshana. I saw it. Let me go back in."

I slowly nodded, saying, "No Pumpkin King unless I ask for it. Understood?"

She grinned and said, "I'm not the Pumpkin King. I told you that."

I'd let her back in to do her magic, and now Kurt was calling before I had any answers to his questions. Except for the one about where I was going next, and I knew he wouldn't like what I was about to tell him.

57

★ ★ ★

Colonel Kurt Hale entered the communications center, finding the duty officer with a scared look on his face and none of the computers showing an active teleconference. Kurt said, "So, Pike coming up here on VTC or what?"

"Sir, he didn't have a computer. He said he'd call back in twenty minutes . . . it's been about fifteen, so . . ."

"He doesn't have a computer? I did a VTC with him yesterday."

"Sir, I don't know what to tell you. He said he's busy."

Kurt nodded at the young communications man, clearly aggravated. The man caught the look and said, "Sir, I gave him your message."

Kurt smiled, saying, "I know you did. Not your fault." What he was thinking was, *What the fuck is Pike up to?*

He turned to exit the room and heard, "Call coming in, sir. Call from Pike."

He rotated around, letting the man do his work with the call, although he wanted to snatch the phone out of the guy's hands.

The man said, "I'm not sure he's here. He might be at dinner."

Kurt smiled, knowing what was about to happen. The man heard the answer over the phone and said, "Okay, okay, no reason to get violent."

He turned, his hand covering the mouthpiece, and said, "It's Pike, and he's not in a good mood."

Kurt took the phone and said, "Probably because you put him through a dick dance after telling him to call." The duty officer said,

"I was just following protocol . . . ," but Kurt had already turned away, saying, "Pike, I need a VTC. We have authority, and I need to brief you."

"Sir, I can't do that right now. I'm in the middle of something, and my computer's at the hotel."

Kurt heard the words and felt the proverbial hair rise on his neck. He said, "In the middle of what? You were going to Durban for Alpha. Why don't you have a computer?"

"Because I'm in the safe house that Aaron was taken to. I have the man who provided it. He's a subcontractor of Tyler. He knows what's going on."

Kurt felt his head about to explode. He put his hand over the mouthpiece and said, "Get George Wolffe in here right fucking now."

The man at the desk said, "Sir?"

"Get his ass in here. I need some adult opinions before I lose my mind."

The man scurried out of the room, and Kurt returned to the phone, saying, "Did I just fucking hear you right? You have the man who owns the safe house in your possession, and you're interrogating him?"

"Yes, sir. But it's not what you think. We were following Stanko, using the intercept you gave us, and Stanko tried to kill him. We interdicted and ended up with the safe house guy. After that, it seemed prudent to question him, since we were already involved."

Kurt was apoplectic. "You *do not have* any Omega authority in Durban. You were supposed to continue Alpha. *Alpha,* you damn Neanderthal."

Pike bit back just as hard. "Sir, did you hear what I just said? What the hell do you guys think we do out here? Let me make it plain: Stanko had a garrote around the guy's neck. He was about to cut his head off with a piano wire. We fucking stopped it.

We have authority to do that. Remember? 'No Taskforce authority will preclude an Operator from preventing the loss of life or self-defense of the Operator involved.' All we did was prevent the loss of life."

Kurt said, "You may have just screwed our ability to continue."

"Well, any operation you want to do is predicated on this guy's information, so fire me."

Kurt took a couple of deep breaths and then said, "We have Omega for Tyler Malloy. The Oversight Council wants you to take him down."

Kurt heard nothing for a moment, then: "Okay, but I have to go to Lesotho first."

"What the hell are you talking about?"

"Sir, the trail leads to Lesotho. That's what he's doing. I need to explore that; then I'll take him down."

Even with the encryption making Pike's voice sound robotic, Kurt heard the conviction.

Kurt said, "Pike, no Lesotho. I need you to return to Cape Town and conduct an Omega operation immediately."

"What's the rush? Is there an immediate threat?"

"He's getting nuclear triggers for the sale to the highest bidder, and that appears to be Hezbollah."

He heard a scuffling in the background, then Pike saying, "Stand by."

He waited for an eternity, and George Wolffe entered the room, saying, "What's up?"

Kurt said, "I'm telling Pike about the Omega authority for Tyler, and he's giving me excuses about Lesotho. I don't know why."

George nodded, then said, "You do know why. It's about Aaron."

Kurt said, "I don't give a shit about Aaron. I care about Americans."

George said, "Maybe Aaron is the key to that."

"This isn't a damn democracy. He's got a mission now."

George smiled and said, "You know what makes us great? At the end of the day? Loyalty. Sometimes the individual takes precedence over the crowd."

Kurt looked at him for a moment, then said, "Saving Aaron isn't going to bring us Tyler Malloy."

"Tyler Malloy isn't the issue. Stopping the triggers from being transferred is. We get Tyler, those triggers are still out there, waiting on someone else. All I'm saying is hear him out."

Kurt nodded, and Pike came back on, saying, "Shoshana just learned that the operation in question is a coup in the country of Lesotho. It's a small country that—"

Kurt interrupted, saying, "I know where Lesotho is, Pike. I don't give a shit about it."

Pike said, "Well, you should, because these fucks are going to take over the country with the help of someone in the South African military."

Kurt said, "And? What's the 'and'? Why do I, as the Taskforce commander, care?"

Pike said, "From what I've seen, Tyler Malloy is fronting the logistics for the effort, and his payment is the nuclear triggers."

"Okay, you're agreeing with me. Take him out."

"Tyler's getting paid by the people in the coup. We upset that and he doesn't get his payday, but those triggers are still out there. Let me interdict the coup, and I'll get the guy who owns the triggers. I'll get them off the table."

Hearing George's earlier comments echo, Kurt glanced at his DCO and smiled.

Kurt said, "This is all about Aaron, isn't it. Tell me you're doing this for the United States instead of an Israeli assassin."

Pike said, "Sir, it's the same damn thing."

Kurt said, "I want Tyler down."

Pike said, "You'll have him. I promise."

Kurt said, "Stand by," then put the phone on mute. He looked at

George, saying, "How far out are we willing to obstruct the Oversight Council? They gave us Omega, yet we determine how that's executed. I could plausibly say that the only way to effect such a thing was to go to Lesotho. But you and I know that's bullshit."

George said, "It'll all be in how you brief it. At the end of the day, the greater problem is the nuclear triggers. I say, let him go. There will be a mess, but nobody will care, if Pike's successful. We have Omega authority. Let him use that to bring this whole fucking thing down."

Kurt said, "But you know that's a lie. I can't hide the fact that I told Pike to take down Tyler and then let him go to Lesotho."

"If the end state is that Tyler loses his triggers, then you've succeeded. And you might free Aaron in the process. Sometimes the little things are, in fact, big things."

Kurt nodded, then spoke into the phone. "If I were to agree with this insanity, what do you need from me, right now?"

Kurt could tell Pike was taken aback. He heard nothing for a few seconds, then said, "Pike, you there?"

Pike came back, saying, "I need an airdrop of an Africa package. The ones with the motorcycles. I'll set up the drop zone, but I need you to get the package in motion. We don't have a lot of time to waste."

Kurt said, "And? How are you going to prevent a coup in Lesotho with a couple of motorcycles?"

"There's only a small team of mercenaries that have set this up. I've confirmed a high-ranking Lesotho military man is involved in the conspiracy, so I'm sure the manpower is from the Lesotho Defence Force, with the mercs providing the leadership. Take them out and take out the coup."

"Can you do that? With only three people?"

"I have four, actually. Shoshana's with me, and we know the location of the safe house they're going to use to stage. Hit that thing and we might get them all, to include the lead on your triggers."

Kurt looked at George, knowing he was now stepping over the line. He said, "You'll have six. Knuckles and Veep will be in that bird with the package. They're at DJ right now, and the L-100 is with them."

Once again, Kurt could almost hear the gears turning in Pike's head. Finally, Pike said, "What the hell are they doing in DJ?"

Kurt said, "For the life of me, I don't know. I put them there because I figured you were going to do something stupid and I needed some sanity on the ground. If I get them moving now, I can have them overhead by midnight tonight. Is that enough time to find and establish a DZ?"

"Yes, sir. That'll be the easy part. You said you had the L-100? Is it still capable of a Fulton recovery?"

"Yeah. Why?"

"I've got to make this guy we have disappear, or he might compromise everything."

"Pike, I can't authorize an extraction for a citizen of another country who's not a terrorist and not an imminent threat. There are boundaries to my authority."

"Okay, I'll just have Shoshana kill him. She really wants to."

Kurt clenched his fist, trying to crush the phone. He said, "All right, all right. Fuck. I'll include a Fulton recovery package. You are really testing the limits here."

Pike said, "I know. But it'll be worth it."

"Pike, don't let me down. I'm hanging it way out, here."

"I won't. Trust me, this way is harder, but in the end, it'll be a much better solution, for everyone."

Kurt smiled and said, "I know. Stop the coup, and prevent the triggers from ever being transferred."

"Yes. Exactly."

"And bring Aaron home. Right?"

Pike said nothing for a moment; then Kurt heard, "Right, sir. Thank you. I won't let you down."

Kurt heard the words and knew he'd done the right thing. Pike was a supernatural predator, and he would move heaven and earth to save Aaron. In between him and that goal was a planned coup of an entire country orchestrated by a highly trained mercenary force.

Kurt almost felt sorry for them.

58

★ ★ ★

I took a wind reading and saw that, while it might be kicking higher than safe above the ring of rock outcroppings, once the team got low enough, below the stone wall, they'd be able to pilot the parachute safely to earth. The wind in this area was constantly whipping, a continuous scream across the hardscrabble ground, and it had caused trouble as we tried to find a drop zone. We'd located a few patches of terrain large enough for a night drop, but the key had been finding one that was protected from the wind. Well, that and one that was hidden from all the damn backpackers running around.

We were at the foothills of the Drakensberg Mountain chain, about three hours west of Durban and within striking range of the border of Lesotho. The problem was that Lesotho was called the Mountain Kingdom for a reason, and the terrain was incredibly rugged, at an altitude of seven thousand feet, which was pretty damn high, and we hadn't even crossed the mountain chain yet.

Deep in the Mkhomazi Wilderness Area—a national forest not unlike Yosemite—was an outdoor enthusiast's dream, with hiking and mountain climbing up peaks with names like the Rhino's Horn, and four-wheel-drive adventures to the Sani Pass, the latter reached only by taking a daredevil switchback gravel road straight up the chain of rock, ending inside Lesotho at the Sani Lodge, and the highest pub in Africa.

Americans like to think of themselves as the wild west outdoorsy types, but they have nothing on South Africans. I don't know where else in the world cage diving with great whites would be advertised like a Ferris wheel ride, and this national forest attracted adventure seekers of all types.

Because of it, the area was dotted with lodges both primitive and luxurious, offering everything from fly-fishing to mountain biking, which made our mission that much harder to conceal. While I most certainly would have liked to take our Land Rovers straight up the gravel to the Sani Lodge, hoisting a beer at the end, we needed to get inside Lesotho without going through any form of immigration. I had no desire to leave any scrap of evidence that we had been there, because I was sure we were not going to remain clandestine.

We were going to get in a gunfight and then disappear. When the inevitable investigation occurred, I didn't want them to have a lead in the form of a customs stamp or border-crossing tax payment. Especially since we had no cover for action whatsoever. While Lesotho, like most of the world, held enough archeological work to allow us to plausibly execute a Grolier cover—to include even actual dinosaur tracks—we'd had no time to establish it, so I was looking for a clandestine penetration.

I'd tasked Brett and Shoshana with finding the crossing, while Jennifer and I found the drop zone, with an eye to infiltrating the country that night. It was certainly an aggressive plan, but we would readjust if we couldn't meet it. There were a lot of things stacked against us, but we knew from Mowgli that the safe house in Lesotho wasn't due to be occupied until the following night, so if we had to wait, we'd do so, using the next day as another reconnaissance day. Shoshana wouldn't like it, but I wasn't going to sprint forward into a foreign country—and possibly get arrested as coup plotters—just because she was antsy.

Jennifer came back from the far side of the field and said, "No obstacles. There's a creek on the left, but it snakes away from the field."

I said, "No roads? No houses?"

"Not that I could see, and I went a good five hundred meters."

"Okay, then, this is it. Let's go back, send the grid, and check what the dynamic duo found."

We walked about twenty feet, and she said, "You think Knuckles is going to have a problem with the ridgeline? If they miss the spot, they'll end up on top of that plateau, and we have no way to get to them."

I turned and looked, seeing an escarpment about a hundred feet high. It *was* a little tight, but I said, "We don't know which direction they'll be coming in from. Look at the bright side: If they come the other way, and the spot's off, the plateau will stop them when they run into it."

She scowled at me, and I said, "Not my fault. You did the DZ survey."

I opened the driver's door and saw Mowgli in the back, shackled to the anchor point of the seat. There had been no way I was going to leave him at the resort to create mischief, and I didn't want him riding with Brett and Shoshana as they tried to penetrate the border, so he came with us. Well, that and I wasn't sure Shoshana wouldn't just beat him to death and leave his body on the side of the road.

He started to speak, and I said, "Rules, Mowgli, rules. No talking. Or I pass you to Carrie."

He scowled, both at his given callsign and at the fact that I wouldn't let him present his case. He was adamant that all he did was provide the safe house. Which was true, but it was enough.

From what I could see, he wasn't a bad guy, as far as assholes go. More like a simple con man. Intelligent, loquacious, and smooth. He'd probably been fleecing tourists at the age of five. Which was precisely why I had brought him with us, and was enough of a reason for me to keep him quiet. Leaving him in our resort cabin would have been asking for him to escape.

We drove through the backcountry on dirt trails, crossing streams and cutting across fields until we eventually hit a two-lane blacktop. After another thirty minutes, we were pulling into our chosen lodge—and not a primitive one, I might add. No way was I sleeping with a mosquito net and no power. I'd probably be using a rock for a pillow in the next few days, so I figured the Taskforce could pay for the night at a lodge with a spa. And I actually had some reasoning behind it. We'd rented one of the "cater yourself" cabins, meaning there was no maid service, but it was expensive enough that nobody would come investigate when we didn't show ourselves for the next couple of days. Money would guarantee some privacy.

I saw our other Land Rover and said, "They're back. Let's see what they found."

Our cabin was at the end of the row, in a cluster of four, down the road from the main lodge facilities. It was two stories and only looked rustic on the outside. Inside, it held every convenience of a modern home—stove, fridge, television, minibar, Wi-Fi, and four separate bedrooms.

I walked up the steps, forcing Mowgli ahead of me, and Shoshana opened the door. She started to speak, and I held a finger to my lips, pointing at Mowgli in front of me. She nodded, but she was smiling, so I knew it was good news.

I took Mowgli to the back bedroom and handcuffed him to the bed. He started to say something, and I held up a hand, then closed the door and returned to the den. Brett was on the computer, working something, and Shoshana was eating an apple. I said, "Okay, what do you have?"

Shoshana looked at Brett, and he said, "Go ahead. It was your idea."

She smiled, and I could tell they'd clicked on their little adventure. Brett had always been wary of Shoshana—like most normal humans—but he seemed to have warmed up to her. Which was good.

She said, "There is no damn way we're crossing through the mountains. It's just too rugged. We could do it on foot, but that would take days—and we don't have that time."

I said, "Come on, there are hiking trails all over the place. All of them big enough for a bike."

"Yes, and we looked at a bunch of the most promising ones, but all the trails, at one point or another, go to literally pulling yourself up rock escarpments, some with ropes. For the most part, they're easy walks, but every damn trail we researched had at least one choke point that prevented its use. We aren't riding a bike up them, and going on foot is a nonstarter. We won't reach Maseru for a week, and that's hoping we can get someone to pick us up as hitchhikers."

"So what are you saying? We need to use the Sani Pass and just risk getting caught after?"

Brett said, "No. Shoshana found another way. One that's not really advertised. There's another border crossing near here called Bushman's Nek, and it's not even manned with immigration folks on the Lesotho side. Just police."

"What is it?"

"It's a crossing that allows the Lesotho folks to enter South Africa to sell their wares. It's got a road that leads to it on the South African side, but there is no road on the Lesotho side. Just a mule trail. It's pedestrian-only."

Shoshana said, "But it's a trail that a motorbike could use."

I said, "What about the police?"

Brett said, "The South African checkpoint is about a hundred meters away from the Lesotho side. We can get around the South African post by using the trails instead of the road. We've already marked them. Once we're beyond it, we can use the road to get to the crossing. The South Africans restrict anyone coming into their country, but Lesotho doesn't have a lot of security on their side. Really, who can blame them? What person wants to sneak *in*to Lesotho?"

I looked at Shoshana and said, "You learn that in the West Bank?"

She grinned and said, "I'd like to say that, but it was a guy at a coffee stand. Brett wanted some water, and I struck up a conversation. That's all it was."

I nodded, thinking the single-night infiltration might actually be possible. I said, "Good work. Really good work. This might actually have a chance now."

She nodded and glanced at Jennifer, liking being part of the team. Jennifer grinned back, and I said, "We need to send in the coordinates for the drop. We've got about four hours to get them prepared."

Brett said, "I know. I was talking with Blaine Alexander about the operation earlier. He's on the ground."

I said, "Wait, what? Kurt said nothing about him coming."

I didn't really mind Blaine taking charge, because it would relieve me of any responsibility when I went apeshit, but I was already trying to sneak in six people on motorbikes past a guard force. One more was asking a bit too much.

Brett laughed and said, "He's in DJ. He'll control from that location. Trust me, we could use him."

I nodded, relieved, and said, "Yeah, you got that right. Get him on the line."

Brett dialed up the VPN, and I saw Blaine on the screen. We'd worked together for years, and I truly liked and respected him. I just didn't want him on a motorcycle behind me, dragging one more person on the operation, but he would understand that.

He'd commanded every Taskforce team in existence on an Omega operation, and yet he said the same thing he always did as soon as he saw me.

"Pike Logan. I was hoping it was you. Looking forward to working with my favorite team."

As always, I said, "I'm the only team that ever makes you look good."

He chuckled and said, "So, I get pulled from Mali by Kurt—from a luxury resort tracking a terrorist with Johnny's team, I might add—to live in the barracks at DJ as a contractor. Thanks for that. Johnny sends his love, by the way. Axe said you're a dead man, because their mission is now on hold."

"Good to see I'm helping keep the officer corps in tune with the common man."

He laughed again and said, "I'm told we got the Africa package you wanted. Six Motoped Survivals, along with a Fulton rig. You ready to execute?"

"Sir, I am. And I'm glad to hear your voice. You ready to do some good?"

"Hell yes. From what I hear, you're about to stop a bunch of assholes from raping the local folk. Doing some *real* good."

Which was the first time I'd actually considered the full implications of the coup. Before, it had been all about the nuclear triggers and Aaron. I'd never considered the innocents who would be harmed by the action, but what he said was true.

I said, "Prepare to copy the DZ information," and then went into a long diatribe of signals, markings, and everything else I could think of. I ended with, "You sure they got the bikes in the package? It's not standard kit in the Africa package."

He said, "I have no idea, but I was told so. I just got here. I'm playing catch-up."

Which was a little confusing. Why not just go to the bird and check? Not wanting to insult him, I said, "Where's Knuckles? Can I talk to him before he launches?"

He said, "Pike, the bird's in the air. It's close to an eight-hour flight. Knuckles left with the package at five, local time. He's been in the air for a couple of hours. He was in the air before I landed."

Shit. Although I knew it inherently, I'd failed to calculate just how far away Knuckles really was. Kurt's saying "I've staged them in Africa in case you need them" made it seem like they were close, but they weren't, any more than someone saying "I've staged them in North America," and the team was in Calgary while I was in Texas.

I said, "So, Knuckles gets a true blind combat drop. Better him than me."

Blaine said, "First time for everything. Now, let's get to business. Give me the plan. Kurt mentioned nuclear triggers, and apparently, I'm supposed to do something about that."

I laughed, liking his attitude. "Yeah, there's an asshole who's getting paid for this coup with castoffs from Project Circle. He'll get his as soon as we're done."

Blaine nodded and said, "And there's a bit of a hostage rescue in here? Kurt's packet mentioned an operator down. An Israeli who's part of the mission profile."

I couldn't believe it. Kurt had made that part of the profile? I glanced at Shoshana, and she couldn't either, her eyes wide. I said, "Yes, actually, there is. An Israeli friend of the Taskforce who stopped a nuclear attack in Brazil. At the World Cup. You remember?"

He said, "I do. And Kurt does, as well. You ready to get to work?"

I looked at Shoshana, and she had her hands held to her face, like she'd just found out she'd won the lottery. Which she had.

I said, "Sir, you don't even need to ask."

59

★ ★ ★

Five hours later we were back at the drop zone, waiting on contact from the aircraft. We had no way to talk to the pilot directly, but with a little bit of planning we could hear him—through our rental car's stereo, no less. Along with the coordination measures for the jump, I'd passed Blaine an AM frequency on the end of the radio dial, which the aircraft would use to transmit in the blind. So we were all sitting in one Land Rover, waiting on the aircraft to give us a disembodied voice like some Mexican radio station skipping across the atmosphere.

After about ten minutes of static, which was annoying the hell out of everyone in the Rover, we heard a squelch. Then, "Prometheus Pike, Prometheus Pike, this is Shadow. Looking for a rope."

Brett bailed out of the Rover as the pilot repeated the request. He began shining an infrared laser into the sky, weaving it back and forth like a cowboy swinging a lasso.

The radio blurted, "Got the rope. Confirm the rope. Coming in north to south."

We all exited at that point, the tension growing. We couldn't see the aircraft, but we knew the risks involved with what was about to happen.

The radio said, "First pass away. Jumpers gone."

We stared into the night sky, trying to identify something that would tell us they were okay, but saw nothing but the stars. Which, honestly, I expected. We wouldn't see a damn thing until they opened their canopies. And maybe not even then.

We waited for three minutes, and then Brett, wearing NODs, said,

"I got 'em." He pointed away from the escarpment and said, "I got two good chutes."

Which was the only thing I cared about. Get past the risk of mechanical failure and the rest was up to the jumpers.

The parachutes circled lower and lower, working turns in the sky. I could tell they were fighting the winds, Knuckles probably wondering how on earth I'd told him it was a safe DZ. They circled right above us, then turned into final approach, heading straight into the wind—and the escarpment.

They dropped below the protection of the wall of rock and immediately picked up speed from the forward thrust of the parachute. The first jumper yanked the toggles of his chute deep, burying them to his waist in an attempt to flare the parachute, but he still hit the ground hard enough to roll into a parachute landing fall. The second one saw the damage from the first and adjusted early, landing upright.

I ran out onto the DZ, finding Knuckles sputtering. He said, "What the fuck? This is the best DZ you could find? The fucking wind is like a tornado; then it disappears completely."

I pointed at the second jumper and said, "He didn't have a problem."

Knuckles shucked his chute and said, "I'm about to kick your ass."

Instead, he fist-bumped me, happy to be alive.

I returned the bump and laughed, saying, "Save it for the bad guys. Can you get the bundle in?"

"Yeah. Pretty sure I can."

Veep came running up, saying, "Holy shit, that was some serious wind."

I said, "Yeah, well, not serious enough to prevent you from landing on your feet. You must be a SEAL, right? Only *they* could do that in this situation."

An Air Force Special Operations member, Veep looked at me, then Knuckles, unsure of what to say without aggravating either of us. Knuckles said, "There will come a time, Mr. Badass, when you'll regret the disparagement."

I said, "Don't make it now. You know, because of the winds." He grimaced and I turned serious, saying, "Can you get our package in safely?"

"Yeah. I can do it. No thanks to your planning."

He pushed a switch on his chest and said, "Shadow, Shadow, we're on the ground. Give me a time hack."

He listened for a second, then said, "Eight minutes. He's circling."

I said, "You saw the winds. Can a CARP release get the package here? Or are we going to go hunting it?"

Meaning would the onboard computer in the aircraft be able to determine an accurate release point, or would the parachute land two mountains over?

He smiled and said, "You know better than that." He pulled out a device that looked a little bit like a gaming controller. "Money is no object to the Taskforce. He's releasing a FireFly."

I nodded, giving a silent sigh of relief. You never knew what technology you'd get in the field, but the drop zone I'd selected would need some serious precision, and the FireFly was exactly that. Basically, some smart guy had looked at JDAM GPS-guided munitions and said, "If we can drop a bomb with that precision, why can't we do the same thing with a parachute?"

And they'd built one. The FireFly was a container system with a ram-air parachute coupled around a GPS guidance system that would read the winds and adjust all the way to the ground. Which would be fine in a normal situation, but ours was a little different. If the GPS computer did its job, the bundle would smash into the plateau once it cleared the break of wind, as had almost happened to Knuckles. Luckily, we could override the system.

Knuckles touched his ear, then said, "Bundle's away."

I looked into the sky and saw nothing for a moment, then caught a flash of dark against the night sky. The canopy was open, much bigger than the one Knuckles had used. Knuckles let the computer do the work as the load came to earth, looking at his screen, then back in the air. He did that repeatedly, until the bundle was about five hundred feet above the ground.

He started working his handset, pushing the parachute to fly slower than it wanted, given the winds at altitude. He brought the bundle over the drop zone, and it sank into the lull of the protection from the mountains, causing the parachute to surge forward at full thrust, headed to the rock wall. Knuckles worked his controller, and the parachute sank to the ground like a child dropping a hanky off a table. Right in front of us.

The container thunked hard, and Knuckles contacted Shadow, telling him the spot was good and to release the second one. Five minutes later he heard, “Second bundle’s away. I say again, second bundle’s away. Standing by for extraction.”

Knuckles repeated his prime video game skills, and the container hit the ground right behind the first. We raced out to break them down. Inside was a veritable Jason Bourne wet dream: six Motoped Survival cycles, a complete communications package, enough cases of MREs to live for a week, high-tech beacons and other surveillance kit, and weapons. Blessed weapons.

I withdrew a Glock 23 pistol and saw immediately it wasn’t Taskforce. With a custom stippled grip, a Trijicon RMR holosight, and a flat-black widened mag well, it was much more of a race gun than we usually used. I held it up to Knuckles and said, “SHOT Show worked out for us?”

He said, “Yep. ZEV Tech came through. Every pistol in that case is tricked out. We’re supposed to be testing them on the range, but I figured a real-world event was good enough. I got to shoot one before I flew today. The trigger is about as crisp as anything I’ve ever fired, and it’s very accurate.”

I grinned and said, “Looking forward to ‘testing’ it.”

He said, "From what I'm hearing, that won't take too long." He withdrew the Fulton recovery system, which was really nothing more than a giant balloon attached to a wire, which itself was attached to a thick full-body suit. He said, "Where's your man?"

"In the vehicle."

Knuckles said, "Veep, let's get this in operation while they break down the kit."

Veep helped him take it to the center of the DZ, then laid out the components of the kit. I went to the Land Rover and unlocked Mowgli, saying, "Time to take a ride."

He had no idea what was about to happen and looked genuinely scared. I said, "Don't worry. You won't be harmed, and you'll get a hell of a story to tell your friends."

I brought him to the center of the field and delivered him to Veep and Knuckles. They forced him to put on the bodysuit, then slapped a helmet on his head. Knuckles said, "You ever seen a video of someone getting hoisted up by a helicopter?"

Mowgli nodded, and Knuckles said, "This is the same thing. Just hold on to the cable."

Veep inflated the large balloon and let it fly, the cable snaking out of its bag as it went higher and higher. The concept was old, and a little bit crazy, but it worked. Basically, our L-100 would drop its rear ramp and fly right into the cable, capturing it with a special collection device. Mowgli would be yanked into the air, swinging behind the bird, where the cable would be snagged and he'd be winched up until he was pulled into the back of the aircraft.

I heard Shoshana say, "What the hell is this? Who called this thing a motorcycle? More like a moped."

To Knuckles, I said, "You got this?"

"Yeah. Get my bike ready."

I left them to their work, going to Shoshana. She'd pulled out what looked like a mountain bike with a very small engine crammed into the space between the top tube and down tube, and a small gas tank behind the handlebars. It was flat-black, with a luggage rack behind the seat, a saddlebag on the left, and a gas can on the right, making it look like it was created for the set of *The Walking Dead*. Called the Motoped Survival, it could be pedaled or driven under power and was robust enough to go just about anywhere but light enough to be carried over obstacles, if necessary.

She said, "This is what we're taking to Lesotho?"

I said, "Yep. It's got a four-hundred-mile range, and we can kill the engine and pedal straight past your Lesotho police station."

I saw Brett and Jennifer breaking out rucksacks, inventorying the gear. Jennifer pulled out a PWS MK109 long gun from a case, a piston-driven M4 derivative with an integral suppressor chambered in .300 Blackout. She slid it into the custom-built holster on the left side of the bike, then bungeed her rucksack on the rack behind the seat. Eventually, all six bikes were outfitted, looking like some Hollywood *Westworld* contraptions for a movie.

Knuckles shouted, "Final pass!" And we all turned to watch. Mowgli was sitting on the ground with his legs in front of him, clinging to the cable for dear life. He turned to look at me and was jerked violently off the ground. One minute he was there; the next minute he was climbing into the sky like he was on an invisible express elevator.

Knuckles waited until he got the call, then he and Veep came back to us.

He said, "Successful recovery. Bird's gone. We're on our own now."

I nodded, and Brett passed out preloaded magazines for both the Glocks and the long guns. I said, "Okay, last chance at the kit. Everyone got what they want?"

Outside of directing a bare minimum of equipment—weapons, night observation devices, an in extremis mechanical and explosives breaching capability, and communications—I'd left it up to the individual Operator to determine what he or she wanted.

I let them dig through the containers one last time, then directed them to store anything sensitive that we were leaving behind inside our Land Rovers. While that was being done, I had Brett and Veep break down the parachutes from the containers, taking them across the stream and stashing them in the thick brush, then breaking the containers down into pieces. If we were lucky, a local would come along and simply steal them.

The entire preparation had taken about three hours, which meant we were running into dawn, and I wanted to be through the border crossing and at a campsite we'd located on the Lesotho side before then. Even so, I was pretty damn proud of what we'd accomplished. Not too many military forces on the planet could have conducted a HALO insertion, complete with equipment, and a Fulton extraction in a single cycle of darkness.

I directed Jennifer and Shoshana to take the equipment-laden Land Rover back to our lodge, parking it out front. The other, empty Land Rover would return with them and remain here for the duration—hopefully not getting stolen.

While we waited, I briefed Veep and Knuckles on everything I knew. I turned it over to Brett, and he briefed our infiltration route. An hour later, now closing in on four A.M., Shoshana and Jennifer returned, and I got everyone together for a final brief and a comms check.

I said, "Okay, Brett and Shoshana have the lead. We cut the engines at the South African checkpoint, pedal our way past them, then do the same on the Lesotho side. No lethal action. If anything happens—if we get compromised—then we evacuate and regroup. Got it?"

They all nodded, and I said, "Brett. Your show."

We fired up the bikes, and they were a hell of a lot louder than I expected, like six lawnmowers attacking a small patch of grass. Brett circled his finger, and he led us out of the DZ, the night split by our headlamps. I brought up the rear, and the sight of the caravan racing toward the border brought a grin to my face.

Missions like this were the one thing that made me feel alive, testing the boundaries of my skill. And the kit was pretty damn cool too.

The only thing that would have made it better was if a couple of velociraptors were racing alongside us.

After entering the gate to their borrowed training compound, Johan directed the driver to the front of the barracks. He jumped out of the cab, went around to the back, and said, "Andy, have the men break down the kit. You take Chris to the medic. I'm going to find Colonel Armstrong."

Andy nodded and said, "I don't think it's broken. He'll still be good."

Johan went up the steps, saying, "We'll see," over his shoulder. He entered the barracks and went to the office in the back, hearing voices. He knocked and waited. Armstrong came outside, closing the door behind him.

He said, "What the hell took so long? It's almost four in the morning."

"The damn driver couldn't find the drop zone even with a GPS. He was supposed to be waiting on us when we hit the ground. We got nothing. The stand-ins you found happened to know the area, and they're the ones who located the DZ. If that happens in Lesotho I'm going to fucking gut him."

"It'll be better in Lesotho. He knows that terrain like the back of his hand, like our stand-ins did here. He won't even need a GPS."

"He'd better not, or he's dead."

Armstrong said, "What else is bothering you?"

"The jump was a bit of a cluster as well. The pilot offset on the wrong side of the DZ, forcing an extra pass, something I don't want to do over Lesotho airspace. Then Chris came in hard. He fucked up his ankle."

"Will he be able to execute the op?"

"I don't know. They're checking him out now, but as far as final rehearsals go, this one didn't give me a lot of confidence."

The door to the barracks opened, and Andy came in. He nodded at Armstrong, saying, "Sir." Then to Johan: "Chris is okay. Bruised patella and sprained right ankle, but the doc says he can wear a brace in his boot."

"Can he jump?"

"Doc said he didn't advise it. Chris said he's going."

Johan smiled and said, "Get me an up on the kit; then we'll do an after-action review. Make sure that fucking driver is there."

Andy left, and Johan said, "Well, sir, I've got other issues to take care of. I'm going to go find that stupid pilot. Straighten his ass out."

Armstrong said, "Before you go, I have someone I want you to meet."

"Who?"

"The new future ruler of Lesotho. Deputy Prime Minister Makalo Lenatha."

"Why the fuck do I have to meet him? He's not paying the bills."

Armstrong scowled and said, "He wanted to meet *you*. He wants to meet the man who's going to receive him on the airfield when I bring him in. He's been waiting up all fucking night for you to get back; now, get in there and shake his hand."

Johan rolled his eyes and said, "He's going to fly in like a king after I've done the killing, and I have to start kissing his ass before that's even happened?"

"Yes. No smart-ass comments."

Armstrong opened the door to the office, ushered in Johan, and said, "Prime Minister Lenatha, this is Johan van Rensburg. He's the ground-force commander for the operation, and the one who will meet us on the airfield."

Johan saw four security stiffs glowering at him, and a man in a suit, about five foot seven, with a narrow hatchet face. Johan took an immediate dislike to him.

Lenatha came forward, sticking his hand out and saying, "It's good to meet the man who will help our country get rid of a tyrant."

Johan shook the hand and said, "So, you're going to bring progress and hope to the country? Or just get rich?"

Lenatha's smile faded. Armstrong quickly said, "Johan's full of humor."

Johan said, "I am. Just try me."

Lenatha smiled again, weakly, and said, "So, was the rehearsal good? You're ready tomorrow night?"

Armstrong glared at Johan, and Johan said, "Yes. It was fine. We'll go tomorrow night."

Lenatha said, "Good, good. I wish you the best of luck."

Johan said, "With those dumb fucks you've given us, we're going to need every bit of it."

Armstrong grabbed Johan's bicep and began ushering him to the door, saying, "Johan's got some final planning to do."

Lenatha said, "I completely understand. I'll see you on the airfield."

Armstrong opened the door, and Johan said, "You will, rest assured."

Armstrong got him back outside, closed the door, and said, "What the hell was that all about? I told you no bullshit."

Johan said, "Sir, I'll do the killing, but I'm not going to make that guy think he's a savior. He's a fucking mercenary, just like me."

61

★ ★ ★

We left the hardball road, taking a gravel track, and the caravan slowed to a snail's pace. Brett came over my headset, saying, "The South African checkpoint is about five hundred meters from here. We marked a path around it. Everyone hold up while Carrie and I go find the route."

I said, "Roger that. Everyone else, kill your engines."

The night grew quiet, the two small engines disappearing into the darkness. Jennifer put down her kickstand and sauntered over to me. I said, "What's up?"

"We've got a long way to go to Morija. We get through the checkpoint and I think we should get some sleep."

I said, "I know. We're going to be running the ragged edge here soon. I've got a campsite picked out, in the Lesotho national forest. We'll get there about dawn and rack out. But I'm worried about them making it to the safe house before we do."

"It's about four hours to Morija once we cross the border. They aren't due to get in until tomorrow night."

I said, "Yeah, I just worry. We're trusting the word of some asshole we just sent into the sky."

She patted my arm and said, "It'll work out. With you it always does."

I said, "I don't know this time." I looked at her and said, "I think Aaron may be dead, and I'm worried about Shoshana. If that's true, and she finds out, she's going to go on a suicide run. She'll kill everyone, and then get killed. I won't be able to stop her."

Jennifer said, "He's alive."

I said, "That's just talk. There are plenty of men I wish were alive who aren't. We aren't special. We bleed like anyone else."

She said, "I know. I remember Decoy. That's not what I meant."

I immediately felt like a patronizing ass for comparing my combat to hers. She said, "I mean, he's *alive*. Shoshana believes it, and she's scary supernatural."

I said, "I hope you're right, because if you're not, I might be putting her down like a rabid dog."

Her eyes widened, and she said, "What do you mean by that?"

Brett came on the net. "We have it. Follow the path we used; you'll see us about seventy meters in."

I said, "Go back to your bike."

She said, "That's not happening. Ever."

I repeated, "Go back to your bike. And remember, we have a mission. Don't make it personal. I promise Shoshana won't."

Knuckles took the lead, and we wound through the woods until we found Shoshana and Brett. They mounted up, and we went about fifteen miles an hour, threading through the brush. Every once in a while, I saw a piece of reflective tape tied to a limb. Shoshana and Brett had marked the entire path to ensure we could get through without a lot of searching. Thirty minutes later, Brett cut to the left, and we were back on a hardball, riding as fast as the bikes could go—which is to say about thirty miles an hour.

Sooner than I expected, he cut to the right of the road, saying, "This is it. The blacktop ends about a hundred meters ahead. There's a small opening with no gate. We need to pedal through, one by one. There's a police checkpoint on the left. It was active in the day, but I have no idea what's there at night."

I said, "Roger all. You leading?"

"I guess I have to, as the black man."

I chuckled and said, "Call when you're through."

He left, and we waited. Ten minutes later, he called, "Shoshana, you're next."

She left, and then one by one, the team pedaled through the small pedestrian gate. Finally, it was my turn. I realized immediately that the pedaling part of the equation left a lot to be desired. It was as hard as hell to get going. Of course, I was probably carrying about a hundred pounds of gear. I wondered why I hadn't heard Shoshana or Jennifer bitch about it.

I huffed, changing gears as I built up speed, finally seeing the gate ahead. I reached it and then heard someone shout.

Not good.

I pulled into the brush and became absolutely still, my head cocked in the direction of the noise. I heard the voice again, and it wasn't from us. I withdrew my NODs and saw a half-dressed man on a porch, shouting into the darkness underneath a single bulb. He had on pants and an equipment belt, but no shirt. Two more men appeared, dressed in uniforms, and they all left the porch. Brett said, "I have an issue. They've seen me."

I pushed the bike through the gate and dropped it in the brush. I said, "Did they see the bike?" It was too late to retreat, and if we had to take them out, I wanted them searching for black men on foot. If they saw the weird motorcycle, there was no way we could risk riding them again.

"No. It's lying down."

"Where's everyone else?"

"Hiding in the brush. They'll be found if they come out."

Shoshana said, "Let them come."

That was the last thing I wanted. I said, "Negative, negative. Everyone but Brett and Knuckles, stay where you are. Lie low. Brett, approach them."

"I don't speak the fucking language. They're going to know I'm not Basotho."

I started moving forward, saying, "Just do it. Knuckles, Knuckles, you see the targets?"

He whispered, "Roger that."

"I got the tall guy on the left. Can you get the guy on the right without him seeing you?"

"Roger."

"Okay. Brett, you got the center guy. Start waving your arms and talking. Get them focused on you. Everyone else, stay the fuck down."

Brett stood up, saying something that was lost in the wind. I circled around to the edge of the porch and began stalking. I whispered, "Knuckles, you good? I'm about to hit."

"I'm good. I'll go on you."

They reached Brett, and he began talking, his hands waving all over the place like he was describing the building of the pyramids. The middle guard pulled a pistol from his holster, and that was the end of the planned assault.

Brett snatched the weapon out of his hand and slammed it into his face.

My target drew his own gun, focused solely on Brett, and I saw Knuckles come out of the darkness behind the far target. I reached mine a split second later, grabbing the barrel of his weapon and hammering a fist into his kidney from behind. He collapsed to his knees, and I jerked the gun out of his hand, then used it to knock him out. I whirled to the other targets, but they were all down.

I said, "Check them for damage."

I felt the pulse of my guy, then watched his breathing, seeing it steady. I explored the wound on his head, finding a crease of blood but no fracture.

I said, "How are we looking?"

Brett said, "My guy is good. Gonna wake up with a headache, but no permanent damage."

Knuckles said, "Same here."

False dawn was starting to bleed its tendrils of light into the woods. I said, "Okay, let's get the fuck out of here. The campsite's about forty minutes due west. Inside the Sehlabathebe National Park. Let's get there and bed down for some shut-eye. We're going to be busy for the next twenty-four hours."

Brett said, "Should we leave a Batman card?"

Turning to go, I said, "What the hell are you talking about?"

"You know, Batman. I'm starting to really like that character."

I said, "Batman's American. If you can think of a Lesetho superhero, I'm all about it."

He said, "Good point," and jogged to his bike.

62

★ ★ ★

Aaron scuffed the mortar of the next brick in the row, close to finishing the work on the entire ring around the window. The noise seemed deafening to his ears. A *scrape, scrape, scrape* that he was sure the lethargic uniformed tribe would eventually figure out and report. But so far they hadn't.

He was working faster than he had before because he knew his time was coming to an end. He pried out another piece of masonry, tossing it through the window.

He had a decision to make, and soon. He didn't want to leave without Alex, but he had the means of escape in front of him. He'd been torn for the last twenty-four hours about his next actions. Escape, leaving her in the prison? Or stay, when he had no control over her fate? He'd decided that his getting out was the best course of action. There was a risk, in that the guards could punish her for his escape, but it was the best chance for the both of them.

He stepped off the bucket, casting a wistful glance out the window, seeing the gloom from the setting sun. He hid the spoon in a crevice he'd created and came from behind the blanket. Thomas was sitting on the floor with his cup, ready to alert if anyone came.

Aaron said, "It's ready, but this is going to be close. If that fuck comes before it's dark, I'm out of luck."

Thomas said, "You want to go now? Is that what you're saying?"

"I can't. There's no way I'll get off this base in the daylight. Not even these guys are incompetent enough to allow that."

Thomas smiled and said, "Then darkness it is, although I still think you're making things worse."

"Thomas, you may not believe it, but you're going to die in here. And I might too, if that damn sun doesn't drop fast enough."

Thomas said, "Maybe, but each day I live is one more day on earth. I don't seek to shorten it."

Aaron said, "Neither do I."

There was a commotion in the front of the room, and Aaron saw Lurch come barreling in with four other guards, the inmates scurrying away.

Shit. Aaron knew he'd just missed his chance.

Lurch marched forward with his phalanx of minions, all swinging batons even as the inmates scrambled away. The only one who didn't run was Thomas.

Lurch stopped in front of them and said, "Jew, it's time to go."

Thomas said, "Why must you use such aspersions?"

Lurch lashed out with a baton, cracking Thomas in the head. He fell to the floor, and Aaron knew something had changed. They had never before directly accosted the suit tribe, and certainly not its leader.

Lurch said, "You'll get yours later tonight, you little worm. For now, I'll settle for the Jew."

He jerked Aaron to his feet, then flicked his head. A man to the left hammered Aaron in the head with a baton, and he fell to his knees. The man cracked him again, dropping him to the floor. Aaron lost focus, vaguely seeing Thomas step in and get brutalized as well. A guard cuffed his wrists, then dragged him on his stomach through the open cell room, the uniformed prisoners laughing and hooting. He tried to stand up, but the pace was too quick. He staggered forward, then fell again, the man jerking on his handcuffs without mercy.

They reached a Land Rover, and a hood was thrown over his head. He was shoved into the vehicle, and they drove for what felt like close to five minutes. Not long enough to leave the base. So they were going deeper. Aaron's mind was working furiously, trying to assess the best- and worst-case scenarios.

He was jerked out of the vehicle and once again forced to move faster than his legs could maintain with the hood on. He fell, was kicked, and stood again. Eventually, he was slammed into a wall, then hoisted up, hooking his handcuffs on an iron bolt that left him on tiptoe, straining to relieve the stress on his shoulders, his ankle chains slapping the wall.

So it's the worst case.

His hood was ripped off, and he found Lurch in front of him. He said, "General Mosebo won't be here for a few hours, but he asked me to soften you up. He wants to know what you know, because tonight is critical. Make no mistake, I have no questions. I'm just here for the fun."

He brandished a bamboo rod and stood back, swishing it in the air. For the first time, Aaron saw a person next to him. A female in bra and panties, hung on a hook just like him, but still hooded. Lurch lashed out, striping her belly, and she screamed.

Alex.

Aaron felt molten fury, wanting to explode in vengeance.

Lurch came back to him and said, "You want me to work over you, or her?"

Aaron gritted his teeth and said, "I'm going to kill the lot of you."

Lurch laughed and said, "I guess that means you want me to work over your partner."

He raised the bamboo lash again, and Aaron said, "No. Don't. Take it out on me."

Lurch said, "Good. Because it won't be fun using that body after we've beaten it."

And the rod came down.

Johan felt the aircraft leave the earth, and it had a feeling of finality. They were in the air, and the mission was a go. He looked at the men around him and had confidence in their abilities, but he was losing conviction in what he was about to do.

The men sat in the web seats of the C-130 aircraft, already in their parachutes. The flight was only an hour and a half, and it wouldn't be long before they exited into the black night. He leaned over to Chris and said, "You sure you're good to go?"

Chris was American Special Forces and had proven to be a good man during the rehearsals. One of the few who understood the limitations of the indigenous men they were training.

"Yeah, I'm good. My ankle is cinched tighter than a virgin's cunt. I'll be fine."

Johan nodded, and, curious, he said, "How did you get into this?"

"What do you mean?"

Johan leaned back and said, "I mean, this doesn't seem to be your skill set. How were you hired?"

Confused, Chris said, "You've seen my skill. I can outshoot anyone here. My ankle doesn't matter. What the hell are you talking about?"

Johan said, "We aren't training anymore. We're taking over a country for money."

Chris squinted his eyes and said, "We're removing a despot. That's what I do."

Johan laughed and said, "When? Where have you removed a despot?"

"I served in Iraq. Afghanistan. I did what was right then, and I do it now."

Johan nodded and said, "Keep telling yourself that."

"What does that mean?"

Seeing he'd hit a nerve about Chris's past service, and not wanting to fight, Johan let it drop, saying, "Nothing. Just do your job and earn the paycheck."

He moved to the front of the aircraft, feeling Chris's eyes on his back. He reached the loadmaster, hearing him talk to the pilot on a headset about the altitude. With the short flight time, they'd spend most of it below ten thousand feet to avoid wasting the oxygen the men held on their HALO rigs.

He sat down in the web seat next to the loadmaster, away from the men, not wanting to think about what he was doing. He closed his eyes, and it was almost pure, the vibration of the aircraft, the smells, the cinch of his harness bringing the memory of just such a flight, on a team that believed in what they were doing, and an end state of something worth gaining. Back when he cared.

He was jolted awake by the loadmaster. "Thirty minutes. Thirty minutes."

He turned to the back of the aircraft and relayed the command, the men standing up and beginning the laborious process of hooking rucksacks and weapons to their gear. He went to the rear to do the same. Ten minutes later, the loadmaster gave him the mask signal. They were climbing.

He relayed, and the men closed the oxygen masks on their faces, checking bottles and making sure they could breathe in the rarefied air of twenty-five thousand feet. The group began doing pre-jump checks on one another, making sure they'd connected all the various attachments correctly and that the container pins were ready to deploy the lifesaving parachutes. Johan talked to the loadmaster one more time. He should have had someone check over his gear, like the others, but he'd done this so many times he didn't bother. Better to focus on his duties as the jumpmaster.

He went to the ramp at the rear of the aircraft, his adrenaline starting to pump, his senses becoming hyperalert. This was it. What he lived for. No matter the outcome or purpose, this moment in time was why he did what he did.

The loadmaster pressed a button, and the ramp began to lower, the sky outside huge. The wind began to rocket into the back of the aircraft, and he glanced back at the men, all now looking at him, their faces covered with goggles and oxygen masks.

He was the single person on earth they trusted now, the focal point of their entire existence. They would do what he asked without hesitation, because he was the jumpmaster. He gave them a thumbs-up and then awkwardly took a knee at the corner of the ramp, fighting his rucksack and the wind, looking for the terrain features he'd memorized.

The beacon he'd emplaced would guide in the aircraft for the jump run, but it was his job—his duty—to corroborate the information. If he couldn't find the landmarks, he wouldn't give the release.

He craned his head out into the wind and stared down, seeing nothing but scrolling hills in the blackness. He waited, then saw a river. The five-minute landmark.

He turned around and gave the command to stand up. The men shuffled upright, crowding to the rear. He could feel the adrenaline, see the vibration in their bodies. He returned to the wind, craning out of the side of the aircraft for the release point.

He saw the lights of Maseru ahead, then the rotating spotlight for the airport, at twenty-five thousand feet looking like a toy flashlight. They were on track.

He turned around and gave the signal to stand by.

The men crowded closer to the edge of the ramp, eyes wide. Sweat pouring. Goggles starting to fog.

He saw the crest of a butte, the release point. They crossed it.

He stood up, turned to the men, and pointed off the ramp, into the vastness of space. They exited without hesitation, the entire team spilling out of the back of the aircraft like lemmings with a death wish.

The last man passed him, and he followed, leaping out of the aircraft with a faith born from a thousand jumps before.

He felt the buffeting wind from the slipstream of the aircraft, then entered the clean air left behind, arching his back and falling flat and stable, looking for the team. He saw the blinking strobes, all in front of and below him, and relaxed, checking his altimeter.

There weren't any Hollywood stunts like linking up and turning points. They were twenty-five thousand feet above the earth at night, each carrying more than a hundred pounds of equipment and breathing oxygen from a tank. If they could all open their parachutes at the designated altitude, that would be success.

All too soon, he reached four thousand feet. He cleared his airspace, making sure nobody was around him, passing through three thousand feet. He arched hard and pulled his rip cord.

He felt the chute kick out but knew immediately something was wrong just by the way it deployed. It partially inflated, whipping him hard to the right. He looked up and saw a tangled mess. He seized the toggles, jerking them down, attempting to fully inflate the canopy. It did no good. He began spinning in a circle, the rotation becoming more and more violent, to the point that the centrifugal force was about to make him black out.

Flying through the air with half lift, falling to earth like a fidget-spinner toy, he felt the rucksack between his legs begin to twist. It caught enough air to flip him on his back, the weapon at his side punching him hard in the jaw.

He shook his head, squeezed his knees, and forced the rucksack back below him. It caught the wind again, flipping him back onto his belly, still spinning. He frantically traced his harness to the cutaway pillow, yanking it out like he was pulling Excalibur from the stone.

The bad parachute jettisoned, and he was briefly in free fall again, a sickening sensation, causing his stomach to lurch. He grabbed his reserve rip cord and ripped it free. The parachute inflated, and he had a brief moment of respite, then saw he was within two hundred feet of the ground and flying fast. He had no time to lower his rucksack. He saw the earth racing to meet him and yanked deep on the toggles. He hammered the ground, bashing his knee into a rock. He screamed, rolled over, and realized he was alive.

He lay in the dirt for a moment, savoring the act of breathing. He worked the fasteners on his rucksack, put his weapon into operation, then stood up, his chute splayed behind him. He realized he was on the plateau, but way off the designated mark.

He saw trucks in the distance and thought, *Not all bad. At least that asshole found the drop zone.*

64

★ ★ ★

The rain started coming down harder and I began to wish the safe house location we'd been given by Mowgli was in the city of Maseru, so I could establish a TOC inside a hotel. But at least I didn't have it as bad as Knuckles and Jennifer. I was sitting in a coffee shop with Shoshana, one of the few local establishments open for business in this small village. Although calling it a coffee shop was probably giving it an air of suburban legitimacy it didn't deserve. It was a thatched-roof cinder-block building with four plastic tables and a small room off to the side where the owner cooked over a propane stove. It was incredibly rustic, something I completely ignored because it was also dry, and the hosts overcame any lack of modern conveniences with their open, friendly attention to us.

Knuckles and Jennifer, on the other hand, were in a hide site dug into a hill across a valley from the Morija Guest House. When Jennifer had learned the safe house was within rock-throwing distance from a set of actual dinosaur tracks, she actually volunteered for the duty, something she was probably now regretting.

I'd placed Brett and Veep in another hide site with a view of the main road into Morija, giving us early warning of any suspicious traffic. I'd kept Shoshana with me, for obvious reasons. I wanted her on a short leash because I was sure putting her in the field would be like dangling bacon in front of a Rottweiler.

The village of Morija was tiny—really nothing but one paved road—but it was the historical heart of the country of Lesotho, with the king's residence only a few kilometers away, the Lesotho Museum and Archives down the street, and the church of the first French mission founded in the country within it. While Maseru had ended up being the capital, Morija was the wellspring of its heritage.

Mowgli had told us he'd coordinated for the rental of an entire establishment known as the Morija Guest House—to include the owner's house—which turned out to be three buildings at the end of a rutted dirt road high in the mountains. Not exactly the Ritz. Getting close had been a little bit of a chore, but once we'd determined we'd beat the force to the location, it gave us time to prepare.

The distance to Morija had ended up being about double Jennifer's earlier assessment, as it took us close to eight hours to get to the village. We'd arrived just prior to nightfall, and I'd determined that the guest house had no easy surveillance positions, as it was built onto the side of a mountain all by itself, at the end of a road only a four-by-four could use. I'd detailed Knuckles and Jennifer to hike into the woods and build a hide site into the brush on the hill across the valley. They'd established an observation post, and they'd been sending negative reports ever since. Then it had begun to rain.

I'd used a Thrane Inmarsat to send a SITREP to Blaine in Djibouti, the owner of the coffee shop looking at me like I was a wizard full of black magic. Blaine had had no additional updates from the Oversight Council, so I assumed I was still good to go with my mission. Which, honestly, I wasn't sure how I was going to accomplish. First on the list was locating and recovering Aaron, but I wasn't holding back on the second and third objectives because of the first. Aaron could be dead for all I knew.

I had a lot of options to pursue. I could hit the guesthouse if anything appeared; I could tag whatever vehicles were there, tracking them for follow-on operations; or I could simply assess and report to Blaine, letting him get the mighty machine of the United States in motion. Either way, I figured we had twenty-four hours to figure it out. The guys weren't going to hit the ground and immediately go into operations. They'd use the guesthouse for planning, and that gave me some breathing room—time to coordinate an appropriate response in conjunction with Blaine.

I focused on my primary twin objectives—finding Aaron and stopping the transfer of the nuclear triggers. The coup really didn't factor into my thinking—I'd let Blaine work that through the State Department or DoD. Or not. That was above my pay grade.

Eventually, the coffee shop closed and we were forced to leave the shelter of the thatched roof for the rain, making me wish we'd driven the Land Rovers through the Sani Pass, compromise be damned. We'd paid the wonderful hostess much more than she'd requested and ended up sitting against an abandoned brick building that was missing its roof. We were within view of the road that led to the guesthouse, looking like a couple of hippies trying to thumb a ride to Woodstock.

With the rain pelting down in an incessant bongo drum against the makeshift poncho hooch I'd built, and the darkness consuming us, Shoshana said, "I should go to the house. Explore it now, before anyone arrives."

"Aaron's not there. We haven't had a single sign of life from that place."

She played with a pebble on the ground between her feet and said, "I felt something bad. Aaron's in trouble. Deep trouble."

I sighed and said, "What, like you felt a disturbance in the Force?"

She said, "What's that mean?"

I said, "Seriously?"

"Yes."

She is not human.

I said, "Nothing. Look, we're sticking with the plan. If we don't get jackpot here, we'll reassess our options, but for now, we aren't tainting the one lead we have."

She said nothing, snuggling into me to capture the warmth of my body. It was a completely Shoshana move, with no overtones at all, and it made me smile. She was without intrigue, a blank slate. She felt cold, and I was providing heat, so she would use it.

I adjusted the makeshift hooch I'd made, stopping a drip, and put my arm around her. She said, "I cannot believe Aaron is in danger because of some American pursuing nuclear triggers. It doesn't seem fair. We left that behind. We don't do that stuff anymore. We do non-threatening work."

I said nothing, letting her words settle. She continued. "I no longer kill just because someone orders me to do so." She shifted, looking up at me. "But I'd kill to save you."

I said, "Shoshana, you don't need to convince me to help Aaron."

She settled back down and said, "I think I do. You don't hold him as important as I do. You don't understand our connection."

I said, "I completely understand. He's your Jennifer. I get it, trust me."

She whipped her head around and said, "You think that? You think our relationship is like yours?"

"Don't you?"

She said, "Don't toy with me."

I said, "Look, it's not jinxing anything to say it out loud. I feel like I'm walking on eggshells with you whenever Aaron's name is mentioned. I know what he means to you. I understand. I was *you* at one time."

I squeezed her shoulder and said, "I'm still you, at my core."

She wormed closer and said, "Well . . . you understand, then. You are also the Pumpkin King."

I laughed and said, "Yes. I suppose I am."

Our earpieces crackled, and Veep came on, saying, "Three SUVs just entered town, headed toward the mountain road. Couldn't see what was in them."

I looked at my watch and saw it was just past ten P.M. Considering we hadn't seen a vehicle the entire time we'd been here, I figured it was them. I said, "Roger all. Knuckles, you copy?"

"Got it."

The SUVs passed by us in the darkness, the headlights reflecting the incessant rain. Twenty minutes later, Knuckles called, saying, "It's them. Twelve men. I got positive ID on Johan."

I glanced at Shoshana and said, "Any sign of Aaron?"

"None. It's the assault force. If I were to bet, they're going to bed down here tonight, do some planning, get situational awareness, and then assault tomorrow night. Maybe he'll show up later, once they're settled."

Which was pretty much what I was thinking. I said, "Okay, stay in place until they bed down. I'll rotate you guys out with Veep and Brett."

Veep came on, saying, "I don't think that's going to happen. Pike, you know that field next to the river we had to forge? The one with the old sign for the cultural festival? Adjacent to the boys' school?"

"Yeah?"

"Five deuce-and-a-half-looking trucks just pulled up. Full of soldiers."

What the hell?

65

★ ★ ★

I clicked on the net and said, "What are the trucks doing?"

"Nothing. They just killed their lights and are sitting in the field."

"Are you secure?"

"Yeah, yeah, they can't see us. We're down in the river, looking over the bank, but this isn't a coincidence."

Knuckles said, "Two of the SUVs are headed back down the mountain, empty."

I tucked the poncho around us, blending in to the darkness of the building. The SUVs passed by, and a few minutes later, Veep said, "They're at the army trucks. A gaggle of men are loading."

Five minutes after that, he said, "They're headed back up."

Shoshana said, "This is it. They're attacking tonight."

The vehicles passed us again, and I said, "No. They wouldn't do it this quickly. They just got on the ground. They need to do reconnaissance. Conduct final planning."

"They have a Lesotho general on the inside of this thing. We know that. How much planning do they need to do?"

I said, "Knuckles, do you have optics inside the building?"

"I can see the den of the main house. The men are all gathered around a table. Johan is talking to them."

"Give me a read."

"They're planning, no doubt. Got the headlights of the SUVs. They're parking. Five men got out. Local nationals."

I waited, then heard, "A lot of handshaking going on. The locals are pairing up with the assault guys."

And I knew Shoshana was right. They were going to attack tonight. My hope to develop the situation was going to hell in a handbasket, along with successfully executing my primary objectives. I couldn't assault the house with a damn company of men waiting down below. Hell, I couldn't assault the house if it were only the mercenaries, as they outnumbered us two to one, and we certainly couldn't chase behind them with our bikes.

And there was still no sign of Aaron.

Knuckles said, "The majority of the package is leaving. They're loading up in the first two SUVs."

Shoshana said, "We should hit them. Right now. Ambush them when they come back down."

I seriously considered it, then said, "We do that and we might break up the coup, but we do nothing for Aaron."

"We capture one of them. Take him alive."

"We don't have the time to plan an assault like that. We'll just end up in a running gun battle. We'll be lucky to escape with our lives." The words were no sooner out of my mouth than we saw the headlights bouncing down the road, the rain now a light drizzle. They raced by us, and I said, "Knuckles, what's up there now?"

"Looks to be Johan and two locals."

I waited for the SUVs to reach the field, then said, "Brett, what's happening?"

"They're loading up. Four of the lorries are turning around."

"Where are the white guys? What are they doing?"

"They've split up. Two to a truck. They left the SUVs behind."

Shit. They were going on the attack, moving much, much quicker than I thought they would have. I'd misjudged them.

"They're leaving the field."

"Knuckles, what's Johan doing?"

"Johan just rolled up a map. Looks like they're leaving as well in the final SUV."

I stood up, breaking down our little hooch. I said, "Veep, Veep, are the first four trucks gone?"

"Yeah. They're clear."

Shoshana stood with me, saying, "What are you doing?"

I raced around the building to where we'd stashed our bikes. I withdrew my long gun from its sleeve, saying, "Following your plan. We've only got one SUV to contend with, and the guy inside it is the one who captured Aaron."

She flashed her wolf smile, and I said, "I'll take front tires. You take rear tires. Do *not* kill Johan."

She nodded, then said, "There's still a lorry full of soldiers down at the field."

I said, "We're shooting suppressed. We do this right and they'll never know." I turned on my holosight as she pulled her own weapon. I said, "You post up here; I'm going to the end of the building. I'll shoot the tires the minute he's parallel to you; you hit the rear as he rolls by."

I got on the net, saying, "All elements, all elements, we're going to ambush Johan's vehicle. Blood, Veep, keep eyes on that truck full of soldiers. Tell me if they react. Knuckles, Koko, give me trigger. When the vehicle's gone, break down the hide and crack that house. Get it ready for reception."

I heard nothing for a second, I'm sure their brains processing the absolute insanity of what I'd said. I took a knee at the end of the building and aimed up the road, past Shoshana's position, saying, "All elements, you copy?"

"This is Veep. We copy."

"This is Koko, copy. Vehicle is leaving now. I say again, vehicle is leaving now."

Two minutes later I saw the headlights bouncing down the treacherous mountain road. It reached the intersection with the asphalt lane we were on and turned toward us. I would have to guess at where the tires were located due to the glare, but luckily, the gravel track was so pitted that the SUV couldn't do more than ten miles an hour on it, which meant he wouldn't be able to accelerate to much faster than thirty when he passed me on the asphalt. It wasn't like he was driving a sports car.

He came parallel to the far edge of the building, where Shoshana was located, and I started firing controlled pairs, pinging first the left, then the right, then back to the left, shooting where I thought the tires would be. I saw a muzzle flash behind the vehicle and knew Shoshana was doing the same, but it appeared to have no effect.

The SUV passed my position, and I pulled my weapon, hiding against the brick and holding my breath. It didn't take long. The vehicle skidded to the left. The driver overcompensated and the SUV jerked hard to the right, the right two wheels sliding over the embankment on the far side of the road.

It wasn't a long drop, but it was enough to cause the SUV to roll over. I sprang from my cover, my weapon raised, racing across the road, seeing Shoshana doing the same. She reached the embankment before me. I heard a shot ring out, then saw Shoshana drop to the ground. I thought the worst had happened, but then she returned fire.

I crested the rise and saw a local national crawling out a window, the truck upside down. He fired a pistol, and Shoshana's rounds slapped him up against the door, his life-force mixing with the rain. I sprang down the embankment, and another man rose on the far side. The other local. All I could see was his head, and he was looking toward Shoshana. I couldn't see his hands but had to assume he had a weapon.

I lined up the red dot and fired, flinging him back in a spray of brain matter. He disappeared from view. I turned on the white light attached to the front rail on my handguard and shined it into the vehicle. It was empty.

Shoshana shouted, "Pike!" and I whipped both my head and barrel to her, fearing somehow Johan had gotten behind me. She pointed, and I shined the light, catching a man running across a rock-strewn lot with an old chimney standing by itself, heading toward the river and the soldiers in the field.

Shoshana raised her barrel, and I shouted, "No! Cease-fire."

My earpiece came alive. "Pike, this is Veep. Soldiers are leaving the truck. They're spread in a skirmish line and headed toward us."

I started after Johan, moving just fast enough to barely keep him in the cone of my light, his figure coming in and out of it as I ran, the rain giving it a strobe effect.

I said, "Johan's coming toward your rear. He escaped. I'm behind him. Break, break, Carrie, Carrie, sweep to the right, see if you can get ahead of him."

Veep said, "You want us to close on you? Meet him in the middle?"

"No. He's clearly in radio contact with them, and I don't want them at our back. We have no exfil platform. How many are there?"

"Looks to be about ten."

Johan went down, then came back up, and for the first time, I noticed he was limping on his right leg. I said, "Remove your suppressors and put down a base of fire. Scare the shit out of them. Make them think you outnumber them."

Brett came on: "You want us to take them on?"

"Yeah, but do it noisily. If they return fire with any skill, or start maneuvering, then fall back. Put the river between you and them. We'll meet you on the other side."

Five seconds later, I heard the crackling of a gunfight, recognizing the noise of our weapons at first, then a couple of desultory blasts from an AK. Johan heard it too and dropped to the ground. I lost sight of him and crouched, killing my light. I cocked my head but could hear nothing over the rain.

There was another round of sustained fire, and Brett came on, saying, "I thought you were insane, but it looks like you're a genius. They're running back to the truck like a band of circus clowns."

I started crawling forward, slowly, a foot at a time, not wanting to bump into Johan by surprise. I knew that whoever got the drop in this contest would win.

Shoshana said, "I'm at the river. The bank is very steep, about twenty feet deep, but there's a concrete footbridge across it . . . wait, wait. Someone's on the bridge. Johan's beat me to it. Johan's crossing."

I stood up and began running as fast as I could, saying, "Blood, Veep, you know that bridge?"

"Yeah, it's to our right about fifty meters."

Shoshana said, "I'm chasing him."

"No. Don't. That's a funnel with no cover. If he chooses to fight, you'll have to kill him. We need him alive. Break, break, Blood, what's the status with the truck?"

"It's bugging out. I'm moving to the bridge. Veep's got coverage on the truck, but it's hightailing it out of here."

I reached Shoshana and ran right by her, onto the concrete of the bridge. She watched me go by, and I heard, "What the hell? Where are you going?"

The bridge was long, about seventy meters, and I saw a figure more than halfway across, limping along. I sprinted about thirty meters, took a knee, hit the figure with my light, and shouted, "Johan! Stop!"

He did, crouching down. Hearing his name must have completely blown his mind. Shoshana reached me and turned her light on him as well. I considered trying to trick him into thinking we were friendly but decided he was too smart for that.

I shouted, "Johan, your troops are gone! Let me see your hands."

He turned and started running as fast as he could to the far side. He got about three steps before he was slammed to the ground by Brett. I heard, "I got him."

We sprinted across, seeing Brett holding Johan in a joint lock, the South African continuing to struggle. I leaned in to him and said, "Johan, I'm cold, wet, and tired, and I don't have the patience for any fucking around. You've done a very bad thing. You took a friend of mine, and I want to know where he is."

"Who the hell are you?"

I took the light off my rail and shined it in my face. The look of shock was priceless. He sagged back, ceased struggling, and muttered, "Fuck me."

66

★ ★ ★

Aaron heard the footsteps in the gravel and knew it was time for another round. The door slammed open, Alex whimpered, and he clenched his stomach, waiting on the blow, as had happened the last three rounds. The strike didn't come. Instead, his hood was ripped off, and he found himself squinting in the bright light.

Lurch stood in front of him, sporting his asinine smile, but now he was followed by two other guards, both armed and also grinning. As if this was simply great fun. Behind them was General Mosebo, his face contorted in a scowl.

Lurch brought his cane over to Alex, who so far had avoided the punishment. He rubbed her naked belly, causing her to squirm and sob. He said, "You've proven tougher than I would have thought, Jew. But we haven't used the salt on your wounds yet. Or our other tools."

Aaron said nothing. Lurch lashed out in a rage, striping Aaron's belly for the hundredth time. Aaron grunted, then panted from the pain, feeling the bamboo split his skin. General Mosebo tapped Lurch on the shoulder, and Lurch retreated.

The general leaned in so close that Aaron could smell his fetid breath. He said, "I have a very, very big night tonight. By this time tomorrow, I will own this country. The only thing standing in my way is you."

He brought up a finger and used it to tap Aaron's forehead hard enough to bounce it against the wall, punctuating what he was saying. "What. Do. You. Know. Of. My. Plans?"

Aaron said, "Nothing. I swear to God, nothing. You can have this place. I don't care. I was in Johannesburg. I was nowhere near Lesotho. This has been a huge mistake."

General Mosebo smiled and said, "Since the planning has continued without a hitch, and my friends who are helping me have actually landed, I almost believe you. But I have to be sure. And unfortunately, that won't end well for you."

Aaron said, "You can beat me to death. You won't get a different answer."

Mosebo nodded, saying, "Yes, I believe that to be true, but I've questioned your prison friend, Thomas, as well. Poor guy has delusions of grandeur. He thinks because he was protected before, he would always be protected—but he is dying tonight as well. Anyway, it seems you have a fondness for this thing."

He backhanded Alex in the belly, and Aaron felt his killing instincts rise into the red. The two guards went to her and hoisted, getting her off her hook. Lurch cleared a table from the middle of the room, tossing it to the side and saying, "Put her right here. Right in front of me."

Alexandra began fighting like a cornered tomcat, until one of the guards smacked her hard enough to render her senseless for a moment. Aaron began thrashing on his hook, screaming unintelligibly.

Mosebo said, "So, I see it's true. You care more about her than your own life. And you can save her. Just tell me."

"I don't know anything! I fucking don't know."

Alex was put on her hands and knees, the hood still over her head. Aaron was close to losing his mind, his impotence to help splitting him apart, and then he focused. Returning to center. Returning to what he was.

He didn't have the ability to escape before, while he was hooded. He couldn't even see to fight. But his hood was removed precisely so he could witness the horror about to occur. All he needed was leverage. Some way to raise himself high enough to remove his hands from the hook above him.

Lurch unbuckled his pants and positioned himself behind Alex. In a low voice, Aaron said, "I'm warning you. Don't."

General Mosebo laughed and said, "Tell me if there's anyone against me, and I won't allow it."

Aaron began thrashing like a shark on a line, screaming that there was nobody against them, doing anything to get someone near him.

Mosebo said, "Don't let him knock himself out. I want him to see this."

The first guard ran over to him, pinning him against the wall. Mosebo said, "You want to change your answer?"

Aaron curled his lips and said, "No. I said I would kill the lot of you. That hasn't changed."

Mosebo looked confused, Lurch sniggered, and Aaron raised his legs, locking them around the neck of the guard, the chains from his ankle shackles working just as efficiently as they had before. He hoisted himself using the man's shoulders, releasing the handcuff chain from the hook, and dropped to the floor with the man's neck in his legs. He felt it snap with the impact. He leapt up, knowing he had to stop the second guard from firing.

The guard raised his weapon, and Alex came up off the floor, head still hooded but realizing something was happening. Something that required her to fight. She whirled her cuffed arms in a circle and connected with the guard, knocking him off-balance before he could fire.

Aaron launched across the room, looping his cuffs around the armed guard's throat, then rotating around and hoisting the guard onto his back like a bag of wheat. The guard dropped his weapon, his arms flailing ineffectually, his mouth squirting out obscene noises. Aaron bounced on the balls of his feet, using the guard's own weight against his throat, and felt the cartilage break. He lowered, then sprang upward, flinging the guard over his shoulder.

Aaron felt the neck vertebrae separate even before the man hit the wall. He whirled back into the room, the two men with weapons out of play, and saw Lurch run like a scalded dog out the door. Alex scurried to the corner, still wearing her hood. General Mosebo backed up, saying, "You stay right there. I am in charge here. Men are coming for you."

Aaron's mouth slowly curled into a smile. He said, "Really? I hate to tell you this, but there's only one thing coming here tonight. And I already told you what that was."

He advanced forward, and Mosebo said, "Wait, wait, wait. There's going to be a coup tonight. This could work out well for you. Lots and lots of money."

Aaron reached him and leaned his face in just as Mosebo had done moments before. He said, "Give me your cell phone."

Trembling, Mosebo did so, saying, "Why?"

"Because I need it to call my wife. She's worried about me."

Confusion flitted across Mosebo's face, and Aaron saw Alex raise her hand to remove the hood. He said, "Alex. Leave the hood on for another couple of seconds."

Her breath hitching, unsure of what was happening, she said, "Why? . . . Are we free? . . . Why?"

Aaron smiled at General Mosebo and said, "It's just better this way. Trust me."

And he snatched the man by the throat, bending him over and slowly choking the life out of him. Aaron savored the death, drawing it out, relishing it much more than he should have, the mighty general gargling and ineffectually thrashing his fists back and forth.

After the body had dropped, he turned to Alex and said, "Take the hood off. Put on General Mosebo's clothes. We need to move."

Alex looked at the carnage, then at the bloody ribbon of stripes on Aaron's upper body. She said, "My God. My God. What have they done to you?"

He ripped a shirt off the guard he'd thrown into the wall and said, "Nothing I wasn't willing to pay, but you need to harden up. We are not out of the woods yet. Get dressed. We need to go." He began digging through the guard's pockets, looking for the keys to their cuffs.

Seven minutes later they were slinking along the back wall, then racing to the woods at the base of the mountains. They were deep inside the military base and had just killed the head of the entire Lesotho Defence Force. Aaron had no illusions about his chances of getting out. All he had was the single AK-47 that had been left behind, with one magazine of ammunition.

He saw a stand of trees and dragged Alex toward it in the darkness, burrowing inside. She said, "What are we going to do?"

"We're going to call my wife. She'll come get us."

Alex started crying, rocking back and forth, saying, "What are you talking about? We aren't finishing a movie at the mall and waiting on our mom. We're going to die. You killed all of them. They won't let that go. We can't get out of here."

Aaron grabbed her chin and said, "Two things have just happened: One, I killed the head of the Lesotho Defence Force. Two, we're fucking free. Start thinking about the future, not the past."

Alex drew strength from his words. She nodded, wiped her eyes, and said, "I'm sorry I wasn't any help. I was so afraid."

Aaron shifted his grip, now cupping her chin. He said, "*Sabra,* your little action in there saved us both. You did everything you were supposed to do."

She gave a tentative smile, scrubbed her eyes again, and said, "What was that about calling your wife? Is that a joke?"

Aaron looked embarrassed, pulling out the cell phone. She said, "What?"

Aaron turned to her and said, "This is going to sound insane, but Shoshana is here. She's looking for me."

Trying to maintain her new positive attitude, but failing, she said, "How do you know? She's in Israel."

"We're . . . connected. I don't know how I know. But she's here, looking for us."

Alex shook her head and said, "This whole thing is crazy. I wouldn't have thought you could get us out of that room. If you believe it, I'll believe it."

Aaron dialed a number on General Mosebo's phone and said, "Belief's got nothing to do with it. Trust me, this isn't blind faith. It's more like gravity. It exists, and she's here. It's time to put her in play."

I circled Johan in his chair, no longer listening to his protestations of innocence. I was growing aggravated. I watched his head swivel around, trying to keep track of my movements. I said, "Johan, I don't want to hear the lies anymore. I know much more than you think I do. Where is Aaron?"

He said, again, "I don't know! I gave him to General Mosebo and I never saw him again."

I said, "Look, I don't even give a shit about the coup. I really don't. What I care about is Aaron, and the fact that you fucks are trading this coup for nuclear triggers. You want to make a profit selling nuclear triggers, that's your business. When you want to sell them to Hezbollah, that's mine. I'm surprised, honestly. I didn't think you were a pure mercenary. I thought you had some honor. Some respect."

He looked shocked, saying, "What the hell are you talking about?"

I glanced at Shoshana, and she nodded, meaning she thought he was telling the truth, using her freaky empath ability. Something I'd grown to trust. I was surprised that she didn't want to skin him alive, but she'd been strangely submissive since we'd caught Johan. She'd just sat in the back of the room, looking subdued.

Brett opened the door to the house, entering and saying, "Got the two Land Rovers running. We can now get out of here."

We'd bundled up Johan on the bridge and then hustled him back the way we'd come. I'd told Brett to hot-wire the SUVs in the field that the locals had abandoned, and left Veep on watch for the return of anything nefarious. It sucked he'd stay in the rain, but I couldn't leave our back door open. We'd returned to the overturned SUV and retrieved Johan's kit, which included weapons, radios, and body armor that he'd never get to use.

We'd marched on foot to the safe house, meeting Jennifer and Knuckles at the door, both prepared to receive us after breaking into the cabin. I'd taped Johan to a chair and had begun questioning him.

To Brett, I said, "Any trouble with that? Any reaction from the gunfight?"

"None at all. Shit, there are only like four houses in this place anyway. With the rain, they probably thought it was thunder."

I nodded and returned to Johan. "You didn't know what this whole coup is about? You didn't know that Tyler Malloy is doing all of this for nuclear triggers from Project Circle? Don't play me. You're not in the position to do so."

Johan became reserved, but I could tell he wasn't surprised at the revelation. If he didn't know, he sure as shit suspected.

He said, "I have no idea what you're talking about."

I looked at Shoshana, and she shook her head. He *did* know something.

I said, "I thought you fancied yourself the white knight. Someone who didn't simply play for pay. Why are you here, working to get nuclear triggers into the hands of a terrorist organization?"

He shouted, "I'm fucking not! This is a strict contract. There are no nuclear triggers. A guy in Israel paid us to cause a coup. All we were doing was changing one prime minister for another. There isn't going to be any effect to the damn country. Twenty-four hours later, it's running just like it did before. All that happens is a guy in Israel gets favored-nation status for the diamonds. That's it."

I began to think he was telling the truth. At least as he believed it. I said, "Jennifer, get me the intercepts."

She said, "Pike, that's classified."

I looked into Johan's eyes and said, "Do it."

She left the room, and I said, "I'm about to show you what you were doing. If I believe you were duped, I might be persuaded not to fucking kill you."

Johan showed no fear whatsoever. He said, "Honestly, something stunk about this mission from the beginning. If what you say is true, you'll get no fight from me."

Jennifer brought out the transcripts we had, along with the photos of him at the Castle of Good Hope. I cut his hands free, letting him survey the reports. He saw the pictures and said, "You've been following me for that long? Why didn't you simply stop it?"

"We weren't following you. We were following Tyler Malloy. He's a shithead, and he's trying to supply a terrorist organization."

He nodded, but I could tell he thought I was trying to trick him. I waited, letting him read all the top secret collection we had. I saw him grow more and more agitated. When he finished, he looked up and said, "Pike, you have no reason to believe this, but I had no idea. I don't care about this country one way or the other. I don't care if the coup succeeds. I *do* care about being used."

I flicked my head to Shoshana, saying, "And you care, of course, about not getting skinned alive by my partner."

He said, "That was nothing personal. That was business. This is not. This is treason."

Jennifer said, "Treason? Against what country?"

"Against me."

He shook his head and said, "I don't expect you to understand, but I don't work for terrorists, and I don't like being used. Colonel Armstrong lied to me. I knew he was lying to me, but I thought it was about diamond concessions or something else innocuous."

He tossed the papers on the table and said, "Maybe I just wanted to believe that." He looked up, staring me in the eyes. He said, "And now I'll pay the price. I suppose I've earned it."

I was a little taken aback at how willing he was to suffer for his sins. I decided to attack from a different angle. "You've earned a ride in my aircraft, going to a black hole while we work to contain Tyler Malloy. Or . . ."

He let the question hang in the air, then asked, "Or what?"

"Or you help us, and you go free."

He rolled his eyes, saying, "I just got played by Colonel Armstrong. I don't need the same from you."

I said, "I'm fucking serious. You help us now and I'll turn you loose. My organization knows nothing about you. I can make that happen."

He said, "Why would you? I'm not stupid. I'm a fucking mercenary taking over a country, and you're going to pretend that never happened? This isn't running a stop sign."

I said, "Because, believe it or not, I like you."

He settled his gaze on me, thinking, and I drove home the point. "Without you, I might not be able to prevent Hezbollah getting those triggers. I might miss. Yes, I have you, but that's not my goal. Tyler Malloy is my goal. You do what you think is best. Fuck the coup. Think of the terrorists. You told me before you don't play that game."

Johan considered my words, then said, "If I do, you can't kill my men. I'll get you Tyler Malloy, but this mission will go. I won't be a traitor to the men I've trained with."

I said, "You think they're doing some good? You think this country is going to be better off because of what you've engendered?"

"I don't give a shit about this country. I care about my men. That is it. They didn't ask for this, don't know anything about the payout, and I won't sell them for my own freedom."

Knuckles, who'd been silent up to this point, had heard enough. He sprang forward and said, "You fucking piece of shit. You care more about the assholes who are going to turn this country inside out than the country itself? What the fuck is wrong with you?"

Johan looked him in the eyes and said, "I care about my men. I will not betray them. That's the end of it. You want to kill me, that's a price I'm willing to pay."

I could see Johan was serious and was amazed he wasn't afraid that his death would be the most horrific thing he could imagine. But then again, I'm sure he'd seen enough to imagine the worst. I was a little impressed.

I said, "I don't understand you. I really don't. You have a moral streak that seems to measure up with everyone in this room, and yet you take pay for a coup that will do nothing but destroy this country."

Johan said, "You know anything about Lesotho? It's corrupt. Changing out the prime minister will do nothing to harm anyone here. Any more than they're already harmed. If I thought this would have been a tragedy, I wouldn't have done it. It's just a change of management, and I was making a paycheck. There isn't any good here."

Jennifer said, "Yes, there is. I did the research. They have a party that truly wants to help. One that isn't in the pocket of corporate diamond or water interests. One that wants to use the natural resources to help the people. Why didn't you fight for them?"

Johan looked at her like she was a liberal nutcase. He said, "Because they can't pay."

I said, "Okay, okay. If I accept your conditions, how will you execute?"

"Colonel Armstrong is going to land here after the coup, with the new prime minister. When we're all said and done, I hand him to you. You do with him what you will. I owe him no allegiance anymore."

He locked eyes with me and said, "I'm serious. I don't work for terrorists."

I said, "So I let the coup go? And then get success afterward? That's my choice?"

Johan nodded and said, "Honestly, I don't know how else I can help you. If the coup fails, he's not landing, and if he doesn't land, you have no proof of what he's done. And without him, you have no connection to Tyler Malloy. You can burn it all to the ground once it's over, but you need to get him here because he's the link to the South African who has the triggers. Otherwise, no matter what happens in Lesotho, he won't be implicated. It's just one more failed coup."

I said, "And this has nothing to do with protecting your men."

He laughed and said, "It has *everything* to do with protecting my men, but it's not mutually exclusive. You get what you want, and I get what I want. My men get on that plane, and you get Colonel Armstrong. Look, I'm not trying to negotiate here. I'm telling you how to get what you want. And I want to help."

I said, "Do you?"

He grimaced and said, "I do, Pike. I do. You can burn me at the stake after. Seeing that fuck get taken down is payment enough. Everyone on the continent knows I don't work for terrorists. *Everyone.* Most certainly Colonel Lloyd Armstrong. He knew, and he still used me."

He said it with so much venom, I actually believed him. I said, "Okay. I get you're a little ticked at him, but how do I know you can execute the deal?"

"Because I'm the ground-force commander of the entire operation. I'm the one calling the shots for the coup. I'm the man that'll bring in that aircraft. You've captured the only man on the team who *could* do it."

I nodded, saying, "Should have known. Good."

I leaned in to him and said, "All that remains, then, is you telling us what you did with Aaron. The Israeli."

He grew cagey, looking at Shoshana. Fearing her. He said, "I told the truth. I *did* question him, but General Mosebo took him. I have no idea where."

I slapped the table and said, "That's not fucking good enough.

We're running out of time. Your damn coup is going to start in a couple of hours, and I'm not leaving here without him."

He said, "I told you what I know. I'm not hiding anything."

I said, "Well, how about I let his wife in on the questioning." I turned to Shoshana, expecting to see the dark angel appear and scare the hell out of him. Instead, I saw her leaning against a bookcase, resigned.

I said, "Shoshana?"

She looked at him, then me. She said, "He's telling the truth. He doesn't know where Aaron is."

I said, "Bullshit. He's hiding it to protect his ass."

She shook her head and said, "He's not. I can see it. He's not. I'd like to kill him right now because of what he did, but it won't get me Aaron."

She was so despondent, I was unsure of what to say. It was crushing. I'd thought Aaron was dead, and now I saw that Shoshana was starting to believe it. Which meant *I* didn't want to believe it. He was *alive*. She'd told me that not more than an hour ago.

Along with the feeling that he was in deep pain.

The room remained quiet, Johan going from one face to the other, and everyone avoiding Shoshana's eyes. A phone began bleating with a ringtone that most definitely wasn't the Taskforce. I said, "What the fuck is that?"

Shoshana began digging in her bag, saying, "It's my phone. Someone's calling my phone."

"Who the hell would have that number?"

She said, "It might be my employer." Meaning the Mossad. She frantically dug it out, hope in her eyes. She looked at the number and said, "It's local."

She physically deflated like a balloon losing air. She answered, all eyes in the room on her.

"Hello?"

I saw her jerk upright, like she'd been hit with an electric current.

She did nothing but listen, then said, "I'm here. I'm right here. I'm close."

She listened a little more, then said, "Don't worry about that. It's not just me. I'm on the way. And I have a force that won't be stopped."

She listened again, and I saw her eyes water. She said, "I've got Pike Logan with me." She nodded at the unheard words coming through the handset, then locked eyes with me. She said, "Yes, he's a wrecking crew. And he has a team. We're coming for you. Stay alive."

She hung up, saying nothing for a moment. She wiped her eyes, breathing deeply. I said, "Well?"

"That was Aaron. He's alive." She couldn't get the next words out, overcome now that her worst fear had been vanquished.

Growing frustrated, I said, "Where? Where is he?"

Tentatively, fearing my answer, she said, "He's in the middle of the military base housing the Lesotho Special Forces, hiding in the woods. He's killed a lot of people, and they're hunting him. He's got Alexandra with him, a single AK, and he's surrounded by the entire base."

She dropped the phone, knowing it was an overwhelming request. She said, "I told him we could help. But it's damn near impossible."

She looked back at me and asked, "Can we?"

She was willing to go on her own, facing a force she had no way to win against, fearing I would say no. But the odds wouldn't matter to her. She was going no matter what I told her.

I nodded, saying, "Yes. Yes, we can."

Her mouth dropped open in surprise. I said, "What? I can't be called a wrecking crew and not prove it."

"You heard the part about him being inside a Special Forces base, right? Surrounded? And you're still willing to go?"

Knuckles said, "Yeah, we're willing. Shit, we've been chasing his ass over half the world. We're not going to quit now. Anyway, it's not as bad as you make out. From what we just saw, the entire Lesotho Special Forces Regiment is being used for the coup."

She said, "I will never forget this."

I said, "You've already told me that. Should I start keeping score?"

She smiled at my smart-ass comment, and I saw Shoshana coming back to life, the killing machine at her core spreading its wings.

I nodded and said, "Everyone kit up. We're going hunting."

Johan said, "What about me?"

I looked at Shoshana, wanting her opinion. She stared at him for a moment, doing her weird thing, then nodded. I said, "You want to make this right?"

"Yes. I do."

I said to Knuckles, "Get him his body armor and radios."

Johan said, "What about a weapon?"

I smiled. "Not so fast. I'll keep you alive defensively, but you'll have to prove good faith with our deal before I'll let you have a bullet launcher."

I didn't wait for the protest I knew was coming. I mean, *I* would have bitched about assaulting a Special Forces base with my fists. Knuckles dropped his kitbag at Johan's feet, and I said, "We roll in five."

69

★ ★ ★

Aaron advanced through the small copse of trees, dragging Alex slowly behind him, the undergrowth grabbing their clothes at every step, the noise to Aaron sounding like an elephant wandering by.

He'd initially tried moving up the mountain, away from the majority of the buildings, to either escape outright or—if they reached a protective fence that proved too hard to cross—at least find a place to hunker down until Shoshana could arrive to help. Instead, they'd run into a mini-city of cement barracks, with men out front cooking over open fires, drinking beer, and using trails to go back down the mountain, winding right by their hiding spot. He'd slowly retraced their steps, fearing they were going to be discovered by accident.

Once they'd returned to level ground, he'd crouched in the undergrowth, thinking. Alex had whispered, "What now?"

"Pretty easy on our part. We just need to stay hidden until Shoshana arrives, but I want to do it as close to the front gate as possible. I don't want to force her to penetrate the length of the base."

She trembled, saying, "I'm not sure how long we can sit here. Those trails are all over the place. Sooner or later, someone's going to stumble over us."

Aaron realized that Alex was barely holding it together, but he didn't fault her for it. Given the complete lack of experience and training for the trials they'd been through, she'd held up pretty well. He said, "She won't be long. She's on the way right now."

Alex nodded, then said, "I'm more worried about what happens when *she* is found. How is she going to sneak in here and then sneak us back out?"

Aaron quietly chuckled. He said, "She's coming with a team. A friend of mine from America. They'll sneak when they can but kill when they can't. They think they're conducting a snatch and grab, then hightailing it off the base."

Alex said, "They 'think' they're conducting a snatch and grab? What's that mean?"

Aaron said, "Well, they *are* doing that, but we're taking out more than just us. We're going to rescue some of the men in that prison."

Alex hissed, "*What?* Are you crazy?"

"Shhh . . . keep your voice down. You heard them talking about killing Thomas tonight? I can't let them do that."

"Yes, you *can.* We can't be responsible for what they do to their own people. This is their country. We can't save everyone." She started vibrating in fear at the very thought. "Aaron, you're going to kill us both trying to do that, along with your friends."

Aaron's face dropped in disappointment. He said, "Alex, without Thomas you would have been gang-raped every hour you were in there. I would be dead. As far as I'm concerned, every minute now is just extra time I would have already lost. He's coming with us."

Alex drew back, the words cutting deep, and Aaron could see the shame fall over her. She said, "I . . . didn't mean . . . I know it's the right thing . . . but we can't . . ." And then she seemed to come to grips with what she was saying, understanding her fear was sealing another man's fate. One who had already saved her life. "Okay. Okay."

She took a breath, then pointed to the east and said, "I think the gate is that way. I was in the front of the prison, and I could see trucks coming and going toward the west through my window."

Aaron smiled and said, "Good. Very good. We'll stick to the woods as long as we can."

She started to say something else, and he patted her arm, saying, "Drop it. Forget about it. I already have."

He struck out in the direction she'd indicated, hoping the woods extended all the way to the fence line. They did not.

He reached the edge of the cover, staying deep enough inside to remain in the shadows of the brush. He saw a rutted track snaking its way around a U-shaped cinder-block building with a single lamp on the far corner.

He heard movement and crouched down. Lurch and another man came running up to the building, shouting something in Sesotho. Two men came out, one short, with a bald head and a thick neck, looking like someone had slapped a bowling ball between the shoulders of a five-foot mannequin. The other was the exact opposite, a tall, thin man, reminding Aaron of a cattail caught in the wind.

Lurch began shouting, waving his arms, and Aaron knew he'd returned to the interrogation cell. He'd found the general.

The bald-headed man rattled off a sentence and then snorted, as if he was trying to clear his nose. They went back and forth, Bowling-Ball Head snorting each time he finished, like he had some form of Tourette's syndrome.

The tall man raced inside the building, and Aaron knew the window for their escape was ticking down. Before the thin man could return, a lorry came flying up the gravel road, screeching to a stop, a cloud of dust enveloping it. The driver leapt out and ran forward, then close to ten men spilled out the back, all armed with AK-47s.

At first, Aaron thought they were the search team, until they unloaded two bodies from the back, dumping them unceremoniously on the ground. The driver began arguing with Lurch, the latter looking confused. Lurch began shouting, gaining control.

Aaron recognized two things: One, Lurch outranked everyone there, and two, nobody but Lurch knew Aaron had escaped. The truck full of soldiers was a reaction to something else, not a planned response, and it would take time for Lurch to develop a course of action.

Aaron grabbed Alex by the hand and began going back the way they'd come, trying to find a path that would allow them to circle around the group. He hit a line of trees that went south, sparsely running between two tin shacks, and took it. He stopped in between them, slowly inching forward, and was overpowered by the smell. The door to the one on the left opened, and a soldier exited, buckling his pants.

Aaron whirled at the noise, and the man shouted at him. The soldier realized something wasn't right and began screaming, a banshee wail that split the night air. He turned to run. Aaron dropped his AK, darted forward, and caught him around the neck, silencing the noise. He cinched the man's upper arm, rotated, and flipped him over his hip, slamming the soldier into the ground. Aaron dropped onto his neck with his knee, using the force of his body to kill him outright.

Aaron surveyed for other threats but found only Alex, crouched with a hand over her mouth, shocked at the violence. Aaron picked up the AK, then heard shouting from the direction of the U-shaped building. The sound of the truck split the night, and Aaron grabbed Alex's hand and began running through the trees. He reached one of the few asphalt roads on the base, seeing nothing but open space and decrepit buildings beyond it, the area sporadically lit by rusted lamps bolted to the roofs. Behind the buildings was an open field full of waist-high grass and undulating hillocks.

He saw headlights to his right and said, "Come on. Fast."

They sprinted across the road, caught briefly in the glow from the truck, then were across, back in the darkness. He avoided the lamps of the buildings, continuing to the field. They reached it, and he dropped to a crouch, saying, "Get low. Get below the grass."

They started moving west, and the truck stopped on the shoulder of the road, the men spilling out. He reached a small ravine and ducked into it, scrambling until he reached the end. He poked his head over the top and saw the fence line about seventy meters away, a ten-foot chain-link barrier with razor wire on top. A guard tower with a lone sentry was spaced every fifty meters. To his right, a hundred meters past the northern tower, he saw the front gate, brightly illuminated, with a drop bar and two soldiers standing guard.

So close.

The northern tower turned on a spotlight, followed by the southern one, and they began randomly sweeping the field, curious about the commotion surrounding the truck. Sooner or later, Lurch would coordinate their actions.

He dropped flat, looking back the way they'd come, and saw the men from the truck spreading out in a line, Lurch giving orders, the Sesotho language floating out in the wind.

The soldiers began moving forward, and Lurch shouted in English, taunting them. "Jew, we will find you. You have nowhere to go. And when we do, the girl will be the searchers' reward. You will be mine. I'll leave your body naked just like you did General Mosebo."

Alex looked at her clothes, and Aaron realized Lurch thought they'd taken them as some kind of statement. A final insult that must have driven him mad with rage.

Aaron dropped the magazine in his AK, pressing down to determine how many rounds it held. It was full. He said, "Get behind me, in the bank of the ravine."

"What are we going to do?"

"Fight."

70

It was a forty-minute drive from Morija to downtown Maseru, but the base happened to be outside the city, so we could be on-site in thirty minutes or less. I used the time to pick Johan's brain. He detailed four primary targets, of which he was tasked with taking the television and radio station down, as well as cutting the primary ISP for the country.

I said, "What will happen now that you're out of the net?"

"When I give the call, they'll execute and won't even miss me. The TV station was to prevent the word from getting out, but truthfully, it's closed at night, and by the time we're through, it should be too quick to even matter. It's a risk, but not much of one. The main thing was keeping South Africa from knowing anything was going on."

"I thought they were in on it? They're giving up the triggers. I heard the guy called 'Colonel Smith.'"

"*He's* in on it, but that's about it. I don't even know who he really is, but he specifically told us that if South Africa thought its water concessions were being threatened, he wouldn't be able to stop the response."

"What about the truck that ran off? The men you were taking as your force?"

"You killed their command. They're just a bunch of privates, and not that good, honestly. The best soldiers went to the hard targets. I got the dregs because our target was really more like a simple breaking and entering. If I were to guess, they're driving around the city wondering what to do."

"Okay, what can you tell me about the base, other than the location?"

He described it as relatively decrepit, with a single drop-bar entry, a couple of guards out front, and buildings spread out as if nobody had a central plan when they constructed it. The barracks for the SF regiment were up on a hillside, and the main headquarters was deep in the woods, off by itself.

I said, "So you've been on it? They know you? Can you get us through on a bluff at the gate?"

He laughed and said, "No. The only reason I was on that base was to be interrogated when I got sloppy on my reconnaissance here."

"Interrogated?"

"Yeah. Mosebo kept his involvement in the coup secret, one, because he knew someone would leak it if it got out, and, two, to protect him if it went to shit. Because of it, I was rolled up when I was doing my targeting work by some counterintelligence guys. I couldn't throw his name out for any help because the only ones who know about the coup are the ones directly involved, and he kept them quarantined on a 'training mission.' I'm sure his plan is to blame the SF regimental commander if anything goes wrong."

"Where's he? The regimental commander? Is he on a target or on the base?"

"He's lying on the side of the road. He was in my vehicle when you ambushed us."

"Okay. Anything else about the base?"

"It's ringed with guard towers, but that's more of make-do work from what I could see. The usual lazy privates baking in the sun for little reason. There isn't a real threat to the place, and they aren't postured for one. There's not much else to it. There's a military intelligence company, some engineers, and the SF regiment. It's spread out, and nobody really talks between the commands, from what I know."

I nodded, then said, "You have some reports you should be making? Something to let everyone know you're good to go?"

He looked at his watch and said, "We're within the window. I get an up, and I can initiate. You want that?"

"Yeah. As long as you aren't going to send a distress signal."

He laughed and said, "What good would that do? All that would cause is the end of the coup. You'd still have me."

I said, "Get to it," then clicked onto our internal net and said, "All elements, all elements, here's the warning order: Knuckles and Veep, you're up first. We're going to drive past the gate-road entrance and let you two roll out. You get in firing position and take out the gate guards. There are supposedly only two. You copy?"

I got an up from both and said, "We'll roll in, and I expect the gate to be open, so don't fuck around. We're going to penetrate and do a quick snatch and grab, wherever we can locate the precious cargo. Break, break, Carrie, that's where you come in. Give Aaron a call and find out where he is on the base. Just a general location. I need to know if we're going to try sneaking in ten feet or run it like Mad Max to the end. You get him on the line, get the information, then keep the line open. When I give the signal—meaning I think I'm close enough for compromise—I want him to fire a double tap in the air, wait a second, then do it again."

We had no way to pinpoint Aaron's location. No beacons, no cell phone geolocation, no nothing, and I wasn't going to trust some long, drawn-out description of what was around him. Firing was risky, but it was the quickest thing I could think of.

She said, "Roger all," and I turned back to Johan, saying, "How'd the radio calls go?"

He put down his hand mic and said, "We're in business. All hell is going to break loose in about ten minutes."

I nodded, and Brett, the driver of our vehicle, said, "We're about to intersect the road that runs next to the base. We're five minutes out before we hit the gate-road intersection."

I nodded and said, "All elements, all elements, five minutes before the intersection. Carrie, what do you have?"

We rolled right next to the perimeter fencing, and I saw searchlights all over the field, a string of men in the distance, double arm's length apart, all armed.

Shoshana came on and said, "Pike, Pike, I just talked to Aaron. He's in an open field and he's being actively hunted. He says he won't be able to wait on a call to fire."

"Why?"

"He's about to start shooting now."

71

★ ★ ★

I hollered at Brett, pointing out the window, "That's them, to the right; he's to the right. Get off this road."

I saw a dirt trail appear to our left, angling away from the asphalt. He said, "Hang on," and jerked the wheel, throwing us all against the side of the vehicle.

The rear vehicle followed, and we stopped out of sight of the asphalt. I got on the net. "Same call, different location. Knuckles, you take the northern tower, Veep, the southern one. Who's got the breaching gear? We need the bolt cutters."

Veep said, "They're in my ruck. I've got 'em."

"Dig 'em out and roll. Get in position, but don't trigger until we've made breach. Knuckles, you good to go?"

"Just give me the trigger. Veep and I will handle it."

Johan said, "Give me a gun. You can't breach with just the two of you."

I stared hard at him. He said, "Give me a gun, Pike. Let me help. I won't hurt anyone but the enemy."

I said, "Brett, give him his weapon. I'm going back for the bolt cutters."

I jogged to the trail vehicle and saw Shoshana kitting up. I said, "Whoa. You're not going anywhere. I need Jennifer and you to drive these vehicles to the exfil point when I call."

She said, "Fuck that. I'm going in. Aaron's right *there*."

She was on fire, and I knew she would be out of control once we broke into the field, which was exactly why she wasn't going to enter. She would listen to nothing anyone said, least of all me.

"Shoshana, I need someone to drive the truck. It's not going to magic to us for exfil, and that someone is you."

Jennifer came around, and I handed her the keys to my truck. She gave me the bolt cutters. Shoshana glowered at me, and I said, "You good?"

She said nothing. Jennifer put her hands on Shoshana's shoulders, leaned in, and with her back to me said, "We're good to go. Standing by for the call. Go get him."

I nodded, clicked on the net, and said, "Knuckles, Veep, you in position?"

I got an up from both. I said, "Johan, Blood, you ready to go?"

Brett said, "This is Blood; I'm next to Johan. We're ready."

I jogged up to them and without preamble said, "Showtime."

We stalked our way through the darkness at a half jog and reached the fence. I started cutting, making a hole big enough for someone to get through carrying a casualty. I reached the top, with Johan pulling on the links as I cut, and I heard the first round crack through the air. I looked out into the field and saw the right of the line shooting at a depression about seventy meters away, then a muzzle flash returning fire.

Aaron.

I heard someone in the depression scream, and the spotlights centered on his location. I said, "Execute, execute, execute. Eliminate the threat in the towers and knock out those lights."

I kept clipping, and both Brett and Johan began suppressing the right side of the line. The fire slacked off immediately, the men dropping flat and shouting. Knuckles came on. "Targets down." One second the spotlights were on the ravine, and the next they were aimed up in the sky.

I said, "Suppress," then ripped the links aside, seated my weapon to my shoulder, and began running to the depression.

The left side of the line saw me and began firing in my direction. I took a knee and returned it. Without commands, we began flip-flopping toward the depression in a bounding overwatch, someone always firing while someone else moved.

The right side of the line gained enough courage to begin fighting again, and I started hearing the unique snap of rounds breaking the sound barrier around my head. I closed within thirty meters of the ravine, seeing the muzzle flash still returning fire, and shouted, "Friendly to the rear! Friendly to the rear!"

I saw Aaron turn toward me, then rotate back to his shooting position, blasting away. I leapt in, and he shouted over his shoulder, "Alex is hit!"

Brett fell in beside me, and I said, "Check her out," then took a position next to Aaron, picking off targets.

I saw a large man screaming at the soldiers to advance on us, and some of them did. Johan leapt into the pit and Aaron's eyes got wide, his barrel rotating toward him. I pushed it up and said, "He's with me."

Aaron snarled, "That fuck is with *them*."

I said, "Not anymore. Trust me. It's complicated."

Johan said nothing, moving to the rear where Alexandra was crouched, Brett over the top of her, bandaging her leg. Johan took off his body armor and put it around Alexandra, saying, "What do you have?"

"Thigh wound. In and out. No contact with the bone. She won't bleed out, but she can't move on her own power."

Johan said, "You ready to get the fuck out of here?" She grimaced in pain but nodded. He turned to me and asked, "We ready?"

I said, "Yeah. Brett, you go with Johan. Aaron, get ready to cover."

Johan said, "Aaron." He turned, and Johan tossed him his rifle. Aaron took it, nodded, and shouldered his beat-up AK.

I shouted, "Go!" and Johan slung Alexandra over his shoulder, leapt out of the ravine, and began running in a zigzag pattern back toward the hole in the fence. Brett followed behind, bounding about thirty meters before stopping and giving cover.

Seeing us escaping, the remaining soldiers put up a ferocious amount of fire, with three having the courage to charge across the field. I dropped one, Aaron hit the other, and the third dove for the ground.

I heard Brett shout, "Go!" and we flipped out of the small ravine and raced past Brett, then rotated around, peppering the area around the truck. The return fire had dropped to almost nothing. I called Jennifer and gave the command for exfil. I saw the fence in front of us, a pair of headlights coming in. We dove through the hole just as the SUVs came rolling up. We piled into the two vehicles helter-skelter, and they sped out, throwing gravel.

Jennifer led us back up the road where they'd staged, then pulled over so we could adjust and reconsolidate. I was crammed into Jennifer's vehicle with Aaron, Brett, Veep, and Knuckles. Shoshana had Alexandra and Johan. Aaron said, "Where's Shoshana?"

I opened the door, saying, "Brett, check out Alexandra. Make sure she's good to go."

He left, and to Aaron, I said, "She's driving the rear vehicle, and trust me, she is a giant pain in the ass."

He smiled and said, "I knew she would come. But I didn't expect you. Thank you."

Jennifer leaned over and pecked his cheek, saying, "It's really good to see you. Alive, I mean. Sorry you missed your honeymoon."

He chuckled, opened the door, and said, "That's the damn truth. Coming to Africa was the worst decision I've ever made."

Jennifer said, "I don't think so. Sometimes you need to lose something before you realize how valuable it is."

He glanced back and saw Shoshana standing outside the driver's door of her vehicle, looking toward him. He said, "I already knew."

"But she doesn't know that you know. And she wants to."

He patted her hand and said, "Thank you again." And exited the vehicle.

We watched like preteens hiding in the woods spying on lovers' lane, with Knuckles passing out NODs to penetrate the darkness.

Watching Aaron approach, Shoshana's face reflected a childlike innocence, full of expectation and hope. Aaron reached her, and she said nothing, simply wrapping her arms around him and burying her head in his chest. He held her for at least ten seconds, then pushed her back, kissed her forehead, and said something in her ear. Even through the green glow of the NODs, I could see the joy on her face.

He cupped her cheeks and kissed her on the lips. She wiped her eyes and stood on tiptoe, leaning into his ear. She whispered and then did something so unlike her it made me wonder if I'd ever known her. She licked his neck, softly, looking for all the world like a lion meeting a mate after a kill. Later, Jennifer said it was a kiss, but I know what I saw.

Shoshana glanced back at us, and we all ducked down, positive she could see us even without NODs.

Hiding below the seat, Jennifer said, "Wow. This is like *National Geographic*."

Knuckles laughed and said, "Don't make any sudden moves. They trigger on movement."

I poked my head back over the bench seat and saw . . . I'm not even sure how to describe it. Serenity? Peace? Triumph? Whatever it was, it was worth every bit of effort we'd expended.

I said, "This is better than *Jerry McGuire*. If she says, 'You complete me,' I'm never letting her live it down."

Jennifer and Knuckles laughed, and I joined in, because we were just a bunch of schoolkids watching a reunion on a deserted road after fleeing a firefight in Africa. We were normal people. And then I said, "Uh-oh."

Because we weren't normal people.

Like an idiot, Johan came around the vehicle and stuck out his hand. Aaron punched him in the face with all of his weight behind it, lifting him off his feet. Johan hit the earth flat on his back and gained some smarts. He remained on the ground. I leapt out of the vehicle, running to the confrontation and jumping in front of him.

I held up my hands and said, "Aaron, I know you had it rough, but you don't understand the position we're in right now. There's more going on than you know."

Aaron let out a breath and nodded. "That's correct on both sides."

"What do you mean?"

He looked at Shoshana and said, "We need to get back in that base. There are men still in the prison that we need to rescue."

72

★ ★ ★

Thomas Naboni heard the crackle of gunfire outside the cell window and instinctively knew it was Aaron. He smiled wistfully, happy for his friend but sad for himself. He knew tonight would be his last on earth. He was simply waiting on the executioner to return.

The uniformed tribe heard the same gunfire and grew restless, pacing about in their cage at each new burst. Their angst was driven by the guards themselves, who'd also begun marching about in confusion, sometimes abandoning their posts for long moments of time.

Everyone in the prison, both the keepers and the kept, could feel danger in the air. The gunfire confirmed it. It didn't last long—maybe thirty minutes tops—but soon after, much farther away, other sounds could be heard. Maybe it was his imagination, or maybe the fight had just moved off the military base, but Thomas was sure he could hear gunfire coming from the city.

The first indicator that something was amiss had been the removal of Aaron and the ominous words from General Mosebo about having a "big night" tonight. The next had been his short, painful interrogation at the hands of Lurch, when he'd broken and confessed to helping protect Alexandra. Now it was the noise of gunfire.

One of his trusted friends, a pharmacist in a former life, placed his back against the wall next to Thomas and whispered, "What does the shooting mean? Good or bad?"

"I don't know." Thomas didn't have the heart to say what he truly felt: For them, it could be nothing but bad.

"The guards keep leaving their posts, like they're trying to find out what is happening. Nobody has seen the captain since he took the Israeli. I think nobody is in charge right now."

Thomas knew his friend was driving at something. "What's your point?"

His friend pointed to the man the guards had been punishing for weeks by withholding food. "Nobi isn't going to live much longer even if we simply remain. But that isn't going to happen. General Mosebo threatened *you* tonight. After you, it will be all of us." He leaned in to Thomas and whispered, "Maybe we should try to escape. We won't get a better chance."

Thomas glanced up at the blanket-covered toilet hiding Aaron's window, thinking about their options. What his friend said was most probably true, but it didn't alter the ultimate problem: They were inside a guarded military base. One that now had active gunfire within it.

Thomas said, "We won't get out of the compound. I'm not even sure we'll get out of the prison. The uniform prisoners may stop us just to curry favor with the guards, and they outnumber us four to one."

His friend remained quiet. Thomas knew he wanted to speak again, but he wouldn't unless given permission. Like every member of the suit tribe, he held Thomas in the highest esteem, with almost reverent deference, because Thomas had kept them alive. It was more than merely survival, though. He'd done so without losing an ounce of his dignity. He'd carried himself in the hell of the prison just as he had when he was leading the revolt against the corruption of the government, the indignities heaped upon him never defining his character.

Because of that loyalty, Thomas felt the pressure like a diamond being formed in the mines of the Lesotho highlands. It wasn't just about him. It was about all of them. Was he serving his men by insisting they remain, or was he simply frozen by his fear for his own survival? And did it really matter? At the end of the day, was getting beaten to death by General Mosebo any more dignified than dying on an escape run across the base?

He glanced at the blanket again, wondering if Aaron had finished his work. He said, "Keep an eye out," then stood up. He glanced furtively left and right but could barely even see the front of the cell in the gloom. He pulled the blanket aside, his pulse beginning to race. He crouched behind it, listening for anyone reacting to his use of the "toilet." What he heard was a scraping above him. He glanced up, seeing the sky through the hole in the wall, then felt a piece of masonry hit him on the shoulder. He brushed it off and continued to stare. One of the bricks disappeared, the hole growing larger. He scrambled up onto the bucket of feces and slowly stood upright.

Outside the window was Aaron, balancing on something below him and working the bricks one by one.

Thomas almost slipped off the bucket in shock. Aaron reached through the window, snagged his arm, then held a finger to his lips. He whispered, "I'm almost done with this. Get ready. You're coming with me."

Thomas's mouth opened and closed, no noise coming out. Aaron pried another brick free, and Thomas found his voice. He said, "We must all go. All five of us. And they go out before me, starting with Nobi."

Aaron smiled and said, "I would expect nothing less." He clicked an earpiece and said, "Pike, Pike, I've made contact. We're starting to remove the bricks."

I heard the call from Aaron and tapped Knuckles on the shoulder. He sidled forward and placed an explosive breaching charge on a side door at the back of the prison, on the other side of the building from Aaron. Our job, should he call for it, would be to assault, coming in hard and killing anyone who opposed us, but the primary course of action was stealth, using a reverse escape plan that Aaron had set in motion for himself before we'd arrived.

At our reconsolidation location, Aaron had told me he was going back in to rescue a guy in the prison, which I'd thought was absolute insanity. Shoshana, for once, felt the same way, but Aaron wouldn't listen, which at any other time would have been sweet justice, because I'd lived with her shit for days. She, like me, felt that attempting to break *back* into the camp, and then into the prison, was absolutely crazy—even for her—but Aaron had been adamant.

A man named Thomas Naboni had kept him and Alexandra alive, and because of it, Aaron felt he owed a debt. He was unwilling to leave Thomas behind, but I was just as steadfast that our mission here was done. All we had to do now was let the coup play out and collect Colonel Armstrong. Risking my life for someone who'd helped Aaron was a noble gesture, but going back in was asking to get everyone killed. And I wasn't too keen on that outcome, noble or otherwise.

Johan had heard the argument going back and forth and said, "Trying to penetrate that base again is not smart. General Mosebo will have it on lockdown after what we just did. I know him. Getting in and getting out will be impossible."

Aaron had said, "You don't need to worry about him. General Mosebo is dead."

"Dead? How do you know?"

Aaron spit out, "Because I fucking killed him."

Johan was speechless for a moment, then said, "You killed the head of the Lesotho Defence Force?"

Aaron turned toward him, the violence held just below the surface, saying, "You have a problem with that? Was he a fucking friend of yours too? The point is that the base will be in complete disarray. There won't be any lockdown, because nobody will order it."

Just being in the presence of Johan left Aaron vehemently angry, and Johan realized it. He backed off, saying to me, "That's the power base of the entire coup."

I said, "Will it affect your plan? Will we still get Colonel Armstrong on the ground if the general's dead?"

"Yeah, it shouldn't alter getting Armstrong. Mosebo had no actual command or decision-making in the assault. That's all up to my guys. He was just supposed to come out to the airport with me for the grand finale of meeting the new prime minister. The problem will be after, in the consolidation of power. The military outnumbers the police, but the police will side with the current prime minister. With a vacuum on the military side, I can see this not being clean. It could drag out and spark into a countercoup."

I went to the natural conclusion, asking, "Which means South Africa could be called in, and the contact with the triggers may balk?"

"Possibly. I guess it depends on how long it simmers. My concern is what I told you before. I wanted a simple change from one administration to the other. I don't want a bunch of bloodshed of innocents, which might now happen."

Aaron said, "Like you give a shit about them. Maybe you shouldn't start brushfires you can't control. Mosebo's dead, and there's nothing we can do about it. Thomas is alive, and there *is* something we can do about that."

I said, "Who is this guy? I mean, why's he in prison?"

"He's the leader of a grassroots political party. One that was fighting the corruption of the entrenched bureaucracy. He got a little too powerful with the people and was removed. In his words, he and his entire inner circle were 'disappeared.' According to the guys in the prison with him, he's their version of Nelson Mandela. The population loved him. Which, of course, is what made him dangerous."

Jennifer looked at Johan and said, "*That's* the guy you should have been backing, instead of just throwing another corrupt idiot in charge."

Johan said, "I don't think you understand how this works. I simply get paid to do a job. I didn't plan this thing. I'm just executing."

Aaron said, "You disgust me."

But Jennifer's words, as usual, were genius and gave me an idea. I said, "Johan, if we get Thomas out, do you think we could install *him* as prime minister? I mean, could we meet the deputy prime minister on the airfield with the police, arrest him on the spot, and install Thomas? Especially since Mosebo's out of the picture to fight it?"

Johan considered for a second, then said, "The police will probably back him simply because he's been jailed by Mosebo. Enemy of my enemy and all that, but he won't be strong enough to remain. We need outside influence. He'll have to be immediately backed by an outside state, because those inside won't back anyone in the confusion, leaving him open. He has no power base."

Jennifer said, "We need to get the United States involved."

Aaron waved his hands and said, "Pike, none of this matters without Thomas, and the longer we wait, the more that base begins to consolidate."

He was right. We could debate the end state all night long, but it mattered little without Thomas in our grasp. I nodded at him, then looked around the group and said, "Okay, this is outside the scope of our mission set. I'm not going to order anyone to go, but I'm game. Anyone want out?"

Aaron watched my team closely, but all he got was Knuckles saying, "You're wasting our time. Same plan as the original?"

I grinned and said, "Same plan. Load up."

73

★ ★ ★

Ten minutes later, we were parked at the intersection of the black-top and the dirt road that led to the front gate of the base, waiting on the call from Veep and Knuckles.

It wasn't optimal, but we'd found an abandoned thatched hut on a deserted road and had put Alexandra inside it. I was a little hesitant to do so, for obvious reasons, but she was completely supportive of the plan—probably because the alternative was coming on base with us and just sitting in the SUV—and so we'd made sure her bandages were swapped and her condition was stable, and we'd left her with Johan's body armor and a pistol.

Besides Alexandra, we had another long pole in the tent: We didn't have enough transportation to get everyone off the base. Aaron had said there were five of them—with one possibly nonambulatory—and all we had were our stolen SUVs. I'd decided to split the force in two: a prison assault force and a transportation location force. The prison assault would be Knuckles, Jennifer, Shoshana, Aaron, and me. The vehicle scavenger hunt would be Johan, Brett, and Veep. Johan knew the base better than any of us, Brett could blend in when they stole whatever they found, and Veep was just good with a gun. The rest of us would attempt the prison breakout—ostensibly the harder of the missions, but I wasn't betting on it.

My earpiece came alive, and I heard, "In position. Stand by," then, "Targets down, targets down."

We began driving down the road, and I saw the drop bar rise. We stopped for barely a second, letting them into our vehicles, and were rolling through the gate, back into the darkness. I surveyed three hundred and sixty degrees trying to identify a response, my finger tapping the trigger guard of my Glock, the adrenaline starting to rise.

Amazingly, I saw nothing. We were in.

Aaron was behind the wheel of our SUV since he was the only one who knew where the prison was located, Brett driving the one behind us. We rolled on the blacktop as fast as we dared without our lights, driving under NODs. Luckily, the base itself had very little outdoor lighting, with most of the weak illumination provided by lightbulbs attached to buildings, so you'd have to be right next to us to see us pass by.

I felt Aaron slow down, then stop, and heard, "Pike. Problem." Ahead of us, at the first intersection on the gate road, I saw a checkpoint. Three men were standing next to a fifty-five-gallon drum with a fire in it, one of them yelling and waving his arms in the air. *Uh-oh.* Aaron said, "The guy shouting is Lurch. The head asshole at the prison. The other two must be guards he's brought out in an attempt to catch me escaping."

We watched for a second; then Lurch stormed over to a Land Rover and drove off, moving deeper into the base.

Aaron said, "Blow through it?"

I glanced left and right, looking for a way to avoid the checkpoint. There was none, only grass fields and woods. I said, "No. That'll just bring a chase. With your plan, we're going to need time. Stealth. We won't get that with a compromise right off the bat. Pull up to it."

I turned around and said, "Knuckles, you got the guy on the left. I'll take the right."

We rolled up to the intersection, and I saw a U-shaped cinderblock building about a hundred and fifty meters down a dirt road, a canvas-covered two-and-a-half-ton truck out front, just like the ones that had shown up in Morija. Probably the same one we had shot at an hour ago. I called, "Blood, Blood, take a look to the left."

He said, "I see it."

"We've got the checkpoint. Stand by. The bodies are staying in the street, so the clock will be ticking."

Aaron pulled up to the barrel on the side of the road, the fire providing flickering illumination. All three of us rolled down our windows. I held my suppressed ZEV Tech down against the door, waiting for the guard on my side to approach. Both were clearly confused, seeing white men in an SUV on their base at two in the morning. The one on Aaron's side approached first and began asking questions, which, of course, we couldn't answer. My target hung back, refusing to approach.

Come on, dipshit, come up to the window.

The tension mounted, until finally, the guard on the driver's side became suspicious. He backed up at Aaron's bullshit explanation and raised his rifle. Knuckles shot him in the head, the suppressor giving off a muted spit. The round snapped him backward like he had a string attached to his skull. I threw open my door, rolled out, and took aim, expecting to be receiving fire from the second guard. Inexplicably, instead of raising his weapon, my guy took off running in a panic. I lined up the holosight and broke the trigger to the rear, twice, the ZEV Tech tracking effortlessly. He tumbled forward, rolling lifelessly on the ground.

I leapt back in and said, "Go, go." I looked behind me and saw Brett take the intersection toward the lorry, pulling into the shadows of the trees. I said, "How much farther?"

Aaron pointed at a large one-story building set back into the woods about a hundred meters away. "That's it. I'll park across the other side, in the brush, and we'll walk in. My window is on the back side to the south. Your position is back side north, on the other end. Let me work it, but if I need you, clear the building all the way to me."

I said, "Hope that won't be necessary."

We exited, softly closing the doors, then approached the building using the cover of the brush, avoiding the main front entrance and circling around to the back. Aaron led us down the cinder blocks for about thirty feet, then stopped, pointing at a hole above him.

I nodded, and we left him and Shoshana, continuing on until we located a wooden door at the northern end. I established security, putting Jennifer on the corner looking out toward the main entrance, and waited. Twenty minutes later, I got the call that Aaron had made contact with Thomas, and I had Knuckles place his charge, leaving Jennifer on the corner pulling security.

So far, so good.

I called Brett, saying, "We've got contact. Starting extraction. What's your status?"

Studying the U-shaped building with his NODs, Brett saw what might have been movement on the porch. He turned his attention to the truck parked off to the side and saw a soldier in the driver's seat. He whispered, "Veep, what do you have?"

Positioned in the wood line on the other side of the road, Veep had a different view. "I have a man in the passenger seat and two on the porch. There's a light in one room on the east side, so I'm assuming someone's in there as well."

Pike came through: "We've got contact. Starting extraction. What's your status?"

"This is Blood. Conducting recce now. It's looking promising, but I'm not committing just yet."

"Roger all. Don't get compromised. That's the priority."

"Understood. Break, break, Veep, keep your eye on the porch. Tell me if anyone else shows up."

Brett touched Johan's sleeve and said, "There's a guy in the driver's seat and one in the passenger seat, and we have to secure that building before we steal it."

The vehicle was an obstacle to assaulting the building, something that had to be passed in order to access a breach point, but luckily, it was parked far enough away that—if they did it correctly—they could eliminate the two men inside the truck without alerting anyone else.

Johan nodded and said, "What about the bed of the truck?"

Brett said, "I don't know. I don't think anyone would be in the back if they're parked at a building, but then again, I wouldn't expect two guys to be up front."

Johan said, "Let me see your NODs." Brett passed them to him, and he focused on the truck, searching for something specific. He found it and handed them back.

"That's the same truck used in the field. It's full of bullet holes. There were about ten or twelve guys in that fight, and we took out at least six of them, so that leaves a max of six, maybe less."

"What if this is a barracks? There could be thirty guys inside, and I don't want to find that out the hard way."

"It's not. It's the headquarters for the military intelligence battalion that supports the SF regiment. I've had the pleasure of being interrogated inside it. The left side of the wing is nothing but classrooms. The right, where the light is on, is the commander's office."

Johan slung his weapon onto his back and withdrew a fixed-blade fighting knife. He said, "Cover me, and I'll check out the truck's bed. If it's clean, I'll take the guy on the passenger's side, you take the driver's side. Good?"

Brett nodded, then said, "Shoot me two flashes if it's clean, three if it's dirty."

They didn't have enough equipment to outfit Johan with Taskforce communications, so they were forced to improvise.

Brett got on the net and said, "Veep, Johan's moving to the truck. Keep your targets on the porch. If they show hostile intent, drop them."

"Roger."

Brett tapped Johan on the shoulder and handed him the set of NODs. Johan lay down, then crawled on his belly to the rear of the truck. He rose into a crouch, listening. When he was satisfied, he slowly peeled a corner of the canvas away and used the night vision on the inside.

He slid back down and stowed the NODS, and Brett saw two flashes. Brett withdrew his own fighting knife and low-crawled to the rear of the truck. He showed the blade to Johan and leaned in to his ear, whispering, "You initiate," then drew a finger across his throat.

Johan nodded and rolled to the passenger side. Brett went left, sliding down the truck bed.

He reached the driver's door and glanced up. He could see the head of his target against the window, asleep. He gently put his palm on the handle, wrapping his fingers around the metal, waiting on Johan. He heard the far door open, the hinges groaning in the night, and yanked down on his handle. The door refused to open. In one painful, panicked microsecond, he realized the man had fallen asleep on the latch, locking the door. He heard a brief struggle on the far side and saw his man waking up. He leapt onto the running board and shattered the window with his elbow, catching the man's head at the same time.

He grabbed the target by his hair and yanked him halfway out, stuck the blade under his neck, and sliced both carotid arteries, a great gout of blood spilling onto the door of the truck.

He dropped to the ground, unslung his weapon, and took a knee at the front tire, searching for threats. He saw the two men on the porch both startled at the noise. One took a single step off the porch, and his head snapped back. He collapsed in a heap, rolling into the courtyard. The other one raised his weapon, and Brett broke the trigger, throwing him against a wall.

Everything grew quiet. Johan appeared by his side, and they both waited to see if they were compromised, expecting a horde to come barreling out of the darkness.

Johan said, "What the hell happened?"

"Fucker had the door locked."

They heard a shout from the lighted room. A question spoken in the Sesotho language floated across the courtyard, followed by a snort.

Johan let out a soft laugh. Brett whispered, "What?"

"I know who that is. I'm going to enjoy this."

On the net, Brett said, "Veep, what do you have?"

"Nothing. I've got nothing. It's quiet."

"Provide overwatch on our side. We're assaulting the room on your side."

He hated the plan, but it was a little difficult to dominate the building with overwhelming force when they only had a three-man assault team. He had a choice: start clearing from one end and moving to the other, or focus directly on the room where they knew a threat existed. He chose the latter.

Brett took aim at the corner of the building, settling his red dot on the lone bulb putting out illumination, and fired. It shattered, plunging the courtyard into darkness. He said, "Let's go," and sprinted down the road. He crossed the courtyard, running to the door adjacent to the illuminated window, leaving the entire opposite side wide open to his back. He prayed Johan was right, because if it *was* a barracks, they were dead.

He stacked on the door, waited for Johan to touch his shoulder, then kicked it in. Two men leapt to their feet, neither one armed. One was a short, bald-headed man, who took one look at Johan and began stuttering incoherently. The other sprinted toward an AK leaning against the wall. Johan's rifle spit two suppressed rounds, knocking the man to the floor.

Brett cleared the rest of the room, then rotated to the door, saying, "Veep, Veep, what do you have?"

"Nothing. All's quiet."

To the bald-headed man, Johan said, "Get on your knees."

The man did as he was told, and Johan said, "Well, Frog, looks like I get to ask the questions this time."

Brett said, "You weren't kidding? You know this guy?"

"He did a little interrogation of me earlier. He thought I was US Special Forces out to do something bad in his country. He was only half right."

Johan walked to the man and got in his face, then theatrically pulled his fighting knife free. He said, "How many men are in this building?"

"Four. Only four." And then he snorted, causing Johan to chuckle.

Brett said, "That's it? Four plus you two?"

The man nodded frantically, saying, "The rest are dead in the field."

Brett clicked on the net and said, "Veep, Veep, bring it in. Break, break, Pike, this is Blood. We have your exfil platform. What's the status?"

75

★ ★ ★

Aaron heard the call and answered for Pike: "I've got three out. Two more and we can exfil. Ten more minutes, max."

Aaron grabbed the jacket of the last of Thomas's inner circle and hoisted the man through the ragged hole in the wall while Thomas pushed from the other side. He slid out, and Aaron lowered him to the ground. Shoshana immediately went to work on his leg shackles, using the key Aaron had given her. That left only Thomas inside, and Aaron knew he would need some help. With no other members of his circle inside the prison to hoist him, Thomas would have trouble reaching the hole.

Aaron said, "Shoshana, one more time, please."

She squatted down, placing her back against the wall and holding her hands at shoulder height, palms up. He put his feet on them and stood, getting level with the hole he'd made.

It had taken more time than he had wanted to extract the weakened men through the window, and it had been a miracle that nobody in the prison had challenged their dwindling numbers. They had been helped by the darkness, as the lone bulb usually used to illuminate the cell had remained off, leaving the inside as black as a cave. Coupled with that, the uniformed tribe seemed content to pace at the entrance, shouting questions at the guard down the hallway, more concerned with what was occurring outside the prison than with the rear of their cell.

Aaron rose up on Shoshana's hands, eliciting a soft grunt. He whispered, "Thomas, let's go."

Thomas's face appeared in the window, and Jennifer came on the net: "All elements, this is Koko. Vehicle just approached the prison's main entrance. Two men exiting; one of them is shouting."

Aaron thought, *Lurch.*

He said, "Thomas, come on. Quickly."

Aaron heard a commotion from inside the cell, the uniformed tribe excited about something. Thomas stood on the bucket, and Aaron heard Lurch coming down the hallway, screaming in a rage loud enough for the sound to penetrate outside the hole. He clicked onto the net and said, "Pike, Pike, execute, execute, execute."

Aaron grabbed Thomas's arm, saying, "Come on. Climb!"

Aaron heard the dull thump of Pike's explosive breach on the far side of the building, and the room blazed into light from the single bulb. Thomas jerked his arm free, giving Aaron a grim smile, his perfect teeth gleaming in the tepid light.

Thomas said, "Go. Get them out of here. I will delay the captain."

"No, you dumbass. Come on!"

Thomas stepped off the bucket and disappeared.

Lurch entered the cell and began raving like a lunatic. Aaron grabbed the sides of the hole and pulled himself back into the hell he'd worked so hard to escape. He heard Shoshana shout, "No!" and then he hit the ground behind the blanket. He withdrew his pistol, took a breath, and tore the blanket aside.

Thomas was on his knees, his hands behind his head, with Lurch facing him head-on and a prison guard off to each side, each holding an AK-47 aimed at him. Instinct and training took over, Aaron's body functioning with the precision of a computer, the focal point being the muzzle of his barrel. He fired a double-tap, hitting the guard on the left in the head, then rotated on his knee to the one on the right, breaking the trigger two more times before the first body had even collapsed, his aim impeccable.

The room erupted into shouting, the uniformed prisoners running back and forth at the front of the cell. Lurch jerked Thomas to his feet, using his body as a shield. He brandished a small Makarov pistol and placed it at the base of Thomas's skull. Spittle flying from his mouth, he shouted, "You! How?"

Aaron said, "You let him go and you live."

To the other prisoners, Lurch said, "Attack him. He's only one man. He can't kill you all. When he's dead, I'll let all of you go free."

Seven of the prisoners stood. Aaron kept his weapon on Lurch, afraid to take his eyes off the Makarov. The prisoners advanced forward, and the lead man's head exploded, flinging him back. Aaron felt movement behind him, and Shoshana appeared, holding her pistol as steady as a rail.

The others stopped in their tracks, looking at Lurch. He screamed again, "Attack them! They can't get you all!"

Shoshana said, "First one to take a step forward will die. I promise."

They shuffled back and forth but refused to advance. Lurch began backing up to the door, dragging Thomas with him. He took aim at one of the prisoners and shot him in the chest, screaming, "Attack them!"

The prisoners recoiled, each trying to use another as a shield. An AK-47 erupted in the hallway outside the cell, and Lurch whirled. Aaron saw Knuckles enter, so close to Lurch he was prevented from bringing his weapon to bear. Knuckles hammered Lurch across the bridge of his nose with his suppressor, dropped his weapon on its sling, trapped Lurch's gun hand, and swept his feet out from under him.

Before he'd even hit the ground, Pike and Jennifer entered, flowing into the room and looking for threats like water searching for low ground. They took up points of domination, and Knuckles punched Lurch in the temple twice, knocking the fight out of him.

Seeing the area was clear, Pike lowered his weapon, saying, "Jennifer, secure the hallway. Knuckles, flex-tie that shithead. Aaron, call Brett for exfil."

He turned to the man they'd just saved and said, "Thomas Naboni, I presume?"

Thomas said, "Yes," then watched Shoshana shadow Aaron, refusing to move more than a foot away from him, pacing wherever he went, like she was afraid of losing him. Thomas made the connection and calmly walked to her, as if the preceding action had been a normal occurrence in his everyday life.

To the room, Aaron said, "Truck's one minute out. Prepare for exfil."

Thomas ignored the words, as if he had all the time in the world. He took Shoshana's hand and kissed it, saying, "Shoshana, I presume?"

She nodded, and he said, "Aaron promised you'd be coming. He thinks quite highly of you. I must admit, I didn't have the same faith."

She smiled, the compliment causing her to glance shyly at Aaron, something so out of character it made Pike laugh. Shoshana's eyes slit, and Pike couldn't resist a jab. "Thomas, don't get too close. She's crazy, and it rubs off."

Shoshana scowled, her essence bubbling back to the surface, but before she could retort, Knuckles finished flex-tying Lurch, saying, "What about this asshole?"

Aaron said, "I have an idea." Lurch watched him approach, his eyes so wide the whites glowed against his charcoal skin. Aaron squatted down, studying him like a child would a bug crawling on a stick. He said, "I think we just leave him here."

Aaron looked over at the uniformed prisoners and said, "You men mind watching him until help arrives? Can you keep him safe? Since he cared so much for your welfare?"

One of the prisoners glanced down at the man Lurch had killed, then, in halting English, said, "Yes, please. We would like that very much."

Jennifer poked her head in from the hallway and said, "Vehicle's here."

Pike said, "Let's go. We still need to get off the base."

Thomas said, "What's the next step? Where are you taking us?"

"Well, there's a little bit of payback for helping you."

Thomas grew wary, glancing at Aaron and saying, "Payback how? What do you want?"

"I want you to run this country."

Thomas's mouth fell open, and Shoshana pushed him forward, the team taking up security positions as they moved, protecting him. Aaron brought up the rear, keeping his eyes on the prisoners who remained behind.

The last thing he saw was Lurch in the center of them, the prisoners circling like a pack of dogs, barking and spitting. One kicked him in the stomach, and the floodgate of rage opened, Lurch lost in the flurry of blows.

76

Sitting in the SUV with Aaron, Knuckles, and Thomas, I watched Johan through the window talking into his radio, the clouds reflecting the feeble light of false dawn.

He waved his arms in the air as he spoke, but it was impossible to tell if he was receiving bad news or just coordinating. I hoped it was the latter, because we'd used up all our luck in the past twenty-four hours. If we had more work to do, it would be asking for Murphy to kick us in the balls.

Getting off the base had proven much easier than getting on—probably because we'd killed just about anyone of rank who was still available—and we'd driven straight back to where we'd stashed Alexandra. She was in significant pain, and Brett—our designated team medic—had set about tending to her wound. He'd pronounced it satisfactory, but he was worried about any future delays and wanted to get her to a hospital. I echoed that sentiment, of course, but I wasn't sure how soon it would occur.

Jennifer and Shoshana were with her in the abandoned hut, keeping her spirits up, while the rest of us talked to Thomas. We'd just given him a complete briefing on what was occurring in the country of Lesotho—leaving out any mention of nuclear triggers and top secret organizations—and he was stunned. Not so much that it was happening—nothing about the corruption of the current government could shock him after what it had done to him and his friends—but that we actually had the ability to alter the outcome.

He said, "I'm not sure I'm the man you seek. I was running for a seat in parliament just to force the conversation. That was all. I didn't expect to win, and certainly didn't expect to become as popular as I was. The fact remains I have no experience in government."

Aaron said, "You want to feed the future of your country to that shithead Makalo Lenatha? He was what you were fighting for?"

"No, of course not. It's just that maybe we should look for someone else. Someone with experience."

I said, "Are you kidding? What do you want to do, check on Craigslist in the help wanted section? Is there another jail around here with political prisoners you want to hit?"

Thomas went from me to Aaron, his mouth opening and closing, the enormity of what we were asking settling in.

Knuckles said, "Thomas, don't take this the wrong way because I would have come for you regardless, but don't let the risks we took for your men mean nothing. You ran into Aaron for a reason. *Seize* it. Your country needs you."

Thomas chewed his thumb and stared out the window. He turned and said, "Can I bring my own team with me? The ones who were in prison?"

I laughed and said, "You're the damn prime minister. It's your call."

"How will we do this? If the military is the power behind this coup, how will we get them to back me? General Mosebo was going to kill me tonight. What's to prevent him from doing the same tomorrow?"

"The military won't back you, true, but that's no longer a concern. They won't back anyone now, because General Mosebo's dead."

"What?"

Aaron said, "I killed him. He's no longer in the equation. You have the police on your side, and that may be enough."

"Then why is the military doing this?"

"They don't know he's dead, and we'll use that to our advantage."

He seemed bewildered. He said, "May I think a moment? Talk to my friends?"

I opened the door, saying, "Sure, but don't waste time. That's a commodity we do not have."

He left, and Johan returned, saying, "It's official. All targets are down, and they're starting to consolidate. Only two hiccups. One, the television station is broadcasting, but so far it's just random gunfire stories. Nothing firm. Two, those idiots killed the prime minister. He was supposed to be taken for a big show trial, but he got caught in the cross fire."

I asked, "How does that affect the coup?"

"It actually helps. He wouldn't stand a chance against Lenatha once he was arrested, but he'd clean Thomas's clock. He had too many allies. He'd be out of prison in hours."

"Good. What's the status on the aircraft?"

"It's circling just outside of Lesotho airspace, waiting on my call. What's up with Thomas?"

"He's overwhelmed, and rightfully so. I'm worried about putting him in place and somebody taking him out immediately. If he can't get support from some block in the Lesotho government, he needs immediate international support."

"What happened with your call to higher?"

Earlier, I'd sent a SITREP to Blaine, detailing what was happening. He was a little shocked at how fast things had progressed but was on board with the *wait for the coup to finish* plan for capturing Colonel Armstrong—and, by extension, Tyler Malloy. I'd asked him to have the Taskforce weigh in, getting the Oversight Council to immediately support Thomas Naboni's legitimacy, which meant leveraging the State Department to do the same. He'd said he would try, but that was about it.

I said, "My higher is going to try to work it, but there are so many layers between me and the power brokers that I don't have a whole lot of faith. I don't want to rescue Thomas only to see him a week later swinging from a lamppost on CNN. We need a reaction right now. Not three days from now."

Johan said, "I have an idea about that."

"You do? What, you think you can get *South Africa* to back him?"

"No, I think I can get the US reaction you want."

And he told us his plan.

77

★ ★ ★

On one side of the hut, I watched Jennifer and Shoshana planning their part of the mission, Shoshana tracing a route on a computer screen. On the other side, Johan was talking with the rest of the team, discussing the second stage of the plan. In the back sat Thomas and two of his friends, looking decidedly uneasy.

I wondered if I should just tell all of them to stop, because I had a feeling Kurt was about to put the brakes on the entire operation.

I'd decided we needed to do a little bit of detailed planning if we were going to try Johan's idea, so we'd turned Alexandra's little abandoned hut into a tactical operations center. A round building about twenty feet across with a thatched roof, it was a typical Basotho structure found all over the countryside, but now it resembled something out of an episode of *Get Smart*—an indigenous shack with four satellite antennae poking out of the straw on the roof.

While the team dove into contingency planning, trying to predict second- and third-order effects, I had called Blaine, connecting with a VPN through my laptop so he could see my face. It was harder to tell a man no when you were looking him in the eyes. Unfortunately, as soon as I'd connected, Blaine had told me to hold on, because Kurt was waiting on my contact.

Which was odd. The only reason we had a commander for Omega operations was precisely because operational decisions rested in his hands.

Half the screen was blank, but the other half was Blaine's face, the background showing plywood. All he'd said was that Kurt wanted to speak to me, and to wait until he connected. Since it was closing in on ten at night in DC, I knew Kurt wasn't hanging around just to say hello.

I said, "Come on, sir, give me a hint."

He grimaced and said, "Your last plan raised some serious concerns in DC. I'll let Kurt explain it."

"What? They were good with waiting on the coup to occur, but the minute I ask for help from the State Department, it becomes an issue?"

He said, "Pretty much. Trust me, this has caused a little questioning of my own ability to command. It's not coming from me."

"What does that mean?"

Before he could answer, the right half of the screen cleared, and I saw Kurt Hale. He said, "Everyone got me?"

I said, "Loud and clear."

Blaine said, "I copy, sir."

I said, "Blaine told you the state of play, right? Am I assuming your vaunted presence on this VTC is because you had some issues getting the Oversight Council to approve?"

Kurt spit out, "Pike, I never took it to the Oversight Council. Not only that, but I'm close to firing Blaine for even considering such a completely insane plan."

He was genuinely angry, taking me aback. He said, "Can you still execute what you briefed before? Letting the coup happen and then scarfing up Colonel Armstrong? Or is this a shit show now?"

Confused at the venom, I said, "Sir, yes. I told Blaine that. We just need some support from State to make sure the new guy isn't assassinated in the first ten minutes. What's the big deal?"

"You didn't hear me. I mean can you execute *without* your chosen replacement?"

What the hell? "What difference does it make?"

"Pike, you're conducting the literal Title 50 definition of covert action. Which means you're breaking the law."

He saw me scrunch up my eyes, because saying the Taskforce was breaking the law was like saying you would get wet if you went out in the rain. He continued. "You are way, way outside the bounds of our charter. I can't believe you even brought this up."

His glance on the computer changed, and I knew he was looking at Blaine through his camera. He said, "And I *cannot* believe that the Omega commander even considered this insanity. You get rope to run missions based on judgment. Of which neither of you apparently own."

I said, "Wait a minute, sir, what's the big deal? Watching the coup is okay, but helping with a good outcome is not?"

"*Precisely!* Precisely. The Taskforce exists within a charter, and I tested the bounds of that charter to give you a chance to get Aaron. I'm glad you got him, but now you've completely left the reservation. You're going to overthrow an entire country?"

"Wait, sir, you knew that was going to happen."

"I knew you were going to watch, sitting on the sidelines. Now you're working the coup."

"What's the difference?"

"Pike, the law allowing covert action was specifically written to require a congressional finding before executing any activity that would affect the political, economic, or military conditions abroad, period. We fall outside of the title because capturing and killing terrorists doesn't do that. Our charter was specifically built around the proscriptions in Title 50. For a *reason.* Now you're running Operation Ajax and want me to sell that to the national command authority?"

Operation Ajax was the code name for the coup the United States conducted in Iran in 1953, when we overthrew Prime Minister Mosaddegh and installed the shah. That action had led to another overthrow in 1979, and a hostage situation culminating in a disastrous failed rescue mission executed by a unit we'd both once served in. He was making a point.

I said, "Sir, we didn't plan or execute this thing. We're just helping to ensure a good outcome. What's the fucking difference? I don't get it."

"Pike, you sitting back and letting the coup happen is like a war photographer just documenting the battle. I can get away with that because the mission—our mission—happens after the fact. We had no play in the coup. Now you're putting down the camera and picking up a rifle. It may sound like splitting hairs with you, but it's a major, major problem."

I leaned back, making sure nobody else could hear what was being discussed, relieved to see they were all engrossed in planning. I said, "Sir, the coup is almost complete, and we had nothing to do with it. All that matters is the outcome now."

"Fine. That's what I like to hear. Conduct our mission and get out."

I glanced at Thomas, seeing him fearfully talking to his friends, the precariousness of his position starkly evident by the trembling in his hands. I knew he would now be dead regardless of his participation. The new prime minister, Lenatha, would see him as a threat and he would disappear, just like he had before, only this time permanently.

"So, no help from the mighty United States? Just let this play out?"

"Pike, get on the airfield and get me Colonel Armstrong. I've already leaned way out on this. Accomplish our mission."

The truth of the matter was I could execute Johan's plan without even reading Kurt on to it. The question was whether I was willing to. I thought about it, putting myself in Kurt's shoes—or more appropriately, putting him in mine. Would he do what I wanted to do if the roles were reversed? It didn't take a lot of reflection to come to an answer. I glanced at the crew, making sure they were still engaged.

Johan had told us that not only had he planned the targets to neutralize but he'd also planned no-fire areas, because the last thing he wanted was a foreign embassy to react on threats against its citizens. First on the list was the US embassy itself, but farther down was a children's hospital in the city. Johan was afraid that if it were threatened, the United States would react, sending troops to protect it, thereby interfering with the coup. His solution to my dilemma for US involvement had been simple: Threaten the hospital. Or at least, tell the embassy it was under threat and get them to react. Get them on the street. As far as I knew, it wasn't under duress, but it *might* be, and that might be enough to get the reaction I needed of American boots on the ground.

Here we go.

I said, "Sir, I'll get to the airfield and accomplish the mission, but there's something else you should be aware of. The coup's gone a little bit out of control, and American citizens are in danger. Do you want me to ignore them?"

"What are you talking about?"

"There's a children's hospital over here, in the city of Maseru. It's the Baylor College of Medicine, and it's caught in the cross fire."

"Baylor? As in Baylor University?"

"I don't know. All I know is that it's full of AMCITs and it's under fire."

Kurt said, "How do you know this?"

"It's uncorroborated reporting. I don't know for sure, but I felt I should bring it up, even though it's not in our charter."

He ignored that last comment, saying, "Can you do anything about it? With the force you have?"

"Not really, beyond a reconnaissance. I can't secure it, but there's a Special Forces security assessment team on the ground here, at the embassy. We could get them rolling, but it'll require release by the RSO at the embassy."

Another Johan nugget. Apparently, he'd been interrogated by some paranoid members of General Mosebo's staff while he was conducting a reconnaissance for the coup, and in their amateurish questioning, they'd let it slip that they thought he was a member of US Special Forces that were on the ground right now.

"How do you know about the team?"

"Found out from Mosebo's boys while we were rescuing Aaron. They thought we were them."

He seemed to buy it. I said, "We're probably looking at a NEO here, regardless of the outcome with Armstrong and Malloy. You might want to start that ball rolling."

NEO stood for noncombatant evacuation operation, a template most US military forces on alert had on their plate. It was usually conducted when a situation in a foreign country went south and American citizens had to be rescued. Like when there's a coup . . .

Kurt said, "I can make that happen, but it'll be a while before any forces can get on the ground. Can you get me information on the hospital without affecting your mission?"

"Yeah, I can probably do that, but I can't interface with the embassy without compromising my mission. That'll have to happen from your end."

Which was an absolute lie. I had every intention of lighting a fire under the embassy's ass. What I wanted was US forces on the ground, waving the flag and providing a visible presence, and in order to do that, I needed to make the coup look like Dodge City.

He said, "Okay, see what you can find out about the hospital. Location, threats, evacuation routes, all the usual stuff. I'll pass that along to the embassy and try to break that SF team free to secure it until follow-on forces can get there."

"Will do."

He leaned back and said, "Okay, how much longer do I need to bite my nails? What's the rest of the plan?"

"It's pretty simple, sir. No real drama at this point. We head to the airport, the aircraft lands with the new prime minister, he takes over the country, and we take Colonel Armstrong into custody. Armstrong is supposed to stay on the ground after the mercenary force flies out, so we let them leave, capture Armstrong, then fly out on the L-100."

I stopped and addressed Blaine: "Sir, that's still good to go, right?"

"Yes. It's waiting on your call in Johannesburg. Thirty-minute flight."

I returned to Kurt and said, "We wring out Armstrong and set up

Tyler Malloy. We get Malloy and the triggers, and Lesotho gets a new government."

"What's your timeline?"

I was a little miffed at the lack of concern for Lesotho. "Sir, what's the difference between putting in Thomas instead of Lenatha? Can't we do that?"

"Pike, *we* aren't going to have anything to do with this coup. If *they* want to do that, it's up to them."

Which was good enough for me. I said, "Roger all, sir. The timeline is within the next two hours. We're going to roll with your final approval."

He nodded and said, "You've got it. Keep us posted, and get me some information on the hospital. The last thing I want to hear is that there are dead Americans because we let a coup go forward. I need to wake a few people up if I'm going to get that SF team rolling."

I said, "Yes, sir," but was thinking, *That SF team will be at the hospital long before you get through the Pentagon phone book.*

78

★ ★ ★

Shoshana tracked the route on her computer and said, "Next intersection, take a left. You'll see the river and a golf course. Parallel it, and follow the signs for the Maseru Bridge crossing into South Africa. You'll run right up to the front gate."

Jennifer said, "Okay, time to win an Oscar. How are you doing back there, Alex?"

From the back seat, Alex said, "I don't think I'm going to have to do any acting."

"Hang in there. The embassy will have a doctor on staff and a medical clinic. You're almost home free."

Jennifer saw the golf course on the left of her SUV, and Shoshana said, "Five hundred meters." The golf course peeled away, and she saw a cutout with metal barriers, then the United States flag.

Shoshana said, "That's it, that's it!"

Jennifer whipped into the turnout, and two US Marines in full combat gear, complete with M16A2s, came barreling out from behind a barricade, holding their hands up in the universal sign to stop.

Jennifer did, and the first Marine trained his weapon on her while the second came to her window. Acting hysterical, she rolled it down and shouted, "There's fighting going on! They're shooting people! They shot my friend!"

The Marine said, "Whoa, wait a minute. Calm down. Who are you?"

"I'm Jennifer Cahill. I'm a US citizen. We work at the Baylor

Children's Hospital downtown. They're shooting all around it, and my friends are still there. You need to help us!"

He looked at her passport, with Jennifer holding her breath that he didn't inspect it closely enough to realize she had no work visa for Lesotho. He did not. He turned and shouted to the gate, "Metz, Blashford, get out here and give me a hand!"

Twenty minutes later they were inside the embassy compound, with Jennifer spilling her tall tale about hostiles threatening US citizens. A man in business casual attire appeared, looking like he was going to attend an embassy briefing, except he was wearing a Kevlar helmet and had a pistol on his hip.

He said, "My name is Ian Tesler. I'm the regional security officer here. What's going on?"

Jennifer was surprised. She'd figured it would take ten minutes of screaming to get him to appear. She had to feign ignorance of embassy operations, but the RSO—the man from the Diplomatic Security Service charged specifically with the safety and security of citizens overseas—was the one person who could create the visible presence Pike needed.

She repeated her story, ending with, "You have to get some Marines over there right now. Protect the people at the hospital."

She knew there was no way Ian would release the Marines, as their specific mission was protecting the US embassy from harm or takeover, but it was her first step.

Ian said, "That's not the reporting we're getting. The fighting is localized to specific areas. Very surgical. In fact, it looks like it might just be a gang war or something like that."

Jennifer pointed to Alexandra, now on a stretcher and being treated with an IV. "Does that look localized? She's shot, for God's sake."

Ian held up his hands and said, "Okay, okay, please calm down. I know the hospital you're talking about. It's not near any shooting that we're tracking. We've sent out a Warden message for people to remain in their homes, and we've had no calls from the hospital."

Jennifer faked being incensed. "Maybe their phones are out. Did you think of that?"

Ian said, "Look, I don't have the forces to secure a hospital. All I can do is ensure the word gets out. My advice is simply to hunker down and let this pass."

She pointed at the Marine to her left and said, "What is that?"

"That man is dedicated to the US embassy."

"So you get protected while my friends die? Why the hell am I paying taxes?"

Ian said, "Ma'am, those Marines have a mission. There's only so much we can plan for. If—"

Another man entered their circle, cutting his speech short. He was dressed in civilian clothes but draped in military kit, and Jennifer knew he was who she'd been looking for. Take away the body armor and weapons and he dressed just like Pike. A shirt with a thousand pockets, and pants made to carry magazines of ammo. The clincher was his beard, a lumberjack thing that Pike would have made fun of. He might as well have put on a nameplate that read OPERATOR, DAMN IT.

The man said, "Ian, you need us to do anything? Can I tell the boys to stand down, or what?"

Looking aggravated, Ian said, "Yes. Just keep them in the break room. Nothing has happened to require an armed response."

Shoshana took one look at the man, then surreptitiously bumped Jennifer like she was trying to get her to introduce them for a date. Jennifer glared at her, letting her know she understood, and said, "Who are you?"

The man glanced at Jennifer as an aside, not worthy of his consideration, then did a double take when he took in who was asking. He became polite, saying, "My name's Clint. Clint Carnegie. Was that your friend who was just evac'd?"

Jennifer said, "Yes, it was. And she's not the last. We need some help. Americans are dying."

Clint looked at the RSO, asking, "What's she talking about?"

"Nothing that we can confirm. She just arrived."

To Clint, Jennifer said, "We need help! They're in danger!"

He said, "Danger how?" His head flicked between Jennifer and Ian, and she knew she'd just earned a seat at the table.

Ian said, "No danger that we can see. The danger is driving around. If everyone stays put, they'll be fine."

"Doesn't look like she's making it up." He turned to Jennifer and said, "What's going on?"

Jennifer felt the first tendrils of shame, knowing she was lying. She said, "I don't know. All I know is that our hospital is in the line of fire of whatever's happening out there. We need some protection."

Ian said, "Wait, wait, your friend got shot on the way here, not at the hospital. You can't say that. You don't know."

Clint looked at Ian and said, "That girl was shot? In a gunfight?"

"Yes, yes, but not in a threatening sense."

"Not in a threatening sense? What the fuck does that mean? Was she shot or not? I thought she was in a car wreck or something."

Ian drew up and said, "She was, but just on the street on the way here. I've given the Warden call. We can't save everyone."

Jennifer said, "But you can save my friends at the hospital! You can do that!"

Three men dressed like Clint appeared, draped in kit and bristling with weapons. One said, "What's going on, boss?"

He said, "I don't know."

Ian said, "You cannot leave here without my authorization. You're working here under my command."

Jennifer pulled the pin on her verbal grenade, hoping it was enough. She dropped it at their feet. "This is just like Benghazi. You guys are going to sit here protecting yourself while my friends die."

The words echoed in the courtyard, the men of the SF team

looking at their commander. She felt Shoshana pinch her, meaning that little devil had read the reaction of the team, and Jennifer had won.

Ian said, "Wait, wait, this isn't Libya, and you guys aren't going anywhere."

Clint said, "It isn't Libya *yet,* and I don't fucking work for you. I work for SOCOM."

Jennifer hid a grin. Shoshana bumped her with her hip again.

Ian said, "Nobody leaves here. Nobody goes out into the street. You could make this so much worse if an American is killed. Let it play out. This isn't Benghazi."

Jennifer knew he was absolutely correct. But also that his order would cause their plan to fail. She said, "Screw you guys. I'll do it myself. I'll be back with whoever I can save."

She turned to the gate, and Ian said, "You're not going anywhere. You said it yourself: Being on the street is dangerous. I can't let you go."

Jennifer gave Clint her most plaintive stare, and he said, "Fuck this. We're going."

Ian said, "You will not go!"

Clint said, "That's the last thing that shithead in Benghazi said. I'm not going to sit here while Americans are slaughtered."

He turned to leave, and the RSO stood in his way. "You do this and I'll fucking fry your ass."

Clint pushed him out of the way, shouting, "Timmons, load up the team!"

Embarrassed for the RSO, Jennifer caught Clint's sleeve and said, "Our vehicle's outside. I'll lead you to the hospital."

Clint nodded, and Jennifer glanced at Shoshana. Shoshana raised her eyebrows and whispered, "What are we going to do when there's no threat at the hospital?"

Jennifer followed the team, all shifting weapons and positioning kit like they were about to assault the Islamic State in Mosul.

She said, "I don't know. Sexual favors?"

The comment actually made Shoshana chuckle. "I don't think Aaron would agree with that."

They loaded their SUV, waiting on the team vehicles to appear through the gate. Jennifer said, "Neither would Pike, but it would serve him right for making up this stupid plan."

79

I said, "So you're rolling now?"

"Yeah, we're probably ten minutes out, but I don't know what I'm going to say to the team leader when we get there and they tell him, one, that they're perfectly safe, and two, that they have no idea who we are."

"We just left there. It'll be okay. It *is* full of foreigners, with a lot of Americans, and they're all scared shitless. You can hear the gunfire from the front gate, and they know something's going down. I talked to the head nurse and she begged for help, petrified that Lesotho is going to turn into Rwanda and they're all going to get their arms chopped off. I told her help was on the way."

"So she's expecting us?"

"Yeah. She'll play ball. I told her I was headed to the embassy to get someone to help, so when you show up, just play stupid. In the meantime, I told her to call all of her American friends and have them consolidate at the hospital. It's about to become the collection point for US citizens. That'll force the embassy to leave the team in place. Kurt's working a NEO option, so with any luck we'll have more American soldiers wandering around than Lesotho citizens. It'll keep anybody who's thinking about a countercoup from appearing anytime soon."

"Sounds good to me. What do you want me to do once I've dropped these guys off?"

"Go back to Thomas and wait for our call. We'll meet up at the airport."

We'd left Thomas and his entourage at the abandoned hooch, telling him we'd come for him when necessary. I didn't like leaving him alone, fearing he'd get cold feet, but I wasn't going to leave a gunfighter behind just to babysit.

"Got it. Will do."

"Koko, one thing: Stay off the main arteries. We just came through them, and Johan was a little premature on the consolidation phase. There is a running gun battle going on at the prime minister's residence. Apparently, that fight has drawn the police force. They have no orders from higher, because the coup decapitated the leadership of the police, but someone at the residence got a call out to them. It's turning into a pitched battle. You finish with the hospital, and you take the back roads, you hear?"

"I thought Johan said the prime minister was dead?"

"Yeah, but apparently that news hasn't received wide dissemination. Johan's guys are pinned down. He's trying to extract them, because at the end of the day the damn firefight is over nothing, but it hasn't happened yet. Just stay clear of the main roads."

Jennifer said, "Okay, okay. We'll do that. We'll be fine. What about you?"

"We're headed to the police headquarters right now, and people are starting to loot and pillage like a Rodney King riot. Johan's got the rest of the teams breaking down and headed to the airport, as planned. The Lesotho Special Forces guys will stay to secure the targets, I guess waiting on General Mosebo to show up."

"So where does that leave us?"

"I'll let you know in twenty minutes. We're either going to be heroes or zeros."

Kurt had gone batshit over the prohibitions for covert action in Title 50 of the US Code, but now I was *really* doing it. The title read, "An activity or activities of the United States Government to influence political, economic, or military conditions abroad, where it is intended that the role of the United States Government will not be apparent or acknowledged."

Change out "United States Government" for "Taskforce" and

that was exactly what I was doing. I was attempting to alter the political conditions abroad right under the noses of my masters, hoping my actions wouldn't be apparent. If I succeeded, I'd be a hero and nobody would even realize it had happened. If I failed, the entire mission would fail, because there was no way I would capture Colonel Armstrong if this blew up in my face. But I honestly felt Thomas was worth it. Aaron had been right about him. Thomas had seen how the other half lived and had realized that Lesotho had been living in a world of poverty it didn't deserve.

Unfailingly friendly, willing to give the very clothes off their backs, the Basotho people had been scraping by hand to mouth for more than a century. In the past it had been just the way of things, as all tribes in Africa were no better off, but it had remained the same even after the exploitation of Lesotho's water and the discovery of diamonds, the government content to sell its people's birthright to corporate interests. Thomas could put a stop to that. But only if we were successful.

What made it worse was that I was doing the mission in the shadow of my own team. They thought Kurt was on board with our plan, but I was hiding my actions even from them. It was a lot of weight to bear on my shoulders, and I really wanted to bounce my insanity against Knuckles or Jennifer—the two sounding boards who routinely kept me on an even keel—but I couldn't. To do so would put them in jeopardy. If this thing went to complete shit, at least they'd be able to claim innocence.

Brett heard gunfire ahead and slowed down. He said, "The headquarters is just around this corner. I thought you said it was secure."

Johan looked up and said, "It is. They're doing some cleanup."

We all knew what that meant. *Cleanup* was code for *vendetta*.

I said, "I thought this was supposed to be surgical. None of the bullshit from a real coup. That's what you told us."

He grimaced and said, "It is. Andy has the police headquarters. He's . . . a little loose."

"And he's the guy you need to convince?"

Johan had already ordered the evacuation of his men on the other targets. The original plan was that they'd leave the objectives in control of the ranking Lesotho Special Forces officer, who'd hold down the fort until General Mosebo and the new prime minister, Lenatha, consolidated control. In the meantime, the mercenary force would flee the country, leaving behind the wonderful new government.

Johan's deviation to the plan was to show up at the police headquarters, order the evacuation of the team there, then free whatever police were still alive, taking them to the airfield for a little surprise when the aircraft with the new prime minister arrived.

Johan said, "I can handle Andy. It won't be an issue. He trusts me. I'll get him to leave, then call you in."

Brett said, "You sure about that?"

Johan said, "Yeah, I can hold up my end of the bargain. As long as this guy doesn't piss his pants."

Going in with Johan was a man named Khosi, one of Thomas's inner circle. Johan was supposed to be colocated with the Special Forces regimental commander and wasn't expected to show up at the police headquarters at all. Him showing up would be a surprise, so we needed to give him every edge he could get. Johan was convinced that appearing alone would raise all sorts of red flags, and he wanted someone to play the part of the Special Forces staff.

Since the guy would have no role other than eye candy, I'd originally tasked Brett, but Johan had axed that idea, saying he didn't speak the language, which could prove crucial if any of the locals threw a question his way. We'd batted the ideas back and forth, and a man from Thomas's circle had stood up. He wasn't Special Forces, but he'd served in the Lesotho military and had volunteered to help. His courage was pretty impressive, given he was going into the lion's den.

All of the Lesotho Special Forces men had assaulted in civilian clothes to prevent anyone from fingering a specific unit when it was over—giving the coup a veneer of a popular uprising—so it was a simple matter of changing Khosi out of his prison rags and into something more appropriate. The charade was complete with a banged-up AK Aaron had taken off the base.

Khosi shifted the AK in his hand and said, "I won't lose my nerve."

Johan said, "You know how to fire that weapon, right?"

Khosi nodded but said, "I thought that wouldn't be necessary."

"It won't."

Brett passed across his earpiece and Taskforce phone, saying, "Don't lose that shit. I'm signed for it."

Johan smiled and opened the door to the SUV. He said, "I'll call when it's clear. You guys come in loaded, because we need to get the drop on whoever is left behind. Worst case, if the comms fail for whatever reason, if you don't hear from me and you see two white guys driving off, come on in."

I nodded, then said what was on my team's mind. "Good luck, Johan. Don't fuck us here."

If he wanted to turn the tables on us, we were giving him the perfect opportunity.

He said, "You still don't trust me, do you?"

Aaron said, "No, I don't."

80

★ ★ ★

Johan left the SUV, went to the end of the street, and took a knee, peering around the corner. He saw four men with AK-47s in the parking lot of the police headquarters, pacing back and forth and looking for trouble. It was enough to prevent him from attempting to walk right in.

The headquarters was a squat one-story building surrounded by chain link and razor wire, with a single vehicle entrance and two pedestrian gates. The vehicle entrance was blocked with the hulk of a destroyed sedan, the interior on fire and billowing smoke. Scattered about were the carcasses of dead policemen, their blood congealing in the morning heat.

Khosi took one look at the carnage and the armed men and said, "Maybe this isn't a good idea."

Johan said, "Yeah, you're probably right, but we don't have a choice now."

Johan got on the radio and was relieved to hear Chris, the American Special Forces man, on the other end.

"Hey, this is Johan. I need to come in and coordinate."

"What's up? Something going wrong?"

"No, no. It's just easier to do it face-to-face. The TV station is only a couple of blocks from here, and I've got everyone else moving out to the airfield. I just want to finalize with Andy before we bring in the aircraft."

"Okay, where are you?"

"Right out front. Can you turn off the gorillas that are pacing the parking lot?"

Chris laughed and said, "Stand by."

Johan saw Chris enter the gravel lot, say a few words, then walk to the pedestrian gate, pushing a body out of the way to get it to open. Johan showed himself, and Chris waved him in.

Johan and Khosi sprinted to the gate, leaping over the broken remnants of the police force to get there. They entered the building, and Johan saw four more bodies, only this time lined up neatly in a row on the floor of the lobby of the headquarters. Each had a bullet hole to the head. Johan said, "What the fuck is that?"

Chris looked embarrassed. He said, "Mosebo's boys got a little out of control. They said it was payback for something."

"Where the hell is Andy?"

He heard, "Right behind you, mate. What are you doing here?"

Johan pointed and said, "What happened?"

Andy said, "Lily Boy, sometimes you have to let the savages blow off some steam to keep them in line."

Johan snarled, "You bloodthirsty fuck. *You're* in charge here. Not them."

Andy leaned against a wall and said, "What's done is done. Now, why are you here?"

"It's time to evacuate. Almost all objectives are secure, and I've got the teams headed to the airport. The only target still hostile is the prime minister's residence."

"That's settled. The prime minister's dead, and the team evacuated. Didn't you hear them on the net?"

Johan showed true surprise. He said, "No, when did that happen? I spoke to them an hour ago and they were still fighting."

"An hour ago. What have you been doing since then? It sure as shit wasn't acting as the ground-force commander."

"I was at the television station, in accordance with the plan. When did they leave?"

Andy ignored the question, saying, "Yeah, speaking of that, why is the fucking station transmitting?"

"What?"

Andy pointed at a television in the corner and said, "They're broadcasting."

Johan said, "That must have just started. I'll take care of it when I get back. Look, it's time to go. We still need to secure the airport for reception of the bird."

"Where's the regimental commander, Colonel Goodluck?"

"He's at the station."

Andy unslung his weapon and said, "At the station, huh? Who's this guy?"

Johan felt the first tendrils of fear. "He's Goodluck's adjutant. His name is Khosi. Now, start packing up your shit. It's time to go. I talked to Colonel Armstrong, and he's preparing to land, but he can't until we secure the airport. Everything's tracking."

Andy said, "You know, Lily Boy, Colonel Armstrong never trusted you. He respects your skill but not your moral compass."

Johan casually brought his weapon up, and Andy said, "Stop. Put the rifle down."

Johan did, slowly, saying, "What the fuck has gotten into you? We need to go."

Andy said, "It's funny you say you spoke to Colonel Armstrong, because I just got off the net with him, and he didn't say a thing about talking with you."

And Johan realized that Colonel Armstrong had been watching him all along. His plan to turn the coup on its head had been defeated before he'd even boarded the aircraft.

He decided to throw everything on the table, hoping to convince Andy to join his side. He said, "Andy, Colonel Armstrong is giving nuclear triggers to Tyler Malloy, and Tyler is going to sell them to terrorists. We can prevent that. We can let the coup go forward, but we can stop that."

Andy said, "I don't give a shit about nuclear triggers. I care about getting paid, which means I need to prevent whatever you've set in motion."

He flicked his head, and two of the Special Forces men descended on Khosi, ripping the AK-47 out of his hands and driving him to his knees. Andy said, "Since I'm sure it would take an awful long time to get you to talk, and, as you say, we don't have any to waste, I'll start with your friend here."

Johan said, "Andy, we don't have to fight. We need to work together."

"We're not fighting. You misunderstand your position. Didn't Colonel Armstrong tell you when you talked to him? I'm now the ground-force commander. Chris, watch him."

Chris raised his weapon, his expression one of bewilderment. Johan realized the turn of events was as new to him as it was to Johan.

Khosi began to struggle, but it did little good. The last thing Johan saw was the terror on his face as they dragged him away.

81

★ ★ ★

We waited for about twenty minutes, and I heard nothing from the Taskforce radio. I called in: "Johan, Johan, this is Pike. Give me a SITREP."

I got silence. I turned to Brett and said, "Go to the corner. Get eyes on the headquarters and give me some intel."

Dawn had finally broken, and the sun was beginning its slow rise into the sky. Up and down the street we could see groups of people roaming, moving about like packs of wild animals, the stores along the street belching looters out of their broken windows.

Brett exited, keeping his Glock low and out of sight. He peered around the brick wall at the corner, then pulled back into cover. Over the net he said, "Headquarters looks like a war zone. Four guys out front with AKs, and about a half dozen bodies near the entrance."

I said, "Roger that. Any sign of Johan?"

Brett stuck his head around the corner and said, "I don't see him . . . stand by . . . there's a vehicle coming out."

He whipped back around and leaned up against the brick, looking at me through the windshield. He said, "They're winching a wrecked sedan out of the way. Two SUVs coming out. The lead has a Caucasian and three locals. The second SUV is nothing but locals. Both vehicles armed."

Five minutes later, I saw the caravan appear at Brett's corner, and we ducked down, letting it pass. I sat back up, staring hard as the vehicles disappeared from view. I said, "Did anyone catch who was in that front vehicle?"

Knuckles said, "I didn't recognize the white guy."

"No, I meant in the back. It looked like Khosi in the back, in the middle."

Brett returned to our vehicle, saying, "We going in now?"

"I don't know. He said *two* Caucasians. That was only one, which means there's another mercenary still on-site."

I called, "Johan, Johan, this is Pike. What's going on?"

We heard two clicks of the microphone, usually meaning whoever was on the other end was acknowledging they'd received the call but couldn't talk.

Aaron said what was on everyone's mind. "You think he's fucking us?"

I opened the door and said, "Yeah, I do. And that bastard is going to wish he hadn't."

We slipped up to the corner, and I saw the four guys Brett was talking about. I said, "Okay, Brett, you cross and conduct a close target reconnaissance. Focus on the southern pedestrian gate, report back, and get ready to join the fight. Veep, Knuckles, same plan as the prison. Remain here and neutralize those guys when I call. Veep, you still have your breaching charge?"

"Yeah. One left."

"Get it." I looked at Aaron and said, "You and I are going down the alley in the back, see if we can breach somewhere without the heavy firepower." Veep returned and handed me the small charge, and I said, "Objective is to clear that target and capture both Johan and the final mercenary. Local nationals are designated hostile threats. We'll leave after we get atmospherics from Brett. Questions?"

Brett said, "I'm getting the CTR because of my lethal skills?"

With a straight face I said, "Yes. That's why."

He tucked his Glock into his pants, dropped his shirt over it, and turned the corner, saying, "Lying sack of shit."

Aaron chuckled, saying, "One of these days he's going to take affront to your taskings."

"Yeah, well, the next time we're hunting mercenaries in Norway it'll be me pretending to be a local."

Brett reached the end of the block and said, "I can see bodies inside, lying execution style. The men outside took an interest in me, but not much of one. No sign of Johan from my vantage point, but I saw two other locals inside. Alley is clear."

Which brought our target deck up to six. I said, "Continue into the alley. We'll meet you there."

To Veep and Knuckles I said, "Drop those targets, then use the primary entrance to breach."

Knuckles nodded, saying, "I'm getting a little sick of the sniper work."

I said, "Do it quickly and there might be some fighting left inside," then patted Aaron on the leg to go.

We went down our building until we hit an alley that ran perpendicular to the police headquarters. Overgrown, with shrubs and weeds fighting a battle with the asphalt, it was full of trash, making our stalk a game of avoid-the-cans.

We reached the intersection of the alley that paralleled the southern end of the headquarters, and I saw the chain link extended another fifty feet before stopping abruptly and joining the brick of the building. Brett was waiting for us, hiding in the shadows of a cluster of trash cans.

He said, "I could only find one breach point on this side. A door about thirty meters down, but I can't tell where it goes. The rest is just brick all the way down."

Shit.

I really didn't like being forced into a single choice of breach, especially since it was an unknown one. Worst case, we'd find we entered into a storage area or some other dead end. It was one of the reasons we usually breached from three or four different directions at the same time.

"No other intel on where it leads?"

"No. I tried, but there aren't any windows in it or near it. It's just a steel door. There *is* a camera above it, so it probably has access to the rest of the building. No reason to put a camera on a breach point unless that breach point is a risk. Besides the door, there are a couple of windows between here and it, but they're barred. Both just offices with nobody inside."

"Can we surreptitiously enter the door, check it out?"

"It's got a triple lock. We can do it, but it's going to take some time."

"Well, the windows aren't an option, and we don't *have* time. Looks like it's an explosive breach on the door. Let's hope we're not leaving all the fighting to Knuckles and Veep when we pile into a paint locker."

We advanced down the alley until we came to the end of the chain link. I could see the door ahead, a camera above it. Aaron said, "You worried about the surveillance system?"

"No. I doubt whoever was tasked to watch it is still alive." I tossed Brett my breaching charge and said, "It's showtime."

He scampered forward and emplaced it in between the dead bolt and the doorknob, a position that would shred all three locks. I called the overwatch team: "Knuckles, this is Pike. At breach. You ready?"

"Roger."

"Go on the sound of the boom."

I checked with Aaron, then nodded at Brett. He pulled the fuse igniter, then raced back to us, getting behind me in the stack. Ten seconds later, the locks were obliterated in a cloud of smoke, and we raced into the building. The first room turned out to be for storage, empty of men, but it spilled into a hallway. On the net, Knuckles called, "Targets down, targets down. Moving to primary breach."

We exited into the hallway and a man sprang out of a room ahead of me, holding an AK. He didn't even glance our way, instead running away from us. He reached the end of the hallway, still running flat out, weapon raised at a threat, and then he flipped in the air, landing on his back like he'd been clotheslined from an invisible I beam across the hallway, his head split open.

Knuckles.

I raced to the door he'd exited, pulling up short. I felt a hand on my shoulder and kicked the door in, going right while the man behind me went left. I saw Johan on his knees, his hands flex-tied behind his back, a Lesotho Special Forces man above him holding an AK. I put a double-tap into the soldier's chest, hearing firing behind me, and Johan tossed his head repeatedly, trying to point with it and screaming, "Behind me! Behind me!"

He was indicating an open door, and I raced to it just as a Sig Sauer MCX barrel appeared, followed by a large Caucasian man. His eyes sprang wide, and he tried to rotate his weapon toward me. I grabbed the barrel, slammed it against the doorjamb, then punched him in the face with the end of my suppressor, a quick bayonet jab that left a circle on his forehead. He lost his weapon, staggered back windmilling his arms, then fell heavily on his ass. I pointed my rifle at his head and said, "Don't fucking move."

Behind me, I hollered, "Status!"

Knuckles appeared at my shoulder, saying, "Building is clear. We've got one room full of police all hog-tied. Another room full of police, all dead."

"Threats?"

"Neutralized."

"Watch this fuck."

I returned to the room, finding Brett at the door pulling security and Veep cutting Johan free. I went to him and said, "What the fuck is going on?"

"We're in a world of shit. Andy is working with Armstrong, and neither one trusted me. Andy has Khosi, and they're headed to our little safe house for Thomas. They're going to kill him and his men. We're about to lose."

82

Shoshana watched Clint talking to the head nurse and prayed she wouldn't make things worse. If they could drive away from this, they'd be home free. She had no idea that it wouldn't be the hospital but Pike who would throw the plan into the gutter.

Clint walked over to their SUV and said, "We can secure this, no problem. It's away from the city and gated. I've talked to my boss at SOCOM, and they've gotten wind of the problem. They're spinning up a Marine FAST team and some Ospreys from the Med. It'll take some time for them to get here, since we're on the bottom of the earth, but you girls don't need to worry anymore."

Jennifer said, "What's the embassy telling you?"

"It's a coup. A real coup. But it's calming down now. The worst is the looting, at this stage. My orders are to stay here and protect AMCITs. Apparently, someone told them to congregate here."

He pointed to the front gate, where Shoshana saw couples and families coming through, dragging suitcases and trunks full of whatever they thought they'd need fleeing a country under fire.

Clint said, "I don't know who's pulling the strings back home, but this is ridiculous. Typical overreaction. You mentioned Benghazi before, and apparently that's solidified like puke on a toilet seat. Now I'll spend my time herding a bunch of cats while the US government wastes billions proving that no crisis is too small to wave the flag."

He spit on the ground and said, "Christ, tomorrow I'll have fourteen dignitaries stomping around proclaiming how quickly they reacted to this nonthreat. It'll be a clusterfuck of epic proportions."

He realized he'd been a little more than crude and said, "No offense. I mean, I saw your friend, but she'll be okay."

Jennifer said, "I'm sorry. We were so scared. I didn't know what to do."

Clint glanced at Shoshana in the passenger seat and said, "I know, I know. Running alone here can be scary, but trust me, I've seen much worse in Uganda. Not your fault."

Shoshana leaned forward, about to say something, and Jennifer pinched her hip. Shoshana relaxed, but only because Jennifer was in the seat next to her. She really wanted to teach the man a thing or two about "defenseless" women.

He said, "You might want to stake out a sleeping place while you have the chance, because it's looking like the good spots will be taken shortly." He tapped the roof of their SUV and walked away, supremely disgusted that there hadn't been a fight.

Shoshana said, "That guy is so arrogant he's going to trip on his own ego."

Jennifer said, "We're good. We did what we needed. A bunch of Ospreys landing here disgorging Marines will prevent anyone from raising a weapon after they arrive."

She patted Shoshana's knee and said, "I'm just glad we didn't have to give him any sexual favors for showing up."

Shoshana laughed, and Jennifer's cell phone rang. Ending the good times.

Shoshana saw her go from proud to worried. Jennifer said, "Is Khosi alive?"

Then: "What can we do?"

Shoshana began bouncing off the seat, with Jennifer holding a finger in the air, her ear still glued to the phone. Jennifer said, "Pike, I don't think he'll execute that."

Shoshana heard snatches of noise from the phone, and Jennifer looked at her, saying, "I've got Shoshana. We'll do what we can."

Jennifer ended with, "I won't. I won't. Get to the airport."

She hung up the phone, looked at Shoshana, and said, "Khosi has been captured. Colonel Armstrong was suspicious of Johan from the start. He didn't trust him. They're going to kill the bunch of them."

"And?"

"And we're a klick away from the safe house. Safe *hut*. They're on the way, and Pike needs us to beat them to it."

Jennifer rolled down the window and shouted at Clint's retreating back. Shoshana said, "Just us?"

He turned around, and Jennifer said, "Not if we can convince that guy to get in a fight."

Shoshana smiled, pulled her ZEV Tech Glock, did a press check to make sure a round was seated, and said, "You might want to ask him his favorite position."

Thomas peeked out the window one more time, seeing nothing on the road. Not even a local walking, which was strange. It had been close to an hour since they'd watched the so-called force leave to execute their plan at the police headquarters, and nobody had come back. The man called Pike had promised him they'd return, and when they did, they'd take him to the airport to arrest the man who'd instigated the coup, and, in a fit of insanity, he'd agreed.

They'd infused him with confidence and plied him with shame, but now, an hour later, the gravity of what they were doing was wearing him down.

Nobi sat down next to him and said, "This is a great day. A day to remember."

He patted Thomas's knee and said, "All of that suffering, every day, you said it was for a purpose. And now that has come to pass."

Thomas wiped his brow, feeling sick, and said, "Don't count on victory until victory is assured."

"What do you mean? You've seen what's happened. It is our time."

They heard a vehicle pull up outside, and a man looked out the window and said, "It's Khosi!"

Nobi's skeletal face broke into a smile. He said, "No more pain. No more hunger."

Khosi entered the hut, his face battered and bleeding. Thomas sat upright, saying, "What happened to you?"

A man shoved him forward, then pointed a wicked-looking rifle at Thomas, saying, "I'm sorry about this, but your friend is wrong. There will be more pain."

I hung up the phone, and Knuckles said, "You sure you want to do that? Get US forces involved directly in the coup?"

Aggravated, I said, "What the fuck was I supposed to do? Let him die?"

Brett said, "I'm with you, but he's got a point. Getting a US Army Special Forces team to rescue Thomas is definitely taking sides on this thing. Going to be hard to explain that when we're done."

"Well, fuck it. It'll be that much harder for the US to back away from supporting Thomas after they saved his ass. They'll come up with some bullshit story, but he'll survive."

I turned to our captive, saying, "What sort of vehicles are here? What do you have?"

The man named Chris, now on his knees with his own hands secured behind his back, said, "We've got a van and a couple of Toyota 4Runners."

Knuckles turned from a window and said, "Street's getting a little crowded. People are starting to shout for a police response to the looting. We need to leave."

I nodded and squatted in front of Chris, saying, "What's the plan now?"

"Andy's talking to Colonel Armstrong. He's landing in the next thirty minutes. The coup is done. He meets General Mosebo on the airfield and we leave."

I said, "Mosebo's dead, you dumb fuck. There is no Mosebo. Get with the program. What are *you* supposed to do?"

Chris's face went slack at the news.

I said, "Wake the fuck up. What's next?"

He said, "Andy's going to call, and I take Johan with me to the airfield." He glanced at Johan, the fear in his eyes, and said, "I was supposed to hand him to Lenatha. He's going to be implicated in some bullshit with the coup. We fly out, and whatever happens here, happens."

Johan said, "Not anymore, you shit."

Chris nodded and said, "I know, I know. I want no part of this."

He glanced at the bodies on the ground, some killed execution-style, and said, "This wasn't part of the plan. I don't murder for money."

Johan said, "Yes, you do, you myopic fuck. You just did."

Chris said, "What makes you so pure? You planned this entire thing."

Johan looked at Pike and said, "I did. No doubt, I did. But I'm going to right my wrongs. The question is whether you're willing to do the same."

"How?"

Johan squatted down to Chris's level and said, "You're going to take me to the airport, just as planned."

Seeing the skepticism on Clint's face, Jennifer turned on the waterworks, saying, "He isn't American, but he worked at the hospital. He just called me and said armed men were surrounding his house. They're going to haul him away and kill him, just because he worked here. Apparently, they hate anything American."

Clint said, "What the hell are you talking about, lady? This isn't Rwanda. All that's happening here is some looting. There aren't any roaming death squads."

"There's clearly at least one. He just *called* me. They're going to kill him and his family."

Clint gave her the side-eye, clearly thinking she was overwrought, the harrowing ride with her wounded friend battering her fragile female sensitivities. After seeing the hospital and the lack of danger, he was sure she was imagining the threat.

Shoshana had had enough of Jennifer's acting. She opened the door to their vehicle, leaned over the roof, and said, "Look, you shit. Get your men loaded up. If it's nothing, it's nothing."

A smart-ass comment formed in Clint's mouth but failed to escape. One look at Shoshana and it died, stillborn. He nodded and said, "You lead, like before?"

"Yeah, we'll lead your team. You ride with us. It's only about one kilometer away, but tell your men to be ready. You wanted a fight, and you're about to get it."

Like all the rest, Thomas was led out of the hut under the watchful eyes of the Lesotho Special Forces members. He saw the mercenary called Andy load up into one of the SUVs, then call for one of the Special Forces men. They held a brief conversation, and then the man came back. He said a few words to his team, then led the line of men behind the small Basotho hut and into an open field, toward a shallow stream at the back. Thomas realized Khosi was in front of him, his face swollen, the blood crusting beneath his nose.

Andy started up the SUV and the vehicle began to roll, passing the men marching in the field, then disappeared. They reached the edge of the stream, and the man who'd spoken to Andy screamed at them to get on their knees. Thomas did so, glancing at Khosi. He mouthed, *I'm sorry.*

Thomas hung his head in shame, waiting on the bullet.

His hands still shackled, Chris put down the hand mic and said, "They've got Thomas and his men. They're dead, or about to be. Colonel Armstrong's inbound. He's landing in ten minutes with Makalo Lenatha. They've seized control of the airfield. It's all in motion."

I said, "Brett, find me a policeman who speaks English."

He came out a minute later with a guy who looked like he was about to throw up, convinced we were going to torture him to death.

Because I was a smart-ass, I said, "You speak American?"

He looked at me quizzically, and I asked, "Where's the captain of this place?"

He pointed to a body on the ground, one of the ones lined up and executed. I said, "Who's the highest-ranking guy you have here? Still alive, I mean?"

He drew up and said, "That would be me. If you must kill again, kill me."

I said, "As much as I appreciate the courage, I'm not going to kill you. I need the ranking man left alive."

My words giving him courage, he said, "Why?"

I pointed at the body of the captain and said, "Because we're about to arrest the man who did that."

His mouth curled into a smile. He said, "It's still me."

Jennifer crested a hill, and two SUVs passed her, headed the other way. Shoshana said, "That was a Caucasian. The mercenary."

Clint whipped his head to the rear, watching the SUVs disappear. He said, "Mercenary? What are you talking about?"

Jennifer said, "Shoshana, to the front. Look across the field."

Clint turned his head back around, seeing a line of men on their knees, seven others standing behind them holding AK-47s. Something straight out of Rwanda.

Shoshana withdrew her ZEV Tech Glock, the RMR holosight and suppressor clearly showcasing the professional piece of weaponry it was, and Clint looked at her with new eyes. He said, "Who the fuck are you two?"

She ignored the question, saying to Jennifer, "Straight in. Go straight in."

Jennifer nodded, saying, "Clint, call your men. Tell them to get ready."

He attempted to do so, but she left the road, cutting straight into the field, the uneven ground causing the vehicle to begin bucking up and down. Clint said, "Jesus Christ, hang on a second. Let me get a plan together."

Jennifer floored it, ignoring the protests of the suspension and the shouting from Clint.

They closed to within fifty meters before the men with the weapons reacted. The lead man raised his AK, firing the first shot of the battle. It hit the windshield between Jennifer and Shoshana, snapped by Clint's head, and exited out the back of the vehicle. Clint dove down in the seat, shouting into his radio.

Shoshana opened the passenger door, stepped onto the running board of the SUV, and began shooting, knowing she wouldn't hit anything but hoping to at least suppress the incoming fire.

Jennifer said, "Clint, get them to flank. Go north."

Clint made the call, and the second SUV broke away from their line of march, streaking north through the field. Jennifer continued straight ahead, and all the soldiers began firing at her vehicle, spider-webbing her windshield.

Shoshana leapt off the running board, hitting the ground and rolling upright, squeezing the trigger as soon as she had a sight picture. The lead soldier of the line screamed, grabbing his shoulder. She broke the trigger again, and he dropped to the ground. The man behind him turned his aim from Jennifer's vehicle to her, chewing up the ground around her. She dove flat and began scrambling to a depression.

Lying on the bench seat, Jennifer slammed on the brakes and screamed, "Get your guys in the fight!"

She heard Clint in the back shouting into a radio, withdrew her Glock, and rolled out of the vehicle, circling to the rear, the steel of the vehicle pinging with incoming rounds. Clint joined her five seconds later, raising his M4 and putting down suppressive fire, ignoring the rounds impacting near him.

Jennifer said, "What about the team?"

Now calm, in his element, Clint took aim, fired, and said, "Stand by."

Jennifer poked her head around the bumper and saw the second SUV had stopped, the men boiling out, all firing. The soldiers in the field had no focus, no command element controlling them, and they paid for the mistake. In seconds, all seven of them were dead.

They watched the team sweep through the kill zone, checking bodies and securing the prisoners. Clint got a call on the radio, looked at Jennifer, and said, "All clear."

Ten minutes later they were fighting off the fawning of Thomas's inner circle, Thomas himself looking bemused at the turn of events.

The team completed searching the dead bodies, and Thomas said, "This is becoming a habit with you two."

Clint said, "What's he mean by that?"

Shoshana said, "Nothing."

Clint had had enough. His voice rising, he said, "What the fuck is this all about? You said they were going to murder a friend that worked at the hospital. *A* friend, as in a single man. You said it was happening at his house." Clint pointed at the abandoned hut and said, "That ain't no fucking house." He turned and pointed to the line of rescued men and said, "That ain't no single man."

He finished by stabbing a finger at Shoshana's Glock. "And *that* ain't no set of nail clippers. I know you didn't bring it in your carry-on bag when you flew here for your bullshit missionary trip to Lesotho. Who the fuck are you?"

Shoshana said, "This might be the time. I won't tell Pike."

Clint glared and said, "What the hell does that mean?"

Jennifer said, "I think it would be best if you just went back to the hospital and provided security. Sort of forgot all this happened."

84

★ ★ ★

I hung up my phone and, shouting over the wind, announced, "Jennifer and Shoshana were successful! Thomas is alive."

Across from me, his feet splayed out, Aaron smiled and said, "Did you have any doubt?"

"Yeah, I did. Like I do for this ridiculous plan."

We were racing to the airport with the team in the bed of a pickup, Chris driving and Johan in the passenger seat. I'd looked for something better, but the pickings at the police headquarters had been pretty slim. The back parking lot was full of SUVs and sedans, both marked and unmarked, but I needed something to hide the team.

Our new Lesotho police friend wanted to take the ones with official markings, but I was having none of that. We'd never get down the street without someone waving us over to stop a looting or prevent some other crime. The city was going a little nuts, the population not knowing for sure what was occurring but everyone understanding it wasn't good, and it had been split between opportunists and dedicated citizens. The longer we remained at the police headquarters, the less likely we'd be able to drive out.

I'd surveyed the lot and said, "This isn't going to work. We need a Trojan horse. Some way to get us all in undetected while showing Chris and Johan."

I clicked on the net and said, "Veep, what the hell is taking you so long?"

Johan had told us he had a commercial drone in his ruck, and I'd sent Veep to go fetch it. I heard, "I'm here. At the front. Where are you?"

"Out back in the parking lot. Get that thing in motion."

He appeared on the lot with a case about the size of a shoe box. I looked at Johan and said, "That drone can reach the airfield?"

He said, "Oh, yeah. It's pretty good."

No sooner had I said it than Veep—our millennial genius—had the drone in the air, a little spider-looking thing floating about, waiting on instructions.

Johan said, "You've only got about twenty-five minutes of air. Get it going."

Veep did something with the controller, and the drone flew away, disappearing as quickly as a stone dropped off a cliff.

I said, "Okay, the one thing we know is they're expecting Johan and Chris. Chris will drive, and Johan will be the prisoner."

Johan said, "Well, I guess first things first." He turned to Aaron, held out a set of flex-ties, and said, "Care to do the honors?"

Aaron took them and cinched his wrists together, saying, "I was wrong about you."

Johan watched him work and said, "No, you weren't. I'm not a good guy. I haven't been one in a long, long time."

Aaron took his knife and slit the attachment for the tie, so that Johan could break it with a simple twist. He held up the blade, letting Johan see it.

He said, "A knife can do both good and bad. It doesn't understand the difference. You do. You will probably die on this mission. In fact, I can't think of any way you won't. Yet you choose to do it. A conscious decision. Before that happens, I just wanted you to know I forgive you."

Taken aback, Johan said, "Thank you for that. I'm sorry for what I did to you."

Aaron said, "Just get this done, and know that no thanks are necessary."

Aaron released his wrists, then said, "But if you fuck this up, Shoshana will skin you alive. And she has every reason to do so."

Johan gave a half-hearted laugh, wanting to be in on the joke, but unsure of what it was. Aaron looked him in the eyes and said, "That wasn't humor."

Veep said, "I'm over the airfield now. And it's not looking good."

We crowded around the screen, seeing immediately what he was talking about. The airfield was out by itself, with a two-lane road leading to the front of the building, the lone landing strip in the back. It was a single-story building without any Jetways or other modern airport conveniences. Basically, it had a drive on the front side for letting people off, and a runway on the back side for boarding a plane. It looked like an airport in 1960s Mississippi.

Veep said, "One checkpoint on the way in, sporadic security at the tarmac."

I said, "Go back to the runway."

He did, and we saw a C-130 on the tarmac, the ramp down and people loading.

I said, "So Armstrong's on the ground. Which means the clock is ticking."

Knuckles nodded and said, "What's the plan?"

Chris's radio squawked, and he answered it, looking at us, knowing any wrong word would seal his fate.

"This is Chris, go."

"Bird's on the ground. Armstrong's here. Crew is loading up on a hot turnaround."

Meaning the aircraft wasn't even shutting down its engines. Chris said, "We're supposed to be on it. Is it going to wait?"

"No. You bring Johan. The bird's leaving without us. Don't worry, Colonel Armstrong will get us out. Lenatha is happy with the reception. Feed these kaffirs a sacrifice and that's all it takes."

The words from the radio caused me to bristle. He was talking about Thomas. Chris said, "So you want me to come out now?"

"Yeah. Get moving. Armstrong's talking to Lenatha about Johan. I think they want another sacrifice. Mosebo should be here soon. I've got his guys from the prime minister's house holding the airfield.

Turns out killing that fuck was a good decision, because we needed the manpower. Johan didn't take into account the security required here. Either way, we're about to knit this thing up."

Chris looked at me, and I said, "Tell him you're on the way but you don't trust the guard force protecting the airfield. Tell him you want to be sure you can get in without being killed."

He did so, and Andy answered, "Just get your ass here. The first vehicle we see is getting through. The next is getting toasted."

Chris said, "Give me five minutes and we're on the way."

He dropped the mic and said, "I did what I could."

Johan said, "Let Chris take me alone. I'll kill Armstrong, Lenatha, and Andy. I promise I can get all three before they stop me."

Chris looked decidedly sick at the suggestion, because he knew he'd be in the middle of that firefight, forcing him to choose a side. I said, "That's not going to cut it. As much as I'd like to see those fucks bleed, it's still mission failure for my team."

Veep said, "Drone's coming back. I'm out of flight time."

I racked my brain, trying to come up with something that would get us in. Every infiltration course of action was foiled by that one lone road leading to the airfield. I had no aircraft for a HALO op, no helicopters for a shock assault, no secret newspaper truck for a clandestine entry.

I said, "We need a Trojan horse."

Knuckles said, "What about that pickup?"

He pointed to a beat-up Ford with more primer than paint. "We can get in the back and cover ourselves with something. Trojan horse."

Brett said, "That's the dumbest idea I've ever heard."

I said, "Yeah, and it just might work. Veep, find us something to cover the bed. Everyone else, load up."

Ten minutes later we were closing on the airport, and I'd gotten the word from Jennifer about Thomas. Knuckles said, "You going to get them rolling here?"

"Yeah. I'll stage them with the police. Aaron, give Shoshana a heads-up. Tell her to coordinate with Veep."

Driven by Veep, the SUV behind us was full of Lesotho police, which I was going to leave on the shoulder of the road at the intersection of the airport entrance. Needless to say, Veep wasn't too keen on the babysitting task, but tough shit. It had to go to somebody I trusted. The intersection was about four hundred meters away from the airport, making it close enough to call them in waving badges when we won.

If we won.

Johan pounded on the glass of the rear window and held up a single finger.

I said, "One minute, one minute. Knuckles, pass to Veep."

Here we go.

We tucked down in the bed, and I dragged the tarp over us, Aaron and Knuckles working their end of the mission. Brett took the canvas and pulled it tight, saying, "I haven't done anything this stupid since high school."

I tucked the tarp over my head, the light now blotted out, and looked at him in our little cave. "How'd that work out?"

He grinned and said, "We went to jail. But I'm sure this'll be different."

85

★ ★ ★

Returning to the hospital in the trail of the Special Forces caravan, Jennifer had parked and then spent her time trying to placate Clint, but he was having none of it. The men of his team had seemed to appreciate what they'd done and treated them with newfound respect, but Clint had been aggravated. He knew he'd been used but still wasn't sure if he should be angry at the subterfuge or happy that he'd accomplished something worthwhile. Jennifer could see the dichotomy play out and recognized Pike in the battle. She knew which side would win. No man like Clint would remain pissed because he'd found a gunfight.

Shoshana's phone rang, and she walked away to answer it. Jennifer said to him, "I appreciate the help. You did a good thing."

He said, "Don't fuck with me. Next thing you'll tell me is that you have an issue with a submarine in a lake in the Highlands, and you need my help because you're a marine biologist."

Jennifer repeated, "You did a good thing. Just take that for what it's worth."

He grinned and said, "You're not going to tell me who you are, are you?"

"We already did."

"Bullshit. You don't work here. You're pretty good at pulling the strings. The Benghazi touch was the coup de grace. If I were to guess, I'd say this whole charade was just to save those men back there."

He was close, but she couldn't tell him that his purpose was simply to show the flag. She said, "I appreciate the help. I really do. Please make sure these people are safe."

He laughed and said, "So I never left here, right?"

She said, "That's right. If you don't mind."

He nodded, and Shoshana hung up her phone, saying, "We need to go." She turned from the SUV and shouted, "Thomas! Get your ass over here. Time to get in the fight."

Thomas came jogging toward them, and Clint said, "What's she talking about?"

Jennifer leaned forward and kissed him on the cheek, saying, "Worry about the hospital. Leave it at that. Trust me."

His men hooted at the gesture, and he said, "Okay, okay. You win. But one day I'm going to find out what happened here."

Shoshana opened the door to their bullet-ridden SUV, letting Thomas take a seat. She said, "Wow. You gave up easy."

She closed the door, and Clint said, "What does that mean?"

Jennifer opened the driver's side and said, "Nothing. She just figured it would take a little more to get you on board."

"Like what?"

"You don't want to know."

He said, "You got that right. She's scary as shit."

Jennifer put the vehicle in gear before Shoshana could say anything crazy.

I felt the truck slow down for the checkpoint, and every man under the tarp tightened his grip on his weapon. If they wanted to check the bed, they'd have to lift the canvas. We all waited, praying for the darkness to remain. One inch of daylight and we were coming out shooting, our surprise lost.

I held my breath, hearing Chris talking through the window, wondering yet again whether it was good policy to put my fate into the hands of two mercenaries who had no loyalty to me or my team. I realized that worrying about someone ripping the tarp off us wasn't the worst case. Johan could tell them to simply start shooting into the bed, and we wouldn't realize it until the first rounds ripped into our bodies.

We began rolling forward again, and I let my breath out. Knuckles whispered, "Okay, they get some credit when we're done here."

And I realized he'd been thinking the same damn thing.

We drove for another two minutes, and I felt the vehicle turn, subtly shifting us in the bed. We were driving around the building toward the flight line.

Not long now.

The truck stopped, and I heard Chris shout out the window.

It was all Johan now.

Johan saw Andy on the airfield, but not Colonel Armstrong. The terminal was to their left, and he assumed the entourage was inside. Which would make it hard for a quick reaction from the men in the bed.

Andy walked up to Chris on the driver's side and said, "So it looks like you and I get to stay in the new prime minister's residence tonight. Not bad."

Chris said, "When are we leaving? I don't like this."

"We'll be out of here tomorrow. Armstrong's got some business with Colonel Smith. Don't worry, he's not hanging around." He pointed at Johan and said, "He's got some business here, as well. Get him out."

Chris exited the door, went to the passenger side, and pulled out Johan. Andy said, "Hold him still."

Chris did, and Andy ran his hands over Johan's torso, Chris saying, "I already searched him."

Andy stood back up and said, "Can't be too sure."

They marched to the entrance of the terminal, and Johan could see Armstrong and Lenatha inside, surrounded by the same four of Lenatha's security men he'd seen when they'd met in Cape Town. One of them opened the door, and he was ushered inside.

Armstrong had a smile on his face, but behind it was a smoldering anger. Johan had seen it once before, when Armstrong had destroyed the teenagers in the park.

Johan was made to stand in front of Armstrong, Chris behind him and Andy off to one side. Johan surveyed the threat matrix, seeing Armstrong and Lenatha were both unarmed, and, while the four-man security detail showed bulges under their suit jackets, they had nothing in their hands—yet. Andy was the only one with a visible weapon out, his Sig Sauer slung at his side.

Armstrong said, "So, Lily Boy, you thought you could teach the master a few tricks, is that it?"

Johan said nothing.

Armstrong slapped him across the face, screaming, "Answer me!"

Johan rolled with the blow, and then said, "You broke the contract. You know I don't work for terrorists."

Armstrong laughed and said, "Is that what this is about? You found out about the payment to Tyler Malloy? I thought it had something to do with the moral high ground of Lesotho. All of this pain, and you didn't stop the transfer from happening. Must really hurt."

Johan said, "What now?"

Lenatha stepped forward, speaking for the first time. "Now, you traitor, you will get exactly what you deserve. When General Mosebo arrives, I'll formally turn you over to him as an enemy of the people. I don't know how long he'll keep you alive, but I do know you'll probably wish it was shorter than it will be."

Johan smiled and said, "Mosebo's dead, you little maggot."

The news came as a shock to everyone but Chris. Armstrong started to speak, when the sound of gunfire erupted outside the terminal.

86

Hidden under the tarp, I heard the conversation stop, then the sound of footsteps retreating. Then nothing but silence. I said, "Brett, take a peek." He did, cracking the tarp near the cab of the pickup and peering out. He said, "They went inside the terminal. I can't see anything through the glass."

"Can we exit?"

"Front's got two security, but they're on the far side. If we were quick, we could get into the terminal alcove and they'd miss us. Knuckles, what about the rear?"

Knuckles crawled to the tailgate and cracked the tarp, then slowly lifted his head. He immediately snapped back down like a turtle withdrawing into a shell. He hissed, "Two security headed right for us."

"Are they going to bypass? Go inside the terminal?"

"How the hell would I know? If I were to guess, since this shit show is your plan, I'd say no."

He laid his rifle gently on the bed of the truck and withdrew his Glock. Brett and I did the same, repositioning our legs underneath us. We waited for what seemed like an hour and then heard the footsteps, the men speaking in Sesotho. They stopped at the tailgate, and we held our breath. Then one of them grabbed the tarp, flinging it back.

Knuckles rose like a jack-in-the-box from hell, drilling the first one in the head, then rotating to the second. The man got off one wild round, and Knuckles put him down.

I threw off the tarp, saying, "Get to the terminal." Knuckles and Brett leapt over the side of the bed. I started to do the same and saw the two men from the far side of the airfield. They'd heard the single round and were running toward us to see what had happened. I laid my weapon on the roof of the truck and seated the buttstock. One of them took a knee and fired at the team scrambling for the terminal. I eased out my breath and broke the trigger. A split second later, he grabbed his chest and flopped on the tarmac, rolling in a death spasm.

The man next to him oriented on me, and I saw him cut down by the team, both now in the alcove of the terminal. I leapt out of the bed and sprinted to them. I stacked behind Brett and heard gunfire from inside the terminal. I looked at Knuckles and said, "Go."

With the sound of the single AK-47 round still echoing in the air, and all eyes focused on the terminal windows, Johan raised his arms to his chest and yanked, hard. The flex-tie split down the middle, freeing his hands. He flicked his right arm down, and like magic, the handle of a double-edged fighting knife slid from his sleeve and into his palm.

Andy caught the initial motion and whirled to him, but not quickly enough. He raised his weapon, and Johan leapt on him, bringing him to the ground and driving the knife low, just above the groin, under Andy's body armor. He sank it to the hilt, then ripped left and right, tearing through Andy's internal organs.

Andy screamed, beating him on the head. Johan heard firing behind him, the room exploding into noise. He slid his left hand up Andy's body, catching him under the chin and pushing out, exposing Andy's neck. Johan jerked the knife free, batted Andy's hands aside, and slit his throat from ear to ear.

He rolled over, snatched Andy's rifle, and rose to a knee, seeing Chris firing at the security men. A bullet hit Chris in the thigh, flinging his leg backward like it had been hit with a bat. He dropped to the ground face-first, and Johan saw multiple rounds tear into the gaps in his armor around his shoulders and neck, a final one cratering his skull.

Johan got in the fight, squeezing the trigger in controlled pairs and taking the life of the security man. The other three surrounded Lenatha, pulling him back to the security point and focusing on Johan. He swiveled his weapon, knowing he was dead, and Pike Logan's team poured through the terminal door, killing every threat in their path.

In the span of a single trigger pull, all three security men were lifeless. Lenatha fell to his knees with his hands covering his head. Johan scanned the room and saw Armstrong running past the security metal detectors, toward the front of the terminal.

He leapt up and said, "I've got him," and gave chase. He reached the entrance lobby of the airport and caught sight of Armstrong running past the single check-in counter. He fired over his head and shouted, "Armstrong! Next one will be in you!"

Armstrong stopped, then slowly turned around, his hands in the air. Johan motioned, and Armstrong walked to him. He put his hands down and said, "I suppose you'll kill me now."

"No. I have something more important in mind."

Armstrong heard the words, and a sneer spread across his face, his confidence growing. He said, "Still the Lily Boy. Sure. Something more important. Maybe you just don't have the stomach for this work."

Johan hammered the butt of his Sig into Armstrong's face, shattering his nose. Armstrong dropped to the ground.

Johan said, "Stomach that, you fuck."

Armstrong moaned, and Johan said, "Get the fuck up."

Armstrong rose, holding his bloody face, and Johan pushed him with his foot, forcing him back into the waiting area. When they arrived, Johan saw a new cluster of men, all wearing police uniforms except one.

Lenatha was on his knees, his hands cuffed behind his back, the police circled around him. One cop smacked him in the head, and the man called Thomas waved his hand, saying, "No more violence. We don't do that anymore. Let the law take care of him."

Lenatha looked up and said, "Who are you?"

Thomas glanced at Pike, and Pike nodded. He said, "Thomas

Naboni." He had trouble getting the next words out but finally did. "The man who is now in charge."

Pike said, "Good. Good. Thomas, it's your show now. Good luck."

Surprised, Thomas said, "That's it?"

Pike smiled and said, "That's it. We've got an aircraft inbound. We'll be taking Armstrong with us, but the rest of this is up to you."

"What if the fighting continues?"

"It won't. Mosebo's dead, and you now control the police. You'll have a ton of US Marines here in short order. I'd recommend as a first step getting in touch with the US embassy for coordination. Get them on your side early."

"Can't you do that? Can't you stay and help?"

His face was so earnest it caused Jennifer to come forward. She said, "Thomas, you have all the help you need. The people love you. You'll be fine."

"But I could use your help. I mean, I trust you. The people will trust you, and so will the Americans at the embassy. I need you to talk to them."

Pike chuckled and said, "Don't read in to our reputation. Just being an American won't help here. I don't think you want me speaking to the embassy. They won't take kindly to us being here. In fact, it'd be good if you just didn't mention us at all."

Confused, Thomas said, "Why? After all you've done here to bring about justice?"

Shoshana said, "Because Pike's an asshole. Nobody likes him."

Knuckles laughed and said, "Thomas, justice is in the eye of the beholder. Trust me when I say the embassy will not appreciate our efforts. Leave us out of this, and make it all internal to Lesotho. You do otherwise—you bring us into this—and it becomes complicated. Let it go."

Thomas reluctantly nodded, and Johan said, "I'll stay."

Pike looked at him in surprise, and he said, "Least I can do. I'd rather be here, working with Thomas, than wherever you're taking Armstrong."

"I told you I'd set you free."

He said, "I trust you, Pike. I do, but I don't trust whomever you work for. And besides, I think Thomas could use the help. I'm from South Africa. I know the continent."

Thomas nodded and said, "Thank you. I appreciate it."

Pike shook his head but understood the sentiment. He said, "As long as you stay on the right side."

Johan said, "Just get those triggers. Promise me that."

Pike looked at Armstrong and said, "Of course. That's what this whole thing has been about."

Shoshana smiled, and Johan knew why. Pike was stretching the truth to the breaking point.

Pike looked at Armstrong and said, "But those triggers will be the easy part. Isn't that right, Colonel?"

87

★ ★ ★

I took another sip of my giant hurricane—if you ordered the big one, you got to keep the glass—and saw Tyler Malloy enter the restaurant. It was okay to booze it up now, because my team wasn't in on the hunt. That had all been turned over to the "proper" authorities, and the restaurant was now surrounded by State Department Diplomatic Security Services and the FBI. Because of Tyler's status as a US citizen, the Taskforce had been pulled from the operation, but nobody could tell me I couldn't get a 'Merican hamburger at a 'Merican restaurant—which was why I was pleased Tyler Malloy had chosen the Hard Rock Cafe for his transfer. Hell, our waitress was even from Texas. Long story, once I asked her, but fascinating all the same.

It had been three days since the L-100 had landed on the Lesotho airfield, and so far, things seemed to be going splendidly for Thomas Naboni. The mighty US Marine Corps had landed about six hours after we'd left and had pretty much secured the entire city from any threats, giving the Lesotho police and military a helping hand at crowd control, all coordinated through the US embassy. Unfortunately, by the time they'd begun operations for the removal of US citizens, the shooting was all over and the people refused to leave.

The commander of the Marine Corps taskforce had been bitching holy hell, trying to put his finger on the idiot who had demanded the NEO. The embassy said it wasn't them—even as they coordinated a response. In their defense, they'd mentioned one wounded person—an Israeli, no less—and a hysterical woman who'd demanded protection for a children's hospital. She had disappeared in the chaos, and nobody even remembered her name. Nobody seemed to know how the rumor of threats to US citizens had snowballed into a deployment order. Well, one person knew—Colonel Kurt Hale—and he was none too happy.

We'd boarded the L-100, dragging Armstrong with us, and I was surprised to find Blaine Alexander on the bird, along with an interrogation team. He'd apparently had enough of Djibouti and had forward staged with the bird. He was in constant contact with Kurt in DC, and I'd spent the thirty-minute flight on a headset, giving Kurt a verbal report on everything that had happened. Well, everything pertinent to our mission.

The last I'd seen of Johan was taxiing down the runway in Lesotho. I had no doubt that Thomas needed the help, but I was a little sad to see Johan go. He'd ended up being a pretty solid guy, despite his seriously flawed employment decisions—to include his interrogation of Aaron. *That* mistake had almost cost him his life, but if he could keep Thomas breathing, I'd call it a wash.

We'd landed in Joburg, and the first order of business had been sleep. I'd left Armstrong in the capable hands of Blaine and his crew, given the team their marching orders, and gone comatose for close to sixteen hours. When I'd awoken and padded down to our hotel TOC, Blaine was talking to Kurt, and Kurt was in a fine mood.

Turned out there wasn't any danger to the hospital, and he'd burned a lot of chips to get the ball moving—all because he'd agreed to let the coup go forward and felt responsible for the threat. Now he was learning there had been no threat to the hospital, and he'd managed to convince the secretary of defense to execute a full-blown NEO, based on my recommendation. He started right in as soon as I sat down.

"You told me the hospital was under fire."

"Now, wait a minute. I told you it was uncorroborated."

"And conveniently, some guy named Thomas Naboni is now in charge of the country. The king's come forward supporting him, which was enough to shut down any bitching by MPs in parliament. Not to mention there's some rumor that a US Special Forces team had something to do with keeping him alive, like some kind of Karzai mission in Afghanistan after 9/11. Because of it, the US embassy is scrambling for a story supporting his rightful position in the government."

"Why are you shouting at me about this? You said yourself, if Thomas was left standing it wasn't any of our business."

"An SF team? Really?" His eyes started to bug out of his head, and he shouted, "It's the same damn team we talked about! They were gone before I even made my first call!"

"Well, you might want to ask the embassy RSO about that."

He'd clenched his fists and sputtered, "I *did*. Two women showed up at the embassy and convinced the team to leave."

"Yeah? That so? Strange."

"Pike—"

Before he could get too worked up, I changed the subject. "Did we get anything out of Armstrong?"

He let out a breath and sagged back, saying, "Yeah, he's setting up a meeting between Malloy and that 'Colonel Smith' guy. We're transferring control over to DSS and FBI, and they're coordinating on a sting with the South Africans. It's a law enforcement matter now."

"So, you got what you wanted. Those triggers will be off the street, and Malloy will be in the bag."

"And you got Thomas Naboni."

"No, sir. I got Aaron. The Israelis thank you. Thomas was just a bennie that worked out."

He said, "The mission was the nuclear triggers."

I said, "The mission was bigger than just the triggers."

He shook his head and asked, "What would you have done if I'd have said no on recovering Aaron?"

I thought about it, then simply said, "The right thing."

He didn't probe what that was, and a day and a half after that, Jennifer and I were having lunch with Aaron and Shoshana, four tables over from Tyler Malloy.

I said, "You guys should really try one of these hurricanes. They're delicious."

Shoshana said, "I don't drink anything that comes with an umbrella."

"Well, you get to keep the glass."

Jennifer said, "So you guys fly tonight?"

Aaron said, "Yes. We have an appointment in the diamond exchange tomorrow with one Eli Cohen."

"Does he know about the coup results?"

Shoshana said, "I honestly don't care." She put a chip in her mouth and said, "Say, you guys should come visit before you go home."

I laughed and said, "What, you need help with Eli?"

She grew cold, saying, "No. We won't be needing any help there."

Jennifer said, "What are you going to do with him?"

Aaron took a sip of his beer and said, "Nothing. Well, I'm going to give him a handgun and then an array of unpalatable options. I'm pretty sure whatever happens to him will be at his own hand. Especially if it keeps his family seat on the exchange."

I said, "Well, good of you to give him a choice."

Jennifer slapped my arm, saying, "Pike."

Shoshana said, "No, he's right. It's a choice he never gave us."

I changed the subject, saying, "Israel's a little out of the way for us."

Aaron took the shift, wanting to get away from the earlier conversation. "Not really. You stretch it a little bit, but you have to fly to Europe first anyway. It's just bending the leg of the triangle."

Before I could say anything else, Tyler Malloy stood up, shaking Smith's hand. I called out to Knuckles, saying, "He's on the move. Get it on tape."

The Hard Rock was located in a patch of concrete called Nelson Mandela Square. Just off the rail line in the Joburg suburb of Sandton, it was a chic place surrounded with art galleries, museums, and restaurants. It was pedestrian-only, which made it easy to box with my team for a follow. Veep, Brett, and Knuckles were positioned outside, lounging wherever they could find spots that covered the avenues of egress.

I heard Knuckles say, "I've got him. He's coming my way. Veep, Blood, on me."

We huddled around the tablet in front of Jennifer while she manipulated the camera view until she had Knuckles's feed. We saw nothing for a moment; then Shoshana pointed to the upper right of the screen. Tyler Malloy came into view, walking rapidly by Knuckles. Knuckles stood, and we got a perfect view of Tyler's back as he walked toward Maude Street and the Sandton Convention Centre.

Jennifer glanced up, then hissed, "Colonel Smith."

We all looked at his table and saw it surrounded by men in suits. Whether they were DSS, South African Special Branch, or FBI I didn't know, but it was a little sweet justice seeing him frog-marched out the back.

We returned to the screen, seeing Tyler had entered an alley. He approached a van, pulled out a key, and opened the back. We couldn't tell what he was looking at, because Knuckles held back at a distance, not wanting to interfere with the inevitable.

Tyler crawled inside the van and began manipulating a trunk. He got it open, and then all sorts of hell descended on him, the van assaulted by a full squad of guys wearing black balaclavas and carrying MP5s. The camera went crazy as Knuckles retreated, calling, "Jackpot. Jackpot. Did you get it?"

I said, "Yeah, we got it. Sort of anticlimactic, though. I was hoping you'd join in and kick him once for Aaron."

Knuckles laughed and said, "See you back at the hotel."

I looked around the table and said, "Well, that's that."

Shoshana stood and said, "We'd better head to the airport."

Jennifer said, "Your flight doesn't leave for a few hours."

"Yeah, but I don't trust being this far away. The rail has an express straight to the airport, and I feel safer once I'm there. That place is a nuthouse."

Aaron pulled out his wallet and said, "Let me get this. It's the least I can do."

Jennifer said, "No, no. It's our gift to you."

Shoshana said, "Big spender."

I laughed and she said, "Come to Israel. I'll give you two a gift."

"What?"

She looked at Jennifer and said, "A date. Jennifer's been wanting one for a while. I can feel it."

I said, "Oh, so now you're giving *us* relationship advice?"

Deadly serious, she said, "Yes, I am. Take it."

Jennifer looked at me with a tinge of longing. I said, "So you're now reading us like the enemy?"

Shoshana smiled and said, "No, Nephilim. You will never be the enemy. I'm just telling you what I've learned." Aaron rose, and she took his hand, saying, "What you two have taught me."

I rose as well and kissed her on the cheek, saying, "Can we go to Caesarea and look at pottery shards? I promised that a few days ago, and it seems to get Jennifer hot."

Jennifer smacked me on the shoulder, then gave Aaron and Shoshana a hug.

Shoshana said, "We'll do what Jennifer wants. But I don't think it'll be about pottery shards. You don't have to be me to read that."

ACKNOWLEDGMENTS

Operator Down is the first book I've written where I began with a blank slate and a plan instead of relying on a news story to spark an idea. I have gone from furiously typing two books a year to having some time to actually ponder, and I used it. I wanted something different. I wanted to move away from trying to chase the latest headlines and just type a story that resonated. That required doing something I've never done before: finding a story that would never make the US news cycle but was still real. Which was liberating. At the outset, I had three goals: one, make it personal vice some world-ending terrorist attack; two, bring back Aaron and Shoshana (just because I love them); and three, set the story somewhere I hadn't before.

From there, I started kicking around ideas that could satisfy those three parameters. I hit upon the diamond trade in Israel and the connection to the plethora of diamond mines in Africa. The idea of a coup began to form, but research into the usual places where blood diamonds are found, such as Sierra Leone, revealed that these were definitely not locations I was looking forward to visiting. I then found the unique land of Lesotho, a country completely surrounded by South Africa, source of some of the largest gem-quality diamonds on earth, and—while relatively stable—also a place with a history of coups.

So, I had an idea, and I took off on my book-research adventure, only this time I got a little more than I bargained for. After spending a few days in Joburg and Cape Town nailing down those areas (yes, the manager of the Hard Rock was from Texas), I met my guide, Khabiso, in Lesotho the first night of arrival, and we planned out the next day's events. What we didn't plan for was getting detained by a counterintelligence unit for "spying" on the Lesotho Special Forces base. After driving around seeing all the specific places I'd requested, we were rolled up outside of the Makoanyane Military Base. Doing things the average tourist would not.

We spent the next six and half hours in solitary interrogation in separate rooms, which I probably deserved since I seriously *looked* like a spy. The book was about a coup, so all the pictures on my camera were decidedly not touristy—the parliament building, the prime minister's residence (a blurry frame taken as we drove by it—with a sign saying "no pictures" *in* the picture), the lone television and radio station, the primary police headquarters, etc.—nothing on my camera was helping my "tourist" story. I had no plausible reason for having taken those photos, I had a retired-military ID card, and there was absolutely no way I was going to tell them I was a writer and have them Google my bio. They'd already told me I'd been trained to "resist interrogation" (Yeah? True, but how do I answer that?) and had called my passport fake because it said I was born in Japan (no idea why that makes my passport "fake"—but you don't argue with the interrogator). I was sure that if they saw my books and bio it would have cemented their paranoid fears. Oh, and there was a US Special Forces team on the ground conducting a security assessment of the USEMB, but they were truly there for a *secret* reason that I alone knew. At least that's what my interrogators told me, because they thought I was spying for them. . . .

In the end, the Johan interrogation scene wrote itself (with a little literary license—nobody ever laid a hand on me—but the Frog is *real*, and I enjoyed giving him some just desserts on the page), and the plot developed with some real-world intrigue that my interrogators managed to let slip during my questioning. I had no idea at the time about the machinations occurring in Lesotho, but everything I learned during that session played out in the book. I'm deeply indebted to Khabiso, who could have left me high and dry but instead became a little spitfire demanding we be released—and who also turned out to have some highly placed friends in the government. After the interrogation was over, Khabiso's sole worry was that I'd give her a bad TripAdvisor review. I laughed and said, "They were stupid enough to take us on the base. Can't get any better research than that." Yes, the building that Brett and Johan assault is real, as is the sheet-draped room I was interrogated in, but the only reason I saw it was because I was careless.

The next day's activities were decidedly more routine—driving to Morija and seeing the museum, with a side trip to a certain concrete bridge that Johan crosses—and I thought about going to the US embassy to let them know that any SF team on the ground needed to watch what they did, but in the end, I just drank a beer at the hotel bar. They were on their own.

In Israel, I'm indebted to my guide, Avraham, who showed me around Tel Aviv. Not only did he give a first-rate historical perspective on the establishment of the city, and the country of Israel, but by the end of the tour, he'd finally decided I was trustworthy. Probably because when he told me about the prison that held Eichmann, I'd relayed I knew all about his capture. A little Jennifer coming through. Sometimes reading history pays off.

I'd initially explained what I was doing there, and that I really would like to talk to someone about the diamond exchange. We finished the tour, and he said, "I have a cousin who works inside the exchange. Would you like to meet her?" Two hours later, I had a call from her saying to bring my passport and no weapons. I assumed that was some Israeli comment made because she believed every American travels with a pistol in his belt, and I thought I was just going to pick her brain at a coffee shop near the exchange, but when I arrived, she'd gotten me clearance to get inside. Yes, I now have a badge for the fabled diamond exchange of Israel, and the education was incredible. So much so, I named a character after her. Alexandra is the name of the cousin who walked me through. I still have the badge, and my wife says we're going to use it—for something she has yet to outline. . . .

As in the Taskforce and life, time marches on in the publishing industry. Retro retired in this manuscript, and my editor, Ben Sevier, moved on as well. He's been with me since *One Rough Man*, and we brainstormed the plot for *Operator Down*, argued about the title, and generally did everything we usually do, and then, while I was deep into it, he was offered a job he couldn't refuse as the publisher of a major house. For the uninitiated, that's like being offered the position of CEO. He'll be greatly missed, but my Dutton Taskforce marches on, with Jess seamlessly continuing to berate me on editing, Liza churning out publicity leads and then forcing this reluctant author to step up, and the rest of the Dutton crew running like a well-oiled machine, making sure my books are the best they can possibly be. As Pike would say to Shoshana, I'm glad you're sweet on me.

ABOUT THE AUTHOR

BRAD TAYLOR is the author of the *New York Times* bestselling Pike Logan series. He served for more than twenty years in the US Army, including eight years in 1st Special Forces Operational Detachment–Delta, commonly known as Delta Force. He retired as a Special Forces lieutenant colonel and now lives in Charleston, South Carolina.